His eyes p  **y don't have** **a man, do** **you so you'll find out."**

Guido's intensity shook her, and then his head descended and his mouth closed over hers. Enveloped in heat, she felt his hands roam over her back and hips, urging her closer so she could feel every hard muscle and sinew in his body.

Though Dea had been with a few men who'd wanted to kiss her passionately, she hadn't fully reciprocated. Something had always held her back... until now.

This was different. Guido was different.

The feel of his mouth slowly devouring hers created such divine sensations she felt she'd been born for this moment and couldn't get enough.

"Guido..." she gasped in pleasure as he drew her into wine-dark rapture.

She clung to him. They were moving and breathing like they were a part of each other. Emotions greater than she could describe had taken over now that Guido had swept her into his arms.

THE BILLIONAIRE'S PRIZE

BY
REBECCA WINTERS

First Published in Great Britain 2016
By Mills & Boon, an imprint of HarperCollins*Publishers*
1 London Bridge Street, London, SE1 9GF

© 2016 Rebecca Winters

ISBN: 978-0-263-92033-8

23-1116

Our policy is to use papers that are natural, renewable and recyclable products and made from wood grown in sustainable forests. The logging and manufacturing processes conform to the legal environmental regulations of the country of origin.

Printed and bound in Spain
by CPI, Barcelona

Rebecca Winters lives in Salt Lake City, Utah. With canyons and high alpine meadows full of wildflowers, she never runs out of places to explore. They, plus her favourite vacation spots in Europe, often end up as backgrounds for her romance novels—because writing is her passion, along with her family and church. Rebecca loves to hear from readers. If you wish to email her, please visit her website at www.cleanromances.com.

PROLOGUE

DEA CARACCIOLO STOOD inside the grand dining hall of the castle on Posso Island. She was ready to flee now that she'd done her part during the wedding ceremony of her twin sister, Alessandra, and Rinieri Montanari.

"Darling? Why are you here by the doors?"

Oh, no. She turned her head in surprise. "Mamma."

"I still need to be in line to greet the guests and would like you to go sit with Guido and his parents."

Dea didn't think she could bear it. "Please don't make me."

"But you're the maid of honor. Your father and I are depending on you to entertain the best man and his family. Alessandra says they love Rini, and Signor Rossano has spoken highly of you since the night you were a model in the fashion show on his yacht. Come on. I'll walk you over to their table."

The mention of the yacht increased her agony, but this was one situation Dea couldn't get out of. Somehow she would have to endure Guido's company for a few more minutes.

During the wedding ceremony they'd gone through

the motions to be civil to each other in order to carry
out their duties, but he'd hardly looked at her and she
knew why. He couldn't help but have a low opinion of
her since that night on the yacht when she'd made the
worst blunder of her life with Rini in front of Guido.
He probably assumed she was still in love with her
new brother-in-law.

The situation couldn't be uglier, but her mother
expected her to be gracious for a little while longer.
When they approached the table, Guido and his father got to their feet before inviting her to sit down.

Guido's mother was a lovely woman and Dea tried
to concentrate on her once they started to eat. "My
sister told me about your generous gift to her and
Rini."

"We thought they should honeymoon on our yacht
to get away from everyone else. Alessandra is perfectly charming, and Rini's a favorite of ours."

"So I've heard."

"I have to say, you looked so beautiful the night of
the fashion show," Signora Rossano continued. "But
tonight you're even more beautiful."

"Thank you," she whispered.

"It's only the truth," a smiling Signor Rossano in-
terjected. "Don't you think so, Guido?"

His son put down his champagne glass. "Papà? As
you well know, Signorina Caracciolo has most of the
Italian male population at her feet."

His father nodded with satisfaction. "That is true."

To his parents' ears, Guido's comment must have
sounded like a supreme compliment. But the choice

of the word *most* let Dea know he didn't include himself in that particular population.

"Signor Rossano, the other models and I were amazed you would allow your yacht to be used for a fashion show backdrop. It was a great thrill for them and they're hoping you'll offer it again."

"I wouldn't count on it for another year," Guido murmured out of his father's hearing, sounding turned off by her comment. She hadn't meant that she included herself in those who hoped to wangle another invitation. But no doubt Guido had assumed as much. She shouldn't have said anything at all.

Feeling more and more uncomfortable, she almost gasped with relief when her aunt Fulvia came over to the table and asked her if she'd like to say goodbye to the Archbishop of Taranto, who'd married her sister and Rini. It was a great honor and Dea excused herself with as much grace as she could muster before clinging to her aunt's arm. Her mother's only sister had saved her from further embarrassment and she would always be grateful.

CHAPTER ONE

One year later

"SIGNORA PARMA IS expecting you. Walk back through the doors to her workshop."

Dea Caracciolo thanked the receptionist and headed for the inner sanctum of the world-renowned Italian opera-costume designer. The only reason Dea had been given this privilege was because her aunt Fulvia and Juliana Parma were such close friends.

Though Dea had met Juliana and her husband on many occasions at her aunt's southern Italian *castello* in Taranto, this particular meeting wasn't social and the outcome—good or bad—would rest entirely on Dea's shoulders.

The sought-after redheaded designer in her late sixties stood surrounded by her staff, giving orders to one and all in her flamboyant style. When she saw Dea, she motioned her to come closer and clapped her hands.

"Everyone?" Their eyes fastened on Dea. "You've all known Dea Loti as Italy's leading fashion model.

She's actually Princess Dea of the Houses of Caracciolo and Taranto and the niece of my dear friend Princess Fulvia Taranto. But while she's here working with me during her spring-semester designer course at the Accademia Roma, you will call her Dea and accord her every courtesy."

Dea was so surprised she blurted, "You mean you're willing to take me on without talking to me about it first?"

"Of course. Fulvia has told me everything I need to know, so I called the head of your department and asked them to send you to me."

Dear Fulvia. Dea loved her so much. "I can hardly believe this is happening."

"Believe it! You're even more beautiful than the last time we were together. Imagine if you were a soprano in the opera too—you would have every tenor in the world dying of love for you."

Heat filled Dea's cheeks. "How awful." Once upon a time Dea would have liked to hear a compliment like that, but not since she'd been in therapy to help her get on the road to real happiness.

Juliana chuckled. "Come in my private office."

The others smiled as she followed the older woman into a small cluttered room that still managed to be tidy. Dea handed her a small bouquet of roses.

"What's this?"

"A token of my gratitude that you even agreed to meet with me."

"*Grazie*, Dea." She inhaled the perfume from the

flowers. "Heavenly. Fulvia must have told you how much I love pink roses."

"I remember your husband giving you some after the opera a year ago."

"You're a very sweet and observant young woman. You're going to go far in this business. I feel it in my bones."

Sweet? That wasn't a word one would apply to the Dea of the past. The old Dea was too self-absorbed. She'd learned a lot about herself in therapy. The new Dea was working on thinking about others.

Juliana put the flowers in a bowl and sank into the chair behind her desk. "Sit down, my dear." Dea did her bidding. "What's this news that you've given up modeling?"

"It's true. I did one show at the end of last semester, but my goal is to become a period costume designer for the opera, like you. As you know, I've loved costume design from the time I was a child. You have no idea how excited I am to work with an expert like you and learn all I can. It's a great privilege."

Juliana's brown eyes sparkled. "You're going to love the project I'm winding up now. It's the costuming for *Don Giovanni*, which will go into production the third week of May. I'd like to hear your comments on this new sketch for Donna Elvira." She thrust a rendering into Dea's hands.

Don Giovanni was one of Dea's favorite operas. But the second she saw the drawing, she shot Juliana a glance. "Don't you mean Donna Anna?"

A smile broke the corner of Juliana's mouth. "Bravo,

Dea. Nothing gets past you. This costume is indeed meant for a younger woman. I've always known you to have a discerning eye. In fact I remember the fashion shows you used to put on at the *castello* with your sister when you were little. They were delightful and, in some instances, brilliant!"

Brilliance was a quality one attributed to Alessandra, not Dea. The unexpected compliment sent a curl of warmth through her body. Juliana handed her another drawing from a pile on her desk. "*Here* is a first draft of the costume for Donna Elvira that she'll wear in the dark courtyard scene. One of the staff worked it up."

Dea studied it for a few minutes. Her brows formed a frown.

Juliana chuckled. "Don't be afraid to tell me exactly what you think. I've always admired your honesty."

Coming from Juliana, that kind of praise meant a great deal.

"In my mind this gown is too frivolous and doesn't reveal her true character. I see Donna Elvira as a mature woman who's ahead of her time. She's hurt and outraged with Don Giovanni for his abandoning her. I'd like to see her gown toned down to convey that she's anything but a fool. She's been on a mission to find him."

"I agree completely. Bring me your version by tomorrow at 11:00 a.m." She took back the drawing and rose to her feet. "That's all the time I can give you for now."

"Mille ringraziamenti, signora."

"Juliana, *per favore*."

Dea rushed around the desk to give her a kiss on the cheek. "I'm more grateful than you know for this opportunity."

After saying those words, she left the building and took a taxi back to her apartment. Located in the heart of Rome, the elegant complex she lived in was in walking distance of the Pantheon and the Piazza Navona. It had been home to her for quite a while. She loved the ancient street, which was over five hundred years old, with its dozens of wonderful shops. On this particular Monday, the lovely April weather matched her lightened mood.

Once she'd eaten lunch she would get to work designing a gown already forming in her mind. But first she needed to make an important phone call to her aunt, who'd made this unexpected meeting with Juliana possible.

When the older woman answered, Dea said, "Zia Fulvia?"

"Dea, how wonderful to hear from you! Your mother is here with me. I'll put the phone on speaker so we can both talk to you."

"Mamma?"

"Darling. I've been anxious to hear from you."

Her heart pounded with excitement. "Guess what? Juliana called my department at the Accademia and has taken me on. I've been given my first assignment. And it's all thanks to you, Fulvia."

"Juliana wouldn't have offered to help you if she

didn't already think you could do the job. When you break out on your own one day, your résumé will be worth its weight in gold because you'll have worked under her tutelage."

"I know that and I'm so thrilled! It's all because of you that I'm finally going to fulfill my dream! Now I've got to prove myself."

"I have no doubt of it."

"Neither do I," her mother said. "I don't think I've heard you this happy in years!"

Tears stung Dea's eyes. "This is the beginning of my new life."

"Your father's going to be overjoyed with this news."

"You've both given me wonderful advice and told me my future is out there waiting for me. Being able to work with Juliana, I know I'm going to find it!"

"Good for you, darling."

"I love you and will call you later."

She hung up, eager to get started on a design that would convince Juliana she hadn't been wrong to do this enormous, unprecedented favor for Fulvia. Dea had meant it when she'd said this was the beginning of her new life.

While she'd been in therapy this last year, she'd been forced to dig deep into her psyche to understand what made her tick. She'd been given several assignments to work on: forget self, put other people first and be kind before blurting out something she'd regret, even if it was true.

But her assignment to let go of the pain of the past was easier said than done. She had to stop dwelling on the fact that her identical twin sister, Alessandra, had been the one to attract the gorgeous engineering magnate Rinieri Montanari, not Dea, in an incident that had brought on Dea's emotional crisis.

She'd met Rini and his best friend Guido Rossano on board the fabulous Rossano yacht during a modeling assignment in Naples. Though Dea had been the first to meet Rini and had fallen for him on the spot—even kissing him passionately in front of Guido before saying good-night—Rini hadn't been interested in her.

When she looked back on that now, she was mortified to imagine what Guido must have thought of her behavior. As for Rini, she'd never expected to see him again. But to her shock, he met Alessandra while he was on business in the south of Italy. That was all it took for the elusive bachelor to fall in love and marry her sister.

Dea had been crushed and her serious loss of confidence had required professional help. Through therapy it became clear that, among other things, she'd always been jealous of her sister's intelligence and scholastic success. Alessandra had already written and published an important factual historical book on their ancestor Queen Joanna.

But it was her aunt Fulvia's comment that had brought her up short and made her realize she needed help.

Dea Caracciolo, do you want to conquer every man you meet? What would you do with all of them? It's not natural.

Her aunt had been right. It wasn't natural. Despite Dea's attempt to flirt with Rinieri, he hadn't been drawn to her. Period.

Following her conversation with Fulvia and her mother, Dea had gotten counseling and had been going through a difficult, painful period of self-evaluation and remembered mistakes. Her darkest memory had involved Alessandra's first love years earlier.

He'd pursued Dea. Part of her had felt guilty, yet another part had been flattered when he'd followed her back to Rome, where she was modeling at the time. But he'd turned out to be a man incapable of being faithful to any woman. A torturous time had followed for her and Alessandra. Only in the last year had they finally put the pain of that experience behind them and had become close in a new, honest way.

Still, trying to find one's self was not an easy journey. Though being a top fashion model had initially brought her excitement and a lot of interest from men, in time Dea hadn't found the fulfillment she craved in a career she'd always known couldn't last forever.

As was brought out in therapy, those deep longings for inner contentment had eluded her. She knew she would have to change her focus if she was going to have a happy life like her parents, or like Alessandra, who was now ecstatically married and a new mother. Because of a soccer injury, Rini hadn't been able to give her children, so they'd adopted little Brazzo. Dea couldn't be happier for them.

After serious thought, she'd chosen to follow her

natural inclination and make her way in a new direction that used her brain and God-given talents rather than her looks, but she was still filled with anxiety.

Forget self.

That's what her brilliant underwater-archaeologist sister had done. In the process, she'd won a wonderful man and already had a family.

Somewhere out there, Dea's prince existed. As her wise mother had promised her, "One day he'll find *you*. In the meantime, work on finding yourself, darling."

Friday afternoon Guido paused at the door of the soccer store adjoining his suite of offices in the Stadio Emanuele soccer stadium in Rome. "I'm leaving now, Sergio. As usual I'll be back Sunday morning before the big game. Have a good weekend."

"You too, boss." His administrative assistant smiled because he thought he knew why, when he could, Guido spent every Friday night and Saturday away from Rome, unable to be reached by anyone. But Sergio would be dead wrong about the reason.

Guido eyed his spectacular soccer mate from the past, whose serious leg injury at the height of his game prevented him from ever competing again. Now that Guido was the owner of a minor national soccer team, he'd recruited Sergio to do a little of everything.

The man knew more about the ins and outs of the national soccer league than anyone. He not only ran their business and ticket sales with meticulous care, but he kept the museum and their soccer store stocked and profitable. On top of that, he handled the phones and kept out unexpected visitors unless they made appointments.

"How come you haven't left already, Sergio? You work too hard. As far as I know you haven't taken a break in months." The man screened Guido's incoming phone calls from the media, but most important, those from Guido's hovering parents.

Being an only child, Guido realized they'd had a hard time accepting that he'd taken a year off from the Leonides Rossano Shipping Company to pursue an old soccer dream. Guido loved them and stayed in touch, but he'd felt smothered and enjoyed the freedom his new career was giving him away from the family business.

"Work saves me from my demons," Sergio commented. Guido could relate to that. "Don't you know there are tons of women calling here all the time after hours, or wanting to order stuff online? You're still a poster hero with those who remember you winning those past championships."

"Even after ten years?" Guido smiled wearily. "I leave all the fans to you. As I see it, you've been divorced long enough and need to find someone who can accept your passion for the sport. You had a big female following of your own."

He scoffed. "That all ended after my marriage. I don't think there is such a woman."

Neither did Guido, but he kept that comment to himself. "Try to enjoy yourself this weekend."

"I know *you* will," Sergio fired back. "Go ahead

and keep it to yourself, but you can't tell me you don't have a woman somewhere."

Conversation over. "Ciao, Sergio," he called to his friend before shutting the door.

There'd never been a lack of women for Guido. In his late teens he'd gotten into a serious relationship with one of the most popular girls at school, Carla, but over time he discovered she loved his celebrity status, not him. From that point on, he was wary of women.

The shock of learning she didn't truly love him changed his perspective on the dating experience. After that, Guido continued to enjoy women, but he didn't get into any more serious relationships. His soccer life had been so full, he'd put the idea of settling down out of his mind.

However, there'd been one woman over the last year who'd taken his breath and was still unforgettable. Dea Loti. Italy's most famous model. Her lesser-known name was Dea Caracciolo.

He'd met her aboard his father's yacht during a fashion show taped for television. It had been galling to realize she'd looked right through him in order to pursue his lifelong friend Rinieri Montanari, and it had aroused Guido's jealousy.

That emotion was something that had never happened to Guido before. He'd tried to put it away because Rini was the best, but it still haunted him.

Guido left the stadium in his Lamborghini and headed straight for the airport. By dinnertime his private jet, with the logo of Scatto Roma—the name of his soccer team, which meant *surge* in Italian—

landed at a private runway just outside Metaponto in Southern Italy. Rini would be waiting on the tarmac for him in the Jeep. They had a lot to catch up on.

Through a quirk of fate, his best friend had married Alessandra Caracciolo, Dea's identical twin sister. Since the wedding, the couple had been spending part of the time at Rini's villa in Positano and the rest of it at her family's island *castello*.

Montanari Engineering, located in Naples, was now drilling for oil on Caracciolo land in Southern Italy, thus the reason for meeting Rini here on the island.

After learning his friend had become a father, Guido had invited Rini for a meal at his apartment in Rome. But this would be the first time Guido had been back to the island since Rini's wedding to Alessandra when he'd been best man. They'd issued him many invitations to come, but Guido had turned them down, using business as the excuse. In reality, he didn't want to take the chance of seeing Dea again.

By now it shouldn't bother him that the woman who'd been so fascinated by Rini while they were on the Rossano yacht was none other than Alessandra's sister. Dea had been her maid of honor. After the wedding ceremony, she'd sat down to dinner with Guido and his parents. While she talked to them, all he could see was her kissing Rini before saying good-night to him on board the yacht.

But that was a year ago. Time had passed and he knew her modeling career took her all over Italy. He was certain she wouldn't be here at the castle. If Rini had mentioned otherwise, Guido wouldn't have accepted the invitation.

As he exited the plane he could see Rini.

"Your team name is perfect," his friend called out the window of the Jeep on the tarmac. "You *are* surging. Bravo."

"Grazie."

When Guido climbed in the Jeep, his first sight of his dark-haired friend said it all. "Fatherhood agrees with you. How is *piccolo* Brazzo?"

"He's going to be a soccer player for sure."

"I can't wait to see him."

"I'm sorry. Not this visit. He's staying with my family at the villa in Positano so Alessandra and I can have our first weekend alone."

"Lucky you."

Rini had found great happiness in his marriage. Guido would give anything to feel that fulfilled. As he sat there, it came to him that he was envious of the happy-ever-after his friend Rini had achieved, a happy-ever-after Guido hadn't thought he'd wanted himself all these years.

He stared at his friend. A spirit of contentment radiated off Rini as they drove across the causeway to the Caracciolo *castello* on Posso Island that jutted into the Ionian Sea.

Only sand surrounded the ancient structure, no grass or trees. In Guido's mind, it was Italy's answer to Mont-Saint-Michel of French fame, with a benign appeal in good weather like this. But he imagined it could look quite daunting during a storm.

Guido found it fascinating to think the beautiful twin princesses of Count Onorato di Caracciolo were born and raised here, away from civilization. From this convent-like place had emerged Italy's most beautiful supermodel. One fashion cover had called Dea Loti "Italy's own Helen of Troy."

The face that launched a thousand ships had done something to Guido...

He'd been so stunned after meeting her in person that he hadn't been able to get her out of his mind. It probably wasn't a good idea to meet Rini here after all because it brought back the memory from the wedding when he'd been watching Dea, who'd been watching Rini. Was she still hungering for him? But it was too late to think about that now or wish he hadn't come. *Get a grip, Rossano.*

"You're being unusually quiet," Rini murmured as he pulled the Jeep up to the front of the castle. "I expected to see you overjoyed with your success so far."

"I am pleased," Guido muttered, "but the season isn't over yet. We've had one loss and still have some tough games to face."

Rini shut off the engine. "You've already brought your team to new heights. I'm proud of what you've done so far."

"Spoken like my best friend," Guido murmured.

He could feel Rini's eyes on him. "How is it going with your parents?"

Guido sighed. "The same. Papà is praying I'll give up this madness and come back to the company."

"Surely not right now."

"Of course not, but he fears I'll stay away from the business for good."

Rini's brow lifted. "Do *you* think you've left the shipping business for good?"

"I don't have an answer to that yet."

"Well, I'm glad you were able to break away and come. Tomorrow we'll go out on the cruiser and do some fishing. I've got some business ideas I want your opinion on. But tonight Alessandra has arranged dinner for us with one of your favorite fish dishes."

To his chagrin, Guido had a problem he couldn't talk over with Rini. How could he tell him that Rini *himself* was the problem? "I'm already salivating."

Filled with shame over his own flawed character, he jumped out of the Jeep and grabbed his gym bag that contained all he needed for this weekend visit. They walked to the front entry. When Rini opened the door, they were greeted by a marmalade cat Guido had played with at the wedding.

"Well, hello, Alfredo."

The housekeeper's pet rubbed against Guido's jean-clad leg. He put the bag down and picked him up, remembering that the cat was getting old and needed to be carried up and down stairs. "Did you know I was coming?"

Rini grinned. "He remembers you—otherwise he wouldn't let you hold him."

"I'm honored."

"Let's go up to your old room." Rini grabbed Guido's bag and they climbed the grand staircase two steps at a time past the enormous painting of

Queen Joanna to the third floor. The windows in the bedroom looked out on the sea. He'd stayed in here before the wedding. "Go ahead and freshen up, then come down to the dining room."

"I'll be right there." Still holding Alfredo, he said, "Thanks for inviting me."

Rini headed for the entry. "I've missed our talks," he said over his shoulder.

Guido watched him disappear out the door. *What in the hell is wrong with you, Rossano? No bear hug for your best friend? What has Rini ever done to you?*

He put the cat on the bed and slipped into the bathroom. When he came out, he opened his gym bag and pulled out two presents. One was a small gift he'd bought for Alessandra in Florence after a match. The other was a baby toy he'd seen in a store near his apartment. A little purple octopus with bells on the tentacles.

"We'd better not keep everyone waiting, Alfredo." He gathered the cat in his arms along with the gifts and went down the staircase to the dining room. The second he walked in, the cat took one look at Alessandra and wanted to get down. Guido lowered him to the parquet floor.

Her gaze darted to Guido and she beamed. "So that's where the cat has been! You're one of his favorite people." She rushed over to hug Guido. He hugged her back and gave her his gifts.

"You want me to open them now?"

"I think I do."

She removed the paper from the smaller box and

lifted the lid. Inside was a small enamel painting of Queen Joanna framed in gold filigree, probably three by four inches. He heard her gasp. "Oh, Guido—"

"I saw it in Florence at the House of Gold and couldn't resist. Consider it a gift to celebrate the publication of your book."

Just then Rini came in the room. *"Caro—"* she cried and rushed over to show her husband.

His friend flashed him a warm glance. "You knew exactly what she'd love."

"I read the book and was so impressed by your knowledge I had to do something to honor you."

"I'm glad you liked it. This is exquisite. I'll treasure it forever." She laid it on the hunt board and undid the large gift. "Oh, how adorable! A purple octopus! Brazzo will love it!" She gave Guido a kiss on the cheek. "Come and sit down. We want to hear all about the team and how things are going."

"First I want to hear about Brazzo."

"He's gorgeous! We'll show you videos later."

No sooner did they get settled and start to eat than Guido heard the helicopter overhead.

"That'll be my parents," Alessandra murmured as they enjoyed their meal. "They've been in Milan."

"For another of Dea's fashion shows?" Damn if the question wasn't out before he could recall it.

"Oh—I guess you didn't know that she has given up her modeling career."

Guido's fork dropped on his plate. *No more modeling?* He couldn't comprehend it. "Since when?"

"Quite a while now. She realized the life of most

supermodels fades after twenty-five years of age and it's past time for her. Dea went back to her true passion and this last year has been finishing her degree at the Accademia Roma. This is her last semester."

Her true passion? Guido blinked. He didn't know she'd ever gone to college. "I had no idea. What is she studying?"

"Period costume fashion design. I'm so thrilled for her. She has an extraordinary gift in that area."

Before Guido could think, he heard voices at the entry. Alessandra's parents walked in the room, but he only had eyes for the gorgeous woman behind them. His heart thundered.

Dea!

She wore her long hair back in a chignon, a style he hadn't seen her in. All that glossy brown hair with streaks of sunlight was hidden. The oval of her face with less makeup than he'd ever noticed before caused him to stare. With those dark burgundy eyes—like the color in a stained glass window—she was beautiful in a brand-new way.

Guido stood up and greeted the three of them. Alessandra begged her parents to join them for dinner, but they said they'd already eaten and were going upstairs.

"What about you, Dea?"

"I'd love some dinner, but first I want to see the baby. I brought Brazzo a present. I hope he doesn't have a bear yet. This one speaks! This one speaks!" She handed it to Alessandra, who opened it and pressed the button. They all listened and laughed.

"Brazzo will love this, but we left him with Rini's father and family. They wanted to give us a break."

"I'm sure you're thrilled, but I'm horribly disappointed."

"There'll be plenty of other times for the rest of our lives."

"You're right, of course." She sat down at the table. "I left work without grabbing a bite and now I'm starving. This dinner looks wonderful. Baked halibut and vegetables with feta cheese. How perfect!"

She was wearing a simple white blouse and a print skirt. Her outfit was so unexpectedly casual that Guido was still trying to make sense of everything when she sat down next to him.

For the rest of the meal Guido was amazed to watch her dig into her food and eat everything. Where was the woman who never ate anything that wasn't on her special diet? Come to think of it, she looked like she'd gained some becoming weight since the last time he'd seen her at the wedding.

Over a glass of wine she turned to Guido. He noticed she no longer wore her fingernails long and painted. "There's a girl at the shop named Gina. She and her fiancé, Aldo, went to the soccer game at the Stadio Emanuele last weekend."

Where was this leading?

"Aldo came in to pick Gina up and she told him I knew the owner. He fell all over me." Guido could believe that. "According to him, you were the greatest soccer player he'd ever seen and he desperately wants to meet you in person sometime, hopefully with my help."

Dea had discussed him with her coworker? He couldn't believe it.

She kept talking. "According to Aldo, the Scatto Roma team is going to win the championship this year. He was a soccer player himself, not on your level, of course. He thinks you walk on water already for lifting the B team to top-tier status."

"Thank you, Dea," he said, attempting to take it all in, but he couldn't understand her interest. "Have you ever been to a soccer match?"

"Never," she confessed without shame. "I've never even watched it on TV. You must think I'm terrible. I had no idea you'd won so many championships for Italy. Aldo said you were everyone's favorite player and the women were crazy about you."

"They were," Rini inserted with a grin.

She hadn't talked to Guido like this at the wedding reception, where she had seemed very stiff. This was something else. He decided to change the subject.

"I understand you're no longer modeling."

"Not for the last year."

"Where do you work?"

"I started at the shop of Juliana Parma ten days ago. She's *the* costume designer for the opera. I've been permitted to shadow her. My aunt Fulvia made it possible. You remember her from the wedding?"

"Of course." The woman had taken Dea away from the table before the wedding cake had been served.

"They're best friends and Juliana took me on as

a favor to my aunt. But now that I'm working there, I'm on my own and I'm terrified."

"How could you possibly be that when you've been Italy's top model?"

"That period of my life is over, and modeling modern-day fashions has nothing to do with being a period costume designer for the opera." Guido still had a hard time believing she had changed her whole life in the last year. To his mind, she was more beautiful than ever. "I have to prove myself in a whole new field. I'm not like you."

"What do you mean?"

"Alessandra said that when you bought that floundering soccer team, you had the satisfaction of being one of the greatest soccer players ever to compete in Italy. With your knowledge and confidence, you've been able to turn your team around. I'm very impressed."

"He's done that, all right," Rini concurred. "So I have an idea. Why don't the four of us go out behind the castle and play a little soccer before it gets dark? Two against two. It works even if we don't have a whole bunch of guys around. Since Brazzo was born, Alessandra and I haven't had a weekend to enjoy like this. Let's team up."

"That sounds fun!" Alessandra chimed in with enthusiasm that sounded real. "I like soccer, but I'd love to learn more about it since Rini is determined our son will be a great player like you, Guido. What do you say, Dea?"

"I'm hopeless when it comes to sports and would hate making a fool of myself, but I'll do it this once."

So she was willing to toss him a bone after she'd just admitted she'd never even seen a soccer game?

"Let me run upstairs to put on my trainers."

Alessandra patted her husband's arm. "I'll find mine too."

Rini got to his feet. "My soccer ball is around here somewhere. We'll all meet in the foyer in a few minutes."

Everyone took off except for Guido, who stood there in a funk. Since Rini's marriage, they hadn't had time to kick a ball around. And now he wanted them to play with the women?

He'd go along with this, but before he went to bed, he intended to have a talk with Rini about what was going on.

CHAPTER TWO

DEA RACED UP the stairs to her bedroom. Rini had no idea how petrified she was when it came to participating in sports. Alessandra was the one who did everything well: tennis, golf, swimming and scuba diving. But Dea didn't dare say no to his suggestion in front of Guido.

The tall, attractive dark blond was not only a recognized national celebrity in the sports field; he was Rini's best friend. Dea didn't want to be a drama queen and create a scene. Those days were relegated to the past. She'd turned over a new leaf and was embracing a different life that meant accepting challenges she'd avoided before now.

She changed out of her skirt into jeans and put on her trainers. No doubt she would fall flat on her face repeatedly for being out of her element, but at least she would be prepared. If Rini allowed her to be on his team, then she'd wouldn't feel so terrible when she let him down. Alessandra would be a much better fit for Guido when it came to sports.

How strange that today of all days Dea's folks had

come to the shop and begged her to fly home with
them after work for the weekend. None of them had
known that Rini and Alessandra had invited Guido.
It had come as a shock to see the three of them at the
dining room table.

Both on the yacht and at the wedding, Dea had
only seen him dressed in a tuxedo. This evening
Guido was wearing a blue polo shirt that emphasized
his well-defined chest, which combined with tight
jeans made it impossible to look anywhere else. Soccer kept him in the sun. His bronzed complexion ac-
centuated the midnight blue of his dark-fringed eyes.

She could understand why female soccer fans
would have gone crazy over him. Guido might not
be playing soccer now, but it didn't matter. He was
an incredibly appealing man.

After the fashion show on the yacht, Guido's father had sought her out. At the time she'd taken an instant dislike to the renowned shipping-company CEO.
He was so full of himself that he was quite unbearable. Dea's modest father was a completely different
type and so easy to be around. Meeting the puffed-
up man's son was the last thing Dea and her friend
Daphne, who had modeled with her, had wanted to
do, but she knew she had to be gracious.

Prepared not to like his son, who was probably an
obnoxious replica of his father, she'd been shocked to
meet his best friend, Rini Montanari, the dark-haired
handsome prince standing next to him. At that moment everything else had left her mind. He wasn't a
real prince, but he'd seemed to have stepped right out

of her childhood dreams. But Rini hadn't responded to her as she'd hoped and her world had fallen apart. Of course, that was ages ago…

Tonight she felt she was truly seeing Guido for the first time and not just as Rini's best friend. It had been unfair to judge him because of his father. This was important to Rini and Alessandra. For that reason she made up her mind to be a good sport and act friendly. Why not? If nothing else, she might be able to talk him into meeting Gina's fiancé after a game, or giving Aldo an autographed team poster or something.

Dea left the bedroom and hurried down to the foyer, where the others had congregated. Rini glanced at her. "While we were waiting, we flipped a coin. You're on Guido's team." He smiled broadly. "My wife is on mine."

"Hmm. I wonder how that happened. Sorry, Guido." Dea rolled her eyes at him. "You got the bad end of this deal."

"Why don't I show you a few moves before we start." He was holding the soccer ball. "Who knows what can happen?"

She chuckled. "I'm game if you are. Let's go."

They left the castle and walked around to the back, where the cruiser was pulled up to the dock in the distance. Rini and Alessandra had moved on to draw boundary lines in the sand.

While Guido explained the basic rudiments of the sport to her, there was no chitchat. He was all business. No doubt the players on his team held him in awe.

"The whole point of the game is to prevent the

other team from driving the ball forward and scor-
ing. One of the first basic moves is to take a big side
step and pull the ball with you to put space between
you and the enemy."

"Show me."

"It goes like this."

Dea watched his hard-muscled body and legs do
the move with sheer masculine grace and speed.
Whoa. She smiled. "Do that again."

He did it five more times. No matter how she an-
ticipated what he was going to do, she couldn't react
fast enough to stop him.

"Again!"

This time she was desperate to succeed. Refusing
to let him elude her, she made a flying leap and tackled him with all her strength. They both went down.
She turned over to look at him, trying to catch her
breath, but laughter kept bubbling out of her. "I'm
sorry."

"No, you're not." He lay there looking at her before bursting into laughter himself. Their faces were
so close she could tell his incredible blue eyes were
smiling. Guido Rossano was a sensational-looking
man. How could she not have noticed before today?

His gaze continued to play over her features. "For
a first soccer lesson, you did well. You'd make an excellent player in American football—tackling is what
they do in their football games. Tackling isn't what
we do in soccer. Who would have thought?"

"Forgive me. I got so frustrated I didn't know what
else to do."

"You've got all the right instincts, but you need to refine your technique to soccer or you'll get thrown out of the game."

"Hey, you two?" Rini called from a distance. "Are we going to play, or what?"

"I need to show her a few more moves before we start," Guido shouted back.

Guilt swept over her as he helped her to her feet. Conscious of their clasped hands, she eased hers from his grip. As his eyes focused on hers, her heart skipped a beat for no good reason. "We'll start with the lift, step and go." He put the ball on the ground. "Use your foot to push it toward me and watch."

Dea was loving this. She started moving the ball toward him. He lifted his foot as if to do a sideward motion. But it was a fake move. He stepped forward and drove the ball away from her. She groaned.

"Let's do that again."

She pushed the ball three more times, but he evaded her every time. "You're amazing!"

"Not amazing. I've been doing this move since childhood."

"No wonder Aldo idolizes you." After four tries she got the hang of it.

"Okay. Now what's the next move called?"

"You're not tired yet?"

"No, but maybe *you* are."

His hard jaw rose a fraction and he put his hands on his hips in a totally male stance. "This one is called the chip shot. Come toward me, moving the ball with your feet."

She did his bidding and thought he would push the ball forward, but he chipped it instead so it flipped up, catching her off guard.

"Oh! I *like* that move. I want to try it." But with her next effort, she used too much force and fell on her derriere. He chuckled and helped her to her feet.

"Try once more."

Dea did her best and stayed upright.

"Bravo. You're ready. Let's try out those moves on them before they decide they want to go home."

"You think I can do it?"

"We're about to find out." The way he smiled made him look like a devilishly handsome blond pirate with a wicked gleam in his eyes. How odd that she'd never dreamed of a tall blond pirate prince before...

The guys played goalie so the girls could battle it out. Guido hadn't had so much fun in years and was silently betting on Dea to outplay Alessandra.

Right away it became clear that Rini hadn't taught Alessandra any special moves. She could run and scrap, but Dea pulled a few moves on her with an expertise that shocked Guido. In the end, Team Scatto Roma took the honors over Team Montanari. Again he was surprised she'd caught on so quickly and he discovered he was proud of her.

Alessandra eyed the three of them. "Now it's the men's turn. You and I will play goalie, Dea."

"I'm ready."

"It's too dark out," Rini protested.

His wife smiled. "Since when has that ever stopped you? I'm counting on you to win for our side."

Guido turned to his friend. "Come on. Let's show the girls how the game is played."

"You're on."

Before they spread out, Guido took Dea aside. "Try not to let the ball get past you. Do whatever you need to do."

"I'm afraid Rini will kick it so hard I won't stand a chance, but I'll try."

He squeezed her elbow. "No one can ask for more than that."

In a minute play commenced. Rini gave as good as he got, but Guido's competitive spirit had kicked in. That's when he realized he was fighting a demon from the past and taking it out on his friend. The score was two to two. Rini went all out for the last play. He gave the ball a kick as fierce as the expression on his face. Dea didn't stand a chance. Or so Guido thought until he saw her catch it midair.

"I did it!" she cried out in unfeigned excitement. Forgetting everything, he ran toward her and swung her around. "Keep this up and I'll sign you on to my team." Before he lowered her warm beautiful body to the ground, there was a breathless moment when even in the semidark her cognac eyes seemed to sparkle. He wanted badly to taste her mouth, but they had an audience and she would probably slap his face.

Alessandra ran up to Dea and hugged her. "I thought you said you've never done sports. What's happened?"

Dea flicked Guido a glance. "I had a good teacher."

"I'll say you did. Come on. Let's go in."

Rini kissed his wife. "We'll catch up with you two in a minute."

As the women walked off, Guido sucked in his breath. The time for the talk with Rini had come. His friend stared him down. "Do you want to tell me what's going on with you? Everything has been different since Alessandra and I have been married, so I'll make this easier for you and start. Why haven't you wanted to get together like we used to do?"

He rubbed the back of his neck. "You really don't know?"

"Guido—" The bleak expression on his face spoke volumes and made Guido feel guiltier than ever. "Talk to me! If I've done something wrong, I'll fix it if I can."

"You can't."

"Why?"

It was hard to swallow. "I'm ashamed to tell you."

"Why?" he demanded again.

Just tell him, Rossano, and get it over with.

"It's ever since that night on the yacht. I'd never known jealousy in my life until then. But I did the moment I met Dea and she took one look at you and fell head over heels."

Rini's black brows formed a line above his dark eyes. "Way back then *you* were jealous of *that*?"

"The force of it hit me like a blow to my gut."

"Are you telling me you were interested in Dea?" He shook his head in total bewilderment. "I thought you'd never met her before that night."

"I hadn't, but her face was continually in the news. Seeing her on deck did something visceral to me. But before I could do anything about it, she walked right into your arms."

Rini shook his head. "I don't know what to say."

"You don't have to say anything. You couldn't help that she was attracted to you. The fact that I knew you weren't attracted to her didn't help me. I've suffered ever since that night because I've held something against you that couldn't possibly have been your fault. You have every right to tell me to go to hell and stay there."

Rini came closer. "That's the last thing I want to do. All this time you've been suffering…"

"And I've made *you* suffer. I'm so sorry, Rini."

To his shock, his friend smiled. "If I don't miss my guess, I believe cupid shot an arrow into your heart when you laid eyes on Dea. The same thing happened to me when I met Alessandra."

"You're right," he murmured.

"*Paisano*—you've been smitten since the night your father brought Dea and her friend over to meet us after the fashion show. After your experience with Carla, I've wondered for years when love would hit you. Little does your *papà* know his endless machinations to find you a wife finally worked!"

Guido threw his head back. "They did."

"Now that I know your secret, I understand what happened out here on the sand just now. You swung Dea around with more energy than I've ever seen in

you. I guess her flying tackle earlier had something
to do with your reaction."

"I've never been so surprised in my life."

Rini grinned. "Contact sports can be fun, especially when it was Dea who initiated that move. You
must be doing something right or she wouldn't have
allowed herself to get in *your* arms."

No one ever had a better friend. Guido cocked his
head. "You don't despise me for being a total fool
this last year?"

"It's forgotten." He gripped Guido's shoulder.
"Listen—I'm going to tell you a secret and I hope
you can handle it. You have no idea the number of
times I envied you for all the women who threw themselves at you. I didn't have that experience growing
up and feared I'd never meet the right woman for me.

"Need I remind you of Arianna, who was so crazy
about you she came to every game and hung around
you for weeks? I might as well have been invisible.
She was gorgeous and I was jealous as hell."

"You're kidding—"

"No. Don't you remember my telling you that I
wouldn't have minded if she'd come after me, but it
didn't happen? And then there was Carla." Guido pre-
ferred not to think about her. "Let's be honest. You
could have had any woman you ever wanted."

"Except Dea...who wanted you."

His dark brows lifted. "Dea didn't want me. We
talked about it. Growing up in a castle together, she
and Alessandra had this idea of marrying a tall, dark-
haired prince. My image filled the bill. But that's all

it was. The image vanished. If you're asking me if she still sees me as her prince, the answer is a definite no. Surely you could tell that at the wedding. I'm now her irritating brother-in-law."

"She seemed to be in a world of her own that day," Guido said.

"That's because she was going through a major life crisis, another thing you're going through yourself taking on a soccer team. In many ways, you and Dea are a lot alike. You had your pick of women over the years but didn't settle. She always had her pick of men, yet didn't end up with any of them. One day she's going to fall so hard that'll be it. Lucky will be the man who captures her heart."

"Wouldn't it be funny if it turned out to be me," he muttered.

Rini shot him a piercing glance. "You and I both know that no matter how bad it looks, you never leave the stadium until the game is over. Astounding surprises happen in the last second."

"True." Guido couldn't argue with that kind of logic. Nor could he doubt that Rini had given him all the truth inside him.

His friend picked up the ball. "Come on. Let's get back to the *castello*. How soon do you have to return to Rome?"

"I have to fly out early Sunday morning for the game."

"I happen to know Dea will be around until then too. Alessandra had planned a day out on the cruiser for the three of us tomorrow. But with Dea still here, it'll be even more fun. Maybe you can teach her how to water ski. She gave up after trying it the first time."

"She hasn't done any water sports?" Guido was incredulous.

"A little swimming. That's it. But the way she got into the soccer match proves to me she's not only game, she's a fast learner. I only have one question. Are *you* game?"

Until their talk a few minutes ago Guido would have said no.

They returned to the castle, where the girls had dessert and coffee waiting for them in the dining room. Guido enjoyed the snack while they chuckled about Dea's tackle, then he excused himself to go up to bed.

"Don't forget tomorrow," Rini called after him. "Once we've eaten breakfast, we'll go out on the cruiser."

"Sounds good." With a smile for the three of them, he left the room.

Alessandra came to Dea's bedroom the next morning in order to French-braid her hair before breakfast.

"Thanks for doing this for me. I can't do it right. Now it won't get in my face."

"As you know, I had mine cut short years ago because I spent so much time in the water scuba diving."

"I'm thinking I might get mine cut too, after I get back to Rome."

"Oh, no, Dea. Your gorgeous long hair? Are you sure?"

"It drives me insane while I'm working. I used to wonder why Juliana wore her hair short. Now I know. Hair gets in the way when you're kneeling in front of a mannequin to work on a hem. We're constantly bending over to examine a drawing or a cut of fabric. All you need is an irritating strand to fall at a critical moment."

"Well, it's your call," Alessandra murmured. "Now let's hurry down to breakfast before the guys eat everything in sight."

"I just hope Guido's forgiven me for tackling him. I don't know what came over me."

"I do. It's called frustration beyond bearing! They're both so good at everything it can drive you crazy! I'm sure no one ever did such a thing to Guido before."

"That's what has me worried."

"Rini laughed about it after we went to bed. He's sure you're the only woman who ever got the best of Guido."

"Now I'm worried he'll pull something on *me* today."

Alessandra's eyes sparkled. "Just don't let your guard down." Her warning excited Dea.

After her sister left the bedroom, she dressed in shorts and a yellow top worn over her orange-and-white-striped bikini. Once ready, she grabbed her tote bag and flew down the stairs in sandals to the dining room. At the entrance, a pair of inky-blue eyes met hers across the room, causing her pulse to race.

"*Buongiorno*, Dea." His deep voice curled through to her insides.

This morning Guido had put on a white T-shirt

and cargo pants that couldn't hide his powerful legs. He held a mug of coffee and looked so sensational she was taken back. A nervous smile broke out on her face. "I hope you didn't wake up with any aches or pains."

"I'm managing to survive," he mocked gently.

Uh-oh. "Where is everyone?"

"Alessandra grabbed a jam *cornetto* and went out to help Rini load the cruiser. Come and join me before we head out."

Since Guido was still here, maybe it meant he'd been waiting for her. Her heart flipped over again.

"Cook makes the best cappuccino in the world."

"I agree," he murmured over the rim of his cup.

Aware of his scrutiny, she walked over to the hunt board and reached for a pastry. After pouring herself coffee, she moved to the table to eat. Once he joined her, she couldn't resist asking, "Are you a champion water-skier too? Alessandra said Rini can't wait to get out on the water and ski double with you."

He sat back in the chair, studying her through shuttered eyes. "I've done a little of everything."

"But soccer is your passion."

"One of them."

A shiver of excitement ran through her. The intimation of what his other passions might be brought heat to her cheeks. With his dark blond hair slightly disheveled, she discovered he had a potent male appeal no woman could possibly ignore. His girlfriends must be legion.

Once they'd finished breakfast, they left the castle for the dock around the back. During their short walk she thought about him and Rini being such close friends since childhood. They were so different, *except* in two major ways. Their masculine charisma was lethal and they both had an air of authority that seemed to be part of their natures.

Dea had met many men over the years, but none of them possessed those extraordinary qualities. She might have known that Rini's best man would be someone who stood out from all the rest too. He wasn't anything like his father. At least she didn't think so, but what did she know?

Maybe if she'd stayed at the table the night of the wedding reception and had gotten better acquainted with the head of Rossano Shipping Lines, she'd have seen similarities that hadn't been apparent at first. Guido was his son after all.

In the past Dea had had a problem with making snap judgments about people. It came from a fear that people saw her as only a superficial narcissist—an unfair label given to models in general. Her mother had pointed out that she put up a defensive shield because part of her felt insecure. Dea had had to learn to give everyone a chance.

Since she'd gone back to school, she'd been making a conscious effort to get along with people. While she and Gina had been at the shop discussing one of the designs that wasn't working, she'd learned the other woman loved the theater. Dea would never have guessed that—all Gina seemed to talk about was Aldo, who lived in her apartment building.

He worked in a garage and wasn't happy because he couldn't make good money. The last thing he'd do was spend the little he had on going to watch a play he had no interest in. Soccer was a different story. Dea had offered to go to the theater with Gina, who was delighted. They planned to see *Othello* at the Silvano Toti Globe in Rome the next weekend. It would give them a chance to study the costuming while they enjoyed Shakespeare.

"Hey, you two," Rini called to them.

When they reached the cabin cruiser, Dea climbed over the side first. After stowing her tote bag below deck, she came back up and slipped on the life belt Alessandra handed her.

Rini took the wheel and signaled to Guido, who untied the ropes. Dea drew in a deep breath, filled with a sense of anticipation that was new to her. She wouldn't lie to herself. Guido's presence was the reason for this feeling, plus a warm sun that portended a perfect day to be out on the water.

Except for a few freighters way off in the distance, they had the sea to themselves. Five minutes later Rini cut the engine. He shot Guido a glance. The other man had already removed his T-shirt. The sight of his hard-muscled body changed the tenor of Dea's breathing.

"Ready to give the girls a show?"

Guido fastened his life belt. "Whenever you are."

The guys tossed two slalom skis in the water and dove off the transom like porpoises. Alessandra turned to Dea. "While I drive, you get in the back.

Keep an eye on the ropes while they're uncoiling. When the guys are up, spot them. In case they get into any trouble, tell me and I'll cut the engine."

With a legitimate excuse to feast her eyes on Guido, she knelt on the banquette and watched them fasten their skis. Then she heard Rini yell, "Hit it!" Alessandra increased the speed and a minute later both men were out of the water like professionals who'd been doing this for years.

They moved in wide arcs and displayed an expertise on one ski Dea marveled over. How would it be to ski like that? "They're fabulous!" she called to Alessandra. "Have you gotten up on one ski yet?"

"No. It's hard."

I want to learn.

Several minutes went by before she saw Rini lift his free arm. "I think they want to stop," she shouted.

"Okay! Start reeling in the ropes and coil them."

Dea did as she asked and wound the rope. Alessandra brought the cruiser around and cut the engine in order to reach for the skis and put them on the transom. With masculine dexterity, the men heaved themselves aboard. Dea couldn't take her eyes off Guido. The sun bathed him in light. He looked like a golden god as he reached for a towel.

"Bravo," she told both of them.

Rini flicked her a glance. "Think you want to do it?"

She finished coiling the second rope. "I'd like to try, but it won't be on one ski. Can you do it on your feet?"

Deep laughter came out of Guido. "I'm afraid it hurts too much."

"Even though you were a soccer player?"

"Even though. Want to go now?"

No…but she *had* to. That was her new rule. Don't hang back. She'd given up before when she'd gone skiing with Alessandra, but her sister was so good at it that Dea had decided not to try anymore. Thank goodness she'd worked out in a gym close to her apartment all these years in order to stay in shape.

"Sure."

"Good for you. There's very little wind right now. It's the best time."

Rini nodded. "I'll drive and Alessandra will spot you."

"Okay," she said on a jerky breath. *Here goes nothing.* Dea undid the belt in order to remove her clothes, then refastened it.

Guido told her to walk over so he could fit her feet in the skis and adjust them. While he hunkered down, she put a hand on his solid shoulder to steady herself. The warmth from his skin crept into her body. Then she stepped out of the skis with his help.

"I'll go first." He jumped in the water and she handed him the skis. Then it was her turn. Once her head surfaced she felt Guido's hands steady her from behind while Rini started the cruiser and slowly pulled away from them. Alessandra let out the rope.

"Grasp it in your hand while I put the skis on you." Guido did everything with ease. "Now I want you to lie back in my arms and brace your legs so they're ready to come out of the water straight. Don't be frightened. When I call out, 'Hit it,' you'll be pulled right up. Just hold on to the rope with both hands. Let the boat do the rest and don't look down. I'll be right here in case you fall."

"Thank you." Saying a little prayer, she watched until the rope was all the way out. Suddenly she heard Guido's voice and the cruiser leaped forward. To her shock she rose right up on top of the water and was skimming across the placid surface.

Dea couldn't believe she was actually water-skiing again, but she was moving fast and made the mistake of doing the one thing Guido had told her not to do. That's when she lost her balance and let go of the rope. The boat swung around and came alongside her. In a second Guido was there and pulled her back against his chest.

"You were terrific."

"No. I blew it because I looked down."

Her sister smiled at her from the boat. "I didn't get up until four tries."

"Let's do it again," Guido urged her. "Your skis are still on. Throw her the rope, Alessandra, and we'll have another go."

Uh-oh. But she refused to reveal weakness in front of Guido.

Once again Rini sat at the wheel and started the engine while Guido put her in the same position as before. He tugged her braid. "Did you know you have a lethal weapon here?"

"I'm sorry if it flipped you."

"I'll live."

His comment brought a giggle out of her, but it was

lost in a cry when she felt the cruiser take off and pull her on top of the water. More used to the sensation, she stayed up rather inelegantly for over a minute, but her legs were tired because she wasn't used to this.

She lifted her arm and immediately Rini cut the engine. This time when she sank in the water, she didn't panic like before. The belt helped her stay afloat. This was fun. So much fun she couldn't believe she'd lived twenty-eight years without knowing the thrill.

CHAPTER THREE

DEA HAD HEARD the others talking about planning a scuba diving trip. She didn't know if she could ever gird up her courage to take lessons and try it, but she wouldn't say no if she got the chance. That was because she had an excellent teacher in Guido, who was fast approaching. The glint of admiration in those dark blue eyes mesmerized her.

"We'll have you on one ski before the day is out."

"Not now. Two are all I can handle, but one day I plan to get there."

After Guido removed her skis, Rini helped her onto the transom and Alessandra was there to hand her a towel.

Now it was Alessandra's turn to ski while Guido spotted her. Dea let out the rope and watched her sister come out of the water on two skis like a champion.

No longer envious of her sister, she admired her. Once Alessandra had done a four-minute run, they brought her in. Dea praised her sister. As for the adoring look in Rini's eyes, it was something to behold. To be loved like that…

For the next hour they enjoyed an alfresco lunch and spent the rest of the day swimming around the boat and fishing with different lures. Dea had gone trolling with her parents many times in the past, so this wasn't new to her. But the company made it an experience she didn't want to end. Guido and Rini exchanged fishing stories and past shenanigans that had the girls roaring with laughter.

They arrived back at the castle having caught a lot of sun and enough cod to feed everyone, including their parents. The cook grilled it for their dinner. Alessandra and Dea helped in the kitchen to speed up the process for all of them, and they sat down to a delicious meal.

In time they retreated to the dayroom, where her father got out the family movies and turned on the TV screen. "First we'll watch the latest videos of Brazzo."

Alfredo wandered in and climbed on her lap. She hugged the cat to her.

The videos of the baby were adorable. Then her father put in another video.

"This shows you girls playing house with your own play castle when you were six."

Dea had forgotten about that one. They used to set it up in the living room with all kinds of props, dolls and clothes. She and Alessandra wore long make-shift costumes and performed as if they were doing a documentary.

"This is where Dea's dream to become a costume designer began," her father informed them. "She was the one to decide what they would wear."

"I was so bossy it's embarrassing."

Her father smiled. "If you'll notice, Alessandra was much more interested in the boat outside the castle she moved around and around."

Everyone laughed, but Dea was mortified. She hoped the videos would end soon. Dea's prayers were answered when her father finally shut off the TV and her parents went to bed. Then Rini and Alessandra said good-night, leaving her alone with Guido. Her heart beat fast.

"I've enjoyed getting to know you today, Dea. Since we're both working in Rome, I'd like to spend time with you again."

"I had a fun time too, and would like that."

"Then I'll call you later in the week. Much as I'd love to stay up and talk to you longer, I've got to get to bed. I have a big game tomorrow and have to be up early."

"Of course. Good luck. I'm counting on your team to win."

"Thank you. So am I." He got to his feet. Alfredo leaped off her lap to follow him.

"No, no, Alfredo." She jumped up and grabbed him. "You have to go to your own bed." Dea lifted her head to look at Guido. "Good night."

His eyes pierced hers. *"Buonanotte."*

Dea took the cat back to the housekeeper's suite, then went upstairs.

After a luxurious shower, she reached for the laptop and climbed into bed to search for the Scatto Roma website. A world of revelation met her eyes.

For the next hour she was entranced and read every bit of information about the history of the team, the new owner, the players, schedules, stats, the soccer museum and the online store.

When she typed in Guido's name, dozens of references came up. There were galleries of his pictures from when he'd been the sensational soccer player of the day. They called him *Cuor di Leone*, the Lionhearted. The explanation stated that it wasn't in honor of Richard the Lionheart but for Guido's father, Leonides Rossano, who was known as Naples's business lion.

Every picture of the striking, fierce competitor took her breath. Guido had worn his hair longer then. In some pictures it resembled a lion's coloring. She went back to the online shop and picked out two large signed posters of him to be sent to her. One was for Gina to give Aldo.

The other poster she'd keep in the bedroom at her apartment. Dea had never been a typical teen who worshipped boys and musical groups. She'd never had posters on her bedroom walls. This would be her first one.

Because of her insecurities, Dea had never handled boys right at school. Since becoming a model, she could never trust the men she dated to see past her looks. Therapy had taught her she hadn't given them a chance. There'd probably been several great guys she might have fallen in love with if she'd understood herself better.

With a deep sigh, she put the laptop on the floor

and got under the covers, but she didn't fall asleep for a long time. Her mind relived those moments in the water when Guido had cradled her in his arms. He smelled wonderful and made her feel safe and confident enough to move beyond the tight boundaries she'd drawn for herself years ago. She'd see him at breakfast before he left. Morning couldn't come soon enough.

At eight the next day she went down to the dining room and found her parents eating. "*Buongiorno*, darling."

She kissed their cheeks. "Where's everyone else?"

"Your sister and Rini drove Guido to the airport two hours ago."

"Two hours ago?" Dea was shocked.

"He had to get back early for the game. The two of them will be back later."

With the disappointing news that he'd already gone, the bottom fell out of her day. "I have to get back to Rome too."

"But your flight won't leave until three. Sit down and eat breakfast with us. We know we're lucky you would come home with us this weekend. Have you had a good time so far?"

"It's been great." That was the truth.

She poured herself some coffee. Guido had told her he'd phone her. She hoped he meant it. There'd been moments this weekend when she'd thought he was attracted to her, but she'd learned from her sister that Guido had enjoyed his share of girlfriends.

He was her brother-in-law's age, thirty-two, yet

still not engaged or married. Maybe he was this way around all women, making them feel special in the moment without having deeper feelings for them. He couldn't have known she'd be coming to the *castello*. Was he glad to discover she'd come? Would he forget about calling her once he was back in Rome?

A tiny moan escaped. There she went again, making this whole situation about her. He'd said he would phone. But until he did, she had work to do. Her mind cast back to what her mother had told her when she was at her lowest ebb. *One day your prince will find you. In the meantime, work on finding yourself.*

Good advice. *Keep remembering it, Dea. Hit the gym before work and concentrate on the fabulous opportunity of learning from the great Juliana.*

Guido waited until Wednesday morning to phone Rini and Alessandra to thank them for the great weekend.

"Are you telling me you had a better time than you'd imagined?"

"You could say that." Thoughts of Dea had been on his mind ever since. "Before I went to bed that night, I told Dea I'd call her, but I don't have her cell phone number."

"I've got it."

Guido wrote it down. "Thanks for that."

"You're welcome. Congratulations on another win on Sunday. Your name is all over the sports news."

"We're on a roll right now. Here's hoping it lasts."

"I have no doubt of it."

"Thanks again for everything. Talk to you soon."

"Ciao."

At noon Guido phoned Dea, but his call was put through to her voice mail. He wanted to meet her for lunch on Thursday if she was available and asked her to call him back. Later in the day Dea rang back. They decided on a little bistro around the corner near her work. She'd meet him there tomorrow at twelve thirty. With the opera's opening coming up in May, they were swamped with work.

Thursday finally arrived. Guido had been living for it. Even in jeans and a top with her hair pulled back in a chignon, Dea was a standout beauty. She drew the attention of everyone when she walked in the foyer, but no one more than Guido, who'd arrived ten minutes ahead of time to wait for her.

A smile lit up her face. "Hi, Guido! I hope I'm not too late."

"I'm early," he explained. "Shall we eat outside?"

"I'd love it. The workrooms tend to suffocate you when we're all in there running around for this and that."

The waiter showed them to a table and they sat down while he took their order. "I'm glad I called ahead for a table. This place is crowded."

She nodded. "It's so popular I've only been here once. And that time we had to wait in line for a half hour, which made us late for work."

"Us?"

"My friend Gina, who works at the shop too. I told you about her. By the way, congratulations on your win last Sunday. You must be feeling on top of the world."

"That feeling lasted until Monday morning."

She chuckled. "So your fears are working up to a frenzy again for this coming Sunday?"

"*Frenzy* is the right word."

Their pasta arrived. "While the waiter is here, would you like some wine?"

"Not during my workday, thank you. Just coffee."

"You're no fun."

"It wouldn't be so funny if I designed the skinny pants for the baritone and they ended up being for the fat tenor, who couldn't pull them on."

Guido burst into laughter. "I see where you're going with this. You've made your case."

Dea was working her charm on him and it made him nervous as hell, but he couldn't identify the reason why until after she'd told him she had to get right back to work. He followed her through the restaurant to the front door.

"Thanks for lunch, Guido. I enjoyed this break with you."

"So did I. I'll phone you again."

"Good. Ciao."

He watched her walk off. So did every other male in sight, many of whom had probably recognized the famous supermodel.

On the drive back to his apartment, he figured out what was wrong with him. Dea wasn't just any woman. She had the title of princess, if she ever wanted to use it, but he couldn't see her doing that.

What worried him was that she'd become his addiction since their unexpected time at the castle. He knew he wanted a serious relationship with her, but would a princess consider what he did for a living to be something suitable?

Guido's father had always been very negative about soccer being a proper career. The comments he had made in the past were never very far from the surface, and they came back to haunt Guido now. For the next few days he let that concern prevent him from calling Dea again.

On Saturday afternoon Guido was getting ready to leave the stadium and found Sergio in the mail room. "How come you're still here?"

"I've had to stay open until the suppliers delivered this week's inventory. A few more orders need to get mailed out before I go to my sister's place for a party."

"That sounds fun. Before I leave, tell me, what's selling the most?"

"Besides T-shirts, our signed soccer balls and autographed posters of our team's stars, of course. We can't keep in enough of the ones of Drago and Dante."

That figured. The two forwards were the current rage. Guido's brows lifted. "How many requests came in for posters of you?"

"Give it up, Guido. None this week, but last weekend someone ordered two posters of you. They picked the one of you making the point that won our game against Team Lancio. I blinked when I saw the name."

"Why?"

"How many women do you know with the name

Dea? You know who I'm talking about. Italy's own Helen of Troy."

Guido's heartbeat skidded off the charts. "I imagine there are hundreds of Deas living in Italy," he muttered in a gravelly voice. Sergio knew nothing about Guido's private life.

"You're probably right."

"Don't keep your family waiting. I'll see you tomorrow before the game."

"Ciao, boss."

He left the stadium and went out to the parking lot for his car. Tonight his parents had invited him for dinner at the family villa in Naples. He'd take the helicopter from the airport.

During the flight he couldn't stop thinking about Dea. It had to be a coincidence that someone with the same name had ordered from the store. Much as he wished he could forget it, he remained preoccupied throughout the evening with his parents. It was good to see them, but he was anxious to get back to Rome before it grew too late.

After his return, he had every intention of driving straight to his apartment. But at the last second he turned off the main route and headed for the stadium. He wouldn't be able to sleep until he knew who had ordered those posters.

The night watchman nodded to him before he let himself inside the store. Once on the computer, he found the week's invoices and scrolled down until he saw a name and address near the bottom that stood out like a flashing red light. *Dea Caracciolo, Via Giustiniani 2, Roma, Italia.*

She'd ordered them the previous Saturday night.

The breath Guido had been holding escaped. That exclusive, pricey address was near the Pantheon, not far from the soccer stadium. She'd ordered two posters of him. He remembered her telling him about her friend Gina, whose fiancé, Aldo, wanted to meet him. Maybe Dea had decided to buy her a signed poster of Guido to give to him. But why had she ordered two?

Guido walked through to the mail room. No tubes or packaged soccer balls were in the out basket. That meant Sergio had taken all the mail to the post office on his way home. She would have received them by now.

The worry he'd felt since their lunch was suddenly replaced by a flicker of hope that his job didn't turn her off. But ordering some posters from the store could mean anything. Guido would be a fool to jump to conclusions until he saw her again.

If he hadn't stopped in to talk to Sergio for a minute, he would never have known she'd ordered something from the store. Every Italian male was halfway in love with Dea's image. It was no surprise his business partner had picked up on her name immediately.

Preoccupied with thoughts of her, he locked up and drove home to his apartment. Morning would come early—he would be meeting with the team and the coaches then. The game against Genoa tomorrow would be critical. Granted, his team had been riding a wave since last November with only one loss, but that could change. A defeat at this stage would tell the soccer world that Team Scatto Roma wasn't ready to compete at A-tier status.

Five more games to go. The season would be over at the end of May. Tonight his father had asked him if he intended to continue for a second season. Guido couldn't give him an answer, but he'd promised to work part-time at the shipping office during June and July. That was as much as he could agree to and still run summer-camp training sessions with the team.

There were other businessmen who would love to buy him out if the team won the national B championship at the end of May. But the decision to sell was still a long way off. Going back to the shipping firm full-time meant signing on as CEO. Guido wasn't ready for that. At the moment he loved the work he was doing. Whether that translated into being fully involved in the soccer world for the rest of his life was a question he couldn't answer yet.

When he'd made the decision to buy a failing team, some element in his life had been missing. It was still missing. The more he thought about it, the more he feared that no matter what path he took, his life would go on to be unfulfilling without the right woman.

Now that he'd spent some time with a Dea he hadn't known existed, the truth of that statement stood out as nothing else could have. He'd lived with her image for a long time, but with that tackle, she'd gotten under his skin in a brand-new way. There was a fire in her he wanted, needed to explore.

Guido fell into bed experiencing alternate waves of

anxiety and excitement at the thought of being with her again. He needed to call her but couldn't handle falling so hard for her only to meet with eventual rejection because his choice of career didn't meet her expectations.

If those posters had been ordered for her friend only, then he didn't want to know about it.

Stadio Emanuele held seventy thousand fans. Dea had researched everything on the website before hiring a taxi to drop her off Sunday afternoon. Tickets for the game against the soccer team from Genoa were still available, but she had to get to the ticket office two hours before the match started.

She'd never been to a sporting event. Men, women, children of all ages made up the massive crowd. They were fired up and so noisy already she could hardly hear herself think. This was sheer craziness.

After standing in line for twenty minutes, it was her turn. She asked for the best ticket on the long side—as if she knew what she was talking about— and was charged 130 euros. Before she went to her seat, she wanted to visit the soccer museum, but she found out it would be open for only fifteen more minutes.

She had to wait to get inside, but by the time she reached the doors, the person in charge announced the museum was closing. If people wanted to see pictures and videos of the all-time best Italian soccer greats, they would have to come another day. People filed out.

Dea stood aside until the last one had gone. "Signor? When will you be open again?"

"Tomorrow afternoon."

"Until how late?"

"Seven o'clock."

"I'll come after I get off work." She wanted to see videos of Guido that couldn't be viewed anywhere else.

The attractive Italian in charge gave her a long look of male admiration and approached her. He'd probably been a soccer player himself, but she noticed he had a very slight limp. "I've seen you before, signorina. You're Dea the model, aren't you?"

Uh-oh. "How did you know?"

He let out a hearty laugh. "Surely you are joking." His hand went over his heart. "Your pictures are on the inside of half the locker doors in the gym here at the stadium."

Heat rushed to her cheeks. "I think you're full of it, but thank you for the compliment. Now I'd better get going and find my seat before the match begins, but I'll be back."

"You're here alone?"

"Yes."

"Is this your first time at the stadium?"

"Yes."

"Be careful. It can get rowdy out there during a game."

"I've heard, but I can take care of myself."

He grinned. "I'll look for you tomorrow."

She thanked him, then left the store to make her way through the crowds to her seat.

The next two hours felt like being on a giant roller-coaster ride, taking her emotions up and down. She'd never sat through anything so riveting. Many times she saw those few moves Guido had taught her. They helped her understand the game a little because she'd been taught by a master. Her admiration for him grew seeing his team play like this.

To her chagrin, the score remained tied until the last few seconds, when Guido's team had a break-through by the crowd favorite Dante. When his kick got past the goalie, the crowd let out a deafening roar. Everyone went wild over the two–one score, scream-ing, "Dante! Dante!"

Dea was elated for Guido, but she barely escaped the pandemonium inside the stadium with her life. Thank goodness she'd arranged for a taxi ahead of time to meet her outside. Otherwise she would have been forced to walk blocks.

She asked the driver to stop at a deli so she could take food home to eat. Later, after getting comfort-able on the couch, she watched the ten o'clock news. The sports segment featured a clip of the soccer game. She heard the announcer praise the rise of the Scatto Roma team and pictures of Dante were flashed on the screen. Guido had to be so proud.

After working up some new costume sketches for tomorrow, she went to bed and got up early to go to the gym before reporting to the shop for work. The costumes for *Don Giovanni* were shaping up. She worked hard and didn't lift her head until five thirty.

Though she'd planned to go to the stadium museum after work this evening, she changed her mind. If she ran into Guido by mistake, he wouldn't believe it was a mistake.

The man who worked at the soccer museum had recognized her on Sunday, and she realized he had to be a friend of Guido's. She should have disguised herself. If he happened to mention that she'd been in the museum, Guido would suspect she'd been looking for him.

Because he hadn't phoned her since their lunch, that was the last thing she wanted him to think. *Let your prince find you.*

By Thursday she was totally deflated that Guido hadn't tried to reach her. At the end of work she found Gina and handed her a tube. "I have a present for Aldo."

"What?"

"Open the end and see."

Gina did her bidding and pulled out the signed poster of a twenty-year-old Guido caught in action midair with the banner *Cuor di Leone*. "Oh, Dea—" She lifted shining eyes to her. "Aldo's going to be thrilled when I give him this."

Dea had been just as thrilled when she opened her own tube and spread the poster on her bed. It now graced her bedroom wall. How she would have loved to meet the dashing athlete back then!

"I'm sorry it was already signed when it was printed."

"That doesn't matter. Isn't he gorgeous? Of course, I don't dare tell Aldo that."

"That might be wise." No man compared to Guido.

"You're fantastic, Dea!" She put the poster down and hugged her so hard she almost knocked her over. "How much do I owe you?"

"Nothing. I wanted to do this for you."

"Ooh." She squealed. "I'm so glad work is over. I'm going to drive by the garage and surprise him with it. You're the best friend I ever had."

Dea watched her run out of the shop. It had made her glad to see her new friend this happy. While she was cleaning up a few minutes later, the middle-aged receptionist came in the back room.

"Dea? There's a man here to see you."

Her heartbeat picked up. She lifted her head. "Did he give you his name?"

"He only said he'd come from the museum at the Stadio Emanuele."

Museum? How had the man running it found out she worked here? "Please tell him I'll be right out."

Most everyone had left already. She hurried into the ladies' room to freshen up and make sure the clip holding her chignon in place was still secure. Her uniform was a pair of sneakers, jeans and a top. Today she'd worn a simple red tee with short sleeves.

She went back in the room for her purse and made her way through the shop past all the racks of costumes to the reception area. Her footsteps slowed. Instead of the dark-haired man from the museum, she spied the dark blond male who'd been haunting her

dreams. He stood in front of a dozen framed photo-
graphs of Juliana taken at various operas.

Dressed in beige chinos and a silky black shirt
with an open collar and short sleeves, his tall, well-
honed physique captured her gaze. She couldn't look
anywhere else. "Guido?" she asked in a breathless
voice. Dea had feared he might never call her again.

He turned to her. Those midnight blue eyes raked
over her from head to toe, spilling warmth through
her body. "I'm glad I caught you before you left," he
said in his deep voice. "My business partner and former soccer buddy Sergio Colombo told me you were
going to come by the museum on Monday. When you
didn't show, I'm afraid he was very disappointed."

Her brows met in a delicate frown. "I don't understand."

"When an order for two posters came in online, he
was the one who sent them out to a Dea Caracciolo.
As soon as you walked in the museum, he recognized
you as the famous model and made the connection.
You're all he could talk about. Surely you know you
made a conquest of him?"

After being in therapy, she didn't like that word
anymore. Was this all about Sergio? "He was very
nice and warned me to be careful in case the crowd
got too boisterous."

"He is nice, but he's become supersensitive since
his divorce. Why didn't you come?"

"Please tell him I had to work later than planned."
Guido probably saw through her lie, but she wasn't
about to tell him the truth.

He moved closer with his hands on his hips. The tension was thick between them. "Did you enjoy the soccer match Sunday?"

"I loved it, actually. Even with the few moves you taught me, I was able to understand some of it and enjoy it. Congratulations on your win. My ears rang with Dante's name all the way home in the taxi."

A glimmer of a smile hovered at one corner of his compelling mouth. He cocked his head. "I was in the dugout. But if I'd known you wanted to see a match, you could have sat in my suite to watch it."

"I should think the last thing the owner of the team would want is to worry about entertaining a guest while you're invested in an important game like that one."

"It depends on the guest. Why didn't you just call and ask me to send you a couple of posters?"

She sucked in her breath. "I didn't want to impose on you. It was easy enough to go online. They were for my friend."

"So I gathered. Now that we have matters clarified, the reason I'm here is to ask you out to dinner. If you come with me, you'll win my forgiveness for being ignominiously tackled. You owe me that much."

Another rush of heat swept through her. Looking at his virile physique now, she couldn't believe she'd done such a thing. "I'll never live it down."

"I won't hold it against you forever," he drawled in a seductive tone. "Do you have plans for this evening?"

"No," she answered honestly. "I intended to go

home for a meal and watch a little television before going to bed."

"You like TV?"

"A good film is one of my guilty pleasures."

"Can you give it a miss long enough to spend the evening with me?"

Thump, thump went her heart. The last time she'd seen him was at the bistro. But her fear that she'd never see him again had vanished because he was standing right here in front of her. Dea wanted to get to know him better and this was her chance.

"I'd like that very much, but I'll need to go home first and change."

"*Bene*. I'll drive you."

"I have my own car."

"Then I'll follow and wait for you in front of your apartment."

At this point he probably knew exactly where she lived. "My car is parked in the alley around the corner. It won't take me long."

"That's good. Plan to wear whatever you like."

Dea felt feverish with anticipation as she drove to her apartment. In the rearview mirror she could see Guido behind the wheel of a sleek black Lamborghini.

She pulled into the private parking area and hurried up to her apartment. Since he wore casual attire, she didn't want to be overdressed. After a quick shower, she put on a silky thin-striped shirtdress in tan and cream with a drawstring at the waist and a curved shirttail hem. The sleeves fell to the elbow, a classic look. She teamed a pearl clip that held her hair in place with a small pair of pearl earrings.

Once she'd slipped on tan heels, she applied lipstick and felt ready. When she left the apartment and approached his car waiting at the entrance, she trembled to think this fabulous man wanted to be with her this evening.

He levered himself from the driver's seat and opened the door for her. She felt his gaze play over her as she got inside. "You look stunning," he murmured near her cheek. His breath sent rivulets of delight through her.

Dea had heard compliments like that for years. But for those words to come from him meant more to her than he would ever know.

"You look great out of uniform too."

Her daring comment caused him to laugh out loud before he closed the door and went around to get behind the wheel. She loved hearing his deep chuckle before he pulled onto the main road. The scent of the soap he used filled the interior. He drove with expertise, maneuvering through Rome's hectic evening traffic with ease.

To her surprise, they ended up at the heliport at the airport. She turned to him. "Where are we headed?"

"It's a surprise. We'll be at our destination within a half hour."

She took a deep breath. "That sounds exciting." Where on earth were they going?

"I hope it will be. Come on. The pilot is waiting for us."

Within minutes they'd climbed aboard the helicopter. She sat in the back while he took the copilot's seat. Dea was no stranger to flights in helicopters. Seeing Rome from the air was an experience she was very familiar with, but right now she couldn't focus on anything but the striking male seated in front of her.

The scenery changed and after a little while the helicopter dipped. She glimpsed Mount Vesuvius in the distance. Her breath quickened as they descended and suddenly the pilot set them down on a helipad. She looked out the windows and realized they'd landed on a *ship*.

Not just any ship.

He opened the door and put out his hand to help her down into the balmy night air. She turned to him in bewilderment. "You've brought us to the yacht."

Guido's jaw tightened perceptibly. Something was going on inside him she didn't understand. He drew her away from the helicopter. "Let's start again, Signorina Loti. Welcome to Naples."

Time stood still while Guido's words sank in. Dea's thoughts flew back to that night on the yacht when she'd been introduced to him. But in her mind, she hadn't been able to see him because his best friend had stood next to him and taken her breath.

"When you look back on that night, do you even remember me?" he asked in a teasing voice.

She swallowed hard. What did he want her to say? Dea needed help. "Rini turned and asked me to dance. I never had a chance to talk to you again."

"Would it surprise you if you knew *I'd* wanted to

be the one to dance with you first? But Rini stood
closer to you."

Oh, no… "I had no idea. Your fath—"

"My father forced us on you and your model friend,"
he interrupted her. "But let's admit Rini was your
choice. You couldn't take your eyes off him and I didn't
stand a chance."

CHAPTER FOUR

DEA STARTED TO TREMBLE. She thought she'd put the memory of that night behind her, but Guido had brought it up because it had obviously been painful for him too. She'd heard it in his voice. "I—I'm sorry," she stammered.

"Don't be. It wasn't anyone's fault and it happened over a year ago. I brought you here in the hope that tonight I could wine and dine you with no other distractions."

He meant Rini.

This was the time for honesty no matter how frightened she was to discuss such a sensitive issue for both of them. "I admit I was attracted to Rini, but it was one-sided."

She heard him take a quick breath. "Are you over him?"

Guido knew how to go for the jugular. It was part of his makeup. She bit her lip. Rini was his best friend. The answer to Guido's loaded question could spell life or death for a future relationship with him. If he wanted one. She lifted her eyes to him.

"His looks filled an image I'd carried in my mind since I was a girl, but it had no substance. I was never into Rini, because he was a figment of my imagination. Amazingly, Alessandra carried that same image in her mind. We're not twins for nothing. But the moment she met Rini, that image took on substance for her and she fell hard.

"The beauty is, he fell hard for her too and pursued her. As you know, they're madly in love and terribly happy. Believe me when I tell you I'm beyond happy for them. I hope that answers your question. Please tell me it does," she pleaded with him.

After a long silence, he said, "Your honesty has blown me away." To her relief, he broke into a smile that melted her bones. "You're good at doing that."

"Am I never to hear the end of it?" she teased.

"I don't know. Come on." He cupped her elbow and walked her over to the covered dining area on the top deck. "Are you seeing another man right now, Dea?"

"No. What about you? Is there a woman in your life at the moment?"

"Only you."

One table had been set for them with candles and flowers. Guido helped her sit down, then poured some wine for both of them.

"I take it we're alone."

"I told you there'd be no distractions tonight."

The steward brought their food to the table and removed the covers. A wonderful aroma of fish with lemon and rosemary wafted in the night air.

She smiled. "In other words, your parents won't show up."

"Not tonight." His eyes searched hers. "Tell me—did they say or do something that made you uncomfortable at the wedding reception?"

"Not at all, Guido. I'm afraid I wasn't myself that day and am sorry if it showed."

But she could tell he wouldn't let it go when he asked, "Was it my father making you uncomfortable? What did he say when he talked to you and your friend after the fashion show?"

She put down her fork. "Nothing. He simply wanted us to meet you and your best friend before we left the yacht."

"Papà came on strong, didn't he?" Dea averted her eyes. "I knew it. There are times when he can be unbearable."

"That's because he loves you so much and is proud of you."

"You were probably afraid I was made in his image."

Guido was so intuitive it was scary. "You and your father bear a physical resemblance. Was he an outstanding soccer player too?"

"He had no interest in the sport."

"But he came to all your games."

"Yes."

"Lucky you."

"He's a hunter."

She took another bite of fish. "Do you hunt too?"

"Maybe once a year when I go with him, but I prefer fly-fishing. What about your father?"

Dea smiled. "Dad would rather camp out with our family."

"That's something else I'm crazy about," he informed her.

"It's so fun."

After the steward brought them a pastry dessert, Guido changed the subject. "What are you doing Saturday night?"

She got a fluttery feeling in her chest. "Gina and I are going to see *Othello*. We made arrangements for it last week."

"Then getting together with you this weekend is out since I have another match on Sunday in Bologna."

He'd be out of town. Maybe he was as disappointed as she was. "When will you be back?"

"Monday."

Dea wanted to see him again too. "What's your Monday evening like?"

A flicker lit up his eyes. "What do you have in mind?"

"After work I'll pick up some groceries and fix us dinner at my apartment."

"She cooks too?"

The warmth of his smile invaded her insides. "I spent years in the *castello* kitchen after school watching and learning from the cook. When she did her shopping in Metaponto on the weekends, I often went with her."

"But you don't have to cook for me."

"I'd like to. It's fun now that I can eat things I long for. The only drawback is cooking for one."

"I know what you mean. I normally eat out."

"So—" she rolled her eyes "—you chip, drop, kick, sweep and cook too?"

The corners of his arresting male mouth turned up. "Tell you what. After you get home from work on Monday, call me and I'll pick you up. We'll go shopping and spend a culinary evening together."

"Be sure to bring a video of your game against Bologna. I'd like to see at least a part of it."

"If we lose, I won't bother to bring it."

She studied him over the rim of her wineglass. "You *won't* lose."

"How do you know?" he whispered.

"Your team played its heart out last Sunday. I imagine they'll do it again and again."

"That's the kind of faith that helps me push them. On that positive note, I'll get us back to Rome."

"This was a long way to come, Guido. We could have gone anywhere to eat."

His features grew serious. "True. But it was important to me that I erase the bad memory of that night from my mind by doing this again."

She moaned inwardly. "I never meant t—"

"I know you didn't," he broke in. "We'll never talk about it again. Thank you for coming with me." He stood up and helped her from the table. They walked toward the helipad at the other end of the yacht with his arm at the back of her waist. The Bay of Naples glittered with lights, making a glorious sight. To be with Guido like this thrilled her.

"Please thank the steward and the cook. The food was delicious," she said before climbing in the helicopter.

"I'll tell them." She felt his hands squeeze her hips gently before she moved all the way inside. He shouldn't have touched her like that. It sent a voluptuous curl of heat through her body.

For Guido to bring her all the way here to clear up something so vital meant his attraction to her was more than skin-deep. Guido was a man of great substance. But he'd been hurt; otherwise he wouldn't have asked if she was over Rini. To embark on a relationship with him, they had to build total trust between them.

His sensitive nature had picked up on her pain at the wedding. If she got the chance, she'd explain to him that she'd been going through her own personal crisis that had nothing to do with his parents or anyone else.

Dea shivered. The whole issue with Rini was hard to explain, but it was long since over. Much as she was dying to get to know Guido better, she realized there were things he was holding back from her about himself. She would work on getting him to tell her what was wrong.

The flight from Bologna touched down at the airport at one on Monday afternoon. Their one–nil win had made the whole team giddy. After a training session at the stadium with the players and coaches, Guido drove home on fire for the evening planned with Dea.

It seemed like months instead of days since their dinner on Thursday night.

He watched the video of the game and made notes. But he kept waiting for the phone to ring and lost his concentration. When it finally rang and he saw the caller ID, he picked right up.

"Dea?"

"Are you back?"

"I've been at the apartment several hours. How are you?"

"Relieved to know you made it home safely." He liked hearing that. "Your win was all over the news last night. You must be ecstatic."

He was ecstatic all right, but she was the underlying reason for this joie de vivre he'd never felt before. "What time should I pick you up?"

"If you'll give me an hour, I'll be ready. But why don't we walk to the market at the Via della Pace? It's close and they'll have everything we need."

"I'll be outside the entrance waiting for you. *A presto*, Dea."

Guido showered and shaved. As he was finding out, anytime he was with Dea, surprising things happened. To go grocery shopping with her would no doubt be an adventure, followed by a casual night at home. It was exactly what he needed after the stressful weekend when once again he thought the team wouldn't win until the last few seconds.

He pulled on a sport shirt and jeans, grabbed the

disc with the video and left. Once he'd found a parking space near her apartment, he walked to the entrance expecting to have to wait. Instead she was outside drawing the interest of every male in the vicinity.

Why not? She was wearing taupe-colored trousers topped with a sheer flutter blouse in a pale blue. The hem fell to her waist, emphasizing the feminine curves of her body. A mesh shopping bag hung from her fingers.

Her long, sparkling brown hair with its gold highlights was tied at the nape with a thin pale blue ribbon. Her natural beauty staggered him. When she saw him, she broke into a smile that lit up her eyes. He moved closer, already feeling out of breath. "I've been looking forward to this evening."

"Me too. Are you hungry?"

She should know better than to ask him a question like that. "Starving. I skipped lunch in anticipation of tonight."

"Good. I plan to feed you well. We only need to buy a few items. It's just a short walk after we reach the corner."

"I want the exercise. It helps me unwind."

"I know what you mean."

Exhilarated to be with her, he headed down the street with her. "What's on the menu for tonight?"

"Chicken Tetrazzini. I thought it would be a nice change from fish."

"I like anything."

"Sounds like you're an easy man to please. Lucky

for me." They rounded the corner and soon arrived at the market. "Help me find chicken breasts, white mushrooms and linguine. I'll gather the rest."

"Like what?"

"Parmesan cheese, fresh garlic, onions, parsley and thyme, and cream."

"We'll need a good wine too."

"Why don't you pick it out."

He knew a Tuscan Chianti that would go well with their dinner. They worked together. She reached for some herb focaccia bread and he found a couple of *baba al limoncello* pastries.

Guido paid for the groceries and carried the bag home. It was bursting at the seams. He slanted her a glance. "Just a few items," he ribbed her.

"I guess I'm a typical woman after all. Sorry if it's heavier than a soccer ball…"

"I'm relieved your apartment is only a couple more steps away. I just might make it."

"Let's hope there's no reporter hanging around trying to take a picture of the famous soccer player in your sad condition." Her comments continually amused him. "Tell you what. Once we're inside, you can stretch out on the couch and watch the game while I cook."

"I thought *you* wanted to watch it."

"I do. I'll come in and out of the kitchen."

"That won't work. We'll cook together, then eat while we watch. I want to hear your commentary."

"It won't be worth much."

"Let me be the judge of that."

"The bathroom is down that hall if you'd like to freshen up."

"Thank you."

Her elegant apartment reminded him she was a woman who had the title of Princess Caracciolo and Taranto. But the way she behaved, you'd never know she came from a long line of aristocrats. She'd worked her way around the market picking out what she wanted and taking her time like any Italian housewife. Surely he'd never seen a more beautiful one.

As he came out of the bathroom, he passed her bedroom, then backtracked in slow motion. On the wall next to the window was a poster. To his shock, it was the one of a younger Guido. She'd kept this one for herself. The sight of it gave him a heart attack.

He checked his breathing before going back to the living room. Within a half hour delicious aromas filled the apartment. She made a place on her coffee table in front of the television. He poured the wine while she went back to the kitchen for their plates.

Guido could see doing this for the rest of his life. Never had he been with a woman who caused his thoughts to expand as far as marriage. Since he'd taken her to the yacht, part of him was alarmed by the depth of his feelings for her because he didn't know if he trusted everything she'd told him concerning Rini.

He had no doubt she'd spoken the truth as much as she could admit. But he sensed there was more she was holding back from him. Since it involved his best friend, he couldn't be satisfied with a half confession any more than he could a half loaf of bread, especially not now, when he knew what was hanging on the wall in her bedroom. The poster's presence had to mean something vital.

He would have to go on seeing her to learn the whole truth. Maybe that would involve digging it out of her soul. Until then he would spend as much time as possible with her because he couldn't help himself. At this point she was on his mind day and night.

They watched part of the game, but she fired questions at him that suggested she really wanted to understand. He was only too happy to oblige.

"Are your players trained into the ground?"

His lips twitched. "Maybe not into the ground. On an individual basis they train by working out hard, running a lot, eating right, practicing skills. If you have a love for it, it isn't so hard."

She sat back against the cushion of the couch. "So what part do you play as the owner?"

"I'm like one of the coaches and get right in there. When we're not out on the field, the players work out in the gym. I work on them to focus on abs and quads. They need to increase their agility and endurance."

A glint of amusement entered her marvelous eyes. "Do they hate to see you coming?"

"Always. When the other coaches are through, I usually make the team run a variety of drills and practice plays. I force them to concentrate on being as fit as possible by combining sprints with long runs."

"Well, it's certainly paying off. You've only lost one game this year."

"True, but we barely won yesterday's. That's got me nervous. I don't want the team to get comfortable."

She took another sip of wine. "Do you have a motto?"

He nodded. "Discipline yourself so others don't!"

"What a great slogan! It makes perfect sense."

"I'm glad you approve."

"Are you kidding? Let's watch the end of the game and see if your team has taken your words to heart."

After fifteen minutes it was over. She wanted to know how many players were on a team, their positions and tactical skills. "How did you train when you were high school age?"

"I started soccer at seven."

"I should have remembered that."

Even if she was being polite, it flattered him that she would show this much interest in the game.

"During the summers, when I had no guidance, I'd start by running hills with my friends. Later on I'd work on sprints and sudden bursts of speed. Then again, I always had to have a ball at my feet so I wouldn't lose touch until soccer practice started.

"I went to as many matches as I could attend and played every position, including defender, goalie and midfield. But my favorite position was forward."

"The position you excelled at until you became the epic champion."

His brows lifted. "Epic?"

"That's you. I'm truly in awe of you, Guido."

"It's past history."

"But that excellence is living on in your team. Are you happy you left the shipping company to do this?"

"Yes, but whether I decide to own and manage a soccer team for the rest of my life isn't a question I can answer yet."

"I bet your father wants you back."

"Yes, but I won't do it unless I can embrace it a hundred percent. Let me ask you a question. Are you happy your modeling career is behind you?"

A shadow entered her eyes. "You want to know the truth?"

"What do you think?"

"I went to college to study fashion design, something I'd always been interested in. But by the time I was halfway through, I couldn't seem to produce something that wasn't mediocre. I felt like Salieri in the film *Amadeus*."

Guido would have laughed if he didn't know how serious this was. "You're referring to the Italian composer at the time of Mozart."

"Yes. As someone put it, you have to squint your ears and listen for the magic. If you can sense a supernatural beauty within, you know it's Mozart. If it's just music, it's not Mozart and probably someone like Salieri."

"You were awfully hard on yourself."

"I know. Halfway through school I was approached by the agency that hired me to model for them. I thought I'd take a year off school and try it."

Guido was fascinated. "Did you love it?"

"*Love* is a strong word. I enjoyed the first year

very much, but after that I sensed a lot was lacking in my life. The problem was, I felt it was too soon to give it up. I knew I could go back to school, but what if I failed to find my true calling? The owners of the agency put a lot of pressure on me to remain with them."

"You made a lot of money for them."

"Money runs the world." She didn't sound happy about it. For once he'd met a woman who wasn't impressed by the Rossano name and fortune.

"So tell me how you came to work for Juliana Parma now."

She shook her head. "I don't want to bore you."

"You mean the way I've bored you for the last two hours?"

A small laugh escaped her throat. She looked at him. "Throughout my life, my parents and aunt and uncle have taken me to the opera. I'd sit in my seat and envy the singers whose voices could bring such pleasure to people, to me. I cried through every opera. I thought if God had given me a great voice, I would go on singing forever."

His throat thickened with emotion. "God gave you another gift, Dea. You've thrilled a lot of people modeling the clothes of famous fashion designers."

She sat forward. "That's the point. It was the designers who created all the haute couture fashions. I envied their brilliance. All I did was walk around to display them."

"But those designers needed a woman like you to carry them off to the greatest advantage."

"Thank you for trying to build me up. In time I realized that the only thing that could make me truly happy was to create something of my own, something that came from me. That's probably how you feel about soccer. It comes from *you*, no one else."

Dea got that right. "When I saw you and Alessandra in that video, even at your young age your father acknowledged that you had an aptitude for design."

"That's because I wasn't good at anything else."

"I could argue with you, but I'm afraid you wouldn't listen. Go on and tell me about Juliana."

"Many times our family went backstage to talk to her. I saw how much she loved her work and I could understand because her creations brought life to the singers on the stage. The richness of the sets and clothes makes the opera so fantastic.

"When you watch them perform in street clothes, it's so different from casting them into their parts with all the trappings. It's a kind of magic she creates.

"After I went back to finish school, I knew I wanted to do what she did." Tears filled her eyes. "My aunt made it possible for me to work under her this semester. You'll never know what a great honor that is."

"I think I do. I've attended many operas in my life. What you've admitted helps me understand why I've enjoyed it so much."

"She designs for the theater too. The other night Gina and I were engrossed in the costuming for *Othello*. Bringing in the Moorish elements made it very exciting. In the future I hope I can be a part of such a project."

"With a drive like yours, I have no doubts." It was getting late and he knew she had work early in the morning. The last thing he wanted to do was over-stay his welcome, but he needed to do this right. He sensed in his gut this woman could change his life. "Let me help with the dishes before I leave."

"Those are my department tonight."

"Your food was fabulous. I hope you know that."

"Thank you." He reached for the disc and she walked him to the door. "I'm so glad you came over tonight."

"We'll have to do it again. I'll be in touch."

She opened the door. "I'd like that."

Much as he wanted to crush her in his arms and kiss the daylights out of her, he didn't dare. He was a greedy man. The poster on her wall still wasn't enough. He wanted to hear her bare her soul to him.

Like Carla, who'd hovered in the recesses of his mind because she'd judged him lacking, was Rini still lurking somewhere in her psyche because he hadn't wanted her? That's what he needed to find out. But that kind of deeply buried secret would take time to emerge—he'd have to get the whole truth from her. He couldn't be with her much longer and not find out.

"Thank you for tonight." He cupped the side of her lovely face with his hand before walking down the hall to the elevator. The warmth of her skin stayed with him all the way out to his car for the drive home.

CHAPTER FIVE

THURSDAY EVENING AT the close of work, Gina and her fiancé, Aldo, were waiting for Dea at the front entrance. After introductions were made, the cute auburn-haired mechanic shook her hand.

"Thanks for the poster. Since you won't take any money for it, let us buy you dinner."

"That's very nice of you, but I have a better idea. How would you like to see the soccer game on Sunday?"

"I can only afford seats behind the goalie."

"I know a better place to sit and have a friend who'll lower the price for you."

He squinted at her. "Are you serious?"

"Yes. Follow me to the stadium and we'll buy them now. You can tour the museum at the same time. It doesn't close until seven." Now Dea had a great excuse to see the videos of Guido without his thinking she was chasing after him.

"That would be wonderful!" Gina hugged her.

"I must be dreaming," Aldo murmured. "I've heard this game is already a sellout."

"One thing I've learned—they always have tickets. I'll get my car."

She hurried off. Before long the three of them arrived at the stadium and parked near the suite of offices. There was a long line of people waiting to buy tickets. "Why don't you get in line while I go in the museum. I'll only be a minute."

When she went inside, she saw that another man was in charge. She went up to him. "Is there any way I can talk to Sergio if he's here?"

His eyes swept over her. "You're the famous model!"

"Past tense. Could you get in touch with him?"

"He's running the ticket booth. Maybe I can help."

"Thank you, but no. He's the one I have to talk to."

"Just a minute." He pulled out his phone and made a call. After a minute Sergio walked in the rear door. She ran over to him.

"I'm sorry to bother you, but I need a favor. There's a couple at the back of the ticket line. He has dark red hair. Give him the very best seats you can for Sunday's game, but only charge him the cheapest price. I'll make up the rest." She opened her wallet and pulled out enough euros to cover it.

"I'll be happy to. Don't go away."

"I won't. After they get the tickets, we're going to spend time in here. Maybe you can give him the royal tour. It would mean everything to him and a lot to me."

"Sure thing."

He left through the same door. Dea thanked the other man and went outside to find Gina. Fifteen minutes later they'd bought their tickets. It wasn't until they headed for the museum that Aldo cried, "Do you know who that guy was who sold me the tickets? Sergio Colombo! He's only the greatest soccer player in Italy next to Guido Rossano. And these are the best seats in the stadium!"

Gina flashed Dea a smile of such gratitude it warmed her clear through.

"Now that you're set, let's take a tour before it closes."

Some moments in life were precious. Sergio gave them a personalized visit with anecdotes about Guido she'd never forget. The videos thrilled her to the core. When they thanked him and turned to leave, the man who stole her breath every time she saw him stood in the doorway.

"Guido…"

He moved toward her. "Why don't you introduce me to your friends."

Sergio must have told him she was here. If he'd still been in his office, then he'd had to come only a few steps. Before she could say a word, Aldo walked toward them. "I can't believe it. Guido Rossano. I've idolized you for years. Gina—" he drew her along "—this is the legend."

"It's an honor to meet you at last." She shook his hand. "Thanks to Dea, this day has come."

"Have you been well taken care of?" No one could be more charming or dashing than Guido.

Aldo beamed. "This is about the best day of my life!"

Dea was touched to see a grown man so happy to meet a boyhood idol.

"They'll be at the match on Sunday," Dea informed him.

"Why don't you two pick a poster before you leave and I'll sign it."

"You mean it?" Aldo's eyes widened. "How about the one at the national championship."

Sergio pulled it out of the bin and put it on the counter. He handed Guido a felt-tip pen. Gina looked at Sergio. "We'd like a signed poster of you too. I'll pay for it."

"No, no. It's on the house."

A minute later Dea saw two people ready to leave the store looking like they'd been given all their Christmases at once. She turned to the first man running the museum, then Sergio and Guido. "Thank you all." But as she started to follow her friends out the door, Guido said, "Where do you think you're going?"

Dea looked around. "Home."

"Do you have to drive them?"

"No. We came in our own cars."

"Good. That saves me a trip. Come to my office with me first."

"All right." After taking a breath, she turned and called to Gina, "I'll see you tomorrow." They waved back.

To her surprise, Guido put an arm around her shoulders in front of the other men and swept her through the back doorway, a shortcut to his inner sanctum. "I don't want the guys thinking they have a chance with you."

She blushed. "They were both so nice."

He took her inside his office and shut the door. "If you want to know the truth, it's not every day the ravishing Dea makes an appearance at a soccer stadium not once, but twice. One more time and their hearts might not be able to take it."

"You idiot." She pushed against his chest playfully and was rewarded by being crushed against him.

His eyes pierced hers. "You really don't have any idea what you do to a man, do you? I'm going to kiss you so you'll find out." Guido's intensity shook her before his head descended and his mouth closed over hers. Enveloped in heat, she felt his hands roam over her back and hips, urging her closer so she could feel every hard muscle and sinew in his body.

Though Dea had been with a few men who'd wanted to kiss her passionately, she hadn't fully reciprocated. Something had always held her back... until now.

This was different. Guido was different.

The feel of his mouth slowly devouring hers created such divine sensations that she felt like she'd been born for this moment and couldn't get enough. "Guido," she gasped in pleasure as he drew her into a wine-dark rapture. She clung to him, and they moved and breathed like they were a part of each other. Emotions greater than she could describe took over now that Guido had swept her into his arms.

She was already crazy about the man, but the sheer

physical feeling at this moment was all consuming, burning everything in its path so there was no room for anything else. Mind, body and soul were on fire for one man who answered the question of her existence.

"My office is no place for this. Come home with me, Dea," he whispered against her lips, swollen from the refined savagery of his kisses. "I need to be with you more than you can imagine," he confessed in a ragged voice.

I want that too, Guido. I'm in love with you. I know I am. But if you only need me, and aren't in love with me, then I can't let this go any further.

After one more long, hungry kiss, he opened the door. She was so dazed she would have fallen if he hadn't helped her to her car.

"I—I don't think I can drive." Her voice faltered.

"Let me. My car is in the private parking area. I'll come back for it tomorrow."

She shook her head. No matter how much she wanted to go home with him and throw away the key, she didn't plan to spend the night with him. "You mustn't leave yours here. I'll follow you."

Guido kept Dea in his sights for the short drive to his apartment. Once she'd pulled alongside him in his private parking garage, they took the elevator to the second floor. It wasn't until they'd entered his apartment that he realized he'd never brought a woman here before.

He turned on the lights. "Forgive my generic apartment that has no personality."

"Oh, yes, it does. You can tell in an instant that a bachelor lives here."

He flicked her an amused glance. "That bad, huh?"

Her eyes smiled. "It tells me you're a practical man. No nonsense about you. You certainly don't have to make excuses to me."

"Nevertheless, I want to explain that the convenience of the location to the stadium makes it ideal, and it serves as my base for eating and sleeping while I'm living in Rome."

"Where did you live before?"

"Naples. But I sold that apartment when I moved here. It would have been pointless to keep it. I'm afraid it didn't have any personality, either." She laughed quietly.

Guido studied her features. "Is that what you really think about me? No nonsense?"

One brow lifted. "When you were teaching me some soccer moves behind the castle, you were all business. But on second thought, maybe the Lamborghini doesn't quite match the profile of the down-and-out bachelor who doesn't need more than a roof over his head."

"Do you know something, Dea Caracciolo? I've never laughed as much with anyone else."

"You should do it more often. It's very attractive."

His pulse raced. If he got started on Dea's attributes, he'd never stop. After those moments in his office he still hadn't recovered from being set on fire. His desire for her was off the charts.

If she was worried he was about to carry her straight to the bedroom, she ought to be. He'd already broken his own rule about not rushing things with her. He hadn't been able to help it. *Slow down, Rossano.* "Have you had dinner?"

"Not yet. Gina and Aldo surprised me as I was leaving work this evening. They wanted to take me for a meal to thank me for the poster. I told him to save his money for soccer tickets and we went straight to the stadium. You and your staff were so nice to them."

"It was our pleasure." Holding on to his last vestige of self-control, he said, "The restroom is down that hall if you'd like to freshen up first."

"I'd love it. Thank you."

"I'll be in the kitchen. I know I saw eggs and cheese in there this morning and will whip something up for us."

"Perfect."

Guido headed there and made tasty omelets they ate at the kitchen table. He produced some oranges to go with their meal.

"Hmm. These are gorgeous." He watched her finish the last section of her fruit and thought he'd never seen or tasted such a luscious mouth. "So were the eggs. You're a terrific cook."

"Thank you."

"Having lived on your own for so long, you're probably a great chef and don't know it."

He chuckled. "What I am is a nervous wreck now that the soccer season is coming to an end. Three more games now that it's May."

"How many at home?"

"One. The others will be in Cagliari and Siena."

She sat back in the chair drinking her coffee. "Has owning this team been fulfilling for you? Can you see doing this for years and years?"

Her interest sounded genuine. If he had his heart's desire, he could see doing just about anything. "I don't know. My father's not getting any younger. His emotional pull on me to come back to the shipping lines is strong."

"You're his only son. That puts you in a vulnerable position."

He nodded. "But Papà has two brothers and they have three sons who also sit on the board. And there's my grandfather. At ninety-five, he still wields influence with my father."

She cocked her head. "I understand from Alessandra that you're the light of your grandfather's life. He believes you're the one in the family to take Rossano Shipping Lines in a new direction."

"But that's my father's decision, no one else's." Guido swallowed the rest of his coffee. Here they were talking in his kitchen instead of picking up where they'd left off in his office. He feared she was thankful for the breathing room between them effectively lowering the heat.

"If you're through eating, let's go in the living

room. I want to talk to you about something important."

Those fabulous orbs narrowed. "I thought that's what we're doing."

Until he learned everything hiding inside her, he knew he would never have peace. "It's more comfortable in there."

She averted her eyes, a subtle sign of nervousness. "First I'll just clear our dishes."

"Not tonight. Remember your rule? It applies at my house in reverse. After you."

Resigned to do Guido's bidding, Dea went through to the living room and sat on one of the chairs near the couch. He'd followed her, but the tension radiating from him let her know something was wrong. "What is it?"

In a surprise move Guido leaned over her and put his hands on the arms of the chair, virtually trapping her. With his lips so close to hers, she couldn't think, let alone breathe.

"We entered deeper waters this evening. Though I want to carry you to my bedroom and make love to you all night, we need to talk before we can no longer feel the sand beneath our feet. I won't be able to go on seeing you until I have all the honesty in you," his voice rasped.

All her honesty? "What do you mean?"

"If you're holding anything back where your feelings for Rini are concerned, I need to know."

After those words he gave her a long, lingering

kiss that left her trembling before he released her and sat on the couch across from her with his hands clasped between his legs.

His eyes had taken on a haunted look, as if he couldn't make up his mind about her. Sickness swept through her.

"I've told you everything! I don't know why you don't believe me. I think what you meant to say is, you need to hear all the dishonesty in me. The problem is, I'm not sure I *could* identify all of it and agree that to go on seeing each other would be a waste of time."

Either Rini or Alessandra had betrayed her and told Guido every ugly detail about her past. One of them had undoubtedly gone so far as to reveal the details of that tumultuous period in the past when Alessandra's boyfriend had betrayed her and chased after Dea. No other explanation would explain why the earth had suddenly tilted.

Now that Guido knew her history, it didn't surprise her that he wanted to understand her behavior from her own lips. If he was hoping it was all a lie, Dea couldn't help him out.

She'd thought she'd put all the misery behind her and was endeavoring to become a better person who had faith in herself. But there'd be no convincing Guido of anything. The damage was too great for her to fight for him.

What a fool she'd been to let her guard down. Now she'd fallen in love with him, and she knew this was the one fatal mistake in life she'd never recover from.

There was no one like Guido, but he was beyond reach.

On unsteady legs she got to her feet and reached for her purse on the coffee table. "There's nothing more for me to say. Goodbye, Guido."

Before Dea broke down and dissolved into tears, she left the apartment and hurried to the parking garage for her car. She could hear him call out to her, but she didn't stop. When she backed around, he stood in her way looking fierce and so handsome it hurt.

"You're not going anywhere."

Her breath caught. "You worded that wrong. *We're* not going anywhere. All the family secrets are out. It could never work for you and me. Please move aside. It's late and I have to be up early in the morning."

In the dim light of the garage his face seemed to have lost color. "I can't let you go until we talk this out. You've obviously misunderstood me."

"No, I haven't," she fired back. "You were crystal clear."

Her words rang in the air. He finally stepped aside so she could drive out to the street. Her last glimpse of him through the mirror reflected a man wearing a mask so bleak she hardly recognized him.

Dea drove to her own apartment. When she walked inside, she was aware that the recent joy she'd been experiencing had left her soul. Before going to bed, she removed the poster of Guido from the wall. Unable to throw it away yet, she rolled it up and put it in the closet.

Once under the covers, she buried her face in the

pillow until it was wet. *No prince is going to find you,
Dea.* From here on out it was work and more work to
get through this life.

Friday morning after sleeping poorly, she got dressed,
skipped breakfast and worked out in the gym. One of
the guys on duty there, who was a big flirt, came over
to bother her. He couldn't be a day over twenty-four.

"When are you going to let me take you out?"

"Never."

"Ooh. That was brutal."

Dea was in a brutal mood. Even if it was her fault,
her experiences with men had brought her nothing
but misery. "I can see three women in here at least
five years younger than I am. I'm sure they'd love
your attention."

"They're not you."

"Lucky them."

Her comment got rid of him for the moment. She
took advantage of the time to slip back out and grab a
cappuccino on her way to the shop. Today they were
having a meeting to discuss a few of the men's costumes for *Don Giovanni*.

She welcomed the busy day so she wouldn't give
in to her agony over losing Guido.

There was no one she could confide in about this,
not even her aunt. It saddened her because she'd been
getting along with her whole family for a long time.
The next time her mom let her know Rini and Alessandra had gone back to Positano for a while, she'd fly
home to visit her parents. Her parents could always
fly here. That was the only way to avoid more pain.

At quitting time Gina came over to her table, her face beaming. "I'll never be able to thank you enough for what you've done. Aldo's a different person. Are you going to be at the game on Sunday with Guido?"

"I plan to," she lied without compunction. She didn't want to talk about him, not ever again. While their heads were together, the receptionist came in the room and approached her.

"Some flowers arrived for you, Dea. At first I thought they must be for Juliana until I saw the card with your name. They're out in the reception room on my desk." Her brows lifted. "Three dozen red roses! Someone's in love."

Dea's heart did a double kick. "I'll be out in a minute. Thank you."

Gina nudged her. "Guido Rossano is absolutely crazy about you. If I didn't like you so much, I'd be horribly envious."

"You've got Aldo."

"Yeah. I do, but there's no one quite like the *Cuor di Leone*."

Her eyes closed. Gina was right. Guido was unique in so many ways she could hardly breathe just thinking about him. Why did he bother to send her anything? He could have no idea how painful this was for her.

"Well, come on," Gina urged her. "It's time to go home. If you're not dying to look at them, I am."

Dea took a quick breath. "Okay." She grabbed her purse and followed her friend. The second they reached the foyer, the heavy perfume from the roses assailed her. They both gasped as she walked over to the enormous spray and reached for the card perched in a little plastic pick. *You have to forgive me. I said everything wrong and want to start over.*

Tears stung her eyelids. She pressed the card to her heart. They couldn't start over.

Gina stood behind her. "If you'll bring your car around, I'll help you put these flowers in the backseat so you can take them home."

Before the flowers could be placed inside the car, Dea and Gina had to tip the vase to pour out the water. Somehow they managed. "Thank you," she said to her friend before driving home.

After parking in her space, Dea had some difficulty taking the roses out of the car so the heads wouldn't get broken off.

"Let me help," sounded a deep, familiar male voice behind her.

She started to tremble. "Guido—"

"I've waited here wondering if you'd bring them home or throw them away at work. I have my answer."

Dea should have tossed them. Now she'd been caught in the act.

"I'll bring them in. You go ahead and open the door for me."

Guido had left her no choice. When they reached her apartment, he carried them out to the kitchen to fill the vase with water. He darted her a glance. "I meant what I said on the card. I need to start over with you by taking you for a drive in the country.

We'll stop at some spot for dinner and talk. Please don't deny me this."

"You already know everything there is to know about me. There's no need for more talk."

"We haven't even started," he came back. His dark blue eyes glittered. "Let's get something straight. We may have been the closest of friends all our lives, but I swear before God that Rini has *never* discussed you with me. Neither has Alessandra, so you can put that misconception out of your head once and for all."

Was he speaking the truth? Dea wanted to believe him.

No matter how hard she fought it, the force of his words and personality cut through her defenses like a sharp knife. Not only that, he was wearing a dusky blue jacket over a cream shirt open at the throat and beige trousers. His masculine beauty melted her on the spot. It wasn't fair. She could feel herself weakening.

"I—I need to shower first," she stammered.

"While you do that, I'll carry these roses into the living room and put them on the coffee table. I want you to see my apology every time you enter your apartment."

Oh, Guido…

Dea hurried to her room and got ready. She chose a dressy peach blouse and skirt. After brushing out her hair and leaving it loose, she joined him in the living room. The red roses had already filled it with their fragrance.

She was probably a fool to go with him, but she'd

promised herself not to make snap judgments anymore. Tonight she would hear him out one last time,
but this was it.

Quiet reigned as Guido drove them a short distance
from Rome to Lake Nemi, which was set in the cra-
ter of an ancient volcano. He turned on some music.
Neither of them felt the need to talk. That suited Dea,
who was waiting for an explanation from him when
he was ready.

She sat back to enjoy the landscape, especially
since she'd never been here before. The lush nature
preserve surrounding the lake came as a pleasant surprise. He took them to a charming restaurant bordering the water and asked for them to be seated in an
isolated area. The waiter led them to a candlelit table
for two separated by ornamental trees.

Guido ordered their meal. Wine and *cacio e pepe*,
a dish of Pecorino Romano cheese and pasta to die
for. Halfway through their meal she eyed him frankly.
"This is delicious. The flowers were lovely too, but
I'm still waiting for you to tell me why you don't
think I've been totally honest with you. That hurt,
you know? More than you can imagine."

He leaned forward. "I believe you've told me the
truth, but—"

"But what?" she cried softly.

"Maybe you're still in denial over deep feelings
you don't realize are there?"

"I take it you're talking about Rini, the prover-
bial elephant in the room." His sustained silence con-
firmed her suspicions. "You're still afraid I'm in love

with my brother-in-law, and you want chapter and verse, is that it?" She put her napkin on the table. "Sorry I can't change history to make it more palatable for you, Guido."

His brows furrowed. "I'm not asking for that," he insisted.

"No? It sounds to me like you're asking for blood, so now you're going to get it. Long before that night, I'd been floundering emotionally when it came to men. Since childhood the image of the perfect man had lived in my imagination, but no man ever thrilled me to the point that I wanted to marry him."

"Until Rini," he grated.

"Yes. I took one look at him and no one else existed for me. The fact that there was no substance to back up that feeling—only a girl's dream—didn't stop me from throwing myself at him. When I say *throw*, I mean I slid my hands up his chest and kissed him with hunger. I'd never done such a thing in my life and assumed he had to feel the same way, but he didn't kiss me back. In truth, he couldn't get rid of me fast enough."

Even with his tan, Guido's complexion had gone ashen. "Stop, Dea—"

"No! I haven't finished. You wanted the unvarnished truth? Well, here it is. I suggested we get together the next evening, but he said he wouldn't be in town. After thanking me for the dance, he walked away without saying anything about seeing me again. I left the yacht in shock."

Guido's grim expression couldn't prevent her from

getting everything off her chest. "He was the second man in my life to do real damage."

"What do you mean, the second?"

"Rini didn't share that with you?"

"I told you. You were never a topic of conversation between us."

"I see. Well, years ago Alessandra's fiancé made a play for me and followed me to Rome. I never encouraged him. He swore he was in love with me, but the minute he got there, he went off with another model. The incident not only put me off taking any man seriously, but made me feel horrible for my sister and it drove a knife in her heart. Both of us had been so hurt it took us years to become friends again."

"You don't have to say another word." Clearly uncomfortable over the direction of the conversation, Guido got to his feet. After leaving some bills on the table, he walked around to her chair. "Come on. Let's go out to the car."

Still fired up, she walked quickly without letting him touch her. The second they got in the Lamborghini, she turned to him. "I know you don't like hearing this, but you wanted *all* of my truth."

"I never meant to cause you this kind of pain."

"Maybe not," she admitted, but Dea was too far gone now. At a glance, his profile resembled chiseled stone, but that didn't stop her from telling him everything.

"Simply put, Rini's rejection put me in the blackest hole of my life. Who could imagine a greater irony than the one where he met my sister and fell madly in love with her? They say lightning doesn't strike twice in the same place, but it did with me. I needed help. If it hadn't been for my family and my therapist, who pulled me out of that abyss, I don't know what would have happened."

"Please don't say any more."

"I have to. You wanted an answer. After many talks I began to figure out my life. Alessandra and I are now closer than we ever were throughout our childhood and have come to a perfect understanding.

"She knows that Rini represented the figment of my imagination that had lived inside me for years. He didn't know me from Adam and had no interest in me. So for me to feel rejected by him tells you the precarious state of my mental health."

Traffic was light entering Rome. It didn't take long to reach her apartment and drive to her parking level on the third floor.

"In time I worked through my humiliation. Rini was very kind and told me to forget it. Whatever he chose to tell Alessandra is their business, but she knows the whole truth. At her wedding I realized any amorous feelings for him had been wiped clean from my heart. Soon after that I gave up modeling and went back to college."

Without saying anything, Guido turned off the car and reached for the door handle. She told him not to bother. "I don't want you to see me inside my apartment. In fact I don't want to see you again. You have a trust issue with me that will never go away. I understand where you're coming from, but I can't be with a man who won't ever be free of his suspicions. Something, someone, has robbed you of your ability to trust."

Dea let herself out of the car. Before she shut the door, she said, "Let me leave you with this thought, which you can choose to believe or not. If you or your parents felt slighted by me at the reception, it wasn't intentional. What you sensed was my shame because you were his best friend and had witnessed my brazen behavior that night on the yacht.

"No one could expect you to forget that. But please be assured of one thing. I've loved getting to know the former *Cuor di Leone*."

"Dea—"

"*Adio per sempre*, Guido."

"Goodbye forever?" he ground out.

"Just what I said." She shut the door. Wild with pain, she hurried toward the entrance leading to her apartment.

CHAPTER SIX

"YOU'RE NOT RUNNING away from me again." Guido caught up to Dea and wrapped his strong arms around her from behind so she was trapped. His breathing was as ragged as hers. "I'm not letting you go until you agree to spend all day tomorrow with me."

She moved her head from side to side. "There's no point."

"Of course there is! You're right about me. I do have trust issues and need you. I want to show you the real me. I know in my gut you and I are good for each other. Give me tomorrow to turn this around, Dea. You can't mean things to end this way. I couldn't take it." He held her tighter, sounding frantic.

Once again she could feel herself giving in to him. "You have a game this weekend."

"On Sunday. Tomorrow is Saturday. I'll be here in the morning at seven thirty. Where we're going, it will be sunny and you'll want to wear something casual. We'll be gone the whole day and won't be home until late. Promise me you'll be ready when I come for you."

His body was actually trembling like hers. Feeling the strength of his emotions made it impossible to deny him. "I...promise."

"*Grazie a Dio.*"

"*Buonanotte*, Guido." Before he tried to kiss her, she reached for the door handle and hurried inside the building.

Once in her apartment, Dea dashed to her bedroom and pulled out her cell phone. There was only one person she could talk to about how she was feeling. She needed her twin. The two of them had suffered through so much. Alessandra, now a married woman with a child, would understand Dea's pain and fear as no one else could.

Her sister answered on the third ring. "Dea?"

"I know it's late, but I need some advice. If Rini is right there, maybe you could call me back later?"

"No, no. I'm back in Positano. He's still with our parents working, but will be home tomorrow."

Dea was glad she hadn't disturbed them. "How's Brazzo?"

"Thriving. I put him to bed several hours ago."

"Then you don't mind if we talk?"

"Are you kidding? I've been dying to know if you've seen or heard from Guido since that weekend when we were all together. But in case nothing came of it, I was afraid to ask any questions."

Her eyes closed tightly. "Quite a lot has gone on, actually."

"Oh, Dea—that's the best news!" She heard pure happiness in her sister's voice. "I just love Guido. He's a fantastic man. You two seemed so great together I couldn't believe it. Rini thought the same thing. To quote him, you were 'like two halves of the same incredible whole.'"

It had felt that way to Dea. "We've been out several times. He's been by Juliana's office and sent me roses. Tomorrow we're spending a whole day together."

"Meraviglioso!"

"I don't know, Alessandra. That's why I'm calling."

"What's wrong?"

"He's been relentless in getting me to bare my soul to him. Now that I have, he—he's afraid I'll always have feelings for Rini," she stammered. "I don't know what more I can say or do to convince him otherwise."

"From what Rini has told me, Guido has always been as closed up as my husband when it comes to the personal. He's a deep one."

Dea shivered. "I've already learned that about him. I'm frightened to spend any more time with him."

"Because you feel doomed to love a man who isn't sure of you, right?"

"Exactly." Dea knew her sister would understand. "I can't think of anything worse than having to prove myself to him over and over."

"I can think of one thing."

"What's that?"

"Never seeing him again."

She gripped the phone tighter. "You're right. The thought of his being gone out of my life is anathema to me."

"He's exciting, all right. Something must have happened over the years that has made him so distrustful. If you want my advice, do to him what he did to you. Stick to him like glue until you uncover *his* secrets. When that day comes, he'll get the point that he's the only male in your universe."

Was that possible?

"Thanks for talking to me, Alessandra. I'll do what you said, but I'm so nervous."

"So was I when I flew to Positano to surprise Rini long before we were married. It was a bad time for us and I was terrified he'd tell me to go home and never darken his doorstep again."

"You knew he wouldn't say that to you."

"No. Not then I didn't. There's no man more forbidding than Rini when he's upset. All I can say is, I'm thrilled to hear Guido hasn't left you alone. Just keep doing the unexpected."

"We'll see." But it took courage she didn't have a lot of. "Give the baby hugs for me until I can see him again."

"I will. And when you're with Guido tomorrow, tell him Brazzo adores the purple octopus. Between the color and the bells, I'm positive it's his favorite toy."

"I'll relay the message. I'm sure it will please him."

"Dea? Do me one more favor. Keep me informed. I'll be dying until I hear from you again."

"I promise. Love you."

"Love you too."

She clicked off. It was hard to believe that after

so many years of pain, the two of them were close again in a brand-new way.

At seven twenty in the morning Guido parked his car in front of Dea's apartment building and hurried inside to ring her on the foyer phone.

"There's no need for you to come up, Guido. I'll be right down and meet you at the car."

Elated that she was ready, he went back outside to wait for her. Though it was semicloudy in Rome, there'd be full sunshine where they were going.

Every time he saw her, she wore something different. Five foot seven and beautifully built, she could wear anything and look fabulous. This morning she'd put on white jeans with cuffs at the ankles and strappy beige sandals. On top she wore a round-necked three-quarter-sleeve cotton sweater in a soft hyacinth color. She left her freshly washed hair loose. It sparkled in the light. Best not to eat her up until they were alone.

"Buongiorno, bellissima." He opened the car door and helped her inside before going around to get behind the wheel. "I hope you haven't had breakfast yet."

"Just coffee."

"Good. We'll eat on the plane." He pulled into the traffic and headed for the airport.

She glanced at him from eyes the color of vintage Burgundy. "Are we flying to Naples again?"

"Si, signorina. But we won't be visiting the yacht."

"Are you going to take me on a sightseeing tour of your childhood haunts?" The question intrigued him.

"Would you like that?"

"I'd love to see the places that helped shape you into the person you are."

"We'll do that another day. Today I don't want to think about the past."

Her brows furrowed. "Why would you say that? Is it so painful?"

"That was an interesting choice of words."

"But the right one obviously. Otherwise you wouldn't question my asking."

He was glad they'd reached the airport so he could avoid an answer until they were on board the plane eating breakfast.

"Before we land in Naples, I'll try to explain myself. I grew up an only child. Since you were a twin, you can't possibly comprehend what it was like for me. My parents couldn't have more children and my father refused to adopt. He wanted a child from his blood. My mother was eager for more children, but it didn't happen."

"I'm sorry for all your sakes."

"My parents' marriage suffered because of my father's refusal to make my mother happy. His intransigence broke her heart. Ever since he said no to the idea of adoption, Papà has been paying for the damage he did to their union."

"So you became the golden child who had to meet your father's every expectation."

Guido nodded. "From the time I could comprehend pressure, I felt like I had to be perfect in his eyes to make him happy. I knew he expected me to follow in his footsteps. But I loved playing soccer and saw the disappointment in his eyes when I had to leave for practice or another game. He warned me that a life of sports wouldn't give me stability."

"That couldn't have been pleasant for you."

"No, but what made it worse was the fact that he was right."

"What do you mean?"

"In my late teens I had a serious girlfriend named Carla."

"You did?" At last he was revealing something vital about himself.

"I imagined us getting married one day after I'd had my run at soccer. But after I gave it up to go back to work for my father, she went off with another soccer player. When I realized it was the celebrity status of being the wife of a high-profile athlete she wanted, not me, I became wary of women."

Her eyes looked wounded as they played over him. "I'm sure that hurt a great deal."

"It made me angry. I did go back to work for my father, but I wasn't happy. The rest you know. Last year I left the company to buy a minor team. Not only have I turned out to be a great disappointment to Papà by leaving the business for a time, I'm a thirty-two-year-old bachelor.

"For the last five years he's been pushing me to get married. I know what's motivating his overzealous methods of throwing women at me. He wants me to provide grandchildren, hoping it will ease my mother's pain."

"So *that* was why he allowed the fashion show to take place on board the yacht."

"Of course. He planned it to coincide with my birthday because he wanted us to meet. Since nothing else had worked over the years, why not introduce me to the supermodel who's been the talk of Italy? With his reasoning, no real man could resist you, certainly not his own son.

"For once in his life, my father was right. Rini and I had been talking when Papà brought you and your friend over to your table. I'd seen your pictures everywhere, but meeting you in the flesh was something else."

Dea moaned. "When you and I were at the wedding reception, I was afraid I'd offended you when I made the remark about my friends hoping to do another fashion show on the yacht."

"I think you know by now that didn't offend me."

She nodded. "I'm afraid I've jumped to too many conclusions."

"So have I. I don't know how much you know about Rini and me. We met at seven years of age and attended the same schools together until college. The two of us went through every good and bad time together. I'll never forget when he learned that his soccer injury left him without the ability to have children."

"That had to have been so terrible for him."

Guido nodded. "When you met him on the yacht

and danced with him, I thought he was the luckiest man alive to meet you after what he'd been through. I also believed he deserved to find an amazing woman like you. But deep inside me I wanted you for myself and was appalled at my feelings of jealousy."

"Oh, Guido—"

"*Oh, Guido* is right! You have to understand that I was at a vulnerable point in my life because I'd decided to buy the soccer team and leave the company for a while. Nothing was a sure thing and I risked alienating my father in a way that might ruin our relationship for good. You talk about floundering while you were at Rini and Alessandra's wedding—so was I."

Before anything more could be said, the Fasten Seat Belt light went on.

"Come on. Let's get back to our seats. We'll resume this talk later."

Dea had wanted secrets from him and she finally had the truth. Now that she knew about his girlfriend from the past and her rejection of him to chase after another celebrity, she understood the war going on inside him where his father was concerned.

When they touched down and got off the plane, he led her to the waiting helicopter and helped her on board. "I promise our flight won't last longer than ten minutes."

Once they were in the air, he used the mic to talk to her. "We're headed for Ischia Island. Have you been there?"

She shook her head. "In my teens Papà drove us past it and the other islands off Naples in the old cruiser, but we never went ashore."

"Then you're in for a treat. We'll be putting down near Serrara Fontana in the mountainous southwest part."

"Does this island have special significance for you?"

"I'll explain in a few minutes," was all he would tell her.

The pilot made a beeline for the highest summit on the island and descended toward an isolated piece of property partially hidden by the vegetation. Soon a helipad appeared and they made a gentle landing.

Guido thanked the pilot before helping Dea to climb out. He grasped her hand and walked her along a path through the grove of chestnut trees. The sound of the rotors grew faint. As they came out the other side to a terraced garden of palms and flowers, he heard Dea's soft gasp.

Her eyes had taken in the two-story pastel-pink villa above the garden with its pool. The ornamental parapets of the balconies overflowed with bougainvillea and hibiscus. "This all looks like something out of a dream." The marvel in her voice told him everything he wanted to know.

He threaded his fingers through hers. "It wasn't like this when I first saw the place sixteen years ago with Rini. We were through diving for the day and decided to explore on rental bikes. After we swam in one of the many hot springs throughout the island, we arrived up here at the top. That's when I saw this wreck of what was clearly once a magnificent villa overlooking the sea, closed up and isolated. Its beauty haunted me."

"You were young to be so affected."

"I agree. Living in Naples all my life, I'd been surrounded by beauty and had traveled to many exotic places in the world. But this spot had such a strong pull on me, I eventually made inquiries of the locals."

"What did they tell you?"

"The original owners had lost their money and were forced to sell. The second owner bought it as an investment but only visited it a few times. Little by little the place fell into more disrepair, and a small portion part of the villa suffered fire damage."

She shook her head, causing her fabulous hair to float around her shoulders. "That's so sad."

He took a deep breath. "Over the years I flew here often. The worse it looked, the more I wanted it. The day it went up for sale again, I bought it and the first thing I did was clear a space for a helipad. Once that was done, I spent all my weekends here restoring the garden and making renovations. To get out of the Naples office and come here to work in the soil was therapeutic for me."

"You did all this by yourself?" She sounded incredulous.

"Most of it, though I did hire locals from time to time."

"When was that?"

"I took possession three years ago."

Her eyes were smiling. "So you could transform it."

"That's one way of putting it."

"Just as you decided to turn a grade-B soccer team into a national champion. I see a pattern here."

He chuckled and drew her into his arms. "But I don't know the outcome of either transformation yet."

"Why not?"

"For the obvious reason that our last three games of the season haven't been played yet. As for the other..." Her mouth was a temptation he couldn't resist. After kissing her long and hard, Guido put his arm around her shoulders and walked her up to the villa. "See for yourself."

He unlocked the main door and drew her inside the large foyer with a curving staircase rising to the next floor and rooms extending on both sides.

Dea walked around the interior, which was devoid of anything but the prepared drywall. She turned to him. "From the outside of the villa, you would never guess this is all unfinished."

He nodded. "It's ready for the right person to take over and create an ambiance of beauty from the flooring to the ceiling."

She eyed him for a moment. "Why not yourself?"

"You've seen my apartment, and I've told you about the one in Naples. This is no bachelor pad and needs the eye of someone with exquisite taste."

"Have you found that person?"

Guido moved closer and put his hands on her shoulders. "How would you like the job?"

Maybe it was a trick of light but he thought her face lost a little color. "Please don't joke about something like that."

"I would never joke about anything this personal. The first time I visited your apartment, I saw a reflection of the real you in everything and loved being there."

"Zia Fulvia helped me decorate when I moved in."

He tightened his fingers around her upper arms and shook her gently. "Why don't you ever take credit for your own genius? Don't you know how wonderful you are?"

"Guido—" Her cheeks filled with color and she pulled away from him.

"It's true. When you were telling me about the opera and how vital the costumes and settings were to making it come alive, I felt *you* come alive. That's the moment I knew I wanted you to see this villa and tell me what needs to be done. I'm sick of apartments and plan to live here for the rest of my life."

"You don't require anyone's help. You've created a masterpiece outside."

"I'm glad you think so, but the real task still awaits me. Come on. After you see the whole house, we'll drive down to the village for lunch and you can tell me what you think."

Not giving her a chance to argue, he grasped her hand and led her up the stairs to see the four bedrooms and bathrooms. The superb view of the Tyr-

rhenian Sea from the master suite held her gaze for
a long time.

A tour of the downstairs included a library and a
separate den off the living room. The large kitchen
and dining room on the other side of the house produced more cries of delight. He could hear her mind
working and knew her imagination had taken over.

A detached garage in the same Mediterranean style
with a tiled roof stood behind the villa. Along with
the gardening equipment, Guido kept a truck and his
Alfa Romeo Spider convertible locked up there. He
helped her get in his vintage sports car and they took
off down the winding road. The smell of roses and
jasmine hung heavy in the air. The woman seated next
to him had no clue what she meant to him. Not yet…

*I'm sick of apartments and plan to live here for the
rest of my life. This is no bachelor pad and needs
the eye of someone with exquisite taste. How would
you like the job?*

"We're coming into Sant'Angelo, an old fishing
village." Guido's deep male voice curled through
Dea's insides. "My sailboat is moored there in the
harbor. One day I'll take you out and we'll sail around
the island."

"Which one is it?"

"The white and blue one, which isn't much help,
since so many boats are the same."

She laughed. "This little town is a panoply of white,
blue and ochre houses all pressed together in a symphony of color. I've lived by the water all my life, but

our family's island has no color, just a dark stone castle."

He threw her a glance. "The severity has a beauty all its own."

"I agree, but this paradise dazzles the eye. The impossible yellows and pinks of the flowers make me think you live in heaven."

"Today I'm there."

She felt the same way as he slowed down and parked the car in a tiny space only someone as daring as Guido would have tried to navigate. He levered himself from the driver's side and came around to open her door. "In a few minutes you're going to taste pasta *arrabbiata* with a spicy kick that is out of this world. Emanuela's is right here on the beach."

For a little while Dea let go of her fear that he couldn't trust her feelings for him and inhaled the experience of being with Guido like this, a man whose background she was only beginning to understand, a man she already loved with all her heart and soul.

The food and wine turned out to be divine. Throughout their meal, his dark blue eyes wandered over her, causing every nerve in her body to throb with desire.

Following a tasty treat of raspberry gelato, they walked back to the car and took a drive around the island on the main road.

Traveling to the quaint, picturesque villages filled her with delight. He was better than any tour director or history teacher. He talked about the local legend of

the giant living in the volcanic rock and the tufa lime-
stone deposits built up around the fumaroles and spas.

Dea learned the island was shaped like a trapezoid
and housed sixty-two thousand people. The larger
towns sold everything imaginable. In Casamicciola
she bought some small ceramic tiles of Ischia for her
mother and sister. It was after five when Guido drove
through the hamlet of Ciglio, close to the villa. They
bought sausage rolls in puff pastry and fruit tarts to
take with them.

After arriving back at the villa, Guido parked the
car in the garage. Then he led her to a wrought iron
bench by the pool, where they ate their picnic. The
helicopter would be coming shortly, but Dea didn't
want to think about that yet.

"Do you know one of the meanings of *alfresco*?"
His eyes gleamed with mischief.

"Besides eating outside?" She smiled. "This garden is no prison. You know very well you've created
a work of art out here."

"Then will you do me a favor and think about my
proposition? While you're getting the costumes ready
for *Don Giovanni*, will you picture the villa in your
mind and tell me what kind of floors you envision
here? A color scheme? Would you work up a rough
draft that will point me in the right direction?"

She swallowed the rest of her pastry. *Stick to him
like glue*, Alessandra had advised her. She had to
prove to him how important he was to her.

"I'm flattered that you want my opinion. Let me
think about it and I'll get back to you."

A look of relief crossed over his striking features. "That's all I ask. I'd like to fly you here again next Friday night after work if you don't have other plans. We can stay over in Ciglio, then spend Saturday here. I'll have to get back to Rome Saturday night because the team is flying to Siena first thing Sunday morning."

"I'll try to get off on the dot of five. Maybe I can drive to the airport from work and meet you at the plane to save time. As it is, we won't get here until nightfall."

They both heard the helicopter coming. Her disappointment that they had to leave this paradise was killing her.

"I'll be counting the hours until we can be here together again, Dea." He cupped her face with both hands and kissed her mouth. "Umm. I can still taste the cherries on your lips."

He kissed her thoroughly before they walked through the trees to board the helicopter. As it rose in the air, she felt like her heart had been wrenched from her body. The villa got smaller until she could see the island where she'd known such great happiness. Dea couldn't bear to go back to her apartment. But she needed to get hold of herself so he wouldn't know how much this day had meant to her.

On the flight back to Rome, she told him one of her ideas for decorating the villa while they were seated in the club compartment of the plane. "When we were in Casamicciola, we passed a store with the most wonderful ceramic floor tiles in various shades from white to cream."

"You noticed all that?"

"Well, you *did* ask me to think about it. I couldn't help but see your main floor and walls as an extension of the outdoors where light sweeps through the interior, even up the staircase.

"One of the bedroom floors upstairs could contain a soft pink pigment to reflect the exterior of the villa. Maybe another bedroom could be done in a subtle gray-blue. Your kitchen would be gorgeous with hints of a lemon motif in the wall tiles to reflect the astounding yellow of the flowers on the island."

His brows lifted. "Wall tiles… You've already envisioned that in your mind?"

She smiled. "You'd be surprised what's going on in there." Dea had already designed a nursery for his children. Her thoughts wouldn't stop. "It's your fault, you know."

A low laugh came out of him. He sounded happy, in fact happier than she'd ever known him to be. This blissful state continued until they landed in Rome and he drove them to her apartment.

"Just pull up in front and let me out. I know you have a game tomorrow and I don't want to keep you."

"You're sure?"

That one question threw her for a loop. Dea had thought he would insist on seeing her inside so he could kiss her senseless. He'd spoiled her today. Now she was a mess, wanting so much more. *You're being selfish again.* He had a huge day ahead of him.

"Good luck tomorrow, Guido." She undid her seat belt to kiss his cheek before getting out of the car with her small souvenirs.

"I'll call you tomorrow night if it isn't too late."

"Don't worry about that." Dea shut the door and hurried inside the building to her apartment. He hadn't asked her if she wanted to attend the soccer match. What did that mean?

Once she'd showered and climbed into bed, she lay there wide-awake reliving her incredible day. Was it another test to see if she cared about him enough to show up uninvited? Should she do the unexpected, as Alessandra had suggested?

Dea wrestled with that question for a long time. Finally she concluded that since he'd asked her advice on how to decorate the villa, she'd take her chances and go to the match. She had to see him again or she wouldn't be able to make it to Monday when she had to go to work.

Guido, Guido. I love you so much I'm in pain.

CHAPTER SEVEN

GUIDO AND SERGIO sat in his private suite next to the press box to watch the game. Maybe thirty minutes had gone by when he heard his phone ring. When he saw the caller ID, he picked up.

"What's going on, Mario?"

"This is important. Someone has asked to be let into your suite, but it has to be all right with you."

He could only think of one person he wanted with him today, but that was a dream that wouldn't happen. "If you're referring to Rinieri Montanari or his wife, Alessandra, you know they always have an automatic entrée."

"I'm talking about the gorgeous supermodel who was here last week with friends."

"You're serious—"

"*Sì*. I swear she's here at the ticket booth."

Guido's breath caught in his throat. He hadn't expected her to show up today.

Last night he'd been tempted to ask her to come to the game and spend the rest of the night with him, but he'd held back, waiting for her to suggest it. When she didn't, he'd suffered disappointment.

As he and Sergio had discussed many times, few women—barring those who played the game or had a family member on the team—could get into soccer in a big way. But Dea had been supportive from day one. Maybe she was different.

"Boss? Shall I bring her up?"

"Please," he said when he could find his voice.

Sergio stared at him after he clicked off. "What's wrong? Is Dante's leg still bothering him?"

He hoped not. "We're about to have an unexpected visitor."

"I thought you said your father would never come to the stadium to watch a game."

"You've got the wrong gender."

"Your mother?"

"Wrong again." He got to his feet.

"Ah… Then it must be your secret woman."

Sergio never let up. Guido moved to the door and opened it to watch for her. In a moment he saw her walking in the corridor alongside Mario.

The dark blue short-sleeved dress with small red poppies Dea was wearing hugged her figure, then flared from the waist to the knee. With every step, the material danced around her beautiful legs, imitating the flounce of her hair, which she wore down, the way he liked it. Talk about his heart failing him!

"Dea—"

Her searching gaze fused with his. "I hope it's all

right." The slight tremor in her voice betrayed her fear that she wasn't welcome. If she only knew...

"You've had an open invitation since we met." Nodding his thanks to Mario, he put his arm around her shoulders and drew her inside the suite. Sergio slipped out of the room and closed the door so they could be alone.

He slid his hands into her hair. "You're the most beautiful sight this man has ever seen." With uncontrolled hunger he lowered his mouth to hers and began to devour her. Over the announcer's voice and the roar of the crowd, he heard her little moans of pleasure as their bodies merged and they drank deeply.

When she swayed in his arms, he half carried her over to the couch, where they could give in to their frenzied needs. She smelled heavenly. One kiss grew into another until she became his entire world. He'd never known a feeling like this and lost track of time and place.

"Do you know what you do to me?" he whispered against her lips with feverish intensity.

"I came for the same reason."

Her admission pulled him all the way under. Once in a while the roar of the crowd filled the room, but that didn't stop him from twining his legs with hers. He desired a closeness they couldn't achieve as long as their clothes separated them.

"I want you, *bellissima*. I want you all night long. Do you understand what I'm saying?"

Before he heard her answer, the noise from the crowd became earsplitting. Within a minute someone unlocked the door and burst in. "Boss? I've been trying to reach you. Though we won the game, Dante's leg may be broken. You're needed in the locker room. *Viene subito!*"

Dante… The game was over… For the last hour he'd been so caught up with Dea he hadn't noticed the passing of time.

After being jerked back from rapture he hadn't thought possible, his brain was slow to digest what Sergio had just told him.

Dea had more presence of mind. She eased herself out of his arms and got to her feet before he did. He stood there for a minute, raking one hand through his ruffled hair. "What happened?"

"He fell hard on his sore leg after getting kicked."

Dea put a comforting hand on his arm. "Go to him, Guido. If you can, come to my apartment later. If not, call me." In the next breath, she ran out the door before he could detain her.

Much as he wanted to go after her, he knew his duty was to Dante. Dea hadn't wanted to leave him; otherwise she wouldn't have told him to come to her place later. Loving her for her consideration, he started down the hall. By now the team doctor would have looked their star player over.

It wasn't until he was on his way into the locker room and saw Dante's family that he realized those hours with Dea had swept him away to a different world where nothing else had mattered. Not even his team. After she'd arrived, he hadn't watched a second of the game. Worse, he hadn't known of their victory until Sergio barged in.

It would all have been taped for Guido, but the news was bittersweet. Only two more matches before the end of the season. They'd have to play them without their star, Dante. For Sergio this had to be déjà vu. Ten years ago he'd suffered an injury that had knocked him out of competition for good. Guido had to pray Dante would heal well enough to play again.

This was the downside of being a team owner. His job was to encourage the rest of the team to carry on to a national victory. Realizing what he had to do tonight, he knew he wouldn't be able to get over to Dea's until long after she went to bed.

After he watched the ambulance take Dante to the hospital, he congratulated the team and had a short pep talk with them. Once the guys left, he phoned Dea. She answered on the second ring.

"Guido. How is Dante?"

"He's gone to the hospital. I'll know more by tomorrow morning."

"You sound exhausted. Don't come over tonight. It's late. Go home to bed and if you can, concentrate on your latest win. You're almost there."

"I don't know. Without Dante, our strength has been reduced."

"I don't think that's true. You have other players who will step up. One of them will realize this is their opportunity to become a new star for the team. Sometimes wonderful things come out of tragedy."

If she was speaking from experience, then she'd

learned a great deal about life. Her fighting spirit was exactly what he needed right now. "Thank you for those words. They mean more than you could know."

"I'm happy you said that. Here I was afraid that my arrival during the game prevented you from watching the rest of it and you resented me."

He let out an exasperated sigh. "What I resented was having to let you go at all. May I have a rain check for tomorrow evening? I'll bring takeout to your apartment after work and we'll watch the game we missed. How does that sound?"

"I'd love it, but tomorrow evening my aunt will be in Rome and we're going out to dinner with Juliana." He had to swallow the bad news that they wouldn't be able to see each other as soon as he'd wanted. "Maybe the next night? I'll show you some of my ideas for your villa. They bombarded me all night long. Where do you keep all your trophies?"

Her mind leaped around and fascinated him so much that laughter escaped his lips despite his disappointment. "My parents' villa."

"How many do you have?"

Guido shook his head. "I don't know."

"Enough to fill a room?"

"Why?"

"You know that little nook off the den? It would be a great place to keep them. Kind of like your own museum. I can see a wallpaper motif of a real lion head with the words *Cuor di Leone* above it. On one side could be family pictures of your parents. On the

other, pictures of you at different ages to immortal-
ize the Rossano name.

"I can hear what you're thinking," she added, "so
here's the plan. You could have double doors hung
that locked and couldn't be opened unless you used
a remote. I know how modest you are, so if you don't
want anyone else to see it, then there's no problem."

He was so touched by her words he had trouble
finding the right response. "I can see you think bigger than life."

"It comes from living in a castle with the enormous
painting of Queen Joanna dominating the foyer. We
Caracciolos can't think any other way."

His throat had swelled with emotion. "I'll call you
Tuesday and we'll make plans. Miss me, Dea." He
hung up and headed to his car. The next time he was
with her, he was going to have the most important
discussion of his life with her.

Miss me, Dea.

She'd heard the huskiness in his tone. Didn't he
know she wouldn't be able to breathe until they were
together again?

Luckily Dea was kept so busy at work the time
flew until she went out for an enjoyable dinner with
her aunt and Juliana Monday evening. During the
meal her mentor praised Dea's work. She also announced that they'd be working at the opera house
for the next three evenings while rehearsals for *Don
Giovanni* were going on. The opera would open the
following week.

Exciting as that prospect would be in the professional sense, it meant Dea wouldn't be able to see Guido until Friday. When his phone call came Tuesday afternoon, she had to tell him news that was hard on her too. "But I promise that nothing will keep me from meeting you at the airport on Friday at four thirty."

A full half minute of silence met her ears before he said, "I don't know if I can last that long."

"I feel the same way," she admitted, but something else was bothering him, evidenced by some nuance in his voice. "How's Dante?"

"He's out for the season."

"I'm so sorry."

"He received flowers at the hospital, among them some roses with a card that was signed by Dea Loti and said, 'A fan who is wishing you back to health as soon as possible.' Do you have any idea how honored he felt?"

"Good. He got them!"

"All the guys have come in and out of his room and read your card. Now his celebrity status has shot through the roof. Sergio and Mario are green with envy."

"Guido…those flowers were meant to cheer you up too."

"You succeeded. How am I supposed to wait until Friday?"

"The same way I am. Work, work, work."

"There's steel beneath all that beauty."

"And a warrior lives inside you! Your team is

going to be superb at their next match, all because
of their legendary owner."

"The things you say," he whispered. "If you were
with me right now…"

"We'll be together on Friday. I'm staying positive
for you. *A presto*, Guido." She hung up before blurting that she loved him, but that day was coming soon.

At four fifteen on Friday, Dea arrived at the airport by
taxi, so eager to see Guido her cheeks were flushed
and she thought she might be running a temperature. She hurried out on the tarmac to the section for
the private planes. In the distance she saw the Scatto
Roma jet. The door was open and the staircase had
been placed against it.

He was here! She ran all the way with her overnight bag and raced up the steps straight into his
arms. Guido put her bag down and buried his face
in her hair. "I saw you coming. Thank heaven you're
early. I couldn't have stood to wait another minute."

"Neither could I!" She pressed her mouth to his,
kissing him so hungrily she almost knocked him over
like she had playing soccer with him. Dea was no
longer the same person. This man Guido—the love
of her life—was eating her alive while he carried her
all the way to his bedroom. For the next while she
lost cognizance of her world. Overwhelmed with the
pleasure he gave her, she hardly realized a voice had
sounded over the plane's PA system.

"Signor Rossano? Do you wish to take off now?"

On a groan, Guido lifted his head and pulled out his phone. "We're ready."

"Bene."

His blue eyes were glazed with desire as he looked down at her. "We have to go to the club compartment."

"You shouldn't have brought me back here."

"I couldn't do anything else." He snatched another kiss from her lips and helped her to stand. Her hair was a complete mess and her lipstick had long since disappeared. She felt herself wobble on the way to the front of the jet, where they strapped themselves in their seats.

His eyes never left hers as the plane taxied out to the runway. Soon the engines screamed and they lifted off into the early evening sun. Once they'd achieved cruising speed, the steward brought them dinner.

"To shorten the time we're in the air, we're flying directly to Ischia and will drive a rental car to our hotel in Ciglio. How does that sound?"

She finished munching on some bruschetta. "I think you already know."

"Tell me how things are going at the opera."

"It's a whole other world. You can't imagine how exciting it is to see the singers get dressed in their costumes. All our hard work is on display, but I have to tell you one funny thing. Gina wasn't given the right dimensions for Leporello's jacket. When he tried it on, his considerable belly prevented it from closing. Gina and I tried not to explode from laughter."

Guido flashed her a broad smile.

"Juliana saved the day by finding a red scarf that she wrapped around him so the front edges would lie flat. When he reached for notes, we were all afraid the scarf would burst, but it didn't. Her ability to innovate at the last second makes her the queen of costume designers."

"I'm looking forward to seeing the opera performed."

"Me too. It starts next week."

"You'll have to show me the costumes you designed."

"I only helped."

"Now who's being modest?"

She finished her coffee. "Do you think your team is ready for the game in Siena?"

His brows furrowed. "They're going to have to be, but Drago can only do so much."

"One of the other players will step up. Have no fear."

"You really believe that, don't you?"

Heavens—in chinos and a sport shirt, the man was so incredibly attractive with that dark blond hair that she couldn't help staring. "Yes. They want you to be proud of them. You're their hero."

He made a protesting sound. "You don't know that."

"Oh, yes, I do. I'll never forget the look of worship in Aldo's eyes when he met you in person. Your team's feelings for you have to be a hundred times stronger."

"Did I ever tell you how good you are for me?"

"I don't know how you can say that when I caused you to miss watching an hour of the game last Sunday evening."

"There's a lot more I want to say on that subject, but I'll wait until we're completely alone."

How wonderful that sounded. A minute later the steward removed their trays and told them they'd be landing soon. Dea sat back, aching to get Guido all to herself. Within three minutes the Fasten Seat Belt sign flicked on and they began their descent. In the dying rays of the sun, Ischia rose up to greet them.

A rental car was waiting on the tarmac. Guido loaded them inside and drove them out to the main road. Guido pampered her to the point she felt sorry for every woman who would never know what it was like to be with a fabulous man like him.

It soon became clear that the island was overrun with tourists. She wished they didn't have to stay at a crowded hotel tonight, no matter how charming it might be. "We should have brought sleeping bags we could put down at the villa."

"On those hard subfloors? Not exactly my idea of comfort, but I'm living for the day when it's ready for occupation."

Dea eyed him covertly. "There's still your sailboat. We could pick up some goodies in the village and sleep on board."

She heard a harsh intake of breath. "You must have been reading my mind. I wanted to take you there in the first place, but it's intimate. Contrary to what you've probably heard about me, I'm not the kind of man who sleeps with every woman I fancy. I would never treat you that way."

"You thought I'd feel more comfortable staying at a hotel with adjoining rooms?"

"I'm trying hard to be a gentleman with you."

"Please try harder not to be."

His deep unexpected laughter filled the car's interior. "There's no other woman in the world like you, Dea. How did I get so lucky?"

"I've been saying that to myself about you ever since our own little soccer game." She ached with love for him. "I'm afraid I'm not known for my subtlety. To be honest, I've never been to bed with a man."

"That's what I thought."

"Does it show so much? Is that why you haven't tried to take advantage of me?"

"A woman who knows her value is more desirable than you can imagine."

"Well, I hate to ruin that image you have of me because it's all I can think about when I'm with you."

"Now she tells me."

His teasing was driving her crazy. "Surely at this point you must realize that if I thought you were a true playboy out to use me, we would never have made it this far."

"I think that's a compliment of sorts. But in case you've got the entirely wrong opinion about me, I'll be honest too. Over the years I've had a few very short-term intimate relationships with women. None since my birthday last year, however."

The birthday on the yacht… "That night changed history for both of us, Guido."

"You're right. That was the night my world underwent an upheaval from which I've never recovered and don't want to." He reached over and put a hand on her thigh. Through the fabric of her cotton pants, she felt his touch electrify her body. "If you really want to spend the night on the boat, there's nothing I want more. We'll head straight to Sant'Angelo now."

"I'd love it," she answered in a trembling voice. "But if you've already made reservations, I—"

"Don't worry about it. I'll cancel them now."

To her delight he pulled out his cell phone and made the call, ensuring a perfect night. All week she'd imagined them alone and away from other people with no pressure. It looked like she was going to get her heart's desire, and she preened like Alfredo when he found a spot in the sun.

Within an hour they'd picked up food and had walked over to the pier. They planned to go sailing in the morning. Dea had brought her bikini in case they decided to swim and sunbathe. But they would stay right here for tonight.

Guido led her to his one-man sailboat moored in its own slip. When she saw the name of it painted on the side, she let out a cry and stared at him. "The *Bona Dea*?"

He nodded. "The *Good Goddess*."

Her eyes rounded. "How long have you owned this boat?"

"I bought it off a fisherman two years ago. He'd

owned it for fifteen years and had named it for the ancient Roman goddess of fertility, *your* namesake, as it turns out."

"I don't believe it!"

"Truth is stranger than fiction. I was in love with your name long before we met. It just took meeting you in the flesh to complete my entrancement."

CHAPTER EIGHT

DEA BLUSHED AND climbed on board. It was no surprise to Guido she knew her way around a boat. She'd lived by the water all her life, even if she hadn't learned to water ski until he'd helped her.

Together they went below with their overnight bags and freshened up. She helped him make the bed with clean sheets and a blanket from the cupboard. After pulling out an extra quilt, he took it and the pillows up on deck so they could be comfortable.

"Come here." He propped himself against them and drew her down so she lay against him on the padded side of the boat. It rocked gently in the water. Once he'd covered them with the quilt, they enjoyed some of the nuts and chocolate they'd bought.

The lights of the village reflected in her eyes. "It's like looking at wonderland, Guido."

He kissed her temple. "You like this place?"

Dea nestled closer. "What a question."

"I've spent many nights right here on the water."

"I can see why."

"Can you imagine yourself living here?"

"That's not a trick question. Or is it?" She lifted her head to look at him. Her glossy hair drifted across his cheek. "What are you saying?"

He kissed every part of her face. "Do I really have to answer that?"

"Guido—" By now she was sitting up. Her body had gone taut with emotion. "Please don't tease me. Not about this. I couldn't take it."

His expression grew serious. "I'm in love with you, Dea. So in love that I never want to be apart from you."

"You are?" she asked in a shaky voice. Tears glistened in her eyes.

"Do you really need convincing, my love? I want to marry you right away and spend the rest of my life on this island with you. I want so many things. I'm bursting with the need to tell you. Forgive me if I'm moving too fast, but I can't help it. I've loved you for too long believing there was no hope."

She put her hands on his shoulders. "I've been waiting, dying for you to tell me. I was afraid I might never hear the words. I'm madly in love with you, Guido."

"I thought maybe I had a chance with you when I saw a poster of me in your bedroom at the apartment."

"You *saw* it?"

He nodded. "I knew you'd bought two posters. The evidence gave me hope, something I badly needed."

"Oh, darling. After our day on the water with Alessandra and Rini, I knew I was truly falling in love for the first time in my life."

"It happened to me when you tackled me."

"But *I* didn't know that! You left the castle that morning before I could say a final goodbye to you."

"You know why. I knew it was too soon to ask for all your passion."

"And all my truth," she reminded him. "You think I didn't want the same thing?" Dea gave him another fervent kiss and shook him gently. "When I discovered you'd already gone that Sunday morning, I felt such pain go through me that I knew you'd taken my heart with you. What if I never saw you again? I was terrified until you called me to go to lunch."

"*Adorata*, I've lived in terror since that night on the yacht. If I couldn't have you, I didn't want another woman. For a while I was out of my mind fearing I would never be able to have my heart's desire."

She kissed him hard. "No more talk about the past. I want to be your wife, Guido. I've already designed our whole villa, complete with the most adorable nursery you ever saw in your life. We're going to have children to keep both sets of grandparents busy. Is this your official proposal?"

The lovelight in her eyes blinded him. "It's official, *bellissima*." He reached in his pocket and put a diamond solitaire on her ring finger.

"It fits perfectly!" She squealed. "Oh, Guido—you've had this all along?" She hugged him around the neck with the same strength she'd shown playing soccer. "It's gorgeous! *You're* gorgeous!"

"So are you. I love you." He covered her mouth with his own, hardly able to believe that she was going to be his wife after he'd lived through so much agony. Later, when he let her up for breath, she said, "Let's go below so I can show you how much you mean to me."

"Dea, before we both lose complete control, we need to talk about our future." He grasped her hands and kissed the palms. "You've made me the happiest man alive. To know I'm going to be your husband is such a privilege. I want to do everything right."

"What do you mean?"

"Just that I want our wedding night to be the first time we make love. After what you've told me, it's my way of honoring you."

"But—"

"No buts." He pressed another kiss to her lips. "I want to be worthy of you."

"Guido, of course you're worthy! We *love* each other. I don't understand."

"I need you to love me always and be proud of me. Especially of what I'll be doing in the future."

Her brows knit together. "I *am* proud of you and whatever you do. You have to know that!"

"You say that now, and I love you for being so supportive of me. But the owner of a soccer team isn't a befitting profession for the husband of Count Caracciolo's princess daughter."

"What?"

"You know it isn't! Hear me out, *squisita*. I couldn't sleep thinking about you last night. I couldn't wait for us to be together so I could ask you to marry me. The fact that you've said yes changes everything."

"In what way?"

"I'm no prospect at the moment. Certainly no father's idea of the right kind of son-in-law. My father never liked it that I fell in love with soccer."

"But that doesn't mean he doesn't love you with all his heart and support whatever decision you make. Where is all this insecurity coming from? Are you afraid I'll leave you if you stick with soccer? I can see that I'm right."

He shook his head. "Whatever the reason, this comes from wanting to take care of you the best way I can and be an example to the children we'll have. So I've decided to sell the team at the end of the season whether we're victorious or not. It's only two weeks away. Sergio and Mario have always been interested in buying me out if I chose not to go on."

"You don't mean it! You love the soccer world!"

"Not the way I love you and the children I want to have with you. Tomorrow I'll inform my father and grandfather that I'm coming back to work for the company. They'll be ecstatic."

"I'm sure they will, but it's you I'm worried about. You left the company last year because you felt stifled and needed to do something of your very own. We've already talked about this. I thought we were going sailing tomorrow and talking more about plans for the villa. I was thinking we could put in an herb garden at the side of the house."

"I love all your ideas, Dea, and want to do everything with you. But this is too important to put off.

If you don't mind, I want us to go back to Rome in the morning."

"Stop, Guido. Can't you hear what you're saying? You haven't worked for the company in almost a year. How can you be sure it's what you want to do?"

"I'm very sure now that I know I'm going to have a loving wife to take care of for the rest of our lives. Nothing's more important to me than you."

"Being CEO won't give you the freedom you've had as a soccer-team owner. Think about the way you felt when you decided to leave the company and do something that made you feel alive."

He crushed her to him. "I didn't have you in my life then. I want our lives to have stability."

"But you have that being the owner of Scatto Roma."

"It's not the same thing. Trust me."

"If your team wins the national championship, you might feel very differently about things then. Give it a little more time, darling. How can you think about all this when you're flying to Siena Sunday morning to play an important match?"

"I'll be able to fit everything in." He pulled her down next to him again. "After we get back to Rome, I'll fly to Naples. My father will be so elated he'll plan to call a meeting of the board and things will be put into motion to make me CEO. I want all that in play before we tell either of our parents that we're getting married."

She lay against him, much quieter than before. "Then I'd better not wear this engagement ring around anyone yet."

He kissed her neck. "It'll be our secret for two more weeks, then we can shout it to the world. For now I'll know you have it and that you've promised to be my wife."

"Tell me what it is you'll do as CEO."

"Find new markets for new ships. The business is constantly evolving."

"How do you go about doing that?"

"Right now I'd rather talk about you and your work. When do you graduate?"

"In June. My internship with Juliana will be over."

"Do you think she'll let you go on working with her?"

"I wouldn't dream of asking her. I need to prove myself and will have to apply elsewhere. It may take time to find a company that will hire me. One day I hope to build a reputation for myself."

"You don't have to wait to do that. I'll set you up in your own business and opera companies will flock to you."

"That's very generous of you, darling, but this I have to do myself. Gina is in the same boat. We're both watching out for each other. While I wait for a bite, I'll be helping you work on the villa."

"Before that we'll be planning our wedding. I already know where you want to be married."

"Since you're an only child, maybe your parents would love to see you married in Naples at your church."

"You're going to be the bride, Dea. It'll be your day and your choice."

"You mean that?"

He drew her closer. "How can you even ask me that question?"

"Then I think it would be lovely to let them give you the wedding of their dreams. They don't have a daughter. My parents have twin girls and they've already had the joy of helping Alessandra plan her wedding."

"It was magnificent," he murmured. "The Archbishop of Taranto even officiated."

"You've told me of your mother's sorrow and your father's pain because he knew she'd wanted more children. When you tell him his plan worked to find you a wife, I have a feeling your parents will get a new lease on life and plan something magnificent too."

Guido looked into her eyes. "You don't have a selfish bone in your delectable body. More than ever I know I don't deserve you, but I'm going to try from here on out to be all the things you want me to be. *Ti amo*, Dea. *Ti amo*."

With Guido's declaration of love, he'd sent Dea the message she'd been waiting for all her life, and eventually she fell asleep. But in the middle of the night she awakened disoriented. It took her a minute to realize she was on the sailboat with him.

Careful not to disturb this man she loved to distraction, she eased out of his arms and got to her feet. The moonlight picked out his striking features and caught the facets of her diamond. Tonight he'd asked her to marry him. On her finger was the proof, yet during her sleep something had bothered her so badly she'd come wide-awake.

She needed another talk with her sister, but that couldn't happen until they flew back to Rome. The night was cool so she went downstairs and slept under the blanket until she heard Guido call to her.

"I'm right here, darling!" She slid off the bed and started up the stairs. They met halfway and Guido swept her in his arms. His kiss was to die for.

"Where did you go?" He sounded alarmed.

Dea rubbed his hard jaw. "Umm. You have a beard."

"Don't change the subject."

"I guess I'm so excited at the thought of marrying you I woke up during the night. You were sleeping peacefully. I didn't want to disturb you, so I came down here and went back to sleep."

"When I couldn't find you, I—"

She hushed the rest of his sentence with her mouth. "It's going to be fun getting to know all the fascinating little things about each other."

He cupped her face. "Except when you scare the daylights out of me."

"What did you think happened?" Dea wanted to understand him.

Guido held her close. "You don't want to know. I feared someone might have come by and tried to drag you off."

"Oh, darling, I'm so sorry."

"No. *I* am for not insisting we go downstairs last night, where we could be totally private and I could better protect you. If you'll gather your things, we'll get going. We can shower on the plane and have breakfast."

She smiled. "Don't shave. I like your five o'clock shadow."

His eyes darkened with emotion. "I don't know if I can wait to marry you."

"You're going to be exciting to live with. Already I know you're an impatient man. It will be a challenge to keep up with you. Come on. Let's get going. I can tell you're hungry. I think there are a few more nuts left on deck to tide you over."

She gave him a kiss on the cheek, then hurried back down to the bathroom to gather her things and straighten the blanket on the bed. Guido brought the quilt and pillows downstairs and put them in the cupboard.

"Pretty soon we'll be getting a lot of use out of that," he said, glancing at the bed.

Her heart raced. "Don't make promises you can't keep." On that bold note she dashed out of the room and up the stairs with her overnight case. His deep laughter preceded him on deck.

Before they got in the rental car, she took off her ring and slipped it in her purse. It wouldn't do if the steward or the pilot saw her wearing it. Secrets always had a way of getting out. Word would somehow get back to Guido's family.

On the way to the airport she brushed her hair and put on lipstick. Guido watched her out of the corner of his eye. "You're going to be my wife, but I still can't believe I'm marrying my fantasy."

"I love you so much. It seems too wonderful to be true."

His hands tightened on the steering wheel. "I'd like to take you to Naples with me. I hope you understand why I need to go alone first."

"I do."

"I probably won't get back to Rome until midnight and then I'll have to be up at dawn."

"Guido? How would you feel if I flew to Siena to watch the game with you?"

"Much as I'd love it, when we're the visiting team I can't see to your needs or make you comfortable."

She could tell what he was trying to do. He had no idea how much this was hurting her. To her grief, there was no dissuading him from his plans. "Then I'll watch it on TV."

"As soon as it's over, I'll phone you and we'll make plans to spend Monday night together."

Once they boarded the plane and were in the air, Guido disappeared long enough to shower and change so he'd be able to fly directly to Naples from the airport in Rome. Dea decided to wait until she got home to her apartment to shower and wash her hair.

The steward served them a delicious breakfast. Guido asked her to show him some of her drawings for the villa. She got them out of her case and they pored over everything. He had his own ideas, of course, but loved most everything she'd suggested except for the *Cuor di Leone* motif.

"That's too over the top, *bellissima*." He squeezed her hand across the table. "Have I hurt your feelings?"

"Yes, but I'll find a way to live with it. In fact I'll put that poster of you on the door of our new walk-in closet, where I can indulge my fantasy about you."

Too soon the seat belt light flashed. They were getting ready to land. This would be their first separation as an engaged couple, but she could tell Guido's mind was in a dozen different places. He was a man on a mission. The wrong one, as far as she was concerned.

When they'd taxied to a stop, Guido walked her out of the plane and down the steps to a waiting limo he'd arranged for her. He helped her in the back with her case and told the driver where to take her.

"The next time we're together, we'll plan our wedding. One more game a week from Sunday, and then we'll tell our families. *Miss me*." He planted a fierce kiss on her mouth before shutting the door.

That was the second time he'd said that to her. Did he honestly think she wouldn't? Didn't he know yet what he meant to her?

She gave him a little wave. The limo drove away before he could see moisture bathing her cheeks. It didn't take long for Dea to get into her apartment. She hoped no one had seen her tear-ravaged face.

The minute she was safely inside, she opened her purse and put the ring in her jewelry case. With that done, she pulled out her phone and flung herself on the bed to call Alessandra.

Please be home. Please answer.

Five rings and her voice mail came on. Of course it

did. On a Saturday she and Rini had to be out somewhere with the baby. Dea asked her to phone her back
when she could without leaving a reason for the call.

This ought to have been the happiest day of her
life, but as it wore on, her pain grew heavier. A trip
to work out in the gym didn't relieve it. All she could
think about was Guido's reason for flying to Naples
today.

She came back to the apartment to shower and
wash her hair. The rest of the day was taken up when
Daphne Butelli, the friend who she'd modeled with,
phoned. Daphne wanted to meet up, so they decided
to see a film and get dinner after. The distraction
didn't help her mental state. She came back to the
apartment still filled with anxiety.

While she was watching the news on TV, her phone
rang. *At last,* she thought when she saw the caller ID.

"Alessandra?"

"Hi, Dea. I'm so sorry not to have gotten back to
you until now. We spent the day with Rini's father
in Naples. It was his birthday. Carlo and his family
came too. As usual we had to take so much stuff for
Brazzo I forgot my phone. Until we got back home
tonight, I didn't realize you'd called me this morning."

"Please don't apologize. Is Rini close by?"

"No. He's in the den taking care of business he
didn't get done today. Are you all right?"

"Yes."

"No, you're not. I can hear it in your voice."

"I'm afraid Rini will walk in on our conversation."

"This is about Guido, right?"

A sad laugh escaped. "Who else?" The tears started again.

"We're safe for a while. Talk to me."

"I'll make this short. In case Rini surprises you, please don't react to what I'm going to tell you and don't tell him anything after you hang up. Make something up. This is for your ears only."

"I promise."

"We spent the night on his sailboat in Ischia. He asked me to marry him and gave me a beautiful diamond ring. But he doesn't want anyone to know we're engaged yet. He plans to sell his soccer team after his last game a week from tomorrow.

"In the meantime, he flew to Naples today to tell his father he's going back to the shipping lines and will accept the position as CEO. When all that is accomplished, then we'll announce our wedding plans."

"What you've just told me has me jumping out of my skin for joy, so why are you so unhappy?"

Dea sank down on the side of the bed. "Because when I see Guido on Monday night, I'm giving back the ring."

A long silence followed. "What am I missing?"

"Guido's afraid I'll leave him."

"I'm not following."

"Maybe this will help." She told her sister about Guido's insecurity where his father was concerned. "He said that the owner of a soccer team isn't a befitting profession for the husband of Count Caracciolo's princess daughter."

"He actually *said* that?"

"Oh, yes."

She heard her sister groan. "I can't believe it."

"Neither can I. Deep in his psyche he thinks he has to work for his father to prove his own worth."

"Oh, Dea, I don't know what to say."

"You're not alone. A year ago he left the shipping business to buy the soccer team. He loves what he does *now*. There's excitement in him. I'm afraid he'll lose all that by giving it up. He's only doing it because of me, Alessandra, and what he thinks his father expects of him. I can't live with him knowing he's giving up what he loves most."

"No. I couldn't, either."

"I'm glad you agree with me." Given the turbulent, painful history between Dea and her sister, only Alessandra could understand her reasoning. "If I return the ring on Monday night, no harm will have been done. No one will ever have to know he proposed and it will all be over before any decisions he's made are final. Then he'll be free to do what he really wants."

"But he wants you."

"He won't want me, not when he knows why I can't keep the ring. And I've made another decision."

"What's that?"

"Tomorrow I'm going to send out résumés over the internet to places needing period costume designers for either the opera or the theater. If it means moving to England or France for a time, I know it will be a good thing. My career is important to me and I'm not going to let this set me back."

"I love you, Dea, and I'm behind you a thousand percent."

"Thank you for listening. I needed to say it out loud." She appreciated her sister not trying to reason with her or talk her out of anything. "I love you too. Take care. Good night."

CHAPTER NINE

IT WAS TEN to twelve Sunday night when Guido arrived back at his apartment. The fabulous game results were in. Team Scatto Roma: 2—Siena: 0

A forward on the opposition side had developed a bad case of stomach flu and couldn't play. Fate was with Guido's team despite Dante's fractured leg. One more win next Sunday and the national championship would be theirs.

Guido quickly phoned Dea. He had so much to tell her, he couldn't wait to hear her voice. But disappointment flooded him when his call went to her voice mail. He'd have to wait until tomorrow to talk to her.

Exhausted from virtually no sleep in the last twenty-four hours, he passed out the minute his head hit the pillow. He woke up at eight and checked his phone. Dea still hadn't responded. Guido left another message, but no results. After showering and getting dressed, he grabbed a quick bite and left for his office at the stadium to do a follow-up after the game.

As the day wore on he called her several times. No phone calls from Dea proved something was wrong.

After telling Sergio he was leaving, he drove straight to her work only to discover she'd already left for home. By now he was feeling close to frantic. He parked and entered her apartment foyer to ring her. If he couldn't reach her, he would call her parents.

Relief swamped him when he heard the buzz that let him inside. He took the stairs two at a time to the third floor. She'd left the door open for him, but instead of running into his arms, she stood in the living room dressed in her workout clothes. He moved inside and shut the door, struggling for the right words.

"What's going on, Dea?" he rasped. "Why in heaven's name haven't you returned my calls?"

"First let me say welcome back and congratulations on another win."

He rubbed the back of his neck, completely bewildered. "What's happened to you since we kissed goodbye at the airport?"

"If you'll sit down, I'll tell you."

"I'd rather stand."

"Guido, I haven't intentionally tried to be cruel by not answering the phone." Her sincerity smote him. "The truth is, I've needed this much time to gather my thoughts before we spoke again. I had to be sure that you'll understand perfectly what I'm about to tell you."

He felt like he'd been slugged in the gut. "You've decided you don't want to marry me after all."

Her unmistakable nod caused such excruciating pain he couldn't breathe. While he stood there in shock, she walked over to the end table and put the ring down.

"More than anything in the world, I want to marry you and be your wife. But I don't want my husband to give up the career he loves for me."

Her first salvo found its target, crippling him.

"I want the Guido I met, who was full of life and excitement, who's still young and has an extraordinary gift that can't be bought. That man has the ability to motivate thousands of younger men who need a hero to model themselves after. A man like that only comes along once in several lifetimes.

"I fell in love with that man, not the man who's going back to a job he'll still be able to do years from now, a job that doesn't fulfill him, a job that squeezes the life out of him.

"Guido Rossano? You're worried you'll never live up to your father's expectations if you don't go back to the company. *I'm* worried you'll never be happy again if you do, so we need our engagement to end."

Zing. Another salvo to finish him off. He broke out in a cold sweat.

She moved to the doorway. "You're welcome to stay here as long as you want. I'm off to the gym."

In the next instant she was gone, leaving her words ringing in his ears. *I don't want my husband to give up the career he loves for me.*

Little did Dea know he'd already come to his senses and she'd been preaching to the converted. But she hadn't given him the chance to talk.

Galvanized into action, he raced out the door to

stop her. But when he reached her parking space, he discovered her car was still there. She had to have taken the staircase to escape him. Where in the hell was the gym? But even if he could find her, the gym wasn't the place to continue their conversation.

Guido went back to her apartment. After locking the door, he pocketed the ring. A quick examination of the kitchen revealed she had enough food for him to make them a meal. But she didn't come home and he ended up putting the food away.

He sat on the couch to watch the evening news and the sports. At five after eleven he heard her key in the lock and she opened the door. Her eyes collided with his across the expanse. She looked drawn and pale. Her hair had been tied at her nape with a band. "Guido! What are you doing here?"

"What do you think? You disappeared on me before I had a chance to talk to you about anything."

She closed the door. "I can smell garlic and basil."

"I made us a meal. If you're hungry, I'll warm it up."

"I ate dinner earlier."

"By yourself?"

"No. With Gina. We met at the gym first."

He'd been lounging back on the couch with his legs extended. "You told me I could stay as long as I wanted, so I took you at your word. If you're too tired to hear what I have to say right now, I'll still be here in the morning."

Her features wooden, she came closer and sank down on one of the chairs.

"Go ahead."

Guido sat forward. "After I flew to Naples to surprise my family, I discovered they were away for the day with friends in Salerno. I was the one surprised and ended up visiting with my grandfather and his nurse. He mostly talked about the war years and his hard life when he was young."

Her head lifted. "You didn't talk business?"

"No. He told me he always wanted to go to sea and travel the world. But he revered his strict father too much and stuck with the shipping company like a dutiful son. He looked me in the eyes and said, 'My life was successful. I had a loving wife and family, but my great regret was that I wasn't happy in my career. Good for you for doing what makes you happy.' With those words he said he was tired and told me to kiss him before he went to bed."

She rubbed her hands over her knees. "That must have been a very emotional experience for you."

"I heard a side of my grandfather I didn't know existed. Yesterday in Siena I underwent another shock when my parents showed up to be with me at the game."

She looked startled. "They actually came?"

"Yes. I knew it was my grandfather's doing, but the fact that they made the effort was a revelation. My mother had always been on my side and would have come to all my games if she hadn't felt it was disloyal to my father. It was an added bonus for them to see that my team won the game."

"I heard the score on the news," she murmured.

"When I saw them off at the airport and thanked them for coming, I told them I loved owning the team. So much in fact that I wasn't planning to go back to the company for a few years. But to sweeten the bad news, I told them you and I were getting married and wanted him and Mamma to help us plan everything."

Dea's eyes went suspiciously bright.

"I thanked him for never giving up on me and finding me the love of my life."

"You did?" She sounded incredulous.

"Do you know he wept? So did my mother, but I've never seen my father break down like that. Before he had a chance to say another word, I promised him that God willing, we'd give them grandchildren. I also invited them to fly to Ischia with us soon so they can see where we're going to live. We'll let them choose the room they'd like to have when they stay with us."

"Oh, Guido—" Suddenly Dea had launched herself into his arms and broke down sobbing. "Forgive me for the things I said to you, darling. You have to forgive me for doubting you."

He crushed her against him, burying his face in her hair. "I can understand why you said what you did. To be honest, when I was talking to you on the sailboat, I was thinking of my own father, not yours."

"I know that now." She half sobbed the words.

"I've always been afraid he didn't think soccer was a worthy job for a son of his."

"I understand it all. I get it, but you have to know he doesn't feel that way."

"You're right."

She covered his face with kisses. "I never meant to hurt you. Where's my ring?"

"Right here." He reached in his trouser pocket and put it on her finger.

"I swear I'll never take it off again."

Their mouths met hungrily. When he finally lifted his head, he said, "Do you think it's too late to call your parents and tell them our news?"

"Yes, but they'd never forgive me if I didn't waken them anyway. And then I want to phone Alessandra and Rini. She loves you and has wanted this marriage since the day we went out on the cruiser together."

"You made that up."

"No. What you don't know is that she and I have had several talks about you, all my doing. Rini's going to be so happy for us too. Now the *four* of us will be joined at the hip forever."

Guido burst into laughter. Heavens, how he loved this woman! What was it Rini had said that evening at the castle when he'd confided in him about Dea?

You and I both know that no matter how bad it looks, you never leave the stadium until the game is over. Astounding surprises happen in the last second.

Astounding was right. At the last second all Guido's dreams had come true. He stretched out on the couch and started to pull her on top of him, but she held back. "If we don't make the call now, it'll be too late."

"You're right."

She went over by the chair to get her purse and pulled out her phone. He sat up and she rejoined him on the couch. Guido wrapped his arm around her and held her close while she punched the programmed number. "I've got it on speakerphone."

"Dea?" her mother cried after picking up on the third ring. "What's wrong, *tesoro*?"

"Not a thing, Mamma. Can you put your phone on speaker so Papà can hear this too?"

"Just a minute. Okay. Go ahead. We're both listening."

Guido squeezed her hip.

"Do you remember the day you told me to concentrate on finding myself? If I did that, my prince would find me?"

"Prince?" he whispered in her ear.

"Of course I do."

"Well, you're full of wisdom. My blond pirate prince has asked me to marry him."

Pirate?

"Grazie a Dio!" her father said in a booming voice.

"Oh—*tesoro*, we've been praying for this day since your sister's wedding."

She stared at Guido. "You have?"

"We weren't the only ones, either."

"What do you mean?"

"When you and Guido stood at the front of the cathedral as maid of honor and best man, Guido's parents smiled at your father and me. We were all thinking the same thing—that our beautiful son and daughter were meant to be together, but you didn't know it then. I'm so happy for you. Guido? Are you there? Do your parents know yet?"

Dea handed him the phone.

"They know, and they think I'm the luckiest man alive, which I am."

"Welcome to the family, Guido." This from Dea's father.

He felt a thickening in his throat. "I'm thrilled to become a part of it. I don't know if Dea told you, but my father arranged for that fashion show on the yacht so I could meet the breathtaking Dea Loti. He thought she would make me the perfect wife. I took one look at her and knew she would."

"That's very touching," Dea's mother said in a tear-filled voice.

"Mamma? How would you and Papà feel about our getting married in the Rossanos' church in Naples?"

"We don't care where you take your vows as long as we're there," her father asserted.

"Darling? Have you picked a date?"

Dea kissed Guido's lips. "Maybe three weeks? A month? By then I will have graduated and the soccer season will be over. We don't want to wait any longer than that."

"Does Alessandra know?"

"We're going to phone them right now."

"You do that and we'll talk more tomorrow. Fulvia will be overjoyed."

"She will! I guess I don't have to tell you that I have the best parents on earth. *Dormi bene.*"

"Ooh!" Dea threw her arms around him, almost knocking him over. "I'm so happy I can't breathe."

"You have to breathe to live, *adorata*. Come on.

Let's get this call to your sister over with. You and I have things to do."

She kissed one corner of his mouth. "Are you going to make us wait a whole month?"

"Yes, you gorgeous witch. Keeping the fires burning will add infinite pleasure to our wedding night and all the nights destiny allows us from then on."

Dea grasped his hands and kissed the tips of his fingers. "So—" she rolled her eyes at him "—you chip, drop, kick, sweep, cook and are an incredible romantic too. What did I ever do to deserve you?"

June 30, fourteenth-century church of San Giovanni, Carbonara, Naples

"There are so many photographers here you'll be late for your own wedding."

Dea clung to her father's arm, trembling with excitement as she carried a sheaf of white roses tied with a white satin ribbon. "I love you, Papà."

His eyes glazed over with love. "You know how I feel about my daughter."

She did. "I don't know what I'd do without you." People had thronged from everywhere to watch, but all she could think about was Guido, who stood inside the church waiting for her. She couldn't get to him fast enough.

"Juliana outdid herself when she designed your wedding dress. Her gift to you is almost as magnificent as you are, my darling girl."

The exquisite lace covering her arms and shoulders

hugged her white princess-style wedding dress. She wore a shoulder-length veil of the same lace and had left her hair long. Guido asked that she never cut it. Since he felt that strongly, she wanted to please him.

Organ music filled the vestibule where Alessandra and Rini were waiting for them dressed in their wedding finery. Her twin's smiling gaze fused with Dea's. They heard the chords of the wedding march at the same time. This wasn't like the pretend weddings they'd staged in their play castle when they were little. This was really going to happen.

Two friends of the Rossano family opened the doors and Dea began the long walk to the front of the church with her handsome father. Alessandra and Rini followed them down the aisle. The church overflowed with guests from both their families. With every step closer to Guido and the priest who would marry them, her heart thudded harder and harder.

Out of the corner of her eye she saw some friends from the college and the models she'd worked with over the years. With another step, she spotted Gina and Aldo and realized everyone from Juliana's shop, including her staff, had come.

Farther on, she saw Sergio and the other men and coaches who worked with Guido. Many of the players on his team had come to honor him. Still others from Rossano Shipping Lines had come en masse.

Closer to the altar she saw the Montanari family, including Valentina and Giovanni, Rini's sister- and brother-in-law. They sat on one side of the aisle. On the other sat her loving mother and aunt Fulvia, plus the staff from the castle. Juliana and her husband sat behind them. The older woman beamed. Dea owed her so much.

Suddenly her father walked her to Guido's side and lifted the roses to hand to her sister. Dea turned toward her fiancé, but she couldn't prevent the slight gasp of awe that escaped her lips.

With his tall superb physique and dark blond hair, he looked so splendid she almost fainted. A white rose decorated the lapel of his wedding suit, the same midnight blue color as his eyes. Guido wore his jacket buttoned over a matching vest with a stark white shirt and pastel gray-blue tie. He flashed her a haunting smile that took her breath away.

"Bellissima," he whispered in a husky tone and grasped her hand. *"Grazie a Dio"* you're no longer a figment of my imagination. If you had any idea how long I've been waiting for this moment..."

She *did*, actually, because she'd been in the same pain.

As the ceremony began, she feared the Rossanos' family priest performing the rites could hear her heart resounding throughout the nave. Very little registered until they'd repeated their vows to love and honor each other.

"I now pronounce you man and wife and ask that you remain faithful to each other. May God bless this union. In the name of the Father and the Son." He made the sign of the cross. "Amen."

Guido didn't wait for any prompting. He reached for her shoulders and lowered his mouth to hers, giving her what she would always remember...the divine kiss of life from her new husband. Unspeakable joy filled her heart.

For three days and nights they stayed in their suite at the villa on Ischia, the only area aside from the bathroom that had been furnished in time for their honeymoon.

This morning Guido had left her arms long enough to go down to the village for more food. So far they'd subsisted on love and little else.

Dea's hungry eyes played over his hard-muscled body as he put some sacks on the table. He was the most gorgeous man on earth, whether in shorts and a T-shirt like he was wearing, or nothing at all.

"I brought you something that will interest you."

"I thought by now you'd figured out that you are my only interest."

A smile of satisfaction lit up his handsome face. He drew a newspaper out of one of the bags and handed it to her. "Look on page two. No doubt my father had a great deal to do with the half-page article and picture in the *Corriere della Sera*."

She smiled up at him. "The paper with the largest circulation in Italy? Of course he did. He's the proud *papà*."

Dea propped herself against the pillows. The second she opened to the article, she let out a cry. There she was in her flowing white wedding gown and veil coming out of the church with Guido in a formal dark suit hugging her waist. The happiness on their faces brought tears to her eyes as she read the article.

On June 30, Signor and Signora Guido Ernesto Fortunati Rossano were married in the fourteenth-century church of San Giovanni a Carbonara in Naples. A reception followed at the Rossano villa. The island of Ischia will be home to the famous couple.

The bride, gorgeous former supermodel now turned opera-wardrobe designer Dea Caracciolo, is the twenty-eight-year-old daughter of Count Onorato Caracciolo and Princess Taranto of Southern Italy.

The groom, thirty-two-year-old Guido, the son of prominent shipping magnate Leonides Rossano and Isabella Fortunati, and the grandson of Ernesto Rossano, is the former national soccer champion of Italy known as the *Cuor di Leone*. At present he is the new owner of the fast-rising soccer team Scatto Roma. The team is tied for first place with Team Venezia, and the two will compete in a play-off for the national championship July 3 at the Emanuele Soccer Stadium in Rome.

Dea put down the newspaper. "I think the reporter got it all in and then some."

"Do you mind? You know Papà."

"Darling, I love him. He's your father and I love

his son so terribly that if you don't get in bed and love me this instant, I won't survive another minute."

"Well, we can't have that." He removed his clothes with startling speed and slid beneath the quilt to roll her on her back. "Dea," he whispered, looking down at her. "I keep thinking we're in a dream and I'm going to wake up. We aren't dreaming, are we?"

"I don't think so, and I'm afraid you're stuck with a wanton for good."

"If every man were stuck with a passionate woman like you, we'd all be in permanent heaven."

"Honestly? H-has it been good for you?" Her voice faltered.

He shook his dark blond head. "Can't you tell what you do to me? For three days I haven't let you leave my arms. You're so beautiful, I'm constantly out of breath. If you could see the way you look with your hair spread out on the pillow, and the way your eyes darken with emotion, maybe you'd understand. But you're not a man."

"Thank heaven for that. You make me thankful I'm a woman." Her eyes filled with tears. "I wish we'd met ten years ago. When I think of the time we've wasted."

"I try not to think about it. What matters is now. You've made me happier than I could ever have imagined. Love me again, *squisita*." He lowered his mouth to hers and began to make love to her with a new ferocity. For the next few hours Dea was shaken by a passion she'd never known.

Her amazing husband had been so wise to insist

they wait until they were married to become intimate lovers. To experience the wonder of lovemaking like this without knowing you belonged to each other first would take away this ultimate joy.

They finally fell asleep again. Later he wakened her with a hungry kiss. "How would you like to sleep on the boat tonight? I thought it was time we christened that bedroom too."

She chuckled. "I agree. Why don't we eat and then go sailing?"

"Are you saying that for my sake?"

Dea gave him an impish grin. "Yes! Because I can tell you're suddenly restless. The game on Sunday is on your mind. I'm thinking about it too. Tomorrow we'll be flying back to Rome. Before we leave, I want to spend our last night on the *Bona Dea*. She *is* the goddess of fertility."

His blue eyes flickered with emotion. "Would you really like to start a family right away?"

"Yes, if we can. But if you don't feel that way…"

He kissed her deeply. "I want it all with you as fast as possible."

"I'm so glad you said that. We're not getting any younger. It would be so nice if we had a baby soon who would become friends with Brazzo. They're planning on adopting another baby one of these days."

"I know. Rini told me."

"When did he tell you that?"

"Yesterday evening while you were in the shower, he left me a message that they were negotiating for another baby. According to Alessandra, it will be the closest thing to having twins. He said he hoped I was doing my own form of negotiation in order to get the job done too. He ended with, 'Hurry.'"

She sat straight up. "He didn't!"

"Oh, yes, he did. Do you want to see my phone?"

"No. You two are incorrigible. Alessandra would have a cow if she knew he'd written that to you."

"A cow?"

"It's an American expression Gina picked up from Aldo's New York friend and she passed it on to me."

He grabbed her hand and pressed it against his heart. "I swear I'll keep it a secret from my new sister-in-law." In the next breath he threw off the quilt. She screamed, provoking his laughter.

"Come on, Aphrodite. Even your lover, who can never get enough of you, has to renew his energy, and I'm starving!"

October 10, Posso Island, Southern Italy

The sun had just fallen into the water. "There they are!" Dea had glimpsed the Jeep behind the castle as the helicopter dipped closer. "This is so exciting to be having a reunion here at last!"

Once they landed, Guido hugged her hips before helping her down. Every time he touched her, her legs turned to jelly. She hurried toward the Jeep and saw that her sister had brought Brazzo with them. He was seated on her lap playing with his purple octopus, tugging on one of the belled tentacles.

Their dark-haired fourteen-month-old toddler was

so adorable Dea could hardly stand it. With coloring like that and olive skin, you'd never know he wasn't their birth son.

"Oh, you cute little thing." She kissed his cheeks and then her sister's cheek before climbing in the back.

"What? No kiss for me?" Rini teased.

"How about a hug instead?" She wrapped her arm around his neck from behind. Guido followed her into the backseat with their luggage.

"It's about time you lovebirds left the nest." This from Rini. Dea saw the secret look the two men flashed each other.

"We've been busy decorating the house," Guido explained.

"Sure you have. Excuses, excuses." Rini kept up the banter.

Alessandra laughed. "I hope you're hungry. Dinner is waiting."

Dea reached forward to tousle Brazzo's curls. "I'm starving. Someone should have warned me that getting married makes you hungry. Are Mamma and Papà here?"

"They will be later." Alessandra looked over her shoulder at Guido. "How does the team look to you for this new season?"

"It's good. They've recovered from the loss in July and are working harder than ever. Dante's back with us and suiting up. Another month and the doctor will clear him to play."

"That's wonderful news."

Rini drove them around to the entrance of the castle. Dea got out behind Alessandra and trailed her into the foyer, where Alfredo was waiting. "Oh, my buddy." She scooped him up. "Have you missed me?"

But at this point Brazzo was toddling around and the cat squirmed to get down. "Well, I just got my question answered. This fickle cat has a new playmate. Look at you walking, Brazzo!"

The men had just come inside with the bags. They all watched in amusement as the precious boy chased after the housekeeper's pet.

"Come on, you two." Rini started for the stairs. "We've put you in the same bedroom Guido has used when he's stayed here."

"Brazzo and I will be in the dining room, won't we, sweetheart. Hurry back down."

Dea hugged her sister, then followed the men upstairs. Excitement rippled through her body to think she'd be sleeping with Guido in her old home.

Rini left them alone while they freshened up. Guido grabbed her from behind while she was looking out the window. "You have no idea how I longed to drag you up here after our soccer match on the sand. The dreams I had about you would make your face turn crimson."

She wheeled around and threw her arms around his neck. "I had my own dreams that night. The thought of sneaking into your bedroom in the middle of the night never left my mind. I guess I don't have to wonder what you would have done. You would have been

the total gentleman and escorted me back to the hallway."

"Don't be so sure. I was on fire for you that night."

"So on fire you didn't even say goodbye to me."

"You know why, my love. Come on. We'll have
all night to finish this conversation. In the meantime,
our hosts are waiting."

They clasped hands and went downstairs to the
dining room. Brazzo was sitting in his high chair at
the corner of the table between Rini and Alessandra.
He banged the tray with a spoon.

Dea chuckled and sat across from them with Guido.
"Umm. I can see the cook has outdone herself with
my favorite salmon and eggplant."

"She knew you were coming and remembered."

"I'll go out to the kitchen later and thank her."

"Now that we're all here, Rini and I have an an-
nouncement." Dea eyed Guido while they waited for
Alessandra's news. "We had to be certain to make
sure everything was going right, but we have just
been told to expect our next baby in a month!"

"I knew it!" Dea squealed in delight.

"It's a girl this time." Rini's smile lit up his dark
eyes.

"There couldn't be better news, *paisano*," Guido
said.

"I agree, but do you think you can stand a little
more?" Dea reached in the pocket of her pleated pants
for a picture. "We've got a little news of our own."

The shocked look on Guido's face was worth all

the trouble she'd taken to keep her secret to herself. "Dea?" he whispered huskily.

"It's Rini's fault."

Everyone looked shocked at her comment, especially her brother-in-law. "You did send my husband a text four months ago. I'll quote it for everyone.

"'We're negotiating for another baby. According to Alessandra, it will be the closest thing to having twins. I hope you're doing your own form of negotiation in order to get the job done too.' Your postscript said, 'Hurry.'"

While quiet reigned, she handed Guido the picture. "Take a look and see what you did, darling."

Her husband looked down at the sonogram like he was in a trance.

"If you'll notice, there are two babies in there."

"Dea!" Alessandra's cry of joy reverberated in the dining room and probably the whole castle. She shot out of her chair and hurried around to look at it over Guido's shoulder.

"There *are* two."

"One is a girl. The doctor couldn't tell the gender of the other one yet. I'm four months along."

"Then our daughters will be less than six months apart. That's so perfect! We'll get out the play castle when they're old enough."

"It'll be déjà vu."

"Wait till our parents hear about this—"

Guido was still processing the information in a daze. He turned to Dea. "I thought you'd been putting on weight recently, but I didn't want to say anything."

"I knew you had to have noticed." She leaned over and kissed him on the mouth. "Sorry if I worried you about that."

"I wasn't worried, Dea."

"Liar. I love you more than ever for not giving me grief about it."

He got to his feet. "Are you all right?" When he put his hands on her upper arms, he was trembling. "Is everything going the way it should?"

"The doctor has given me a clean bill of health."

Alessandra ran the picture around to show Rini. While everyone was occupied, their parents walked in. "What's going on?" their father wanted to know.

Dea smiled at him. "We all have news, Papà. You go first, Alessandra."

Once her sister told them that they would be getting a girl within the month, she ran back around to give Dea the picture. "Now it's your turn."

The moment was surreal as she handed her mother the sonogram. She watched her parents study it.

Suddenly her mother pressed a hand over her heart. "Twins… You're going to have twins."

Her dad smiled broadly. "Well, what do you know. Fulvia said twins ran in the Taranto side of the family. Thanks to the Montanari side of the family, we're going to have a set of twins before another set comes along."

Dea loved her father intensely for making Rini feel included in a very real way.

"Let's break out the champagne, but you won't be able to drink it, Dea. No alcohol until after the babies are born," her father informed her. "Your mother and I know every rule."

Dea lifted shining eyes to Alessandra. "But you, my dear sister, can have all you want."

Rini hugged her. "I'm afraid it's wasted on my wife."

"Dea?" Guido whispered in her ear. "I need to be alone with you. Can we go upstairs soon?"

She nodded and kissed his jaw. He'd just found out he was going to be the father of twins. That had to be staggering news for any man. Perhaps even as staggering as it had been for the woman who carried them.

Her mother seemed to understand what was going on. "Dea, honey, you look tired. I think you should go up to bed. We'll celebrate in the morning."

Bless you, Mamma.

"Bed does sound good. It's been a long day."

Now that the evening had come to an end, everyone said good-night. Guido put his arm around her waist as they climbed the stairs to the bedroom on the third floor. "Oh, I forgot the picture."

"We'll get it in the morning. Right now I want to take care of you."

She hadn't realized that having to keep her news a secret from Guido had drained her. Suddenly she felt relaxed and couldn't wait to drift off with his arms around her.

As soon as she brushed her teeth and undressed,

she fell into bed. "I know you want your parents to know. Why don't you give them a call? Then I'll answer every question. I'm sorry I didn't tell you before now, but when the doctor detected two heartbeats, I wanted to wait until he could take a picture and make sure the babies were healthy. I couldn't see worrying you until I had to."

"I'm not upset with you, Dea. If anything, I'm glad I didn't know before now. We've had to deal with the villa and work, your graduation. But now that I know, I'm going to make certain you take perfect care of yourself. We have two precious babies growing inside you. It's a thrill I still haven't fully comprehended yet."

"That's the way I felt when the doctor first told me. Go on and phone your parents. They'll be ecstatic."

He put the covers over her and sat on the edge of the bed to call his family. The joy in their voices rang out through the phone. Dea reached for it. "We don't know if there's a boy or another girl in there. Maybe by the next appointment the doctor will be able to tell us."

"You're going to need help," his mother said through the tears.

"We'll need a lot of it," Dea assured her and meant it. "I'm so thankful we already have your room ready at the villa. Here's Guido back."

She waited while he finished talking to his parents. By the time he'd hung up and gotten into bed, she was half gone.

"You know that song…he had the whole world in his arms… Those words were written for me."

Dea turned into him, loving his hard, solid strength. "It works both ways. She had the whole world in her arms… You're my whole world, Guido Rossano.

"My whole glorious world. *Ti amo.*"

* * * * *

The smile grew, even if it didn't quite catch in his eyes.

"Your father was crazy, I hope you know."

This was said so gently, and with so much love, Deanna's eyes burned. But before she could recover, Josh said, "I know why he sent you away, Dee. Or at least, I can guess. And no, he never talked about you all that much afterward. But when he did…" Looking away, he shook his head. "It was obvious how much he loved you." His gaze met hers again. "How much he loved you. *Missed* you—"

"You mind if we don't talk about this right now? About Dad?"

His cheeks pinking slightly, Josh straightened, turning to look out over the pasture. "Sorry. I'm not real good at this."

"At what?"

"Social graces. Knowing when to keep my trap shut. I hear this stuff in my head—" he waved in the general direction of his hat "—and it just falls out of my mouth."

"I remember," Deanna said quietly, then smiled, not looking at him. "I think that's why we were friends."

"Because I have no filter whatsoever?"

"Yes, actually." She let their eyes meet, and her heart thudded against her sternum even harder than the baby kicking her belly button from the inside.

* * *

Wed in the West:
New Mexico's the perfect place
to finally find true love!

THE RANCHER'S EXPECTANT CHRISTMAS

BY
KAREN TEMPLETON

First Published in Great Britain 2016
By Mills & Boon, an imprint of HarperCollins*Publishers*
1 London Bridge Street, London, SE1 9GF

© 2016 Karen Templeton-Berger

ISBN: 978-0-263-92033-8

23-1116

Our policy is to use papers that are natural, renewable and recyclable products and made from wood grown in sustainable forests. The logging and manufacturing processes conform to the legal environmental regulations of the country of origin.

Printed and bound in Spain
by CPI, Barcelona

Karen Templeton is an inductee into the Romance Writers of America Hall of Fame. A three-time RITA® Award–winning author, she has written more than thirty novels for Mills & Boon. She lives in New Mexico with two hideously spoiled cats. She has raised five sons and lived to tell the tale, and she could not live without dark chocolate, mascara and Netflix.

Once again, I have to give a shout-out to
Kari Lynn Dell
For her patience,
Friendship,
And willingness to answer probably some of the
dumbest horse-related questions she's ever heard.
I hope your eyes don't hurt TOO much
from rolling so hard.

To Carly Silver
Editorial Assistant Extraordinaire
It's with very mixed feelings that I congratulate you
On your promotion.
Because you, my dear, have been a true godsend
To this beleaguered author.
So. Much. Love.

Chapter One

The baby walloped her full bladder, jerking Deanna Blake out of a mercifully sound sleep and scattering wisps of agitated dreams into the predawn gloom. Her heart hammering, she scooched farther underneath the soft Pendleton blanket, cradling her belly…

"A-*choo*!"

Gasping, Deanna heaved herself around just as the small child fled the room, awkwardly yanking shut the bedroom door behind him.

For what felt like the first time in weeks, she smiled, then clumsily shoved herself upright. Spearing a hand through her short, undoubtedly startled-looking hair, she frowned at her old room, coming more into focus as the weak November sun gradually elbowed aside the remnants of a dark country night. She'd been so wiped out from her cross-country flight, as well as the three-hour drive up from Albuquerque after, she hadn't even turned on the light before crawling into bed. Now, taking in the old *Gilmore Girls* poster, its curled edges grasping at the troweled plaster walls, she wasn't sure which was weirder—how long it'd been since she'd last slept here, or that the room was exactly as she'd left it more than ten years ago. Then again, why would Dad have changed it—?

Deanna squeezed shut her eyes as a double whammy of grief and guilt slammed into her, even stronger than the next kick that finally forced her out of bed and into the adjoining bathroom where she studiously avoided glancing at the mirror over the chipped marble sink. Between the pregnancy puffies and an unending series of sleepless nights, in the past few weeks her complexion had gone from fair to vampiresque. Meaning it was simply best not to look.

Teeth brushed and comb dragged through hair, she wrestled into a pair of very stretchy leggings and a tent-sized sweater before, on a deep breath, opening her door. A child's laughter, the comforting scent of coffee she couldn't drink, tumbled inside.

As if everything were perfectly normal.

Through a fog of sadness and apprehension, Deanna crept down the Saltillo-tiled hallway toward the kitchen, hoping against hope that Gus, her father's old housekeeper, was just looking after the little boy while his daddy tended to some ranch duty or other. Just as Gus had watched Deanna from time to time, as well as Sam Talbot's boys whenever the need arose. In some ways it'd been like having four older brothers, both a blessing and a curse for an only child living out in the New Mexico boonies.

She hesitated, gazing through a French door leading into the courtyard centering the traditional hacienda-style house. A light snow sugared the uneven flagstone, sparkling in the early morning sun. Save for the spurts of laughter, the house was as eerily quiet as she remembered. Especially after the constant thrum of traffic, of life, in DC. A pang of something she couldn't quite identify shuddered through her. Not homesickness, she didn't think. She palmed her belly, where the baby stirred.

Uncertainty? Maybe.

No, definitely.

The cavernous kitchen was empty, save for a huge gray cat sitting on a windowsill, calmly ascertaining Deanna's worthiness to share its breathing space. The room hadn't been vacant long, though, judging from the softly crackling fire in the potbellied stove at the far end of the enormous eat-in area, anchored by a rustic wood table that easily sat twelve. Even though the Vista Encantada's century-old main house had long since been converted to natural gas, Gus had always lit the old stove, every morning from early October through mid-May. The dark cabinets and hand-painted Mexican tiles were the same, as well, even though the vintage six-burner range's lapis finish seemed a little more pitted than she remembered. And for a moment she was a kid again, scarfing down one of Gus's breakfast burritos before catching the school bus in the dark—

"Dee?"

She turned, immediately trapped in a pair of moss-colored eyes that had at one time been very dear to her. Dear enough to prompt her father to send her clear across the country when she was fifteen, to live with her mother's sister. And oh, how she'd initially chafed at Dad's assumption that something was going on between her and Josh Talbot that wasn't. And wouldn't. Because Josh had never been like that, even if Deanna hadn't fully understood at the time what "that" might have been.

Somehow, she doubted he'd appreciate the irony of her current situation.

"Hey," she said, crossing her arms as Josh dumped an armful of firewood into the bucket beside the stove, his mini-me peeking at her from behind his legs. It'd been over a decade since she'd caught more than a glimpse of him on her occasional visits home. And the tall, solid cowboy whose sharp gaze now latched on to her belly, then her hair, was nothing like the skinny, spindly teenager she used to sneak off to see, prompting her father's conclusion-jumping. Although the shy, lonely girl *she'd* been, still reeling after her mother's death, had only been seeking solace. A refuge. Neither of which, looking back, Josh had been under any obligation to give her—

"I didn't expect..." Deanna shoved out a breath. "Where's Gus?"

"Went into town with my mother for groceries. For... tomorrow."

"Oh. Right."

"I'm sorry," he said quietly, but with a decided, *And where the hell have you been*? edge to it.

So much for thinking her heart couldn't be more shredded than it already was. Irony, again, to find herself facing exactly what she'd avoided by *not* coming home, that look of disappointment. Confusion. Not from her father, no, but still.

"Same goes," she said into the awkward silence. Because she could hardly explain things with a child in the room, could she?

His mouth set, Josh nodded, and pain knifed through her. Josh'd been the only one of the former manager's sons to show any real interest in ranching. Or, later, the horse-breeding operation. Even so, when medical issues forced Sam's early retirement a few years back, her father's asking Josh to take his dad's place had surprised her. At least until she realized how close Josh and her father had become, despite that business when she and Josh had been teenagers. That Dad clearly thought of her childhood friend like a favorite nephew. If not the son he never had.

A feeling she'd gleaned had been mutual.

Blinking away tears, Deanna cleared her throat and

smiled for the little boy, who kept peering at her from behind his daddy. Her father had told her about the child, that his mama wasn't in the picture. Her hand went to her belly again, as if to reassure the little one inside.

"Hey, guy," she said softly. "I'm Deanna. Mr. Blake's daughter. Although you can call me Dee if you want. What's your name?"

The child ducked back behind Josh and muttered something unintelligible. Sighing, Josh twisted to haul the boy into his arms. "How about trying that again? Only so she can actually hear you this time."

"Austin," the kid got out, giving her a sweet, heart-squeezing smile. Dark hair, like his daddy. Same eyes, too.

"Pleased to meet you, Austin—"

"How come your tummy's so big?" he said, pointing to her belly, and Josh's face blazed.

"Oh, jeez…"

Deanna laughed, even as she thought, *At least one person in the room is being honest.* "It's okay, I'm used to it." Returning her gaze to Austin, she bent over as much as she could and whispered, "There's a baby growing inside me."

The kid frowned. "Like the horses?"

"Exactly. Except this baby doesn't have hooves."

"Oh. Is it a boy or a girl?"

"A girl."

Austin frowned at her belly again. "What's her name?"

"Haven't decided yet."

The kid gave her a maybe-you-should-get-on-that look that made Deanna's chest tickle as she bit down on a smile. Then, heaving a breathy "Okay," he wriggled out of his father's arms and took off to mess with the cat, who'd thudded to the tiled floor then flopped in the morning's first sunbeam, belly bared to the world. Or in this case, little boys. Brave cat.

"Sorry about the interrogation," Josh said, and Deanna turned to see his mouth pushed into something reasonably close to a smile.

"Hey. At least he didn't ask how the baby got in there."

"Give him a minute," Josh muttered, and for a second she saw the boy who'd kept her from losing it, all those years ago.

The boy she might have loved, if she'd been inclined to such foolishness.

"Austin's adorable. He looks like you."

"So everyone says." He frowned. "Your…the baby's father let you come alone?"

"We're…not together."

There was no denying the judgment in his stony expression. And not only about her pregnancy, she guessed. The baby kicked; stifling a wince, Deanna glanced over at Austin before meeting that penetrating gaze again. "I had no idea Dad was even sick. I swear. Because he'd made *Gus* swear not to tell me. Because if I'd known, nothing would've kept me from being here. And the worst thing is…" Her eyes stung. Tough. "I can't even tell Dad how angry I am. How…hurt."

The staring continued for several seconds before Josh said, "I know he didn't tell you. But if you'd bothered to pay a visit in the last six months—"

"And why would I do that when Dad made it more than clear he didn't particularly want me to?"

And why was she was even trying to explain something she didn't entirely understand herself?

A long, tense moment passed before Josh said, "For what it's worth, it happened pretty fast."

"So Gus said." Deanna glanced over at Austin, now lying beside the cat and apparently telling it a story, before facing Josh again. "Although I gather the only reason he did was because he figured I'd see the death certificate, discover the truth whether Dad wanted me to or not."

Another breath left Josh's lungs. "I suppose he didn't want you to worry—"

"What he did," Deanna said, not even trying to hide the bitterness in her voice, "was unfair and selfish. Kind of a major thing to keep from me."

Josh's eyes once more dropped to her swollen middle, and Deanna's face warmed. Especially when he looked back up.

"Just like I'm guessing Granville had no idea about his granddaughter."

"I didn't intend to keep her a secret forever, for cripe's sake! But I did know…" Her lips pressed tightly together. "That the circumstances surrounding my condition wouldn't exactly make Dad happy. At least not…not before he had a chance to meet her. I had a plan," she said over the stab to her heart. "Unfortunately it didn't jibe with the Universe's."

That got a hard stare before Josh walked away to open the fridge.

"What would you like for breakfast?"

Deanna frowned, confused. "You don't have to—"

"When was the last time you ate?"

"Um…lunch yesterday? But cereal's fine, don't go to any trouble—"

"Not planning on it. But Gus left pancake batter, and even I can scramble eggs. The squirt already ate, an hour ago."

"Eggs, then. If you're sure—"

He shot her another look that shut her up…a look that said they only had to get through the next few days. Then everyone could get back to their regular lives.

Or whatever.

Another wave of grief shunted through her, as she

thought about the ramifications of her father's passing, not only for her but for the entire community. Weird, how she'd never thought much about what would happen to the ranch after his death, mainly because that'd always seemed so far in the future. Even though he'd been significantly older than her mother, somehow Deanna had always thought of Dad as immortal, like some Greek god. Especially since he'd never discussed the disposition of the property with her—

A sudden burst of voices from the mudroom shattered her thoughts. "Gramma!" Austin yelled as he abandoned the probably very relieved cat and sprinted across the room, where the woman who'd so often filled the gap in Deanna's life, and heart, after her mother died dumped several recyclable grocery totes on the counter, then swept her grandson into her arms. Gus, the belly cantilevered over his giant belt buckle nearly as big as Deanna's, followed a moment later, hauling several more bags which landed unceremoniously on the floor. Her long ponytail a mass of delicate, staticky silver wires against her back, Billie Talbot turned, her expression softening when she spotted Deanna.

"Oh, sweetheart..." she crooned, and fresh tears sprang to Deanna's eyes. A moment later she was wrapped in the older woman's arms. "I'm so sorry...so, *so* sorry..."

Unable to speak, Deanna nodded against Billie's shoulder, the coarse fabric of the older woman's poncho scratching her cheek. "Such a good man, your daddy," Billie whispered into her hair. "Whole town's gonna miss him like crazy...and oh, my goodness!" Holding Deanna apart, Billie grinned. "Seven months?"

"More or less."

"And they let you fly?"

Scrubbing a tear off her cheek, Deanna smiled, remembering that Josh's mother was a midwife. "Believe me, the flight attendants all breathed a huge sigh of relief when we landed," she said, and Billie chuckled.

"I'll bet they did." Then she sighed. "It's so good to see you, honey. I just wish it weren't under these circumstances."

"Me, too."

Another gentle smile curving her lips, Josh's mom tucked her hands underneath the poncho, seeming to see the rest of her for the first time. "Your hair…adorable. The darker color suits you."

Deanna flushed. "Thanks."

"And on you, the nose stud totally works." A low laugh rumbled from her chest. "Although I can only imagine your daddy's reaction. But listen, you need anything while you're here, anything at all, you let me know. I mean it."

"I know you do. And I'm grateful."

A wordless nod preceded another hug before Billie turned to Josh. "Why don't you let me take Austin back to the house for a while? Y'all don't need a four-year-old underfoot right now."

Josh seemed to hesitate for a moment, then smiled for his son. "Wanna go with Gramma?"

"Yeah!" the kid yelled, wriggling like somebody'd put bugs down his pants, and Deanna smiled, too, over the sadness cramping her heart. For the most part, and despite the events of the past little while, she loved her life back east, a life filled with art and dance and music with more instruments than a couple of guitars and a dude on drums. And no matter what, she had her father to thank for that, for giving her opportunities she would've never had if she'd stayed here. Even so, as she watched Josh softly talking to his mother and little boy, as the love and good-will she'd always associate with this kitchen, this house, this godforsaken little town, washed over her, she had to admit it didn't exactly feel terrible to be back.

For a little while, anyway.

Although there was no real reason to walk Mom and Austin out to her car, seeing Deanna again—especially an extremely pregnant Deanna with pointy black hair and a diamond in her nose, for godsake—had rattled Josh far more than he wanted to admit. He could only imagine what was going through his mother's head.

"I think we've got everything for tomorrow," Mom said after buckling Austin into one of the three car seats that were permanent fixtures in the back of her SUV. At the rate they were adding kids to the family, though, one of those wonker vans was looking good for the near future. Straightening, Mom swung her gaze to Josh's. "Although Gus said there's already a dozen casseroles and such in the freezer?"

"Wouldn't know."

A chilly breeze tangled his mother's ponytail, pulled off her high-cheekboned face. "What *do* you know?" she asked, and Josh smiled drily.

"Meaning about Deanna?"

"Yep."

"Not a whole lot. Since she's only been back for five minutes. Also, it's none of my business. Or anyone's."

"True. Although I did notice there's no wedding ring."

He paused. "She said she and the father aren't together. And again...none of our business."

"Hmm." Mom squinted out toward the Sangre de Cristo mountains, their snowy tops aglow in the early morning sun, a harbinger of the winter breathing down their necks. Then she looked back at him, a little smile tilting her lips. "I know how much it annoyed you boys, the way your father and I were always up in your business." The smile turned into a grimace. "Especially for Levi and Colin." Both of whom had flown as far from the family nest as they could, even though Josh's twin, Levi, had returned several months ago. "Still," Mom said, "seeing the obvious pain in that little girl's eyes, that she never got to say goodbye to her father…maybe *your* father and I didn't do such a bad job, after all."

"Like I'm gonna give you that much ammunition," Josh said, and she swatted his shoulder.

Then she frowned. "I'm guessing Granville didn't know about the baby?"

"It would appear not."

Looking away, Mom slowly wagged her head. "I don't get it, I really don't. What would make one of the most generous human beings on the face of the planet disconnect from his only child?"

Crossing his arms, Josh sneaked a peek at his son, happily banging two little cars together. A question he'd asked himself many times, though even as a child Dee's discontent with small-town living had been obvious. As though Whispering Pines wasn't big enough to contain all that Deanna Blake was, or wanted to be…a malaise that only increased as she got older, if her periodic bitching to him had been any indication.

And certainly Josh would've never been enough for her, a truth he'd thankfully realized before he'd said or done anything he would've most certainly regretted. So her excitedly telling him on her fifteenth birthday she was moving to DC hadn't come as all that much of a surprise, even if he hadn't let on how much it'd killed him. Especially since he'd known in his gut she'd never come back. Not to live, anyway.

Even so, her father's basically giving her up…it made

no sense. Then again Austin's mother hadn't seemed to have an issue with leaving her son behind, had she? So maybe this was simply one of those "there's no accounting for people" things.

Josh realized his mother was giving him her *What are you thinking, boy?* look. A smile flicked over his mouth. "I guess we'll never find out. About her father, I mean."

"Guess not." Mom glanced back at the beautiful old house, which, along with the vast acreage surrounding it, the barns and pastures and guesthouses scattered along the river farther out, had been in the Blake family since before New Mexico was a state. "I suppose this will all go to her."

Josh'd be lying if he said her words didn't slice through him. Yeah, by rights the Vista was Dee's now, she could do whatever she wanted with it. But Josh had never lived anywhere else. Or wanted to. So *by rights* the place was *his* home far more than it had ever really been Dee's.

"I suppose we'll find out tomorrow," he said, trying to sound neutral. "After the memorial, the lawyer said."

"Granville's request?"

"Apparently so." Just as his boss had been adamant he didn't want a funeral, or a burial, or "any of that crap." So he was probably looking down from wherever he was, pissed as all get-out about the memorial service. No way, though, was the town gonna let his passing go without *any* acknowledgment. As much as the old man had done for everybody, it'd be downright disrespectful to pretend as though nothing had happened. Meaning for once Granville Blake wasn't getting his way.

"Well," Mom said, opening her car door, "I'd best be getting back. I've got a couple of mothers to check up on later, but no babies due in the next little while, thank goodness. I told Gus I'd be there early tomorrow to get started on the food for the reception. I'll bring Austin back then."

"You don't have to keep him—"

"I know I don't. But something tells me Deanna's gonna need a friend over the next couple of days." She paused. Squinting. "And I don't mean Gus."

Josh sighed. "That was a long time ago, Mom."

"So? It won't kill you to be nice to the girl."

Thinking, *I wouldn't be so sure about that*, Josh stood in the graveled driveway, waving to Austin as his mother backed out, taking his buffer between him and Dee with her. But when he got back inside, where she was sitting at the table inhaling the breakfast that Gus had whipped up for her in the nanosecond Josh had been gone, it wasn't his mother's pushy words ringing in his ears, but Granville's.

Because two days before he'd died, his boss—the boss who'd guarded his privacy so fiercely he'd refused to discuss his illness—happened to mention his suspicion that Dee was in some kind of trouble but wouldn't tell him what. Mutterings Josh had chalked up to the illness, frankly. Or, more likely, Granville's own guilt and regret that he'd kept his daughter in the dark about his condition. Talk about apples not rolling far from the tree.

Except obviously the old man's intuition had been dead to rights, resurrecting all manner of protective feelings Josh had no wish to resurrect. Especially when she lifted those huge, deep brown eyes to his, and he was sixteen again, sharing one of those soul-baring conversations they used to have when they'd tell each other their dreams and hopes and fears, knowing there'd be no teasing, no judgment…

"If anybody needs me," he said to the room at large, "I'll be out working that new cutter I bought."

Then he got his butt out of there before those wayward thoughts derailed what little common sense he had left.

Chapter Two

Apparently, pregnancy made her nostalgic. At least, that's what Deanna was going with as she waddled outside after breakfast, bundled up against a morning chill laced with the scents of her childhood—fireplace smoke and horse-flesh, the sweet breath of piñon overlaying the slightly musty tang of hoof-churned earth. It was always a shock, how clear the air was at this altitude, how the cloudless sky seemed to caress you, make you feel almost weightless. Even when you were hauling around thirty extra pounds that could never quite decide how to distribute itself.

A dog she didn't recognize trotted toward her, something with a lot of Aussie shepherd in him. "And aren't you a handsome boy?" she said softly, and the pooch dissolved into a wriggling mass of speckled love, dancing over to give her hand a cursory lick before trotting off again—*Sorry, can't dawdle, work to do, beasts to herd.*

Other than the dog, little had changed that she could tell. The old, original barn still stood in all its dignified, if slightly battered, glory not far from the house, even though it'd been decades since any actual livestock had been sheltered there. She smiled, remembering the July Fourth barn dances her father had sponsored every year for the entire

community, the cookout and potluck that had always preceded them. The fireworks, down by the pond. How much
she'd loved all the hoopla as a child, even if she'd grown to
dread it after her mother died of a particularly aggressive
brain tumor when she was fourteen, when she'd never felt
up to being the gracious hostess Mom had been. A role far
more suited to someone…else.

Although most of the fencing around the property had
been long since converted to wire, the pasture nearest the
house was still bordered in good old-fashioned white post
and rail…another bane of her existence when she was a
kid and Dad had insisted she help repaint it whenever the
need arose. Which had seemed like every five minutes at
the time. She let her cold fingers skim the top rail, smiling when a nearby pregnant mare softly nickered, then
separated herself from a half-dozen or so compadres and
plodded over, almost as though she recognized Deanna.
And damned if the jagged white blaze on her mahogany
face wasn't startlingly familiar.

"You're Starlight's, aren't you?" she said gently, and
the horse came close enough for her to sweep her fingers
across her sleek muzzle, for the mare to "kiss" her hair.
Same sweet nature as her mama, too, Deanna thought,
chuckling for a moment before releasing another sigh.

It hadn't been all bad, living out here. Boring, yes. Stifling, definitely. But as quickly as she'd acclimated to—
and embraced—living back east, there'd been more than
the occasional bout of feeling displaced, too. Even if she'd
never admitted it. She'd missed riding, and the sky, and
the deep, precious silence of a snowy night. Greasy nachos
at the rodeo every fall. The way the mountains seemed to
watch over the plains and everything that lived on them.
The way everyone kept an eye out for everyone else.

Josh.

She spotted him, working a sleek chestnut gelding in the distance, as homesickness spiked through her, so sharp she lost her breath.

Homesickness, and regret. Choking, humiliating, taunting regret.

Shivering, Deanna wrapped up more tightly in the giant shawl she'd scored for ten bucks at that thrift store near her apartment—

Crap. She had no idea where she belonged anymore, although *here* certainly wasn't it. *Here* was her past, which she'd long since outgrown. But her life *there*, in DC, had collapsed like a house of cards, hadn't it? All she knew was that she'd better figure something out, and soon, before this little person made her appearance. Kinda hard to bring a baby home if you weren't sure where home was.

Still caressing the mare's sun-warmed coat, Deanna looked out toward the other horses grazing the frosted grass, their coats gleaming in the strengthening morning sun as bursts of filmy white puffed from their nostrils. Then she started as she realized Josh was headed her way. His own breath clouding his face, he came up beside her, digging into his pocket for a piece of carrot for the mare.

"I see you two have already met."

Deanna drew back her hand, wrapping up more tightly in the shawl. "She's Starlight's, isn't she?"

"Yep."

"What's her name?"

"Star*fire*. One of the best cutters I've ever ridden. Her babies should fetch a pretty penny. This one's already spoken for, in fact."

"When's she due?"

"Late January or thereabouts."

After a moment, Deanna said, "So she actually gets to carry her foal to term?" and Josh softly chuckled. She knew many "serious" breeders only used their prize mares to jumpstart an embryo, then transplanted them into surrogates. She supposed in some ways it was less stressful on the mare that way, but it'd always seemed to her so... callous. Like the horses were only things to be used.

"Not to worry. Your daddy would've killed me, for one thing. Not to mention *my* daddy. No, we do things the old-fashioned way around here," he said, stroking the mare's shiny neck. "Don't we, sweetheart?"

The horse nodded, the movement knocking off Josh's hat.

"Hey!" The horse actually snickered, making Josh shake his head before scooping the hat off the ground.

Deanna smiled as Josh smacked the old Stetson against his thighs to knock off the dust, then rammed it back on his head. "She looks so much like her mama it's uncanny."

"You seen her yet?"

"Ohmigosh—she's still here?"

Something like aggravation shunted across Josh's features. "Until the day she crosses over. Why would you think she wouldn't be?"

"Because I'd told Dad to sell her, since I wouldn't be riding her anymore. At least, not enough to warrant keeping her. But he kept her anyway?"

Leaning back against the fence, Josh folded his arms over his chest, releasing another little puff of dust from his well-worn barn coat. "He came to talk to her every day. Sometimes twice a day, until...well." A small smile curved his lips. "To tell her all about what you were doing. I even caught him showing the horse your picture on his phone once."

"Get out."

"Of course, then he got all embarrassed when he realized I'd seen him." The smile grew, even if it didn't quite catch in his eyes. "Your father was crazy, I hope you know."

This said so gently, and with so much love, Deanna's eyes burned. But before she could recover, Josh said, "I know why he sent you away, Dee. Or at least, I can guess. And no, he never talked about you all that much afterward. But when he did…" Looking away, he shook his head. "It was obvious how much he loved you." His gaze met hers again. "How much *missed* you—"

"You mind if we don't talk about this right now? About Dad?"

His cheeks pinking slightly, Josh straightened, turning to look out over the pasture. "Sorry. I'm not real good at this."

"At what?"

"Social graces. Knowing when to keep my trap shut. I hear this stuff in my head—" he waved in the general direction of his hat "—and it just falls out of my mouth."

"I remember," Deanna said quietly, then smiled, not looking at him. "I think that's why we were friends."

"Because I have no filter whatsoever?"

"Yes, actually." She let their eyes meet, and her heart thudded against her sternum even harder than the baby kicking her belly button from the inside. "Because I knew you'd always be straight with me. Because…because you never treated me like the boss's daughter."

Confusion flitted across his face for a moment until he punched out a laugh. "Oh, trust me, I always treated you like the boss's daughter."

Now it was Deanna's turn to flush. Partly because she got his drift, partly because she'd had no idea there'd been a drift to get. Or not, in this case.

Another subject she didn't want to talk about, one she'd had no idea was even on the table until thirty seconds ago.

However, at this rate they'd have nothing left to discuss except the weather, and wouldn't that be lame?

"Didn't mean to abandon you," he said, and her head jerked to his again. "A little bit ago. For breakfast?"

"Oh. Right. It's okay, Gus took over. As Gus does. Although I ate so little he threatened to hook me up to an IV."

"So much for eating for two."

"Yeah, well, one of the two has squished my stomach into roughly the size of an acorn. Not to mention my bladder. Anyway, I assured him that since I'd eaten everything that wasn't nailed down in my second trimester I doubted the kid was suffering."

Josh's gaze lingered on her belly for several seconds before he turned to prop his forearms on the top rail. "So how long are you here?"

"Not sure. A couple of weeks? I figured…" Deanna cleared her throat, then clutched the fence, stretching out her aching back. "I figured," she said to the ground as she willed the baby to shift, "there'd be…" Standing upright again, she met Josh's gaze. "There'd be things to discuss. Handle. Whatever. So I left my ticket open-ended. Long as I'm back the week before Thanksgiving, I'm good."

"And what happens then?"

"Among other things, an all Mahler concert at the National Symphony I've been looking forward to for months. But also an installation at my gallery. Well, not my gallery, but where I work. Young Japanese painter. I…" Her face warmed. "Through a weird confluence of events, I sort of 'discovered' him. This will be his first US showing, so we're all very excited…and your eyes just glazed over, didn't they?"

"That's the clouds coming in, they said it might snow later." She chuckled. Josh crossed his arms. "You like it? What you're doing?"

"I adore it. It's what I'm good at. What I love. That I'm actually employed doing something related to what Dad coughed up four years' tuition for is a bonus."

When she reached behind her to massage her lower back again—because her daughter's favorite position involved ramming her skull into the spot right over Deanna's tail-bone—Josh's gaze dropped to her stomach again, then away.

"This must feel weird. Being back."

"You have no idea. Like I'm having a dream where I'm a kid again. Because so little has changed."

Josh gave her a funny look. "Did you expect it to be different?"

"I'm not sure what I expected, truthfully."

"You're not what I expected, either." His eyes narrowed as he scrutinized her hair. "What's up with that, anyway?"

She laughed. "It was decided I needed to look—" she made air quotes "'edgier'. As in, customers are more likely to buy contemporary art from someone who actually looks contemporary to the twenty-first century. So buh-bye long, blah brown hair, hello—"

"Edgy."

"Yep. And this is *not* the pic Dad was showing Star-light. Trust me."

"Since you never sent him one of you looking like this."

"Oh, hell, no."

Josh crossed his arms. "So this is, what? A costume?"

"It's called dressing the part. And everybody does it. Seriously—if you rode into the rodeo ring in a business suit, would people take you seriously?"

Grinning, Josh looked away. "Point taken."

Starfire's breath warmed Deanna's face when she reached up to stroke the mare's nose again. "Gus said Dad had hospice come in, at the end," she said quietly.

"The *very* end," Josh breathed out. "That last week or

so. Gus was his main caregiver. The rest of us filled in when we could, of course. Or I should say, when Gus let us. Since according to him we never did things right."

Her jaw tight, Deanna looked back toward the house. "And as I said, Dad could have clued me in, anytime. Or let Gus do it." Her mouth pulled tight. "I can tell how much it sucked for the old guy, caught between loyalty to my father and what he clearly felt he should've done."

"And obviously you were in no condition to be nursing someone—"

"First off, between Gus and me, we would've managed. Secondly, also as I said, Dad didn't know I was pregnant." Her tenuous grasp on a good mood slipped away. "And this is a dumb conversation."

She felt Josh stiffen beside her. "Just like any conversation that gets too close to reality, right? Seriously, if there's some kind of prize for avoiding a subject, you'd win hands down."

"And you might want to think about picking a fight with a pregnant woman."

"I think I can handle it. And have. *And* since I have absolutely nothing to lose here, I may as well say this—whatever's going on with you, whatever kind of relationship you and your father had is none of my concern. I know that. But this keeping secrets crap is for the birds. Especially since your dad knew something was going on with you, even if he didn't know what. And that *was* my concern, since I worked for the man."

Deanna gawked at him for several seconds before averting her eyes again. "That's ridiculous."

"My concern?"

"No. That you think he knew something—"

"Because he told me, Dee. He was worried about you. I'm not making that up."

Annoyance surged through her. "If he was so worried about me, why didn't he say something? Why didn't he simply *ask* me?"

"Oh, I don't know—maybe because he knew you wouldn't've told him, so what would've been the point? Because God forbid the two of you actually talk to each other. And you know what?" he said, pushing away from the fence. "You're right, this is a dumb conversation. And I've had enough of those to last me a lifetime."

"Dammit, Josh—don't be like this!"

"Like what?" he said, a frown digging into his forehead. "Who I've always been? The dude you could *count on* to be straight with you? Fine. You don't wanna talk, I can't make you. But you're not gonna shut me up, either." He shrugged. "Just how it goes."

Then he stalked off, his boots thudding in the dirt, and Deanna sighed.

This was going to be the longest two weeks in the history of the planet.

His toddler stepdaughter balanced on one hip, Josh's twin, Levi, came up beside him in the ranch's formal dining room, where the dark, highly polished table contrasted with the troweled plaster walls and beamed ceiling. But after probably half a century Josh wouldn't have been surprised to find the table's graceful feet had taken root in the pitted grout between the old handmade tiles. He remembered, because his brain was being a real sonuvabitch today, hiding in here with Deanna when they were little— really little, like before he'd even started school—sitting under the table and pointing out "pictures" they'd see in the uneven tiles—

"You doing okay?" Levi asked, frowning at some unidentifiable finger food before picking one up and popping it into his mouth, anyway.

"Sure," Josh muttered, doing some frowning of his own at Deanna through the wide, arched doorway between the dining room and the vast great room where she sat on one of the leather sofas, Mom watchdogging beside her as people offered their condolences.

His brother's gaze followed Josh's, but thankfully he kept his mouth shut. For the moment, anyway. Levi offered the toddler one of the…things, but with a vigorous shake of her dark curls and an emphatic, "No!" Risa shoved away his hand. So Levi ate it for her. As one did.

"Nice service," his brother said, like they were distant cousins who hadn't seen each other in twenty years. Josh glowered; Levi shrugged. "Well, it was. Simple and to the point. Granville would've approved. Doncha think?"

"Except he didn't want a service at all. People making over him and stuff."

"Yeah, well, we don't always get our druthers, do we? And if you stare any harder at Deanna somebody's gonna melt."

"I'm not—"

Levi snorted. Josh sighed. Levi snorted again.

"You know, I do remember a few things from when we were kids. Like how you two were joined at the hip. Okay, bad choice of words," he said when Josh glared at him again. "But you spent a lot more time with her than you did with any of us."

"Because you all were jerks?"

"There is that." The baby hugged his neck, yawned, and settled her head on his chest, giving Josh a sweet little smile before her dark eyes fluttered closed. Levi smoothed her thick hair away from his chin and said softly, "But I seem to recall you used to be pretty damn protective of her. I'm guessing that hasn't changed."

Blowing out a breath, Josh picked up one of the whatever-they-weres and ate it. Except for the green chile—which found its way into 90 percent of the food around here, with red the other ten—his taste buds weren't really cluing him in. "*Everything's* changed, Leev," he said, chewing. "Seriously—are *you* the same person you were at seventeen?"

"No. Thank God. But I still love the same woman I did then," he said with a glance at his still-very-new wife Val, who gave him a little wave. Softly smiling, Levi met Josh's gaze again. "Only now we're good together. When we were teenagers…" He shook his head. "Would've been a disaster."

"Which has nothing to do with anything."

"Do you even realize how pissed you sound?"

Behind the teasing—and okay, the truth—lay a genuine concern that only proved his brother's words, that Levi wasn't the same live-for-the-moment bad boy he'd been as a kid. Or had seemed to be, anyway. But after six years in the army and taking on a ready-made family, nobility sat a lot more comfortably on his shoulders than anyone could have possibly imagined back then. Which only proved his point that people changed. Sometimes even for the better.

"I don't like unresolved issues, Leev. That's all."

Levi's brows lifted. "Deanna's an unresolved issue?"

"Not for me, no. *No*," he said to Levi's skeptical look. "But I suspect *she's* got them. And I…" He shoved out another harsh breath.

"You still care. Which makes you feel like an idiot. Hey. We're not twins for nothing," he said, when Josh gave him the side-eye.

"Fraternal. We're not clones, for godssake."

"And you don't share womb space—not to mention a

bunk bed—for as long as we did without getting a pretty good feel for what the other person is thinking. Besides, I'm only returning the favor." He nodded toward his wife again. "Considering how you didn't exactly stay out of my face about Val, either."

"And remind me to never say anything to anybody in this family about anything, ever again."

Hiking the toddler higher on his chest, Levi chuckled. "Like that's gonna happen," he said, his gaze swinging toward their father, in conversation with Gus on the other side of the room. "You know what's hell?" he said softly. "Being the child of fixers. Inheriting that gene. Because the truth is, we can't fix everything. Hell, we can't fix most things." From his tone, Josh figured Levi was referring to his tours in Afghanistan, a time he still didn't talk about much. At least, not to Josh. "The trick is," Levi said, facing Josh again, "knowing which battles are yours to fight, and which aren't. And sometimes…" He picked up another appetizer, gesturing with it in Deanna's direction before taking a bite. "And sometimes it's simply about showing up. Being there. Even if you know you're not going to win."

Josh felt another frown bite into his forehead. "Win? Win what?"

"The battle," his brother said, then walked away to rejoin his wife and older stepdaughter across the room.

Yeah, not making him feel better. Especially since, as far as Josh could tell, the battle was in Dee's head. Where it would undoubtedly stay, he thought irritably. And whether or not that made sense—his irritation even more than her reticence—it simply *was*.

Because this wasn't his first rodeo. As it were, he thought grimly.

What was it with women, anyway? At least, every woman he'd ever known. Either they shared every single thought that floated through their brains, or they kept what they were really thinking locked up like it was a state secret. Only it wasn't really a secret, oh, no. Because damned if they didn't expect you to somehow magically *know* what they wanted or what was bugging them. And then what you were supposed to do to make it better. Like you didn't really care unless you could read their minds.

A real stretch considering most men didn't completely understand what a woman was saying when she did tell him. Because there were always these…subtexts. God, he hated subtexts.

Josh took another sip of his beer, not even sure why he was trying to figure this—her—out. Except… Deanna Blake had been the only female he'd ever known—with the possible exception of his mother—who'd always been open with him. Not rudely, or oversharing all the girl stuff he really did not want to know about. But he'd always known where they stood with each other. So her clamming up now was pissing him off. Big time.

A rough breath left his lungs around the same time Dee's gaze wandered to his. His mother was nowhere to be seen, meaning Dee was alone, looking very brave. And, weirdly, very small. Since at only a few inches shorter than Josh, she wasn't.

She smiled, after a fashion, and his gut cramped, remembering how bright that smile had once been. The way it'd light up her whole face…and Josh's insides. How, for every time she'd rant and rave about something, she'd laugh five times more. These huge, completely unladylike belly laughs that sometimes got so out of hand she'd have to cross her legs so she wouldn't pee herself.

But only when she was with him, she'd said.

So he was guessing her obvious unwillingness to talk about what had led to her current predicament—and he had no doubt it was a predicament—was basically a defense mechanism for when your life has gone to hell in a handbasket and you're too damn embarrassed to talk to anybody about it. Especially when—he heard his son giggling, playing with his other cousins near the fireplace—it was kind of hard to ignore the consequences of that handbasket ride.

Not to mention the hell part of it.

Tossing his empty bottle in the plastic-lined bin by the table, Josh marched his sorry ass into the other room and over to Dee, where he dropped onto the sofa beside her like he actually knew what he was doing. Even though, aside from the fact he doubted he could fix things for her any better now than when they were kids, he also imagined they were the worst possible combination of two people in the entire world right now.

And quite possibly the only two people who'd really understand what the other was going through.

He thought this was called working with what you had. Or were given.

Something.

By this point Deanna was so drained, both emotionally and physically, she was basically numb. She'd told herself she wouldn't cry, but that had been a lost cause. Shoot, there were tears when she scored her favorite ice cream in the freezer case; what on earth had she expected at her father's memorial service? Stoicism? And right on cue, her chest fisted. Again.

And Josh was not helping. But asking him to go away would be mean. Not to mention self-defeating. Since as much as she wished he hadn't come over, she didn't want him to leave, either. Actually, what she *really* wanted was to curl into as much of a ball as her massive middle would allow and sleep the merciful sleep of the oblivious. Lord, pregnancy brain was a bitch. However, even if Josh hadn't planted his large self beside her on the couch there was the will reading to get through. Honestly, it was like being in some old black-and-white movie, what with the drama and all—

He'd leaned forward, his elbows planted on his knees. Not looking at her. Just being there, like the old days.

"You doin' okay?"

"Mostly. Sure."

One side of his mouth lifted. "If you say so," he said, and she sort of laughed, rubbing her belly. Babypie was apparently snoozing, thank God, although that hard little head still relentlessly gouged her lower back.

But anyway, Josh. Whose scent immediately brought back a slew of memories—maybe not so numb, at that— that made her think of things she'd refused to let herself think about then, and for darn sure shouldn't be thinking about now. Or ever. God knew not all cowboys smelled that good—and there'd been plenty of times when Josh hadn't, either, to be real—but right now it was all about leather and fresh cotton and something piney and yummy and her extraspecial pregnancy smeller was having a freaking field day.

"You need anything? Food or whatever?"

"No. Thanks. Your mom made sure I ate."

"She's good at that."

Josh sat up a little straighter, scrubbing one palm over his knee. Jeans, of course, although his "good" ones. Paired with a black corduroy shirt with silver buttons, a tan sports jacket, the guy didn't look half-bad. This late in the day a beard haze shadowed his jaw, giving him a sexy male model look, God help her.

Then he laced his hands together between his knees,

frowning at the tops of his boots—also his "good" ones, dirt- and dung-free. "When'd Steve say the reading was again?"

"He should be here any minute," Deanna said, and Josh nodded. The last of the guests—a couple from a nearby ranch, she didn't even remember their names, so sad— stopped to give her the obligatory, "If you need anything, anything at all, please let us know," before walking away, and Deanna huffed a tired little breath. From the time she'd heard until this very moment, everything had felt oddly surreal, familiar and yet not, like being in a play she ought to know her part in but she didn't, really. Now, for some bizarre reason, it felt as though the stage lights were being shut off, one by one, leaving her and Josh on a bare stage, lit only by the eerie glare of a single, stark light. The good news was, she could stop pretending now, if she chose.

The bad news was, she still had no idea what her reality was. Or was supposed to be. But when she looked at Josh's profile, saw that set jaw, the grim set to his mouth, it occurred to her she wasn't the only one whose world was about to turn upside down. Or inside out. Heck, Josh had given his entire life to this ranch. Meaning whatever came next would probably affect him a lot more than it would her.

From the kitchen, a murmur of voices floated into the silent, cavernous room—his parents and Gus, she thought. Austin came over to climb in Josh's lap; Josh wrapped his arms around his son from behind as though nothing, *nothing*, would ever come between them, and suddenly Deanna wanted to know so badly what'd happened between Josh and Austin's mother it almost made her dizzy. She'd asked Gus, actually, but he'd said it wasn't his story to tell.

"Hey," she said softly, and Josh angled his head to look at her, the obvious worry glimmering in those soft goldygreen eyes punching her insides harder than the baby's foot. Even though she knew she shouldn't, she reached over—awkwardly—to lay a hand on his knee, right beside Austin's little sneaker. "It's gonna be okay."

He actually chuckled. "You telling me that? Or yourself?" he said, a moment before the lawyer arrived, looking a little windblown from the short walk from the driveway to the front door.

"Sorry I couldn't make the service," he said breathlessly as Josh stood to shake his hand. "Got summoned to a surprise court appearance in Santa Fe." Sweeping hunks of unruly silver hair off his forehead, Steve Riggs gave Deanna a sympathetic smile. "I'm so sorry, honey, I really am. Your daddy was a good man. We'll all miss him."

The same words she'd heard no less than three dozen times in the past two hours. Still, she knew the sentiment was sincere.

"Thank you."

"Well," the attorney said, looking a little relieved at being able to move on, "I suppose I'm ready when you are. Do you need help?" he asked when she tried to cantilever herself to her feet. But Josh was already on the case, having set Austin down to come around the side of the sofa, bracing one arm across her back to hoist her upright.

The attorney's brows spiked over his glasses. "My goodness. When are you due?"

Because she was not one of those women who only gained fifteen pounds and looked like she was carrying a cantaloupe. "Six weeks or so."

"Well." Steve's favorite word, apparently. "If you gather the others, I suppose we can do the reading in Granville's office. Unless…" His gaze swung to Deanna's. "You'd rather do it elsewhere?"

"The office is fine."

It didn't take long. Her dad had left modest bequests to various people in the community who'd be notified in a few days. Gus got an annuity, Dad's old Caddy and the right to live in one of the guesthouses as long as he wished. Since Dad had already given Josh's parents a house in town after Sam's retirement, his gifts to them now included a few stocks and bonds and a small Thomas Moran landscape painting Sam had always admired…and which Deanna knew was worth big bucks. Then, aside from a modest savings account which went to Deanna, there were a few disbursements to various charities Dad had always supported, particularly ones that worked with the local Native populations.

"And now," Steve said, peering over his glasses at Deanna, then Josh, before clearing his throat. "'I leave my ranch, known as the Vista Encantada, including the house, the land, any and all outbuildings and whatever livestock on said land at the time of my death, equally to my only daughter, Deanna Marie Blake, and my employee Joshua Michael Talbot.'"

A moment of stunned silence preceded a dual *"What?"* from Deanna and Josh.

"Congratulations, kids," Steven said, angling the will toward them so they could see for themselves. "You're now co-owners of one of the prettiest pieces of property in northern New Mexico."

Chapter Three

"But I don't *want* the ranch," Dee said later, after everyone else had left so she and Josh could ostensibly hash things out. She shifted in the corner of the tufted leather couch in the office, clearly miserable. Physically *and* emotionally, Josh guessed. "I never did. And Dad knew it."

Leaning his butt against the edge of the Depression-era desk, Josh crossed his arms. He'd initially assumed her shock had been because Gran had left half the ranch to him. Apparently not. "You told him that?"

"Yes!" Then, rubbing one temple, she sighed. "Or at least I thought I did. In any case—" her hand dropped to what was left of her lap "—I never made a secret of how much I hated being stuck out here. Why on earth would I want the place?"

"And what'd you think he was gonna do? You're his kid, Dee. The ranch was his most valuable asset. Of course he'd leave it to you. I'm only surprised he didn't leave you the whole thing." Because she hadn't been the only one in shock there. Truth be told, Josh still was. And would be for a good long while, he suspected.

Dee's eyes lifted to his before she shoved out another sigh. "I can't...this isn't my home anymore, Josh."

"Well aware of that." His forehead pinched, he glanced down at the floor, then back at her. "But it's been mine all my life. And the breeding operation…sure, I was only an employee and all, but your dad hadn't had a hand in it for some time. He'd left all the decision making to me—"

"I know, Josh. I know." She paused. "He obviously trusted you. And it's not as if you don't deserve it. But—"

"Look, you don't want to stick around and help me run the Vista, I completely understand. We can still be partners, if *you* trust me enough to handle things on this end, and we can split the profits. There's money to be made with the cabins, too, plenty of hunters would be happy to fork over the bucks during elk season. You know Steve'll look out for your interests, make sure I'm not screwing you over—"

"It's not that," she said, sagging into the couch's deep cushions. "It's…" Her mouth thinned. "Okay. It's not as if I'd really given this much thought, since I didn't figure it'd be an issue for a long, long time. But since he did leave me half the ranch…oh, Lord. I can't even say it."

Josh's veins iced over. "You want to sell it."

A long moment passed before she said, "It's more that I need to."

"You sound like you've got gambling debts."

She almost smiled. "No. But I do have a baby on the way. A baby who's going to be applying to colleges eighteen years down the road." Her mouth twisted. "Would be nice to have one less thing to worry about. Sure, the place might be profitable now. But there's no guarantee it'll stay that way. Not in this economic climate. If we sold it…"

Birds in the hand and all that. Yeah, he got it. Josh sighed, realizing he could hardly argue with her. About that, at least. God knows plenty of ranches went under, through no fault of their owners. And he'd be a fool to guarantee her that the Vista wouldn't. Also, out of curiosity Granville had had the property appraised a couple years back, information he'd apparently shared with Josh because he'd been too stunned to keep it to himself. Even taking into account normal fluctuations in the real estate market, the figure was staggering. To somebody like Josh, at least.

Still, for him, it wasn't about the money. It was about the ranch itself. It was about *home*.

"What about her father? I know you said you're not together, but—"

"He's not even part of the equation," she said quietly, then heaved herself to her feet and walked over to the window facing the mountains. "For reasons I'd really rather not get into right now."

Anger spurted through him. "Or ever, right?"

A frown crumpling her brow, she turned. "My situation is really none of your concern—"

"You want to sell the only place I've ever called home, Dee. A place I'd never, ever in my wildest dreams thought might be mine someday. So now that I'm this close—" he held up one hand, finger and thumb a quarter inch apart "—to seeing those wild dreams come true, you want to yank it from me. So tell me how the reason behind that isn't any of my concern?"

Her arms folded, Dee pivoted back to the window. "You could always buy me out."

"Seriously? Like I've got that kind of cash lying around. For a down payment, maybe, but no way in hell would I ever qualify for a loan big enough for the rest of it—"

"But if we sold it and split the proceeds..." She faced him again, a thin ridge between her brows. "You could buy your own place, right? No, it wouldn't be this big—"

"It wouldn't be the Vista."

"—but you don't need this much acreage to start up your own operation. And you've already got a great reputation, I'm sure everybody knows it's you behind the breeding business. It's *you* who's won all the rodeo titles. And besides, then it'd really be yours. Yours and Austin's. And who knows? Maybe someday down the road you can buy the Vista back from the new owners. Especially since you know as well as I do how few outsiders stick around once the romance of owning a ranch wears off. And you can take whatever livestock you want, nobody's talking about selling the horses. Only the property."

"Except I know for a fact there's nothing available in the area."

"Then broaden your parameters, for heaven's sake!"

Josh's knee-jerk reaction was to say *But I don't want to do that*! Except even he knew he'd sound like Austin having a hissy fit over not wanting to put on a coat, or go to bed, or anything else the kid decided was against his druthers at any given moment. Even so...

Even so.

He swept a palm across his hair, then hooked both his hands on his hips, trying to ignore the plea in her eyes, for him to understand. Probably similar to what was in his.

"I hear what you're saying. I do. But home isn't just about place, it's about people. Family. Although maybe that doesn't mean the same thing to you it does to me."

Deanna jerked. *Sonuvabitch.*

"Crap, Dee, I didn't—"

"No, you're right. I mean, of course I loved Dad, but..." She angled back toward the window, where the stark, late fall light brought the worry and exhaustion on her face into sharp relief. "But we definitely didn't have the kind of relationship you and your brothers did—do—with your parents. My aunt and uncle have always been...concerned for me, and my cousin Emily's a good friend, but…" A tiny, sad smile curved her mouth.

"I'm sorry."

A quick shrug accompanied, "It's what I know. Although…" The smile grew as her hand went to her belly. "Although my plan is to do better by this kid." She almost laughed, but her eyes told an entirely different story. "At least I can dream, right?"

Josh slugged his hands in his front pockets, waiting out the next, even stronger, wave of sympathy. At least he'd had great examples in his parents, when it came to his own relationship with his son. And that still didn't stop the fear that he'd screw up…

Ah, hell. Because sometimes it wasn't about what you wanted, it was about what was best for everybody. And tying Deanna down to someplace she'd never wanted to be to begin with, simply because Josh had other ideas…

And those eyes…

"Okay," he pushed out.

"Okay, what?"

"You wanna sell, we'll sell." She seemed to sag in relief. "Although…" He glanced around before meeting her eyes again. God, this was shredding him. All of it. "No sense putting it on the market without sprucing it up a bit first. Otherwise we're likely to get a bunch of lowball offers. I'm sure you don't want that." At her wide eyes, a tight grin stretched across his face. "Yeah. Not as dumb as I look. I'd also like to do one last Christmas party. For the community. If that's okay with you."

Like the annual Fourth of July party, Granville had also hosted a Christmas bash at the house every year, even playing Santa for the children. To yank that out from under everybody this close to Christmas…well, it just didn't seem right.

And judging from Deanna's slow nod, she apparently agreed.

"Except…" Her brow knotted. "Who's going to bank-roll the fixing up?"

"Doubt we're talking anything major. I can probably do most of the work myself, in fact. Since it's my slow season."

Still frowning, she cupped her hands under her belly, like she was trying to ease the weight of it. "And you do realize my window for getting back home is getting nar-rower by the second?"

"I figured as much. So if you'll trust me to oversee the reno, let us throw that last party…" Josh waited out the sharp pain in his sternum. "We could list her right after the New Year. Shouldn't take long to sell. Especially since your dad regularly got offers for the ranch—"

"I know," she said on a breath. "That much, he did share." Another beat or two passed. "You're really good with this?"

"Good?" Josh slipped his hands into his pockets again. "Not at all. But you taking care of that little girl," he said, nodding toward her middle, "is far more important than me being nostalgic or whatever. Besides, kinda hard to regret losing what was never really mine."

Her eyes glittered. "I'm so sorry, Josh…"

"Nothing to be sorry for. I swear."

A moment passed before she waddled over to wrap her arms around him and give him as much of a hug as her belly would let her. "Thank you," she said softly, then re-turned to the desk to rummage through the drawers until she found a legal pad and a pen, after which she awkwardly lowered herself into her father's old swivel desk chair and started making lists.

As Josh felt a dream he hadn't even known he'd had slip from his grasp.

He grabbed his coat and gloves off the hall tree on his way outside, getting all the way over to the stables before he slammed his gloved fist into the splintered siding, making Starfire turn her head and give him a *What the* hell *are you doing, boy?* look. Just once in his life, it'd be nice to have something go—and stay—his way.

And maybe one day he'd discover a hitherto unknown immunity to a pair of sad female eyes.

Today, however, was clearly not that day.

Muttering an ugly curse, Josh slammed the wall again, then leaned his forehead against the cold, unyielding wood, trying desperately to steady his breathing.

"Uncle Granville did *what*?"

Deanna eased back a little more in her father's desk chair to almost smile at the computer screen. Or rather, the completely flummoxed expression in her cousin's bright blue eyes. "You heard me. Left the property to me and Josh equally."

Emily swept a hunk of soft, sorority-sister-perfect golden brown hair behind her perfect little ear, looking both curious and concerned. "So what now? You're hardly going to move back there, are you?"

"Not to worry." Although, strangely, she wasn't nearly as thrilled with Josh's acquiescence as she would've expected. Then again, living with a tiny skull lodged against her spine tended to leech the joy out of most things these days. She loved this baby more than life itself, but she'd be extremely glad when they no longer shared a body. "We're going to sell the ranch and divide the proceeds. Well, Josh is, I'll be home in a few days."

Em frowned. "And he's okay with that? Selling, I mean?"

"He…agreed it's for the best."

"Huh." Emily delicately bit off the end of a raw baby carrot. "So how *is* Josh, anyway?"

"Good," Deanna said, deciding not to go into the whole he's-got-a-kid-now thing. Because, pointless?

"I remember him, you know."

Of course she did. As one tended to remember when that first, blinding hormonal rush swarms your brain so hard and hot and fast you can barely breathe. Like a simultaneously thrilling and scary-as-hell amusement park ride.

"He's changed, though," Deanna said.

"I'm sure. It's been…oh, gosh. About eleven years, huh?"

"Yep."

Only once had Emily and her parents visited the ranch after Deanna's mother's death, the summer before Deanna turned fifteen. Why, she never had figured out, since it'd been no secret Aunt Margaret thought her sister insane for hooking up with "that cowboy" after—or so the story went—Deanna's grandparents had taken their two daughters skiing at the nearby resort, and there'd been a dance, or something, where the twenty-one-year-old Katherine Alderman had met a handsome, older rancher and fallen in love. And then chose to live in the middle of nowhere. So to say that last visit had been unexpected was a gross understatement.

In any case, her thirteen-year-old cousin immediately crushed on the sixteen-year-old Josh, following him around like a puppy dog. And Josh had been the epitome of patience and kindness, which had melted Deanna's heart— even as it drove her aunt straight to Crazyville, clearly panicked that her daughter would somehow suffer the same

fate as her baby sister. But although Deanna had rolled
her eyes—since Emily was an eighth-grader, for heaven's
sake—considering her own feelings about living on the
ranch, and what she remembered of her mother's chronic
wistfulness, she sympathized with her aunt's concerns
more than she might've otherwise.

She therefore could only imagine Aunt Margaret's relief that Emily was now engaged to a senator's son, thus
realizing the *proper* happy-ever-after so rudely snatched
from her younger sister.

"Anyway," Deanna said, "I need to go—" Literally,
before she peed right there in the chair. "So I'll be back a
week from Sunday, I'll take a taxi in—"

"Like hell. I'm coming to get you. And don't even think
about arguing with me."

Deanna smiled. She really did love her cousin. Even if
she was...Emily. The poster child for impeccable social
graces and never putting a foot wrong. Then again, Emily
put up with Deanna, too, so there you were. "Fine," she
said, laughing. "I'll see you soon—"

"That *designer* from Santa Fe is here," Gus said from
the office door, not even trying to hide his disgust. As far
as the housekeeper was concerned, designers and decora-
tors and their ilk were for outsiders who wanted to make
sure their ridiculously overpriced houses looked authenti-
cally Southwest. Gus thought the place was fine as it was.
Gus thought she and Josh were nuts to hire someone to fix
something that didn't need fixing.

But mostly, Gus was ticked as hell they were selling.
In fact, he'd barely spoken to either her or Josh for a good
twenty-four hours after they told him. Yes, *they*. Since
even though Deanna tried to take blame for the decision,
Josh insisted it was mutual. Never mind that more than
once over the past couple days she'd catch him staring at

the mountains, or one of the paddocks or barns, with a pensive expression that pulverized her heart. And if she hadn't had this baby to think of—if she wasn't the only person *to* think about the baby—maybe she would've rethought things.

But not only was she her little girl's only champion, she'd let her heart rule her head for far too long. So this time, it was about being logical. Practical. A grownup. And Josh was a big boy, he'd land on his feet. Or someplace even better than the Vista.

If there was such a thing.

"I'll be there in a minute," she said. "Did you offer her coffee?"

"Since I didn' fall down a well in the last little while," Gus said in his heavy New Mexican Spanish accent, "yes, I did. You wan' me to call Mr. Josh? I don' think he's far."

"Please. Thanks. Since the Realtor should be along any minute."

The old guy tromped out on bowed legs that attested to his many years as a ranch hand before opting for inside duty, and Deanna felt a rush of affection for the man who'd done his fair share of mothering her, too, once her own was gone. Another, much sharper rush of feelings followed, as it occurred to her once she left she'd probably never see him again.

Then, as she came out of the powder room she caught Josh in the entryway, brushing fresh, light snow off his shoulders, and she realized she'd probably never see him again, either. Which *logically* shouldn't've bothered her, considering how little she'd seen him, anyway, in the last several years. Hadn't even thought about him all that much, to be truthful. But in the past few days…

Deanna released another breath. Just another hyper-emotional preggo, nothing to see here, move along. Sure, being back had stirred a lot of memories—how could it not? And she was vulnerable and shaky and more grief-stricken than she probably even realized, and not only about losing Dad, although that would've been enough by itself. And dammit, Josh was about to sacrifice something *for her* that obviously meant the world to him—

"Dee?" he said, frowning. "You okay?"

"You bet," she said, girding her achy loins. And back. Lord, if the kid would *move*, already, that would be good—

The doorbell rang. Josh let the Realtor in, shaking his hand, polite as hell. Even when the man's cold blue eyes swept over the great room with the practiced ease of a lion checking out the savannah for prey. Honestly, the dude was practically licking his chops.

The designer—a dark-haired beauty swimming in suede and turquoise—stood as they entered, grinning for the Realtor, who'd actually recommended her. "Toby!" she said, opening her arms for the much taller man to walk into. "So nice to see you!" Then, still smiling, she turned to Deanna, and something in her deep brown eyes put Deanna immediately at ease. Unlike her sidekick whose presence sent chills down her spine.

"Ohmigoodness," the other woman said after introductions were made, her gaze landing on Deanna's middle before lifting again. "We don't have much time, do we? Before the baby comes?"

"Oh. No. I mean, yes, she's due soon. But I'll be home long before that happens—"

"And I don't mean to rush you folks," Toby said, making Deanna blink in the glare of his too-white teeth. "But unfortunately I've got a showing at eleven in Taos, so if you don't mind…?"

The smile lit on Josh, standing off to one side with a

scowl so deeply etched it took a full two seconds to let go
of Josh's face. At which point he smiled—not as brightly,
thank God—and gave a little nod. "Of course. Right this
way..."

An hour later, his head spinning with words like *com-
parables* and *resale value* and *vintage charm*, Josh sank
onto the sofa in the office, his arms tightly folded over his
chest and his mood the darkest since the day he watched
Jordan walk out to her truck without even looking back.

On a sigh, he leaned into the cushions to glare up at the
hand-forged chandelier, half wishing it would drop on his
head and put him out of his misery. Out in the hall he could
hear Deanna and Tessa the designer softly laughing. The
gal seemed nice enough, and at least she hadn't wanted to
"update" every damn thing in the place, although she did
have some valid suggestions to make things look a little
less like you might find Billy the Kid's bones behind one
of the doors. Even if he was gonna stay, he'd probably go
along with most of her suggestions.

The Realtor dude, though...jeebus. Like a villain right
out of a Disney cartoon, complete with dollar signs in his
eyes. Said he'd have an appraiser come give them an ac-
curate number, but the ballpark figure he'd suggested was
even more than Josh had figured on. No wonder the man
was practically drooling. Hell, maybe Josh should ditch
the horse business and take up selling real estate. At least
houses didn't kick if they got pissed at you.

Finally he heard the front door close; a moment later
Deanna joined him in the room, carefully lowering herself into a wingback chair a few feet away.

"That went pretty well, don't you think?"

Josh grunted.

Deanna tapped her fingers on the arms of the chair for a

moment, then said, very gently, "At least they didn't think we needed to change much."

"Not sure what difference that makes if we're selling it, anyway."

"True, I suppose. And why are you looking at me like that?"

"You really have no attachment to the place? None at all?"

A long moment passed before she said, "No. I don't. But even if I did, I'm in no position to let the past bog me down about decisions I need to make now. For the future." She smoothed an oversize plaid flannel shirt over her belly for several seconds before looking over at him again. "For *her* future."

"And I still say her father—"

"He's married," she said softly, and the rest of his sentence logjammed in his throat.

"Oh, jeez, Dee—"

"I didn't know. Obviously. He was—is—French. Older. A diplomat. And yes, that much was true. Why he was in the States, I mean. I sold him a painting, he asked me out…" She blew a short laugh through her nose. "We even talked about marriage at one point. Or maybe it was only me talking about marriage and he didn't have the guts or whatever to stop me. In any case, it was all fun and games until the diaphragm failed."

"And don't you dare blame yourself for this."

Her gaze slammed into his. "He didn't seduce me, Josh."

"No, he just lied. Same thing. So if you think I'm gonna judge you, you are definitely barking up the wrong tree. Seriously. Like I've got room to talk?"

She almost smiled at that. "Austin?"

"Yep. And Jordan and I were being careful, too. Or at least thought we were. Having a kid had definitely not been on the agenda. But at least I wasn't involved with someone else. Let alone married. And when she told me she was pregnant…let's just say I grew up *real* fast."

"And she took advantage of your big heart."

He felt his brows shove together. "What else would I have done?"

She almost laughed. "Really? After what I just said?" Then her eyes watered. "I'm so sorry, Josh. You deserve so much better than that."

Her sincerity, her *kindness*, stole his breath. Not to mention a good chunk of his earlier irritation, if not his disappointment.

"Thanks."

"I'm serious. You're a prince, dude. Own it."

Clearing his throat, Josh leaned forward, linking his hands between his knees. "Hardly a prince. In fact, looking back, it was probably stupid, her and me hooking up to begin with—okay, so no maybe about it, I knew better and I did it anyway—but at least I acknowledged my kid. Took responsibility for him. What that jerk did to you…" He shook his head, unable to finish his sentence.

"Oh, it gets worse."

From her tone alone, he knew what she meant. "He asked you to get rid of it."

"Demanded, actually."

"Before or after he told you he was married?"

"After. But before he admitted he already had three kids. Yep," Dee said to Josh's softly uttered obscenity. "However, no matter how much I might wish I hadn't let myself get caught up in the fairy tale, that I'd been more alert to the signs I now realize were there all along, the fact is I still made my own decisions. And now I have to deal with the consequences of those decisions. Same as you did…crap," she said, her breath suddenly catching.

Josh jerked to attention. "What?"

"Nothing. Well, not nothing, my back's killing me. But it'll pass." Then she frowned when he dug out his phone. "What're you doing?"

"Calling Mom. Because I've heard way too many going into labor stories not to know a hurting back's not a good sign—"

"Then I've been in labor for the past two weeks. So put your phone away—"

"Hey, Mom," he said when she picked up. "Deanna says her back's hurting pretty bad."

"Oh?" Mom said, her voice kind of echoey. "How bad?"

"Bad enough she's making faces—"

"I'm not in labor, Billie! Your son's overreacting!"

Mom laughed in his ear. "You probably are. But if it makes you feel better, I'm on my way back into town—I had clinic this morning—so I'll swing by, no problem. If that's okay with Dee?"

"You're on the phone while you're driving?"

"Hands-free, not an idiot. And no other cars for probably ten miles. Well?"

He looked up from the phone. "Mom's gonna come check you out, if that's okay."

She glared at him. "If it gets you to shut up, sure. But I'm not. In. Labor."

Mom chuckled again. "I'll be there in fifteen minutes," she said, then disconnected the call.

Billie stuffed her stethoscope back in her bag, then straightened, her hands on her hips. "You're not in labor," she said, and Deanna released a half relieved, half annoyed sigh.

"*Thank* you—"

"You are, however, about fifty percent effaced and a

couple centimeters dilated. Not to mention that baby's sitting real low. As in, engaged already. Probably why your back's been giving you grief."

Deanna felt her forehead crunch. "I thought none of that happened with first babies until much closer to the due date."

"So either your date's wrong—"

"Two ultrasounds. Not wrong."

"Or this child has a mind of her own. In which case, steel yourself, because that's not gonna get better once she's out. Which might happen sooner rather than later," she said to Deanna's undoubtedly horrified expression. "In any case—and you're *really* not going to like this— you might want to rethink getting on a plane right now."

The horrified expression instantly morphed into panic. "I can't stay here, Billie."

"You might not have a choice. Unless you want to risk giving birth at thirty thousand feet with a couple hundred strangers as witnesses."

Struggling to her feet, she shook her head. "Nononononono… I have an installation to oversee, and I haven't finished setting up the baby's space—" Such as it would be, a corner in her dinky little bedroom. "And…" Deanna sagged back onto her bed, defeated. "Really?" she said in a small voice.

Billie sat beside her, wrapping a strong arm around her shoulders and tugging her close, like she used to after Deanna's mom died. "I know, sweetie," she whispered into Deanna's hair. "Like you didn't already have enough on your plate. And it's not like we *know* you'd go into labor— could be you'd make the trip just fine. But it's not a chance I'd want to take. Or want you to take. And if you do give birth early, at least you'll be back home by Christmas, right? Maybe even Thanksgiving, who knows?"

Deanna felt the blood drain from her face. Thanksgiving was less than three weeks away. Suddenly this all seemed very real. As in, in less than a month she could be holding a baby in her arms.

No—her *daughter* in her arms.

Billie rubbed her shoulder, giving her a little squeeze. "It's up to you, sweetie. It's not like I'm saying you can't fly, I'm only saying you probably shouldn't. So let's get a second opinion, and you can think about it." She gave Deanna another quick hug, then stood and collected her things. "But if you do decide to stay, at least there's people here to look after you, right?"

Not as great a selling point as you might think.

Chapter Four

On the other end of the line, a long, aggrieved breath preceded, "You're absolutely sure you can't fly back?"

No sympathy, then. Not that this was a surprise. Her boss was stingier with her compassion than she was with her salaries. But at least Alita—grudgingly—shared commissions. And Deanna was damned good at matching up potential buyers with exactly what they were looking for. Even if they didn't know it when they first walked into the gallery.

"The general consensus—" as in, from the ob-gyn backup at the clinic Billie worked with "—is that it wouldn't be a good idea. I can email you my notes if that'd help—"

"Don't bother—I'm sure somebody else here can get up to speed. However, if you're not back by the beginning of December, you do realize I'll have to replace you?"

Because clearly the woman had never heard of the Family and Medical Leave Act. Or specialized temp agencies. "I was planning on going on maternity leave by then, anyway. I'm only adding a few weeks to it." Not that it was paid. Although at least the cash part of her inheritance would see her through for a while. "You can't fire me for being pregnant, Alita."

"More's the pity," the woman muttered, then disconnected the call.

Yeah, *that* really cheered her up.

And she'd yet to call Emily, let her know what was going on. Or not.

"But we're supposed to go bridesmaid dress shopping next week!" were the first words out of her cousin's mouth...followed by a sucked-in breath. "Oh, God, Dee—I'm so sorry! It's just I was counting on you to keep the other girls on track when we went to the salon. You know how they can get."

She did, indeed. Although she wondered if it ever occurred to Emily that perhaps the slew of sorority sisters and fellow debutantes that made up her cousin's entourage weren't really the "besties" she wanted to believe they were. Or how they'd react to Emily's heavily pregnant—and unringed—maid of honor. A moot point now, she supposed.

"You'll be fine," she said, and Emily sighed. Then chuckled.

"Which I assume is Deespeak for grow a pair?"

"It is. And no, I don't give two figs what you choose. I totally trust your taste." In fashion, anyway, if not in friends.

"Thanks. But...crap. This means I won't be with you when the baby comes. And that sucks. And ohmigod, I haven't even thrown you a shower yet! Okay, seriously, the instant you get back, you are so getting showered. Like no new mother has ever been showered, ever. I swear."

Deanna had to laugh. What her cousin sometimes lacked in focus, she more than made up for with generosity. Not to mention enthusiasm. And she'd never forget how the younger woman had instantly become Deanna's champion after Phillippe's betrayal, not only insisting she come stay with her in her tiny Georgetown one bedroom so she wouldn't eat her weight in Häagen-Dazs, but also standing up to her mother. Who hadn't exactly gotten behind her daughter's public support of her cousin.

And Emily, bless her sweet heart, hadn't wavered even in the threat of her mama's yanking closed the purse strings on the wedding. "No," she'd said with a knowing smile, "It's Mom who'd be mortified if this wedding doesn't come off. Trust me." And sure enough, Aunt Margaret apparently decided a pregnant niece was far less of a social faux pas than letting her daughter get married at city hall. In rags.

"Dee? Did I lose you?"

"No, no… I was just thinking…" She smiled, listening to little snow BBs clicking against the window. Perfect baking weather, she thought, her mood lifting at the thought. "Okay. You're on. For the shower."

"As if you have any choice?" Emily said, giggling. Then she said, very gently, "I love you, you know," and something twinged inside Deanna.

"I love you, too, goof," she said, holding the phone to her chest a moment before shoving herself off her bed, then tucking the phone into her back pocket. A miraculous feat in itself, considering how tightly even maternity denim stretched across her prodigious butt these days—

From down the hall she heard Gus's deep laugh, then Austin giggling, the infectious sound banishing the normally suffocating silence to the dark corners tucked behind the rafters, and she smiled, momentarily content. She knew Austin was in the Baptist Church's preschool program three mornings a week for now, meaning Josh had to cobble together day care however he could manage. Although Gus said these days Josh let the kid hang out with him more and more as he went about his chores. Which was how it was with ranchers' kids, many of whom were homeschooled, working their education around the needs of the ranch.

Not in Deanna's case, however, since her mother, clearly worried about Deanna becoming completely cut off from any social life whatsoever, insisted she attend school in town.

Thank God.

"Dee!" Bellowing her name, Austin scrambled off the chair where he was presumably having lunch and ran to her, arms outstretched. Because bonding happened whether it made sense or not. Laughing over the twist to her heart, Deanna lugged him into her arms and kissed the top of his head, earning her a scowl from the housekeeper.

"You really think you should be doin' that?"

"Billie didn't say I couldn't." Grinning, she tickled the child's tummy, breathing in the scents of little boy and burning logs, the fire's crackling glow banishing the late fall gloom. "So we're fine. Aren't we, hotshot?"

His baby-toothed grin warmed her far more than the fire. "Uh-huh. Daddy went somewhere, so I'm stayin' with Gus. And you!"

Chuckling, Deanna looked over to Gus. "Somewhere?"

"To check out a potential buyer. Josh don' sell his stock to jus' anybody. Jus' like your daddy. You want somethin'? Tea, maybe?"

"I'm good, thanks. And I remember. Hey," she said, giving the little boy a squeeze. "Whaddya say we bake something, you and me?"

"Like what?"

"Well… I'll have to see what's on hand, but you can help me decide. Unless…" She looked at Gus. "I'd be in your way?"

"You kiddin'? Trust me, by now I'm more'n ready to hand over the kitchen duties to someone else."

"Oh, Gus…" For the first time, she realized how tired he looked. That the bags under his eyes weren't only from age, but exhaustion. She hiked the little boy higher in her arms, her eyes stinging when he laid his head on her shoulder. *Falling in love is not an option*, she thought, although she suspected that ship had set sail from the first moment she saw him. "Are you okay?"

The housekeeper looked insulted. "Of course I'm okay, I'm probably healthier'n you. But I'm old. Done. Especially with…" He sighed. "With taking care of people. Not you, buddy," he said quickly, reaching over to ruffle Austin's wavy hair. "But everybody else…" His eyes met hers again as he shrugged.

The stinging got five times worse. "I still don't understand why Dad didn't get full-time nursing care. He could've afforded it—"

"Only that would've meant not everyone would've gotten their full inheritance. I swear, that's what he said. And anyway, it would've made me nuts, strangers around all the time, gettin' in my space." His dark eyes glittered. "Only I forgot I'm not seventy anymore…"

Then his gaze scanned the kitchen, and Deanna sucked in a little breath before setting Austin down, giving him a smile. "Why don't you go find Smoky? I think he's on my bed."

"'Kay," the little boy said, sneakers thudding down the hall. Deanna told herself she wouldn't be around long enough for the cat to exact his revenge. Then she turned back to Gus.

"You're leaving, aren't you?" she said, and a sad smile pushed at the housekeeper's wrinkles.

"My niece and her husband down in Cruces, they've

been after me for years to come live with them. To come home. Still got a bunch of cousins down there, too, their kids, grandkids…" He scratched the back of his head, making his thick, gray hair stick out like a duck tail. "And it don' snow there but once in a blue moon. After sixty years up here, might be a nice change. So I said I'd give it a shot, see how it goes."

Deanna smiled, even as her eyes burned. "You'll be missed."

Gus shrugged. "I know the will said I could live in one of the guesthouses, but nothing's gonna be the same, you know? Somebody else ownin' the Vista…" He crossed his arms over his belly, his head wagging. "I figure if change is happening, I should at least have some choice in what that change is, right?"

"Absol-lutely."

"Aw, don' you go gettin' like that," he said, chuckling as he briefly pulled Deanna into his arms, the soft flannel of his shirt smelling like chili powder and Old Spice and her childhood.

Deanna pulled away, wiping at her eyes. "When?"

"Soon as I get packed," he said as Austin stormed back into the kitchen, clearly bummed.

"Smoky got under the bed where I can't reach him." Chuckling, Gus bent at the waist, his hands on his knees.

"So let's go see what we've got in the pantry, huh? Because this pretty lady's right, this is perfect baking weather…"

"So Deanna's really stuck here until after she delivers?"

Josh took his eyes off the road for a microsecond to dart a glance at his older brother Zach, who'd come along to ensure Josh's latest rescue was going to a good home. One of the perks of having a veterinarian in the family.

Of course, that also meant another brother up in his business. And they had a good twenty minutes yet before they got back to town.

"Yep," he said, ignoring Thor's hot panting in his ear. Dog had breath like a damn dragon.

He sensed his brother's frown. "She good with that?"

"What do you think?" Because even Zach would probably remember Deanna's glee when she'd been "sprung" from the confines of living in—or at least near—a town too small to even have a movie theater. "Not like she has a choice, though."

"S'pose not." Zach paused. "She got anything for the baby? Like a crib or bassinet or something? Clothes? A car seat?"

"And since when did you become a mother hen?"

"Since the moment I realized I *was* the mother hen," Zach said quietly, and Josh flinched, since Zach's wife had died in a car wreck when his own boys were still small. Heck, Liam had barely been a year old. Granted, his brother was recently, and blissfully, engaged. But there'd been a long time when, despite their parents' hands-on support, Zach had also known what it was like not only to be a single parent, but the *only* parent. Still, Josh felt like an idiot, that the full ramifications of Deanna's forced extended stay hadn't dawned on him sooner. As in, babies needed *stuff.*

The dog slurped his tongue back into his mouth and flopped on the backseat with a huge sigh. "I've got Austin's crib somewhere," Josh said. "I suppose that'd work. Although I gave away his baby clothes—"

"She's having a girl. Girls need pink. And…" His older brother waved his hand. "Frills."

"I doubt the kid will care. Or Dee." Since she'd never been a girly-girl even as a kid. Far as he could tell, that hadn't changed. In that respect the big city hadn't rubbed off on her. But then, what did he know? Maybe the Goth-meets-lumberjack look was all the rage in the nation's capital these days.

"You'd be surprised," Zach said, like he was suddenly some wise old woman, jeebus. "We can ask Val, maybe? See if she's still got Risa's baby clothes?"

While Josh imagined his sister-in-law would be only too happy to donate to the cause—if she still had anything to donate—suddenly that didn't seem right. Or fair. A used crib was one thing. Nothing wrong with used clothes, either—God knew Austin had worn whatever Josh could scrounge, and both he and the kid were good with that, he thought as he pulled up to his brother's little house in town, next door to his veterinary clinic. But somehow…

"So maybe we should give her one of those parties where people bring things for the baby."

"A shower?" Zach said.

"Right. That. Then we could ship most of it back east when she leaves."

Because that's where her life had been for more than ten years, and whatever they'd meant to each other before had only been a childhood thing. Period. Whatever Josh felt for Dee now…it was empathy, most likely. Knowing what it felt like to be abandoned, to get stuck with the full responsibility for something—someone—someone *else* had an equal hand in creating.

Pushing open the truck's door, Zach nodded. "That might work," he said as his own two streaked out the front door and down the steps to rush the truck, while grinning, eleven-year-old Landon—Zach's soon-to-be stepson—hung back on the porch with his hands plugged into his hoodie's pouch, clearly enjoying his new role as big brother. Zach hauled his youngest boy up into his lap, ruffling Liam's bright red curls. "You want to get Mom on it, or you want me to?"

"No, I'll talk to her."

A half hour later, the dog racing ahead, Josh walked through the hacienda's front door to relieve Gus of baby-sitting duty, fully intending to take the boy back to the foreman's cabin where they'd been living since his father's retirement. Except all manner of cooking smells greeted him, tangling with the most exuberant rendition of "Deck the Halls" he'd ever heard. What he *could* hear, that is, over Deanna's and Austin's laughter.

In fact, the pair were making so much noise they never even noticed Josh leaning against the door frame with his arms crossed, taking in the various pots bubbling on the stove, the loaves of fresh bread cooling on racks on the counter…the six-inch high chocolate cake on a stand beside the bread, the swirled frosting gleaming like satin in the overhead lights.

And in the middle of the kitchen, a very pregnant woman and his little boy, belting their hearts out to the cat, who was lying in front of the woodstove with a pained expression. Never mind nothing was keeping him there other than his own stubbornness.

A million feelings knifed Josh right in the chest, half of which he couldn't even define, the other half of which he didn't want to. But when the music—coming from Deanna's phone propped against the Mexican-tiled back-splash—stopped, Josh slowly applauded the pair, making Deanna clamp a hand to her chest and whirl around, as Austin beelined for him like his nephews had his brother a little bit ago.

"We made dinner!" the kid said, all bright-eyed and flushed, and some of those feelings twisted a little harder. "An' cake! An' I helped!"

"I can see that," Josh said, giving his son a big, sloppy kiss—the giggles slayed him, every time—before setting him down again and meeting Deanna's equally bright eyes, glittering underneath her crazy, spiky hair almost as much as that tiny diamond stud in her nose. "Where's Gus?"

"I kicked him off the island." At Josh's puzzled expression, she laughed. "For his own good. He finally admitted how hard the last several months have been on him. So I made him go take some Gus time."

"And he actually did?"

"But only after I convinced him I could use the practice. With a kid, I mean. Did you know about his moving back to Las Cruces?"

Josh nodded. "He told me this morning, before I left. Although I figured it was coming."

"Because we're selling the Vista."

"I'm sure that played a big part in his decision."

"I'm sorry—"

"Things are what they are, Dee. Although…" He glanced around the kitchen the designer had pronounced "retro chic." Whatever. "It's hard to imagine the place without Gus. Hell, it's hard to imagine…"

"*You* not being here," she said gently.

God knows he didn't want to do a guilt trip on the woman. But he wasn't gonna lie, either.

"I'm not sure I'm real good with change."

"Don't underestimate yourself," Dee said, nodding toward Austin, down on his knees a few feet away, vroom-vrooming a little truck. "Seems to me you adapted just fine to that little surprise."

Maybe, maybe not, Josh thought, as, after a huge, toothy yawn and a big stretch Smoky finally decided he'd had it, swiping up against Josh's leg before stalking out of the kitchen. Josh halfheartedly brushed fur off his jeans, then faced Dee again. "Thought you were supposed to be taking it easy. Yes, Mom called me," he said to her frown. "Deal."

Dee swatted in his direction, then clump-waddled back to the stove, where she started lifting lids and stirring things and generally making him crazy. In what might've been, under other circumstances, a very good way. The sweater underneath her flannel shirt was less baggy today, hugging her breasts and belly and reminding him how insanely sexy a pregnant woman could be. Even in hiking boots. From her phone, about a thousand people started singing "Joy to the World."

"I think babypie finally shifted—my back's not hurting as much. Besides, I've always found cooking..." She dipped a wooden spoon into the bubbling concoction, lifted it toward Josh to taste. "Very therapeutic. Helps settle my thoughts." Josh came closer, curling his fingers around her wrist to steady the spoon before taking a taste, ignoring the not-so-slight *Oh, yeah?* in his groin when her pulse and his fingertips collided. However, back to the food. He had no idea what it was—although vegetables and a whole mess of spices were involved—but his taste buds were very happy campers right now. Even if other parts of him...weren't.

"Wow. What is it?"

"Just something I whipped up from what was around. Kind of a Southwest ratatouille."

"Rata-what?"

"Never mind." Her brow crumpled. "And your verdict?"

He took the spoon from her to scoop up another bite, nodding and grunting out, "It's okay," and her smile warmed him even more than the spices. Which suddenly kicked in, setting everything on fire between his mouth and his stomach. Perfect.

Handing back the spoon, Josh yanked open the fridge for a bottle of water, gulping half of it down before twisting the cap back on and getting out, "Might be a bit too much for the kid, though."

"There's a milder version on the other burner. Already kid-tested and approved. Huh, sweetie?" she said when Austin sidled up to her and she tugged him close.

"It's dee-LISH-shus!"

Josh looked at her, noticing her flushed cheeks, how her eyes were the color of root beer. So of course now he was craving root beer. "You got him to eat vegetables? What are you, a magician?"

She shrugged, her eyes twinkling. "Maybe." Her gaze followed Austin as he ran off to play with the dog now, then swung back to Josh, a soft smile curving her lips. The music changed, to some carol he couldn't name offhand. "I decided I could either sit and mope about how absolutely nothing is playing out the way I envisioned it, or I could cook a fabulous meal—and eat it—and hang out with the cutest four-year-old, ever…" She grinned. "And decorate the hell out of this house for Christmas."

"Um…you do realize it's two weeks yet until Thanksgiving?"

"Hey, once Halloween's over, I'm good." She reached for three bowls from the cabinet closest to the stove. "Besides, we'll have to decorate for the party, right? Might as well get an early start. Since I'm not going to get *less* pregnant."

His stomach rumbling and his brain churning, Josh silently watched her ladling her concoctions into the bowls. "You're really okay with this, then?"

Dee shot him a funny look, then gestured for Josh to sit at the head of the big table before calling Austin to join them, pouring the kid a glass of milk.

"I'm *making* it okay," she said, lowering herself into her own chair. "Especially since you're right, the community needs this party. I know they probably think I didn't care about them, since I haven't been around much, but…"

She glanced down, a wave of color washing over her cheeks. "My wanting to get away was never about the people." She twisted her fork over her bowl for a moment, then lifted her eyes to his. "Never."

"Then…" Josh winked at a wiggling Austin, who grinned around a mouthful of food, before meeting Dee's gaze again. "Let's go all-out, maybe even hire a band. And, hey, fireworks. It's the end of an era," he said to Dee's lifted brows as Austin yelled, *"Fireworks?"* between them, instantly on board with the idea. "Might as well go out with a bang, right?" He chuckled. "Literally. So whaddya say?"

"I think…" Dee smiled. "I think it sounds perfect. The perfect way to honor Dad—oh, sweetie!" she said as a tsunami of ice-cold milk washed across the table…and straight into Josh's lap.

"I'm sorry, Daddy!" Austin said, eyes huge with tears as Josh jumped to his feet and Thor dashed under the table, lapping up the puddle faster than it formed.

"It's okay, buddy, not to worry." Never mind that his nuts were shrinking faster than the polar ice caps. *Damn*, that was cold. "I used to spill my milk at least once a day when I was little." Josh grabbed his napkin to blot at least some of the moisture, palming Austin's shoulder with his other hand. Out of the corner of his eye he caught the blur that was Deanna, gathering towels and a sponge, then zoom-waddling back to the table, kneeing the disappointed dog out of the way to drop towels on the floor. Then, grunting, she lowered herself onto her hands and knees. Which couldn't be good. Could it?

Wringing the sponge into a little bowl, she looked up at Josh, mischief sparkling in her eyes. "You spilled a glass of milk every day?"

"I did. Until my mother wised up and found one of those lidded cups with a straw...*dog*! No!"

Desperately trying to fend off Thor's milky kisses, Dee toppled over onto her butt, shrieking in laughter, her howls only egging the dumb dog on and dissolving his little boy into a torrent of giggles.

"Honestly, mutt—" His own mouth twitching, Josh grabbed the dog's collar and hauled him off his "victim," at the same time tugging the front of his jeans to get the damp away from his junk.

With that, Dee lost it completely, now laughing so hard she was snorting. An instant later Austin threw himself in her arms...and like somebody'd flipped a switch the laughter died as suddenly as it'd started. Dee wrapped his little boy close, laying her cheek in his hair and rocking him, and Josh felt like he was being crushed from the inside.

"It's okay, baby," she said. "It was an accident, it's okay."

Except it wasn't okay, was it? At all.

"I need to get out of these wet pants."

A crease wedged between her brows, Dee glanced up at him, giving Austin's noggin a quick kiss before gently pushing him off her lap.

"I'm sure," she said, then lifted her hands so Josh could haul her to her feet, and her belly grazed his, and her crazy-sweet laughter still rang in his ears, and the image of her cradling his son was burned into his brain, and Josh thought, *Hell.* "So why don't you run on back and change," she said, as the dog checked out the floor again in case Dee'd missed a stray molecule or two. "I'll watch the little guy—"

"Actually we should probably go."

Not even a boisterous rendition of "God Rest Ye Merry, Gentlemen" could pierce the silence now throbbing between them. Until Austin's tiny, "Is it because I spilled my milk?" shattered that silence.

Ah, jeez...

"Not at all, guy," Josh said, scooping the kid into his arms.

"Then how come we have to go?"

"Yeah, *Daddy*," Dee said, her expression as confused as his son's. With a generous dose of *pissed* tossed in for good measure. "How come?"

God knew she deserved an explanation. But how could he give her a reason for his sudden about-face with Austin right here? Especially since Austin *was* the reason?

He was pretty sure, anyway.

"By the time I change it'll be close to this guy's bedtime. No point in coming back over only to leave ten minutes later."

Her eyes narrowed. Because he was a lousy liar. And nobody knew that better than Dee.

But all she did was grab their bowls and tromp back to the kitchen, one hopeful dog at her heels. "Let me pack some of this up for you, then—"

"You don't have to—"

"I can't possibly eat it all, Josh. It'll just go to waste."

"Okay." He swallowed. "Thanks."

A few painful minutes later she handed him a bag bulging with plastic containers, as well as a cake carrier with most of the cake, before walking him to the back door, rubbing her belly. A gust of frigid air swept in when he opened it; boy and dog streaked off toward the foreman's house.

"Well. 'Night—"

"All I wanted," Dee then said in a small, brittle voice, "was to be useful. *Helpful.* To do something good for somebody else. For you. And Austin. But mainly for you. Because I'm long overdue saying thank you."

"For...what?"

"Being my friend when we were kids. Because you didn't have to do that." Her eyes veered to his, their brown depths bottomless in the half light. "So what'd I do wrong now?"

"Nothing," he said quietly, looking away.

"You sure?"

"Positive," he said, screwing his hat back on before walking out into cold night, feeling like crap and not having clue one what to do about it. Because whether his fears were valid or not, the idea of somebody else suffering for them wasn't sitting well. Wasn't until later that night, after he'd cleaned more frosting off Austin than there'd been on the cake and gotten him tucked into bed, that he remembered his promise to Zach, to handle the shower.

Standing at the front window looking toward the Big House, Josh sighed, making Thor come up to lick his hand, wanting to make it better. Maybe one of these days, Josh thought as he stroked the dog's smooth head, life would be easy. Or at least, eas*ier*.

But he wasn't counting on it.

Chapter Five

By the week before Thanksgiving, winter was teasing northern New Mexico with longer and more frequent visits. Cold, white stuff had fallen from the sky more days than it hadn't, although rarely hard enough to close school. Just enough to turn the countryside into a sparkly winter wonderland and for the ski resort to open early, much to the town's delight. Since, Deanna remembered, a longer season meant more tourists traipsing through town and subsequently more moola trickling into Whispering Pines' coffers.

So between the weather and the various worker bees readying the house for sale this was the first chance she'd had to reacquaint herself with the little village she'd called home once upon a time, its shops and little galleries, the quaint town plaza that would shortly wear its holiday finery, every pathway and roof lined with luminarias on Christmas Eve.

She'd have a baby by then, she realized, the thought zinging through her like a jolt of electricity. Although whether or not she and Josh would have mended things between them, she had no idea. A thought that, on top of

Gus's departure a couple of days before, made her very sad. And lonely, truth be told.

Brushing snow off her head and shoulders, Deanna hurried into Annie's Place, the only eating establishment in town that catered to locals more than *touristas*. The fare was time-honored and hearty and heartily chile-infested— red, green or that combination of both known in New Mexico as "Christmas"—and as soon as Deanna entered she felt catapulted back in time. The classic diner decor, if you could call it that, hadn't changed one iota from when she and Josh would come in as kids, for burgers and fries and shakes as thick as cement. Smells were the same, too, mouthwateringly spicy and greasy and perfect, she thought on a smile as she unwrapped herself from her shawl and slid into a booth next to a window facing the plaza.

She recognized the waitress from the memorial, as the blonde apparently did her, her bright blue eyes sympathetic as she set down a glass of water, along with a straw and a menu large enough to shelter a stadium. "I'm Val," she said with a bright grin, yanking an order pad out of the pocket of the black apron allowing little more than a peek of a boldly striped sweater, tight blue jeans. "Levi's wife?"

"I know, I remember. Although I didn't realize you worked here—"

"Only the lunch rush these days. Although today's crazy slow, for some reason." Still smiling, Val nodded toward the menu. "You need a minute?"

"Actually, no," Deanna said, handing back the menu. "Green chili cheeseburger, well done. Double order of fries, chocolate shake."

Humor danced in Val's eyes. "Anything else?"

"As if I'll ever be able to eat all of that," Deanna said, and Val released the chuckle she'd clearly been holding in.

She called out the order to the bald black dude behind

the counter, then turned back to Deanna. "Josh told us, about you being grounded here. I'm so sorry. About everything. I know what it's like, when life throws you for a loop."

Deanna imagined she did, since Val's first husband had died while deployed to Afghanistan, leaving her a widow with two small children. Definitely put her own situation in perspective. But all she said was, "Thanks. I didn't really know Tomas," she said gently. "But Levi's a good guy. Crazy as a loon, but good."

Val chuckled. "True on both counts. My girls and I are very blessed—"

"And it's about time you dragged your skinny butt in here!" Annie called out, sweeping across the restaurant to haul Deanna out of the booth and against her skinny chest, only to then gift her with the Annie Stink Eye underneath a messy updo that was grayer than Deanna remembered. "What? You think you're too good for us now?"

"Not hardly," Deanna said, laughing. "But I've been insanely busy, getting the house ready to sell. It's taking a lot more time than Josh and I had expected."

It was fleeting, granted, but the disapproval that flashed across both women's faces made her immediately regret mentioning an obviously sore subject. Even though they had to see that without her father, the Vista was only a ranch. A place. A *thing*. Then again, she knew that tradition was often what held little rural communities like this together, that what some people might call progress others saw as a threat. But then, as if reading her thoughts, the older woman took Deanna's hands in hers, her freckled skin so pale as to be almost translucent.

"Change is never easy," she said softly as Val left to tend to her other customers. "But I know you and Josh will do what's best. Well. That husband of mine'll have your food ready in a jiffy. It's so good to see you, Dee." She gave Deanna's hands a quick squeeze. "You've been missed."

Missed? Deanna thought as she wedged herself and her little passenger back in the booth. Since she'd never felt much like a real part of the community as a kid, she somehow doubted it. She did wonder, though, why she'd never really felt connected to the place her father had obviously loved with his whole heart and soul. What made her feel so itchy now, fighting that same trapped feeling that had plagued her adolescence?

And yet—her gaze drifted out the window, toward the little square where a half-dozen toddlers, under the watchful eye of their caregivers, were having a ball in a small playground that hadn't been there before—her life back east this past little while hadn't exactly been all that, either, had it? Obviously not, if she'd been so quick to grab at a Something More that turned out to be nothing at all.

As her other customers headed out, Val brought Deanna her order. Along with, apparently, a side order of conflicted, since the waitress seemed hesitant to leave after setting down Deanna's food. Grasping her burger, Deanna looked up at Josh's sister-in-law.

"Is something wrong?"

"No, not at all. It's just…well, I was wondering if you'd like company. Except then I thought if I asked and you didn't, then you might feel obligated to say yes, just to be polite. And how awkward would that be?"

"I'd love company," Deanna said, smiling. "And no, I'm not just saying that to be polite."

"You sure?"

"Positive. The funny thing is," she said as Val slid into the booth across from her, "I used to think I was a loner. Probably because I was an only child so I was used to it—"

"Yeah? Me, too. And please, dig in. Before the fries get cold."

Deanna took a bite of her burger, savoring the exquisite little explosions of green chile bliss on her tongue. "But there's a difference between needing alone time and feeling cut off from the world."

"You talking about then? Or now?"

Heh. She'd set herself up for that one, hadn't she? Never mind how gently Val had asked the question. Angry with herself for coming perilously close to dumping on someone she didn't even know, for godssake, Deanna stabbed her fry into that puddle of ketchup, hot tears pricking at her eyes.

"Sorry."

"For what?"

Unable to speak—let alone eat—Deanna shook her head.

"Hey." Val stretched across the table to clamp a warm hand around Deanna's wrist, her eyes full of *Don't mess*. "You're pregnant and your daddy just passed and you're stuck someplace I'm guessing you don't really want to be. I'm also guessing you have no idea what comes next. So you clearly need to talk to somebody." She leaned back again, crossing her arms over her stomach. "And right now that somebody's me."

"But—"

"Oh, hell, honey—why'd you think I came over here?"

Fighting a smile and tears, both, Deanna grabbed her napkin and blew her nose. "Because you're nosy?"

At that, the blonde belted out a laugh far too loud for somebody that tiny. "I'd be lying if I said no. But like I said, I've also been where you are. Not exactly the same circumstances, but feeling like your whole world's just imploded? Hell, yeah. And I was pretty cut off, too, as a kid. Again, different reasons. Still. I know what it's like, needing to talk to *somebody* before your brain melts. For me it was Annie," she said, nodding over her shoulder at the older woman, chatting with a slightly grizzled-looking, bearded man at the counter. "In fact, if it hadn't been for her I doubt I would've survived my teen years. Before I met Tommy, anyway. And of course now poor Levi gets the brunt of my emotional upchucking—" smiling a little, Deanna finally stuffed that fry in her mouth "—but it rolls right off his back. Then again, that's how the Talbots are. All of 'em. Listeners. Real good ones, too."

Deanna tried the shake, but it needed to melt a little before she could actually drink it. "True. In fact, I used to bend poor Josh's ear something awful when we were kids."

"So Levi said. And now?"

Blowing a short laugh through her nose, Deanna poked a crisp fry in the blonde's direction. "And now we come to the real reason for this little chat," she said, which got another brief chuckle.

"What I said, about knowing how you feel? Meant every word of it. But, you're right, Levi's also concerned about Josh. It's a twin thing, apparently."

"No, it's a Talbot thing."

"That, too."

Deanna's own smile faded as she sighed. "I know Josh doesn't really want to sell the Vista. And I completely understand why. So now I get to add guilt to all the other crap in my head."

A moment passed before Val got up to get herself a cup of coffee from behind the counter, then brought it back, stirring in enough cream and sugar to turn it into basically hot ice cream. "Actually Josh hasn't said much to Levi about it, although we can guess how he feels. But to be honest, I'm of two minds about all of this. On the one hand, heck, he's never lived anyplace else. So of course he's attached to the Vista. On the other..."

Val sipped her coffee, then squinted out the window, cradling the stoneware mug in her hands before facing Deanna again. "It wouldn't be a bad thing, either, for him to start over somewhere that would be completely his from the get-go. Make his own name from his own operation, rather than continuing to live in your father's shadow. Although this is strictly between you and me, since it's not exactly a popular opinion."

"Pretty much what I said to him, actually. But why are you telling me this?"

After another sip, Val set down the mug, staring at it for a long moment before lifting her eyes again. "Because I think this is fixing to blow up in everybody's face, and since my husband is part of that 'everybody' I'd like it all to work out without *too* many hurt feelings."

"In other words, they all think I'm the bad guy for wanting to sell."

"Didn't say that—"

"Didn't have to." Deanna pushed out a sigh. "I can't afford to hang on to some place where I'm not even going to live. As wobbly as my life might feel right now, I know I can rebuild it. There, not here. Because I simply can't see..." Her gaze returning to the square, with all those little kids running around and laughing, she huffed out another, much more aggravated breath. "I almost wish Dad had left it all to Josh."

"No, you don't," Val said, so sharply Deanna looked back at her. "Your first duty is to that child. If selling the ranch means ensuring *her* future, then nothing else matters. Being a single mom is *hard*. I should know. And what anybody else thinks...tough."

Deanna was stunned. "You're really not on their side?"

Val smirked. "I'm on the side of whatever happening that's best for all concerned. Especially when a baby's involved. Besides, Josh is a big boy, he'll figure it out. And get over it. Speaking of whom…he said the renovation's gotten more involved than you guys had hoped? Something about the home inspection turning up a bunch of problems?"

Still reeling from the idea of having possibly found an ally, Deanna's mouth pulled tight. A few little tweaks, the designer had said. The vintage look will work to your advantage, she'd said. Some paint, some furniture rearrangements, boom.

Boom was right.

"Lead pipes," Deanna breathed out. "'Nuff said."

"Ouch. But the more that gets fixed, the higher price you'll get. Right?"

"In theory, anyway."

"So there you go. And again, Josh will deal. Since it's not like he has any choice."

Maybe not. However…

Crap. Everything told her not to go where her brain was yanking her like an overeager puppy. But talking about Josh and the house naturally led to her thinking about his bizarre reaction the night of the dinner fiasco, as if he'd come face-to-face with something he hadn't realized was lurking in the shadows, ready to pounce. Whether Val was the right person to talk to about it, Deanna wasn't entirely sure, but she was here and seemingly available. As opposed to Josh, who for obvious reasons couldn't be her go-to person anymore. Not about this, anyway. Or Emily, up to her eyeballs in wedding planning—

"Do you have any idea what happened between Josh and Austin's mother?"

Val's brows lifted. "He hasn't told you?"

"No. Which is weird since he's all about being honest and open and stuff."

That got another laugh. "When it suits his purpose, most likely. Like most men. Unfortunately I'm not sure how many blanks I can fill in. I know what Levi told me, but I don't really know how much Josh shared with him. Or how much of that Levi shared with me." Val crossed her arms again. "Why? What's going on with you two? Aside from the house stuff, I mean."

So Deanna told Val about Josh's abrupt departure the other night, about how every time she'd offered to watch Austin since then, he'd give her a polite but insistent, "Thanks, but I've got it covered."

Frowning, Val snitched a fry from Deanna's plate. "Okay…" she said slowly, "after I came back to Whispering Pines with the girls, and Josie immediately latched on to Levi when he started hanging around…" Chewing, she glanced out the window, then back at Deanna. "I might've lit into him at one point, so afraid she'd get attached and then he'd decide he'd fulfilled his duty to Tommy—they were best friends, did you know?" Deanna shook her head. "Yeah. Anyway, they enlisted at the same time, and Tommy made Levi promise…" She swallowed. "He made Levi promise to check up on me and the girls if anything happened. Which I didn't know. So when he showed up, I wasn't entirely sure what his motive was. And frankly I don't think Levi did either, at the time. In any case, my daughter had been through enough, losing her daddy. That last thing I wanted was for her to get hurt. Again."

"So you think Josh feels the same way about Austin."

"I don't know for sure. Obviously. But it makes sense, right?"

It did. Especially since the very thought had occurred to Deanna one night when she'd gotten up for the umpteenth time to pee and her defenses were down along with her panties. She did remember, however, letting out a little "Oh…" and the cat meowing back at her in reply, as if to say, *Took you long enough, dimwit.*

Deanna sighed. Since God knew she understood how it felt to have all the responsibility for another human being dumped in your lap. "Although Austin wouldn't even remember his mother leaving, would he? Gus said he was still a baby—"

"No," Val said slowly, snagging another fry when Deanna pushed the plate toward her. "But Josh remembers. Besides, the little guy's older now…"

The last part of Val's sentence faded into the roar inside Deanna's head, where the first part painfully, and persistently, echoed.

That *Josh* remembered.

"So this isn't about Austin at all."

Val smiled, then slid across the booth's faux leather seat, grabbing her mug as she stood. "You wanna take the leftovers? I'll bring you a box."

"Um…sure. Only…what's Josh's favorite thing on the menu?"

That got a funny look. "You really want to go there?"

"No. But anything's better than this impasse between us."

"Got it. Then same as you, pretty much. Except he likes onion rings on his burger. And he usually tacks on a piece of my peach pie at the end."

"Then pack up an extra order to go," she said, handing over her credit card. "With two pieces of pie. Oh, and whatever Austin might like, too."

"Coming right up."

A few minutes later, Val returned with a stuffed plastic bag, as well as a foam box for Deanna and the credit card slip.

"You know what's crazy?" Val said as Deanna signed the slip, then packed her leftovers into the box. "That you and I were both raised right here in Whispering Pines, and yet we never knew each other."

Slipping the box into the bag with the rest of the food, Deanna looked up. "You never came to any of the parties out at the ranch? The Fourth? Christmas?"

"Not until after I met Tommy, nope. And you were gone by that time."

"Too bad." Deanna gathered her purse and the bag, grunting a little as she heaved herself out of the booth and onto her feet. "I could've used a girlfriend back then."

"Same here," Val said, then gave her a hug, whispering, "Well, you got one now, honey," before letting her go. "I love the Talbots, I really do, but they are definitely a force to be reckoned with."

"I remember," Deanna said, gathering the bag. "Thanks again. For everything." Then she cocked her head. "So how'd you handle the situation with Levi and your daughter?"

A slow smile spread across Val's mouth. "I married him," she said, then crossed the restaurant to take care of a couple who'd just come in.

Josh almost jumped when he opened his door to a snow-flecked, grinning Dee, her cheeks flushed from the cold as she held up the diner's take-out bag. Thor, naturally, swarmed her like she was carrying balloons and a check for five million dollars. Or hamburgers. Thor's needs were simple.

"It's…three thirty." Because the *time* was the most re-markable thing about all of this.

"Which is exactly when we used to eat these after school, as I recall."

On the odd occasion when Gus would pick Deanna up from the private school in Taos where she went after the sixth grade, then Josh and Levi from theirs in town, before dropping them all off at Annie's. Not every day, no—Granville was more likely to chauffer his daughter himself—but often enough that memories now flooded back. Especially of those days when Levi would claim he had other/better things to do, leaving Josh and Dee sitting across from each other, Dee talking his ear off as they inhaled their burgers, oozing with gobs of melted cheese and piled high with green chili and onion rings. His lips twitched, remembering how even at twelve, thirteen, beanpole Deanna could pack it away as well as any cowboy.

How at that point he'd thought of her as a sister.

Josh caught a whiff of what was in the bag and his mouth watered; he caught another whiff of something sweeter, her perfume or hair stuff or whatever, and his hormones wept. Then he remembered how he'd treated her that night and he shut his eyes, listening to his son playing in his room down the hall.

"Josh—?"

Sighing, he opened his eyes again, almost cringing at the confusion in hers. "You shouldn't've done this."

"Because you really don't want to hang out? Or because you were basically a jerk?"

He grimaced. "Do I have to answer that?"

"No. Although you do need to let me in before I freeze. And I promise," she said as she came inside, shedding that blanketlike thing she wore, "I won't speak to Austin, let alone touch him."

"Dammit, Dee—"

"I'm serious." She turned around, her eyes wide. Innocent. Except anything but. "I totally get why you wouldn't want us to bond. Because it wouldn't be fair to him, since I'm not staying. I can hardly be mad at you for wanting to protect your son, can I?"

And again, reality slammed into him, that once the house was sold she'd have no reason to return. Ever. Funny, how even though he'd only seen her a handful of times since she was fifteen, he now realized how he'd never really let go of that tiny flicker of possibility, way in the back of his brain, that they wouldn't lose contact entirely.

And, yes, his knee-jerk reaction—also again—was to put distance between them. But for one thing, he was starving, middle of the afternoon or not. And for another, maybe it was time he grew up already, and stopped getting mad every time something didn't go his way, or when life got bumpy. Because there would always be bumps, there would always be challenges and disappointments and aggravations, and what kind of father would he be if he didn't show his son how to handle the crap with at least a *little* grace?

"I think we can work it out," he said, going into the tiny kitchen where his mother had prepared countless meals for four growing boys and a husband, now basically reduced to the place where coffee, cold cereal and Hamburger Helper happened. "As long as he knows you're only visiting, we're good."

"You sure?"

"No. Then again, he's got his grandmother, and two new aunts now—"

"So plenty of maternal influences," she said, awkwardly levering herself up onto one of the two stools in front of the peninsula dividing the kitchen from the living space. "So I won't be missed. Got it."

His stomach jolted. But Josh turned to see humor sparkling in her eyes, and he thought, *Like hell, you won't be missed,* immediately followed by *Dammit.*

Because he remembered, how much he'd missed her when she'd left before. How he'd missed her dry humor and energy, even her excitement about her upcoming adventure. How her absence had left a huge, honking hole in his life he eventually realized he'd tried to fill in all the wrong ways, with all the wrong females.

Except even then he knew he had nothing to offer that could possibly compete with a world he couldn't even begin to fathom, let alone understand. Because they'd texted, at first, her messages filled with details of her new life, about museums and art galleries and concerts, about seeing this ballet company or that opera. Eventually, though, the texts had stopped. When, exactly, he couldn't remember. But he sure as hell knew why—because whatever they might have had in common before pretty quickly got whittled down to nothing. And now? After almost a dozen years?

He somehow doubted the chasm between them had *shrunk.*

"I guess," he said, pulling plates down out of the cupboard, "we can look at things one of two ways." He carried the dishes—survivors from his parents' "old" set—over to the small dining table behind her, making her swivel on the stool. "Either from the standpoint of what we lost..." He set down the plates, then turned to her, sliding one hand into his front pocket. "Or what we've gained from that person being part of our lives."

Her eyebrows lifted. "Wow. Not what I would've expected, considering—"

"How I acted the other night? Me, either. And to be frank, that's a fairly recent revelation."

"How recent?"

"Thirty seconds ago?" he said, and she laughed, her smile softening a moment later.

"It's a good philosophy. I like it. Seize the moment and all that."

"I guess." He sighed. "I apologize for being a punk, Dee. Really."

Her gaze wrestled with his for a long moment. "And I doubt anybody would blame you, considering everything that's happened in the last little while. I sure as heck don't. But I'm glad…" The smile came back, brighter. Steadier, maybe. "I'm glad we're friends again."

"Yeah. Me, too."

She gave him a thumbs-up, then finally seemed to really see the house, methodically rubbing her belly. Between her hair, the tunic-like thing stretched over the bulge and her cuffed boots, now she looked like a pregnant elf. Except her ears were a lot cuter. "Holy moly. And I thought the Big House was in a time warp."

"The way I see it," Josh said as he opened the bag of food, nearly passing out from the heavenly smells, "if it still works, why replace it? I swear the sofa's upholstered in steel." Thor whined, slurping his slobber back in when Josh glared at him. He pointed to the dog's bed in the far corner of the living room; hanging his head, the dog trudged off, collapsing with a huge, dramatic sigh and giving Josh eyes to match.

"True," Dee said. "But dude, the stove is poop-colored."

He laughed, and for a moment it was like it used to be between them, before his voice lowered and Deanna grew breasts and he was suddenly very, very aware of said breasts. And even more aware that Granville noticed Josh's awareness, no matter how hard he tried to pretend nothing had changed, that he and Dee were still just friends.

And the thing was, on the surface it was true. Josh had

never tried anything—he wouldn't have dared—and she'd never indicated she wanted him to. But if she'd stayed...

"Austin!" he called out. "Come see who's here!"

"Who?" his son called as he ran down the bungalow's short hall, actually gasping when he saw Dee, his entire little face lighting up. How on earth had she made that much of an impression on the boy, that quickly? And yet, when he ran into her arms—she'd somehow slid off the stool to squat in front of them, laughing when his enthusiasm and her shifted center of gravity collided—it was obvious she had.

That thing he'd said, about being cool with the moment? Easier said than done.

Her puffy feet propped on the banged-up ottoman in front of the deeply cushioned chair from which she was probably going to have to be excavated, Deanna watched the flickering flames in Josh's fireplace, smiling at the blended giggles and laughter floating down the hall from Austin's bedroom. Although, despite a tummy blissfully crammed with the rest of her lunch and a huge piece of the best peach pie she'd ever eaten—as well as no small relief that she and Josh had apparently mended a few fences between them—neither could she deny the melancholy scratching at the door of her consciousness, whining for attention.

Because as gratifying as it was to see how much Josh clearly loved his son, watching and listening to their interaction only brought her own situation into even sharper focus. In a few weeks' time she'd be a single parent herself, with all the complications that entailed, piled on top of a life that was already a tangled mess. Hell, she seriously doubted her father would have been nearly as disappointed in her as she was in herself.

Except—her mouth pulled flat, Deanna stroked her belly, only to smile when a little foot pushed against her hand—she could either see this as a failure, or an opportunity. So let's hear it for Door #2, right? Somehow, she'd land on her feet, give her baby girl the life she deserved. And you know what? She'd be stronger for figuring it all out on her own. Maybe this wasn't how she'd ever envisioned becoming a parent, but since this was the hand she'd been dealt, at least she could be the best damn possible example to her daughter she could.

So there, world.

Josh came back into the living room, chuckling and shaking his head at her before squatting in front of the fire to poke at the logs, sending a cheerful spray of sparks up the chimney.

"What's so funny?" she asked, trying not to stare at the way all those muscles bunched and shifted underneath his flannel shirt. Because Skinny Dude had definitely left the building.

More muscles shifted—just kill her now—when he stood to set the poker back in its stand by the hearth. Swiping his palms across his bum, he turned, his grin warming her far more than the fire. "You look like you might not move until spring."

"I *feel* like I might not move until spring." Ripping her gaze away, she stroked the chair's soft, worn arms. "Was this always so comfortable?"

Josh went into the kitchen to pour himself a cup of coffee from the old-school Mr. Coffee. "You don't remember, then?" he said, taking a sip before setting down his mug on the peninsula, and she found herself considering that a pair of soft, kind eyes set into a hard-angled, beard-shadowed face was quite possibly the deadliest combination, ever.

"Remember what?"

He hesitated, then said, "It was right after your mama died, and Granville was…well, kind of a mess."

Her eyes burned. "That, I do remember. Then again, so was I."

"Exactly. So Mom brought you over here to give you a break. Dad made a fire, and you crawled up into that chair, all wrapped up in that very afghan…and you cried yourself to sleep. Nobody wanted to move you, so we didn't." His gaze lowered to the cup for a moment before lifting again to her. "For the next, I don't know, several weeks, maybe? That was your chair. You'd come straight here when you got home from school, crawl up in it and pass out."

"You're kidding?"

"Nope." He picked up the mug and came into the living room, lowering himself into the middle of that godawful plaid sofa a few feet away. Thor immediately crawled up to curl into a ball on the cushion next to Josh, smashed up against his thigh, sighing when Josh's hand absently went to his ruff. "Doesn't even ring a bell?"

"Vaguely. Maybe." Deanna blew out a breath to rival the dog's, hiking the afghan higher on her chest. Not because she was cold, but because…oh, hell—who knew? "I guess I blotted a lot of that out." Then she pulled a face. "That must've been when it started. Or ended, actually."

"What?"

"My relationship with my dad." Frowning, she looked away, picking at a piece of grass or straw or something on the afghan. "We never talked about my mother, really. And certainly not her death." She expelled a harsh half laugh. "A family trait, obviously. In any case…" Her eyes went all tingly. "I used to wonder if Dad sent me away because he simply didn't want to deal with me. Or couldn't, anyway." Another strangled sound erupted from her throat. "And I've never said that to another living soul."

Deanna sensed more than saw Josh take another sip of his coffee before leaning sideways to set down his mug on the end table, his brows drawn. "You seemed happy enough to leave."

"Shoot, Josh—I was fifteen and bored out of my skull here. Which you know. I'd only been back east a couple of times but compared with Whispering Pines? DC was like Oz. Full of wonder and possibilities."

A small smile twitched at his mouth. "And this was Kansas."

"Exactly. But now…well. I'm thinking maybe my problem with feeling isolated had more layers than I could have possibly realized, let alone understood, when I was a kid. I know I was only fourteen when Mom died, but I'd like to think I still could've helped Dad through our grief. Somehow. That we could've helped each other. I mean, I tried my best to be a good girl, to make him proud of me…" She shook her head. "But if he wouldn't let me be there for him…"

"He was proud of you, Dee," Josh said softly. "That I can promise you."

"It would've been nice to hear it, though. At least sometimes. You know?" Her hand went to her cheek, swiping away a tear. "I just wish I could ask him what he was thinking. Why he pushed me away when we needed each other the most. We should have grown closer. Not even more apart than we had been."

Josh shifted on the sofa to cross his arms high on his chest, the move making the dog grunt, then sigh back to sleep. "I guess I didn't realize it was that bad."

"That makes two of us. Don't get me wrong, I never doubted Dad loved me. But why he seemed to have such a hard time showing me how he felt…" Her forehead pinched; she shook her head. "He was so generous to the community, to everyone else…" A tear escaped the corner of one eye; Deanna swiped it away. "I also don't know why I never tried to break down whatever the barrier was between us. Because it wasn't as if I didn't have a great example, right under my nose, of what a normal family looked like."

"And who was that?"

She barked out a laugh. "You guys, doofus. Yes, I know there were issues with Colin, with Levi. Later, anyway. But not for lack of your parents' trying. Not for lack of them *loving* you guys. So why was I so afraid to claim that for myself?"

Josh's eyes darkened. "You were a *kid*, Dee. It wasn't up to you, it was up to your father. You—"

He surged to his feet, making the dog jerk. "God knows I loved your dad. He was very good to me. To all of us, like you said. But I'm gonna say something I've never said to anyone else, either, which is that…" Looking up at the ceiling, he sucked in a breath, then brought his gaze back to hers. "That when it came to you, he screwed up. Epically. And I'm sorry…"

His mouth thinned. "When you first got back…it wasn't you I was mad at, it was him. Only I couldn't tell him why I was mad, so I took it out on you. Because you're right, I wasn't raised to give up on the people I love. Or am supposed to love, anyway. And my parents drummed it into our heads that a person's obligation to those people went way beyond making sure their physical needs were met. Which is why…"

He dropped back onto the couch, and Deanna's heart turned over in her chest.

"Which is why it still hurts that Austin's mom walked away?"

His eyes bored into hers. "How much do you know?"

"That your son's here with you. And she's obviously not."

A ragged sigh left his lungs. "Did you know Jordan's never, not once, even bothered to check up on him, ask how he's doing?"

"Never?"

"Nope."

"And you had no idea this was coming? Her walking out, I mean."

"I knew she wasn't exactly happy, that she felt like we were in limbo. Or she was, anyway. Not really together," he said, cupping the back of his neck as he sat forward again, "but forced to deal with each other because of the kid."

The dog, clearly annoyed at Josh's constant shifting, abandoned him for Deanna, wagging his tail as he laid his chin on her knee and gave her the most pitiful brown eyes in the history of dogdom.

Josh watched the beast for a moment, then said, "Still. I thought the arrangement was working as well as it could. And sure as hell I would've thought her own son might've been worth more to her than a mumbled *Sorry, I can't do this anymore*, when she dropped him off that last time." His gaze met Deanna's as she stroked Thor's head. "So when you told me about your baby's daddy…swear to God, if he'd been standing there? I would've punched his lights out." At her laugh, a smile tugged at his mouth. "Okay, maybe not. But I sure as hell would've told him off."

"I would've paid good money to see that," she said, and he snorted. From down the hall, they heard Austin laughing at something. Josh frowned.

"Is it weird, how much he likes to play by himself? I swear he'll go in there and I won't hear from him for hours. Seems like it, anyway."

"It's an only child thing," Deanna said quietly, rubbing

her tummy. "We're good at entertaining ourselves. We also need alone time, to recharge."

"I guess." He didn't sound convinced. Deanna smiled.

"You didn't lock him in there, for goodness' sake. When he wants you, he'll come out, right?"

"True."

"So…the thing between you and Austin's mother…it wasn't serious, then?" Josh's puzzled gaze swung to hers, and she shrugged. "Just wondered."

He pushed a sigh through his nose. "What it was, was a mistake. Plain and simple." A half smile played around his mouth. "But I expect you know how that goes."

"Lord, yes," she sighed out, and the smile stretched a little…followed by one of those no-big-deal guy shrugs that means anything but.

"Not exactly how I'd planned on becoming a father, though. Especially at twenty-four. And my folks…" He sagged back into the couch's cushions, his hands linked behind his head. "Oh, they rallied, of course they did. For Austin's sake. But I know they weren't happy. Dad, especially."

"And maybe you're being too hard on yourself. Or them—"

"Dad literally didn't speak to me for a week after I told them."

"Oh."

"Yeah. Although at least I did tell them," he said, nodding toward her belly.

Guess he had her there. The dog jumped onto her lap, even though there was no room—

"Thor!" Josh snapped his fingers, pointing to the floor. *"Down."*

"No, it's okay," Deanna said, laughing, as the dog shoved his hindquarters in her face, clumsily trying to find purchase until they figured it out: dog butt wedged between her hip and the chair's arm, dog front draped across her knees, baby belly shoved against dog head. Whatever worked.

"I'm not sure which of you is crazier," Josh said, shaking his head. But at least he was smiling. Sort of. "What about you? Was it serious between you and what's-his-name?"

"Phillippe. And it was on my end. Obviously. Although obviously not on his."

"And let me guess—you're beating yourself up over not being able to spot his douchebaggery."

"Pretty much, yep. I assume you've dated since then?" she said, desperate to shove the conversation back into his court.

His eyes narrowed—nice to see his BS meter was still in good working order—before his mouth turned down at the corners. "I'm a single dad who works twelve hours a day most days. When would I do that?"

"Oh, and like you couldn't find a babysitter. Please. That's an excuse, Josh. And you know it."

That got several seconds of hard staring before he said, "Maybe. But if nothing else, the whole thing—with Austin, with his mother—woke me up. Because life sure as hell got real, didn't it? What I was doing before—and believe me, I'm not proud of it—wasn't going to work anymore. It wasn't right. Especially now that there's this little person who one day is gonna be a big person who's gonna need to look up to his dad. Only thing is, I'm still not sure what *is* right. Or at least, how to go about making *right* happen."

"I know what you mean," she said with a tight smile. "Oh, boy, do I know what you mean."

"Is this the beginning of a whole 'men are scum' tirade?"

Scratching the space between the dog's shoulders, she smiled. "No. Not really. Although I guess Phillippe was. Is. God, I feel so bad for his wife. Since I doubt I was his first...dalliance. And I seriously doubt I'll be his last. Although who knows?" She frowned down at the now softly snoring dog. "Maybe they have an 'understanding'—"

"Daddy! Look what I made!"

Austin thundered into the room—the dog didn't even twitch—holding out a plastic block masterpiece that was rather...impressionistic. Josh hauled the child onto his lap, suitably—and seriously—admiring the creation. "That is so cool, dude. Can you tell me about it?"

With that, the child launched into a rapid-fire description of what was apparently a robot-weapon-vehicle hybrid, then snatched it from his father's hands to demonstrate its many amazing features. A second later Austin turned, holding it out to Deanna with that adorable baby-toothed grin.

"It's for you."

Deanna's heart stuttered. "Me?"

The child shook his head so hard his waves wobbled. "Uh-huh. 'Cause you brought me food."

"Jeez, the woman'll think I never feed you," Josh muttered, and a laugh bubbled up inside Deanna's chest. Especially as Austin's face turned into one big frown as he tried to process this information. Then he brightened.

"*Good* food."

The laugh exploded, startling the poor dog awake and off her lap. Still chuckling, Deanna held out her arms so the boy could take the dog's place. She shifted him on what was left of her lap, admiring her gift. And thinking how this would be her with her own child soon. *So* soon. "Thank you, sweetie," she pushed past what felt like a rock in her chest. "I love it."

"Really?"

"Really truly cross-my-heart."

"Okay, good. Hey—maybe the baby c'n play with it, after she's borned."

"Well, maybe not right after—she'll be too little. But later, absolutely." Deanna tugged Austin to her and planted a kiss in his curls. "I'm sure she'll love it."

"*Ex*cellent," he said, then wriggled off her lap and scampered back to his room. Deanna watched him zoom down the hall, then shoved one hand into the chair's arm to push herself to her feet, carefully holding the Duplo creation with her other. Josh rose as well.

"You don't have to keep that if you don't want—"

"Are you kidding?" she said, clutching the blocks to her bosom. "When a four-year-old gives you a present, you treasure it forever. Jeez…what rock were *you* born under?"

And the grin that slowly, steadily, spread across Josh's cheeks nearly did her in.

"You need me to walk you back?"

"I think I know the way. Besides which that would mean either leaving Austin here alone or dragging him with you, neither of which I'm about to let happen. But thanks. Good to know chivalry isn't completely dead."

There went that darkening thing in his eyes again. "I've always known how to treat a lady. It's how to have an actual relationship with one I seem to be a little sketchy on."

"And maybe that would depend on the lady?"

"You might have a point at that." He slid his fingers into his front pockets. "I know the reason you're home really sucks. But it's good to have you back, Dee. Even if only for a little while."

"Thanks," she said, then hauled her double-wide butt out of there before he could see the ambivalence in her eyes. Because while he was right, the reason she was back sucked, *being* back didn't. At least not nearly as much as she might've figured it would. Except…that wasn't necessarily a good thing.

Since what *would* suck, would be getting sucked into something neither she nor Josh wanted or needed or could even remotely deal with right now.

Or ever, actually.

Chapter Six

"So how do you want to do this?" Billie said, re-draping her stethoscope around her neck before hoisting Deanna back up to a sitting position on the exam table. "Home, hospital—which means a trek into Taos—or here at the center?"

Tugging down her getting-tighter-by-the-second top over her enormous middle, Deanna screwed up her face. "You're not going to yell at me about my blood pressure?"

"Since yelling at you, as you put it, would hardly reduce your stress…no. And in any case, being as it's not insanely high, I'm not worried. So. Decision time, sweetie. What's it gonna be?"

Dee smiled. She'd toured the facility, which easily rivaled the one in DC she'd planned on using. "I guess… here."

"Good," the midwife said, then helped Deanna down before sitting at her desk to add notes to Deanna's chart. Lowering her prodigious form onto the molded plastic chair beside Billie's desk, she caught the poster on the opposite wall, illustrating—in great detail—the birth process. At least the baby looked happy enough.

"Aside from that slightly elevated BP," Billie was saying, "everything else looks fine, no obvious risk factors, baby's in perfect position. And you'll be at thirty-seven weeks right before Thanksgiving." She looked up, her brown eyes twinkling behind her glasses, the lenses reflecting a dozen colors from her brightly patterned cardigan. "So you're good to go."

At Deanna's nervous laugh, Billie smiled.

"You scared?"

"Of giving birth? Not really." A flat-out lie, but whatever. "Of knowing what to do after? I've never even held a newborn before, let alone taken care of one. What if I screw up?"

"Oh, you can count on it. The good news is, the baby won't notice. Or care."

"Greaaat."

The midwife's eyes softened. "You having second thoughts? About keeping her?"

"Billie! Ohmigod, no! Of course I'm keeping her! Okay, so maybe doing this on my own hadn't been part of my game plan. And I have no illusions about how hard it's going to be. But..." Her eyes filled. "But I already love her."

"Then wait until you meet her," Billie said gently. "And once you do? That intuition will kick in harder than you have any idea. Of course you'll make mistakes. Sometimes even insanely stupid ones. Like the time I was so sleep deprived with the twins I forgot to strap Josh into his baby seat and he squirmed right out of it onto the floor. I bawled for a solid hour, convinced the Baby Police were going to come take my children away. He survived, *I* survived, and so will you. And as long as you're here, you'll have all the support you need. I promise."

Words that arrowed Deanna right between the eyes. Because who would've helped her in DC? Heaven knew not her aunt. And Emily was even more clueless than Deanna—

"Josh said at least the house is all done?"

"Um...yes," Deanna said on a released breath. "As of a couple of days ago." And Josh had been as good as his word, patching and painting walls and whatnot while Deanna kept Austin amused, mostly watching the baby's in utero interpretive dance routine. Man, what she wouldn't give to bottle those little boy belly laughs.

Not to mention the image of a paint-speckled, soft-eyed Josh, chuckling at his laughing son.

"And how's the nursery coming along?"

Nursery. A way too permanent-sounding word for a room she didn't dare let herself think of as *her* baby's. Then again, how permanent was anything in her life, really?

"Josh set up Austin's old crib the other day. So at least I have some place to put Katie after she's...out."

"Katie?"

"Or Kate, maybe. Whichever seems to fit."

"Your mama's name. That's lovely. Your dad would be so touched."

Deanna's thoughts, exactly. Except wasn't it ridiculous that she was still trying to please him, even though he wasn't around to appreciate it?

Josh's mom handed her the chart, then clasped her hands together on the corner of the desk. "So the shower is coming up..."

"Listen, about that..." Because there was support, and there was suffocating. A thin line Deanna worried was about to be crossed. Even though she'd been speechless for several seconds after Billie told her. "Seems like a lot of trouble to go to for someone who's not sticking around."

"And clearly you've forgotten what it means to live in a small town," Billie said, complete with the sharp look of a woman who's raised sons. "And the baby's going to need at least a few things while you are here. So unwad your panties, girl and feel the looove."

Deanna chuckled, then sighed. "Except my cousin's going to throw me one when I get back. Two showers just seems...excessive."

"Your cousin..." Billie adjusted her glasses to peer at Deanna's chart again. "That's who you put down as next of kin, right? Emily Taylor?"

"Yes."

"She came out here to visit a couple of times, didn't she? When you were still kids?"

"She did. She's..." Deanna cleared her throat. "She and I are very different, but she's been my rock through this. I've been very blessed."

A gentle smile brought Billie's high cheekbones into full relief. "So why limit those blessings? Don't see any reason why this munchkin can't be showered twice, do you? And by the way," she said, standing. "You're coming over for Thanksgiving—no, no arguments. Because no way are you gonna be in that big house all by yourself on the holiday." She gave a little laugh. "Although it'll be crowded this year, what with all these new people coming into the family." The midwife frowned. "And why are you giving me that look?"

"Because..."

Because she was clearly insane. Although that was a given, wasn't it?

"Why not have Thanksgiving at the Vista?" Deanna said, struggling to her feet. "It's all fixed up, for one thing. And the dining table could seat half the town, for crying out loud."

Even though it'd never been more than her parents and her for holiday meals. Except for that single Christmas when Emily and her parents had come out, when she was ten. The Holiday from Hell, as she recalled.

Billie's head tilted. "You sure?"

"Absolutely." And the longer she thought about it, the more the thought of experiencing a huge, Norman Rockwell–style holiday dinner made her giddy.

Especially since this might be her only shot at such a thing.

"Seriously—why cram everyone into your little house when there's this great big one just begging to be properly used, for once? Besides, it's Josh's house, too." At least, for a while. "And please," she said as her face heated, "let me help with the cooking. Unless you get off on doing the whole thing?"

"Are you kidding? I've been threatening for years to buy one of those ready-made meals from the grocery store. If for no other reason than to see everybody's appalled expressions. But you're very pregnant, in case you hadn't noticed—"

"What's the worst that can happen? I go into labor with a dozen people around who can get me to the birthing center. One of whom could actually deliver the baby."

Billie gave Deanna a speculative look before saying, "Okay. You're on. Now, I'm sure Val will bring pies—"

"Ohmigosh, I had a piece of her peach pie the other day. I'm still on a high from it."

"Then wait until you taste her pumpkin. And apple. And coconut cream. We can talk in a day or two about who does what with the rest. Although I call dibs on the sweet potatoes."

Deanna laughed. "They're all yours."

Then Billie's eyes softened. "After you moved to DC, Sam and I tried I don't know how many times to get your daddy to join us for the holidays. He never would."

"Even though he threw that big Christmas party for the town?"

"Even though. Just never wanted anything for himself." Her brows dipped. "Pardon me for saying this, but your daddy was a strange man. A good man, all told. But strange."

"You're not telling me anything I don't already know."

"Even so, it was obvious how badly he wanted to make everything perfect for you." Another smile touched the midwife's lips. "Same as he did for your mother."

Deanna hiked her purse higher up on her shoulder. "Only it didn't work, did it?"

"Not that I could tell, no," the older woman sighed out. "Then again, Katherine and I weren't exactly besties. No one's fault," she added quickly. "And she was never less than kind to me. But we really were from different worlds, we simply didn't have much in common. And she seemed to prefer keeping to herself. Well," she said, seeming to shake off the thought. "I guess I'll see you Saturday at the shower. In the meantime, stay off your feet!"

As if, Deanna thought, letting Billie hug her again before trudging back to the reception desk to make her next appointment, then out to the small parking lot to heave herself up into the truck's cab.

Where she sat, thinking about her mother. Her sweet, doting mother who hadn't done nearly as good a job at hiding her malcontent as she probably thought she had. Even though Katherine Blake had obviously loved Deanna's father, Deanna guessed she'd never adjusted to life in a small New Mexican town, either.

The day was as brilliantly sunny as it was bitingly cold, the frosted mountain tops glittering against the cloudless, impossibly blue sky. The aspens and cottonwoods were bare now, of course, but as she drove back to the ranch it struck Deanna how simultaneously vulnerable and brave the skeletal branches were, stripped down to their essence.

As she approached the house, she spotted a tall male figure alongside the post and rail fence, clearly focused on the horses inside it, including the pregnant mare. Then the man turned and she recognized Sam Talbot, the boys' father... and she sighed. Because truth be told, the appointment— not to mention all the musings it had provoked—had left Deanna feeling like a toddler in desperate need of a nap. Why on earth was he here?

Not stopping, however, would've been rude. So she pulled up alongside the fence, praying, as she got out of the truck, she didn't look as much like a walrus as she felt.

His smile now splitting his face in two, Sam Talbot opened his arms as she approached, engulfing her in a brief, hard hug that almost brought tears to her eyes. Like most men around here he smelled of horse and earth, overlaid with an aftershave scent that would always remind her of her childhood. It wasn't until he let go, however, that she realized the hulking man she remembered had lost probably half his weight since she'd last seen him. But while his size was diminished, the sparkle in eyes more silver than gray hadn't dimmed in the least.

Except...

"Not sure I deserve that hug," Deanna said, facing the pasture herself, her hands stuffed into the pockets of her own down vest. Which she hadn't been able to zip for weeks.

"Because you want to sell the place, you mean?" When she snorted a laugh, Sam chuckled in return, then leaned his folded arms on the fence's top rail. "You raise four kids, you get pretty good at cutting to the chase. Makes for much more efficient conversations."

A frigid but surprisingly gentle breeze stirred the piñons

bordering one side of the pasture before floating across the pale grass to soothe her hot face. "I know how much the ranch means to all of you—"

"Actually I'm not sure you do," Sam said, not unkindly. "But if that's the start of an apology, you can stop right now. You don't want it, and it's far more than Josh needs. Which I think deep down he knows. Whether he wants to admit that or not." When she gawked at him, he chuckled. "Surprised?"

"You might say."

Sam squinted out over the pasture, his hands knotting in front of him. Gearing up to say something Deanna guessed she didn't want to hear, most likely. Although what that might be, she had no idea.

"What gets me, though," Sam said, "is that Granville knew that, too. All of it."

Frowning, Deanna turned to the older man. "I don't understand."

"Neither do I, to be honest. Since a major reason Gran sent you away was to separate you and Josh—"

"Because he thought something was happening between us. I know."

"You saying it wasn't?"

Deanna picked at a splinter in the wood for a moment before shaking her head. "Josh and I were friends. Good friends, yes, but that's all. I swear."

Another soft laugh preceded, "Yeah, that's what Josh said, too. Even so, your dad wasn't taking any chances that things might change on that score. Since it was pretty obvious the two of you had completely different goals in life. Last thing he wanted was for you…" His mouth drawn in a tight line, Sam looked away again. "For you to end up as miserable as your mother was…"

Clearly the subject du jour. For whatever reason.

"…only somewhere along the line…" The older man's gaze bored into hers. "He apparently changed his mind."

Deanna's head jerked around, her forehead pinched. "Wait. Are you saying my father left the place to both of us—"

"To bring you together. Yep."

In a lame attempt to stop the world from spinning, Deanna grabbed the fence's top rail. "He told you that?"

"More or less."

"More or less?"

Sam released a breath that frosted around his mouth. "The last time I spoke with him, all he talked about was wanting to fix at least some of the mistakes he'd made."

"And you somehow deduced from that he wanted Josh and me to get together." Deanna barked out a laugh. "Seems a bit of a stretch, don't you think? Especially considering—"

"I know, I know. But why else would he leave the ranch to both of you?"

A question she couldn't answer. Or at least didn't want to.

"I knew your father my entire life, remember. We both grew up here, on the ranch. And what I noticed, even when we were kids, was that while God knew Granville could be stubborn as all get-out when he latched on to an idea, he also had no trouble switching loyalties if what seemed like a better idea came along. Not that it happened often," Sam said with a half smile, "but it did happen. So my guess is, as time went on, he regretted coming between you and Josh. Especially once Josh got over his wild oats phase after Austin came along, and your daddy could see what a responsible young man he'd turned into." The man's gentle gaze met hers again. "And I think he suspected you weren't all that happy after you left. And for sure Josh wasn't."

Now it was Deanna's turn to look away. She had no idea how her leaving had affected Josh, since they'd hardly discussed it. But she'd also never had another friend like him. Not even Emily, even though she loved her cousin to death.

None of which changed the fact that her father had, once again, obviously attempted to strong-arm events to his own ends. Or that she was in no position to do whatever her father had expected of Josh and her. Or, apparently, the man standing beside her. However, one meddling parent at a time...

"So Dad thought that by leaving the Vista to both of us we'd fall madly in love and get married and that way the ranch would stay in the family?"

"Stranger things have happened." Sam's voice softened. "Although I do think it was about more than the ranch. He really was trying to make amends, in his own way—"

"Or manipulate my happiness. My *life*." She scoffed. "Except that's what he'd tried to do all along, wasn't it? And what if she—" she pointed to her belly "—had come with a daddy to throw a monkey wrench into his plans?"

"Since he didn't know about that, not sure how that's even part of the equation."

God, she hated when people were logical. Still... "Wow," she said again, then blew out a breath. "So how come Billie didn't mention it?"

"We decided she'd handle the pregnancy. I'd handle this. Teamwork," he said, and Deanna released a soft laugh. Then she sighed.

"I assume Josh has no idea."

"Only what I told you. And that was maybe two or three days ago. So I take it he hasn't said anything?"

She wagged her head. "But why even bring this up? Since we've already decided to sell. No, wait...let me guess—you wouldn't mind seeing Josh and me together, either."

That got a quiet chuckle. "Mind? Not at all. Except even I know that parents rarely get a say in these matters. One of the downsides to kids having minds of their own. So no expectations here, trust me. But…"

A sleek black mare plodded over to the fence to nudge at Sam's chest. He obliged, fishing a piece of apple from his pocket. "But it occurs to me," he said over the horse's crunching, "there's been too damn many secrets around here over the years. Too much truth-dodging. Not that I've got a lot of room to talk when it comes to keeping the lines of communication open with my own boys. I'm not perfect. But…"

His eyes went soft. "It nearly killed Josh's mother and me to watch the chasm grow between you and your father, after your mother died. But what could we do? It wasn't our place to take *his* place. Or even your mother's. That doesn't mean we didn't love you like one of our own." His lips curved. "The daughter we never had."

"Hence the not-minding thing about Josh and me getting together."

Sam chuckled, then sobered. "Even more than that, though… I guess there's nothing standing in our way now, to show how much we care. And always have."

Deanna's eyes filled. And this time it had nothing whatsoever to do with hormones. Of course she'd always felt a connection with the Talbots that went way beyond simply being the boss's daughter. That whole thing about her falling asleep in their armchair, for example. But the thing was, she now realized she'd never fully let herself feel the connection with them she so desperately wanted to forge with her own father. Because yielding to what was obviously a natural pull would've felt way too much like giving up.

And yielding to it now would feel an awful lot like giving in. To what, she wasn't entirely sure. But after a lifetime of being buffeted by external forces beyond her control, was it so wrong to want to claim at least *some* dominion over her destiny?

Although since Josh hadn't brought up the subject she was probably worrying—if she could even call it that— over nothing. Then again, nobody knew better than she how dangerous assumptions could be.

"Well," she said, pushing away from the fence. "Thanks, I guess? I mean, it's not as if this changes anything—"

"Didn't expect it to. Just thought you should know."

Nodding, Deanna gave Josh's father another short hug, then returned to the truck, wondering what, exactly, she was supposed to do with this information. Not to mention what Josh thought about all of it. So the question was…did she have the cojones to bring up the subject? Or the even bigger cojones not to? One thing she did know, however, which was that as much as she ached for her father, she was now even madder at him than she had been.

She slammed shut the truck's door and revved the engine, hot tears biting at her eyes.

At the sound of the old Chevy's tires crunching into the driveway, Josh glanced out the living room's picture window to see Deanna bang back the door and clumsily disembark. Even from here, he could tell she was upset. And knowing she'd had an appointment with his mom, his heart bolted into his throat: was there something wrong with the baby? Or her? But then, wouldn't his mother have said something when he talked with her a little while ago? Then again, maybe not—

"Dee looks mad," Austin said beside him, practically lost in a sea of old, dusty Christmas garlands.

"It's okay, buddy, ladies who are going to have babies sometimes get like that."

A tiny, scrunched up face lifted to his. "How come?"

"I guess because it gets uncomfortable with the baby inside. Like when you eat way too much and your stomach feels all tight?"

"You mean like when it feels like you gotta poop only it's not ready to come out yet?"

Josh nearly strangled on his laugh. "Maybe. But you probably shouldn't say that to Dee, okay?"

"How come?"

"Because girls don't generally like talking about stuff like that."

"You mean poop?"

"Yeah."

"Oh. Okay," he said. Although with one of those grownups-are-just-weird faces that made more and more regular appearances these days. "But maybe this'll make her feel better, huh?"

Josh glanced around at the chewed-up-looking bags and boxes scattered around the room, most of which Austin had already opened and pawed through. Now Josh wondered if that had been the best idea. Not because of Austin, but maybe it would've been better to let Dee have first crack at it, since it had been her idea—?

The front door opened; Dee actually jerked to a stop, her expression a millimeter away from thunderous. "What the he…ck?"

Grinning—and mercifully oblivious—Austin ran up to her, draped in fake pine garland. "We got out the Christmas stuff! Daddy said we could! There's a *lot*!"

At that, some of the clouds dispersed. Maybe not enough

to see the sun, but at least the immediate storm threat had apparently passed. "There certainly is, sweetie." Shrugging off the vest that covered very little, actually, Dee dumped her purse on a table by the front door. Josh could have sworn her belly was twice as big now as it had been a couple of days ago, but no way was he pointing that out. How on earth women even *walked* when they were that pregnant was a mystery. At least horses could spread the load over four legs instead of two.

"So how'd the appointment go?" he asked, and her mouth twisted.

"Fine. More or less. What's all this about?"

"You said you wanted to get a leg up on the decorations. So since the shower's the day after tomorrow…" He shrugged.

Her eyes lifted to his. In which he saw questions. And not, he didn't think, about the decorations. Or the shower. Especially since his father had given him a heads-up roughly thirty seconds ago about their little chat. Which probably explained the pissedness, being as his own reaction, when Dad told him his suspicions about Granville's motives behind the will, had been pretty much the same. Although truth be told her venomous expression when she'd first walked in hadn't done his ego any favors. And wasn't *that* nuts? Because for damn sure the whole idea of them getting together was. For *damn* sure.

However, she then lifted those query-laden eyes to the rafters ten feet overhead, and he assumed the questions would wait. If they ever got voiced at all. Because no way was he bringing up the subject, nope.

"You don't think it's too early?"

"Just following your lead," he said, and a few more of the clouds dispersed.

"I guess I could use some help," she said—reluctantly,

he thought—her hand going to her lower back. "Since your mother would kill me if I got on any ladders right now."

"She'd have to go through me first," Josh said, and something close to a laugh popped out of her mouth…the kind of laugh a smart man knew often preceded a melt-down. You know, a little too high-pitched, a smidgen too forced.

But she didn't melt down, even if the gaze that now swung once more to his radiated with a sadness so deep it took his breath. A sadness that solidified the idea that had been shimmering in his thoughts ever since he'd talked to Mom from *maybe* to *do it*. Whether it would work out or not, of course, Josh had no idea. Dee's lips curved up at the corners. Barely.

"Besides," she said softly, "it's your house, too."

The words almost stuck at the base of his throat. "For the moment, anyway."

"Yes. For the moment."

A weird, sticky silence shuddered between them for a second before Josh said, "You know what you want to do about the tree? There's that big fake thing in a box in the toolshed—"

"Oh, God, no." She looked positively appalled. "Real, definitely. Later, though. Closer to the big party. So." She smiled, trying *so* hard to make it look genuine Josh's heart twanged. "Who wants hot chocolate?"

"Me!" Austin bellowed, his screechy little voice echo-ing off the rafters, ouch, and making Thor bark. Because clearly *something* was afoot the dog needed to stay on top of. Rubbing her belly, Deanna laughed, then cocked her head at Josh. "And yourself?"

"Sure. Then you can sit—" he pointed to the overstuffed chair closest to the ceiling-high fireplace "—and tell me where you want stuff to go."

"You're on," she said, then shuffled off down the hall to the kitchen…only to return a second later.

"Do you remember how my mother used to drape the garlands around the chandeliers?" She pointed up to the pair of huge black wrought iron chandeliers that Josh and she had decided, a million years ago, looked like giant pre-historic skeletons. Both the realtor and the designer had been adamant they stay. And since neither Josh nor Dee had really cared, there they were, looking all rustic and "authentic" and crap.

"Enough. That what you want?"

Her eyes squinched, slightly, when she looked up again. Then she shook her head. "Actually…no. I don't. I trust you," she said, then disappeared again.

Josh seriously doubted she had any idea how much those three words had just affected him. Hell, when was the last time a woman had said she trusted him? That's right. Never.

However.

Whatever Deanna needed, he wasn't it. Not any more now than he had been when they were kids. Less, probably, since they'd grown up. Or, more to the point, grown apart.

So. Decorations, he could put up, sure. A real tree, he could get her. A secret phone call, he could make. Anything more than that…

No.

Because the first time she'd left, at least it hadn't been her choice. This time, however, it would.

And that was a hell he wasn't about to put himself through again.

Chapter Seven

Even though Josh had outdone himself with the decorations—without even a hint of man-grousing, bless his heart—something had clearly shifted between them. Again. And it was probably not much of a stretch to pin that "something" on what they both obviously now knew about Dad's will. Of course, they *could* get the whole thing out in the open and simply talk about it, like actual grownups. Then again, what would be the point—?

"Ohmigosh," Val said from her perch by a garland-swagged window when Deanna pulled out an adorable, ruffled-bottom sleeper from one of the many, many gift bags stacked at her feet. "I'm hearby putting y'all on notice, if I have another girl, I want one of those. And no, I'm not pregnant, so you can lower the eyebrows already."

But the twinkle in the blonde's eyes said she and Josh's twin were doing everything they could to make that happen. And, yes, Deanna had to tamp down the spurt of envy, at how freaking adorable the newly married couple was, their happiness whenever they were together spilling all over the place like glitter.

Not that she wasn't grateful for the outpouring of affection—and gifts, oh, my, goodness, the gifts, including a bassinet to tuck right beside her bed—this little group was showering her with today, Annie from the diner and Billie and Josh's two sisters-in-law. Or soon to be, in the case of Zach's fiancée, Mallory. But honestly, she didn't even know Val except for that one conversation in the diner. And Mallory not at all. Still, being made to feel like she was actually one of them, even if only for this little while, warmed Deanna's heart. So the green-eyed monster could go screw itself.

As could the unexpected heartache from missing her mother far more than she thought she would. After all, she'd had thirteen years to reconcile herself to the fact that Mom wouldn't be around for any of those milestones a girl expects to share with her mother, and she'd managed just fine up till now. More or less. But something about opening presents for what would have been Katherine Blake's first grandbaby was doing a real number on Deanna's head. That her father wouldn't see little Katie, either...

Hell. It was a wonder she wasn't blubbering into a wad of pink tissue paper by now.

Sitting beside her, Billie squeezed Deanna's wrist, as if knowing what she was thinking. Deanna clutched the tiny pajamas to her chest, her breath hitching when it hit her that in a few weeks the tiny person inside her would be *wearing* the pajamas.

Her eyes burning, she smiled for Annie. "This is *so* stinkin' cute—thanks so much."

The menfolk—yes, this was a forward-thinking bunch—were scattered throughout the house, refilling munchie trays and tending to assorted small children, keeping the mayhem in reasonable check. Except for Josh, who'd had to go into Albuquerque for reasons he hadn't made entirely clear, either because baby showers really weren't his thing, or he was simply trying to avoid her.

Considering how little they'd seen each other in the past couple of days, she was going with Option 2. However, Deanna was just as glad none of the men were present when she opened Mallory's gift—a top-of-the-line breast pump.

"That's the brand I used when I had Landon and had to express between takes when I was on the set," the former actress said, pushing her wheelchair a little closer. "Works like a charm. Although…" She chuckled. "Do you even plan on breast-feeding?"

"Yes, absolutely." At least, she figured she'd give it a shot. Deanna opened up the box and lifted out the gadget, trying to imagine fitting the contraption on her boob—

"What's that?"

At the sound of Austin's reedy little voice, Deanna hurriedly stuffed the pump back in the box. "It's, um…" She smiled for the kid, who was wearing an expression so much like his daddy's her heart knocked against her ribs. "A horn."

Val belted out a laugh, only to cover her mouth, muttering, "Good save," from behind her hand.

Big green eyes met hers. "C'n I try it?"

"No, sweetie, sorry…it's for the baby."

Oblivious to the laughter floating around him, the little boy came closer, frowning, to inspect the box. Which thank *God* did not have a picture of how to use the thing. Over the crackling fire in the stone hearth, she heard Josh's truck pull up out front. Great. Just in time to witness her contributing to his four-year-old's delinquency. "What's she gonna do with it? If she's gonna be too little to play with toys when she's born—?"

"Can't wait to hear you answer that one," came a very familiar voice from the entryway. Deanna jerked and twisted around, releasing a little gasp when she saw a grinning Emily, decked out in gray cashmere and designer jeans.

"Ohmigosh—Em!" Bags and tissue flying everywhere, Deanna shoved herself to her feet to meet her cousin half-way, throwing her arms around her. "How did you...? I don't understand—"

"This guy," Em said, nodding back toward Josh, stand-ing a few feet off with his hands in his pockets and mis-chief in his eyes, clearly pleased with himself.

And instantly turning Deanna into the most confused pregnant woman on the face of the planet.

"You're staying for Thanksgiving, right?"

Reclining on the guest room's four-poster bed with Smoky snuggled up beside her, Emily laughed and bit off the end of another cream-cheese-stuffed jalapeño pepper.

"I'd love to, but I can't," she said, pulling a face as she plucked a blob of the gooey mixture from the front of her satin pajamas. "Command appearance, Mom and Dad and me with Michael's parents. I tried to get out of it, but Mi-chael nearly had a fit. As it was I was lucky to snag a flight back on Wednesday...hey. You okay?"

"Just uncomfortable," Deanna said, shifting in the nearby overstuffed armchair. "The baby's already en-gaged."

"What?"

Deanna laughed. "As in, ready to launch. It's a good thing. And I still can't believe you're here," she said, and her cousin smiled, then bumped noses with the cat, who'd decided to see if whatever the human was eating was worth begging for.

They'd talked virtually nonstop since the shower ended hours before, mostly while Em helped Deanna unpack half of Deanna's clothes. *Because when an airline allows you two free bags*, Emily had said, chuckling, *you take advantage of that*. Which apparently meant also bringing a few things for after the baby came, although Deanna seriously doubted she'd fit into her fave pair of skinny jeans right off the bat. But she'd been beyond touched by her cousin's thoughtfulness…even as she still hadn't wrapped her head around Josh's getting her here. Even paying for her plane ticket—although according to Em, Deanna wasn't supposed to know that—since getting one this close to Thanksgiving, and on such short notice, was beyond pricey. Especially for a kindergarten teacher. Yes, a kindergarten teacher whose parents subsidized her apartment, but whatever.

"Well, I am, so deal," Em said, sitting up and reaching for her diet soda on the bedside table, her hair a deep gold in the flickering firelight. A great selling point, the Realtor had said—fireplaces in all the bedrooms.

"But…why?"

Setting down the can, her cousin gave her a pitying look as the cat thudded onto the Navajo rug by the bed. "Because Josh asked me to come?"

Deanna shifted again, willing the baby to move. No dice. "That's what I'm why…ing. I mean, what did he say? Exactly."

Emily's mouth twitched. "I didn't record the conversation, Dee. But as I recall, he said you seemed…unsettled. Being stuck here and all. And he thought it might be nice to have something or someone from home to make you feel better. Even if for only a couple of days."

Only, as thrilled as Deanna was to have her cousin here, Josh's bringing that about sure as heck wasn't making her feel *less* unsettled—

Em took another bite of the pepper. Because clearly the threat of late-night heartburn held no terror. Tougher than she looked, that one. "So what's going on between you two?"

Yeah, she'd figured that was coming. "Nothing. At least, nothing different. Josh and I are friends. Same as before."

"A *friend* who just laid out a not insubstantial wad of cash to get me here."

Deanna turned to stare into the flames, figuring the glow from the fire would mask her blush. "The Talbots are a generous lot." At Emily's chuckle, she faced her cousin again. "What?"

Em shrugged, then glanced around the room. "This was where I stayed all those years ago, isn't it? Is it me, or has nothing changed?"

"The sheets, maybe," she said, and her cousin chuckled again. "Because rustic charm is apparently all the rage these days."

That got another short laugh before Em's deep blue eyes met Deanna's. "Josh said he'd take me riding tomorrow, if I want. Unless you can't bear me to leave you for an hour or two." Deanna threw a pillow at her; on another laugh, Emily threw it back. "Seems a shame to sell it, now that it's really yours. Especially since you have no idea how much I envied you, getting to live out here. All this space. All this…" Emily glanced around, sighing. *"Quiet."*

Deanna snorted. "I think the word you're looking for is *solitude*."

"What's wrong with that?"

"Nothing. In measured doses. Twenty-four/seven, however…" Her shoulders bumped. "But in any case, it's not all mine, remember? Besides, what on earth would I do with it?" And no, she had no intention of telling her cousin about her father's "plan." "And my half of the sale will go a long way toward taking care of this little girl until she's not so little anymore."

"But it's your heritage—"

"I'm not a rancher, Em. And did you hear what I said?"

"Then let Josh do his ranching thing and you could open a gallery. Taos isn't that far, right?"

"And where on earth did that come from?"

"Oh, I don't know…maybe from the eleventy billion conversations we've had about it?" Emily grabbed a down pillow and hugged it to her middle. "You've got the eye, that's not even a question. And you know that's what you want to do."

"Eventually, sure," Deanna said, tamping down a spurt of something that felt more like panic than she wanted to admit. "In DC, maybe. Or some other city with an actual population. In New Mexico—?"

"Only it would be a helluva lot easier to start one out here than in a big city, wouldn't it?"

"Except without selling the ranch, how on earth would I do that? Even here. It's not as if your parents would bank-roll me, is it? I didn't think so," she said at her cousin's sigh. "And anyway… I'm not nearly ready to take on my own gallery. And I don't know when I will be. So…"

"Fine, so maybe the logistics need some tweaking. The timing. But honey…" Emily ditched the pillow to reach for Deanna's hand, all those soft brown waves tumbling over her shoulders. "It's perfectly obvious you need a change. Because you're not happy in DC. And you haven't been in a long time."

"Cripes, Em—I was just dumped—"

"Yes, I know," her cousin said gently. "And you're preg-nant. But you weren't happy before Phillippe, either." Her mouth twisted. "Or *during* Phillippe, for that matter."

"I never said—"

"You never had to. I know you, Dee. And I know…"
Sitting straight again, Emily bit her bottom lip for a mo-

ment before saying, "You were...dazzled by Phillippe. Not that anyone would blame you, God knows. Older, charming...the man is pretty damned dazzling. A douchecanoe, but dazzling. But obviously what you had with him...it wasn't real. And be honest—did you ever really trust him? Completely?"

Blinking away the sting in her eyes, Deanna sagged back in the chair, half smiling when the cat jumped up on the arm to give her a penetrating look. *Yeah, can't wait to hear how you answer* that *one.* And if this had been anyone other than Emily, or if her defenses hadn't been worn to nubs, she might've taken offense. But how could she, since it wasn't as if she hadn't asked herself the same thing a hundred times since the breakup? The thing was, though...

"Yes," she said, a tear slipping down her cheek. Emily plucked a tissue out of the little square box on the nightstand and handed it over. "I did trust him. And that was my mistake. Like you said, I was dazzled. And so, so flattered that he thought..." She blew her nose, then let out a strangled little laugh. "Okay, that I *thought* he thought I was...special."

"Oh, jeez, Dee..." Emily got off the bed to kneel in front of her, taking both Deanna's hands in hers, soggy tissue and all. "You *are* special. He was the jerk. Obviously."

"Then why couldn't I see that? Why couldn't I..." She blew out a breath. "How do I know I won't make the same mistake again?"

Now she noticed her cousin's eyes were wet, too. But instead of spewing more platitudes, Emily only got to her knees to pull Deanna into her arms, rubbing her back when she finally let the tears come.

One of the problems with doing a good deed, Josh thought on Thanksgiving night after most everybody had left and he found Deanna in the kitchen chowing down on the remains of Val's pumpkin cheesecake pie, was that you never knew what the consequences of that good deed might be. Or when it might come back to bite you in the butt. In this case, the good deed being getting Dee's cousin here, the consequences being Emily's talking his ear off on the long, *long* drive back to Albuquerque yesterday morning. Yeah, he strongly suspected Dee would kill her cousin if she'd known how loose-lipped she'd been.

Of course, it was obvious Emily was only worried about Dee, so he couldn't exactly take issue with her lack of discretion. Especially since God forbid Dee would ever open up to him. These days, anyway—

"Oh!" she said, catching him and Thor watching her. Well, Josh was watching her, the dog was most likely watching food disappear into her mouth. "You're still here!"

"I am."

With a sheepish grin, she waved her fork at the mangled pie. "So come keep me from making a total pig of myself."

See, that was the thing, Josh mused as he dug another fork out of the "everyday" drawer and sat next to her, the dog joining them as though he'd been issued a personal invitation. As he'd already noticed, Dee wasn't a bitcher. Not anymore, at least. Although if half of what Emily had said was true, the woman had more than enough to bitch about.

And whether he was still mellow from being stuffed to the gills, or simply couldn't face returning to his empty house—since his parents had taken all the grandkids for the night—suddenly the thought of sharing a pie with the woman who'd once been his best friend sounded like a damn fine idea. He also supposed, despite his earlier reluctance, they needed to address the business about her father's will, if for no other reason than to clear the air. Move on.

After pouring himself a glass of milk, Josh sat at a right angle to Dee, smiling when she inched the pie closer to him. By his knee, Thor whimpered.

"You don't like the crust?" he said, noticing she'd eaten the filling right up to the ruffled edge.

"Not really much of a crust person. Have at it."

"Done," he said, breaking off a big chunk. His sister-in-law used butter in her crusts, so they melted in your mouth like the world's best cookie. Although he shared with the dog, just to be fair. "Don't tell my mother, but your turkey? Best I've ever eaten."

Forking another bite into her mouth, Deanna burped out a little laugh. Her eyes were practically glowing tonight, like maybe she was feeling pretty mellow herself. "Thanks. I got the recipe online someplace. It was brined overnight in apple cider and all sorts of spices and stuff. Although if you hadn't've put it in the oven for me it wouldn't've happened."

"Glad to be of service."

Smiling slightly, Dee sucked on her fork for a moment, then set it in the plate and leaned back, her arms crossed over the bump.

"You done?" Josh asked. Hopefully.

"My mouth says no, but my stomach has other ideas. It's a little crowded in there. So it's all yours." Thor laid his chin on Josh's knee, and Dee laughed, then sighed. "And we need to talk, don't we?"

"About?"

"Why Dad left the house to both of us."

Even though she'd spoken softly, there was no missing the edge to her voice. Wasn't directed at him, though, he didn't think.

"I agree." Josh took a swallow of milk, then shoved in another bite. "What'd my dad tell you?"

Her mouth twisted. "That my father wanted to 'fix things.' The implication being, that he was sorry he broke us up—even though we weren't really 'together'—by sending me away. And now…" She shrugged, then almost laughed. "God, I can't even say it."

Because, Josh assumed, the whole thing was too preposterous to even consider. Of course.

"If it makes you feel any better," he said, matching her position as he chewed, "your father sure as hell never mentioned his *plan*, if that's what it was, to me. And two, since it's not actually a condition of the inheritance— which probably wouldn't stand up in court, anyway—I think we're good to keep on the way we are. Or, aren't."

After a good two, three seconds of steady staring, Dee finally nodded. "That's what I figured."

"So your dad never said anything to you, either?"

"Not a word." Frowning, she stroked her hand over her belly—he could see the baby moving underneath her sweater—then released a breath that was more laugh than sigh. "You don't think…oh, this is crazy—"

"What?"

"What if *your* father made it up? Because *he'd* like to see us get together?"

"What?"

She shrugged. "Just a thought."

"If a totally off-the-wall one. Because Dad…no," Josh said, shaking his head. "In any case, even if he did, neither one of us is…well. It just wouldn't work, that's all. For so many reasons."

"*So* many," she said, nodding. "So we can just forget about all of that, right?"

"Absolutely."

Dee gave him a funny smile, then picked up the fork again, only to wince, her other hand going to her back. Josh frowned.

"You okay?"

"Probably on my feet too much today. Nothing a hot bath won't fix. And a good night's sleep. Although not holding out much hope for that. And why is your face all pinched like that?"

"Because I don't like the idea of you being here by yourself."

"Um... I've been alone since Gus left?"

"And you're not getting *less* pregnant, are you?" He tapped his fingers on the table, then pointed at her. "So Austin and I are moving over here tomorrow."

"Excuse me—"

He got to his feet. "Actually, make that tonight."

"Now hold on, buster—"

"Yeah? What? You gonna tell me I can't move into my own house?"

That got her, apparently. "Oh. Well. No, of course not. But—"

"Don't worry, not gonna encroach on your space."

An actual eye roll preceded, "What I meant was, I don't want to put you out on my account." She plucked her phone off the table, wagged it at him. "That's why God made these handy little devices."

"And you've clearly forgotten how sketchy the service can get up here. Especially if the weather's bad. And there's no landline at my place. At least if I'm here I can hear you scream when you go into labor."

She gawked at him for a long moment, then burst into laughter. "One, there will be no screaming—"

"Yeah, ask Mom how that works out for most of her patients," he said, which got a glower in response.

"And *two*," she said, "unless you're planning on gluing yourself to my side, whether or not we have cell service when the time comes is moot. So thanks for the offer, it's very sweet. But I'll be fine. Really."

His arms still crossed over his chest, Josh narrowed his eyes, trying to decide which path to take as he watched that stubborn little mouth. Oh, sure, he was well aware that sometimes the best thing was to step back and let a gal make her own decisions. He wasn't a total moron. But neither was he gonna let pride—hers more than his, he thought—get in the way of doing what was smart. And wouldn't it be nice, at least once in his life, to be around a woman who'd just let him be a man, for the love of God? To be protective like his daddy had taught all his sons they were supposed to be?

Of course the irony was that his mother wasn't exactly a delicate little flower, either. This was not a woman who freaked out and called her man to come rescue her from spiders and snakes and bears and such. On the other hand, his father had enough White Knight genes coursing through his veins for three people. So Josh wondered how Mom and Dad had worked that particular little issue out.

But what his parents had or had not done wasn't the issue. What Josh was going to do, however, was. Whether Dee was on board or not. "This isn't about me being 'sweet,' or whatever you want to call it. It's about common sense. Besides which, Mom said I should keep an eye on you." A sort-of lie, but whatever worked, he wasn't proud.

Judging from the ravine gouged between her eyebrows, he guessed there was some pretty intense wrestling going on underneath those spikes. She picked up her fork again, even though the pie was long gone. As long as she wasn't planning on using it on him, he was good.

"It's just…" A breath left her lungs. "It wasn't until

this last…fiasco that it occurred to me that…" She sighed again. "That all my life I've looked to some man or other to take care of me. Make the decisions for me. And I finally realized if I ever expected to actually be an adult someday I had to start thinking for myself. Taking care of myself. Instead of the easy way out. Whatever Dad's reasons for sending me away, the fact remains that in his attempt to rescue me, to keep me safe, he kept me from learning how to handle…life."

"But you've been on your own for how long in DC?"

"In reality? Not so much. God, Aunt Margaret and Uncle John were even worse than Dad. They wouldn't even let me live on campus, for pity's sake. So when I finally worked up the gumption to move into my own place after graduation—and they were not pleased, believe me—I guess the freedom sort of went to my head. And I made some bad choices." One side of her mouth lifted. "Although at least they were my choices."

"I take it we're talking about Phillippe?"

"And did you not catch the plural, there? Choices. You are looking at a serial screwup. At least when it comes to picking men. Although the irony was that, after some of the dirtwads I'd dated? I felt like I'd won the jackpot with Phillippe. Because he was all urbane and crap, I guess," she said on a humorless chuckle. "A *man* instead of a boy. Someone who'd actually look at *me* when we went out to dinner instead of his cell phone. Of course the problem was I was so naive I didn't realize what a fake he was."

"We've all been there, Dee."

"Maybe. Except…" She grimaced at her belly before once more lifting her gaze to Josh's. "Some of us get taken in more than others."

At that, Josh had to laugh. "And it's about the cute four-year-old I live with? I love the kid to death, you know that.

But he wasn't 'supposed' to happen, either. So you don't exactly have the market cornered on stupid."

"And you do realize you're probably the only person in the world who could say that to me and live?"

"Only echoing your words, darlin'," he said, and she sighed.

"Even so…" Her mouth twisted again. "What became really clear to me, after Phillippe dropped his little bombshell and winged back to his wife and kidlets in the French countryside, is that it's way past time I learn to love my own company. I don't mean living by myself—I can do that, no problem. I mean, really being okay with not being part of a couple. Or defining myself by my relationships. Or expecting someone else to rescue me when things get tough."

"Wow. You've been thinking about this a lot, huh?"

Her hand passed over her belly. "Ever since the stick turned pink. Although to be honest the seeds were planted a while ago. Just took them some time to germinate." Her eyes glittered. "I want to be tough, you know? And I want, more than anything in the world, to be an example to this little girl. For her to be the ballsiest kid in nursery school," she said, and Josh smiled.

Only to sober a moment later. "So let me get this straight—me wanting to move in is somehow a threat to *you* wanting to be your own woman?"

Dee blew a short laugh through her nose. "Woman, hell. *Person.*" She finally put down the fork. Thank God. "You know what's funny? When we were kids, what I most hated about living out here was how cut off from the rest of the world I was. How…incomplete I felt. Or at least, how incomplete my life felt. As if I knew there was more 'out there,' even if I didn't know what that was. Now I realize it's only when we stop being afraid of being alone that we find completeness the only place we ever really can—within ourselves."

Josh frowned. "And that's way too heavy for a simple country boy like me." Even though, if he thought about it for longer than two seconds, she was right.

"It's true. Although don't kid yourself, bud—" Her mouth curved. "There is nothing even remotely simple about you. There never was."

"That supposed to be a compliment?"

Dee angled her head, her eyes narrowing slightly, like she was studying him. "It's just…you. Who you are." She hesitated, then said, "For what it's worth? You were the only thing about here I regretted leaving."

Her words ringing in his ears, Josh frowned some more at the decimated pie tin before asking, "Even though I was one of the people who overprotected you?"

A second or two passed before she pushed herself to her feet, a soft smile pushing at her lips. "You were there for me. And I'll always be grateful for that. For the way you put up with me. For *you*. But…"

"What?"

"Let's just say Dad wasn't coming entirely out of left field when he sent me away. Because you were definitely something I needed to be protected from."

He felt like the breath had been punched out of him. "You were always safe with me, Dee. Always. I would've never—"

"Oh, I know."

Josh's forehead creased. "Then—"

"Figure it out, country boy," she said, then started slowly out of the kitchen.

"So does that mean Austin and I can move in or not?"

One hand braced on the door frame, she turned. "It's not as if I can stop you," she said softly, but with a steely undertone that definitely made him sit up and take notice. Because damned if he didn't feel like he'd just been issued a challenge.

Even if he wasn't entirely sure what that challenge was.

Chapter Eight

As she stood at the stove flipping grilled cheese sandwiches, Deanna heard, coming from the hallway, the little boy's high-pitched giggles tangling with Josh's pretend dinosaur roar. She smiled, despite feeling pretty tangled up herself. About, well, everything. Josh moving in and her being stuck here and feeling like she was about to explode and all those jumbled feelings about her father—

"Something smells incredible," Josh said, and she turned to see his still-giggling son clamped like a koala bear around one calf as Josh dragged him along the tiled floor.

"Just grilled cheese." Josh tried shaking Austin off his leg. More giggling ensued. Deanna smiled. "And don't look now, but there's something stuck to your leg."

"You're kidding?" All wide-eyed, Josh raised his leg enough to bump the kid's rump on the floor, making Austin laugh even harder. "I thought that leg felt awfully heavy," he said, scooping his son into his arms and growling into his neck before grinning at him. "Where'd you come from?"

"Right here!"

"You sure about that?"

"Uh-huh. You're so silly, Daddy!"

Chuckling, Josh kissed the top of Austin's head, then set him down again. "Looks like Dee's got your sandwich done. Go get up in your seat."

But as long as that let's-mess-with-Deanna's-head list was, Josh and her living under the same roof definitely topped it. Precisely because of stuff like this, watching him be unabashedly goofy with his little boy, effortlessly straddling the line between responsible adulthood and childlike innocence. No wonder Austin adored his daddy. Because it was equally obvious how much Josh adored his son.

And the more she witnessed all this mutual adoration, the more her heart ached for something that had always felt just out of reach. How tempting it was to see Josh with Austin and think, *Maybe...?*

Which is precisely why she needed to stick to her guns about claiming her own selfhood and independence and ability to make her own decisions. About ratcheting down her expectations, bringing them more in line with that thing called reality. Because her very survival depended on it. Then again, for all she knew Josh was looking at her and thinking, *Oh*, hell, *no.* For sure he was thinking *something*, if those weird glances he shot her every so often were anything to go by. So moot point, most likely.

By now Austin had scrambled into his chair, grinning up at her when she set the sandwich in front of him, cut into four triangles, crusts on the side. Another Talbot charmer in training; God help every female in the county with a beating heart. "Thank you, DeeDee!"

It'd grabbed her breath when the child started calling her that yesterday, out of the blue. No one but her mother had ever called her that.

"You're welcome, big guy," she said, ruffling his hair, then turned to see Josh grab his denim jacket off the hook by the back door, shrugging it on over a black fleece hoodie she'd like to burn, frankly.

"I won't be gone but two, two-and-a-half hours at most," he said with a brief glance to her super-sized middle. He'd sold a horse the week before, to a young barrel racer right over the Colorado border, and—as usual—was delivering the horse himself to personally check out the prospective accommodations. Although he was clearly conflicted about leaving Austin with her.

"And we've been through all this," she said, handing him a paper sack with his own sandwich, a bottle of water, a bag of chips. It wasn't much, but tonight's steak-and-potato casserole would make up for it. "It doesn't make sense taking Austin all the way to your folks when you're going in the opposite direction. And as you said, it's only for a couple of hours. The chances of my popping out a baby in that time span are slim to none. Didn't your mother teach you anything?"

"But you have her number, right? Of course you do, what am I saying? But I'll leave Thor, just in case."

In case of what? she wondered, even as she said, "I'm fine, Josh. We're all fine. And will be fine. Honestly, you'd think no pregnant woman ever had another child to look after. Right?" And she even sounded confident. Yay, her. "Besides, Val said she's coming over in a bit, so we won't even be alone for all that long. So go, get out of here."

He still hesitated—jeez—but finally walked over to Austin to drop another kiss on the boy's head before giving Deanna a funny little smile. And for a moment—not even that, a millisecond—she almost thought he was going to kiss her goodbye, too. And wasn't that totally nuts?

Then he was gone, taking what felt like half the air in the room with him. Not to mention a good chunk of her bravado. Because the only other time she'd been alone with a little kid was that day when she'd shooed Gus off, when the old man hadn't been more than a few minutes away and she knew Josh would be back soon and she hadn't been this pregnant.

Yeesh, overthinking much? she thought on a sigh, then carted her own sandwich over to the table, along with a glass of milk and a bowl of red grapes. Which Josh had specifically told her Austin wouldn't eat. Never mind the kid had eaten vegetable stew, for godssake. And loved it.

"What're those?" Austin asked, suspicion colliding with curiosity in his scrunched up face. Somehow, Deanna swallowed her laugh.

"Grapes."

"Oh. I don't like those."

"Yeah, your dad told me. That's too bad," she said, popping one in her mouth and mentally patting herself on the back for not pushing him to take a taste. Because, for one thing, she remembered when she'd visit Aunt Margaret when she was little, and her aunt would force her to take at least two bites of everything on her plate, even if it made her gag. *Yeah, I'm looking at you, liver.* And for another, if she'd learned nothing else from five years of selling artwork, it was that you never gave the potential buyer the chance to say no.

She might've, however, made a few these-are-*so*-yummy noises as she munched.

Austin frowned at her. Then the grapes. Then her again. "Are they good?"

"Well, I like them. But I thought you said you didn't."

"Actually… I don't think I ever tasted one." Which would naturally beg the question, *Then how do you* know *you don't like them?*

"I see." Deanna tossed another grape into her mouth. Austin frowned harder.

"C'n I have one?"

Deanna looked at the grapes. "Huh. I don't know..."

"But we're supposed to share. Daddy says. Grandma, too. Please?"

Oh, God—were those *tears*? For heaven's sake, she'd only meant to see if she could get the kid to try a grape, not break his spirit. Deanna practically shoved the bowl toward him. "Of course, sweetie. I'm sorry, I was only teasing."

After shooting her a way too grown-up look, Austin twisted a grape off the cluster and took the tiniest nibble imaginable. Then he nodded. "I guess it's all right." He took another, only marginally bigger, nibble. "But it's not nice to tease."

Deanna's face flamed. "No, it's not. I'm sorry."

"It's okay," Austin said with a shrug as he finally shoved the rest of the grape into his mouth. And took another one. "Daddy said you're not used to being around little kids, so I should go easy on you."

And if she'd had any food in her own mouth, she would've choked on it. "He actually said that?"

"Uh-huh. C'n I have more milk, please?"

"Sure, sweetie." Feeling slightly dizzy, Deanna pushed herself to her feet—yes, by bracing both hands on the table and shoving with all her might—grabbed his plastic cup and lumbered to the fridge. Four, hell. Kid was sharp enough to hold office. And probably more so than most people who did—

"Knock, knock—anybody home?"

"It's Aunt Val!" Austin yelled, morphing back into a little kid as he practically fell out of his chair to streak out of the kitchen, his sneakered feet thundering down the hallway. Judging from the high-pitched jabbering that followed, Val had her two munchkins in tow. Probably why the cat, who'd been asleep in his bed beside the woodstove, took off for parts unknown. Because you never knew with toddlers. Especially that one, Deanna thought, smiling, remembering Val's youngest's nonstop energy and curiosity two days before on Thanksgiving. *And that's gonna be this one in a year or so*, she thought, and she gulped down her smile.

She was so not ready for this. That. Her.

And she should probably get over that *real* quick.

"In the kitchen," she yelled as she cleared Austin's plate, shoving in one of his leftover crusts as she trudged from table to sink, trying not to wince. But damn, her daughter had the hardest head in the history of hard heads, which Deanna prayed was not prophetic for the kind of teenager she'd be.

And maybe she should worry about knowing when to feed and change her before fretting about adolescent angst—

"Oh, my goodness—did you decorate even more?" Val said from the doorway, grinning, her long staticky hair floating around the shoulders of a denim jacket worn over a heavyweight hoodie.

"I might have a slight…problem," Deanna said, and Val laughed.

"So I see. But the house looks incredible. Even in here. That tiny tree on the buffet is seriously adorable. Although you do realize how high you've set the bar for the rest of us?"

"Sorry. But the waiting suuuucks. You guys want me to come decorate your places, just let me know."

"I might just take you up on that, considering how busy I am these days baking pies for the resort." Although Val's glowing expression said she was clearly thrilled. "Might even have to scrounge up an assistant sometime soon. Since child labor is frowned upon, go figure. But the reason we're here is…" She held up two overstuffed plastic bags. "More baby clothes, ta-da! Because there will be those days when between the urps and the poops, there aren't enough onesies in the world…hey. You okay?"

"Back," Deanna got out, pointing, and Val nodded.

"Yeah, Risa was like that. I swear if I could've reached inside to shift her, I would've. But…" The blonde's pale brows dipped. "You sure that's all it is?"

"Unfortunately, yes. The pain is constant and dull, not—"

"Like a blowtorch to the crotch?"

Deanna burbled a little laugh, then realized that would be *her* crotch, in the not too distant future. Fun. "Is it really that bad?"

"It ain't no hayride, honey. Although at least there's a kid at the end of it. Unlike, say, acute appendicitis. And thank *God* for epidurals. So I'm guessing you pulled baby-sitting detail today?"

"I did. Because Josh is schlepping a horse across the border."

"Which you realize sounds vaguely illegal," Val said. "But how's it going with the kid?"

"Other than feeling like I'm keeping company with a six-hundred-year-old gnome? Fine."

"Get used to it, kids definitely say whatever they're thinking. And they think a *lot*, jeebus. Josie comes up with this stuff that regularly makes me wonder, Who *are* you?" Then she swung the bags toward the table. "So sit, sit, lemme show you what I brought—"

From the great room came shrieking. And bellowing. And giggles. And more bellowing.

"You sure it's okay to leave the kids on their own?" Deanna said, lowering herself to one of the chairs about as gracefully as an elephant with piles.

Plopping into the seat closest to Deanna, Val upended the bags on the table between them and a million wee baby things came tumbling out. "You kidding? I sometimes think Josie's a better mama at eight than I've ever been. Kid doesn't let 'em get away with anything. And Austin thinks she walks on water. Anyway..." She spread out the loot, patting one particularly faded, splotched sleeper. "This stuff is not pretty. Which is why I didn't bring it to the shower. But like I said, there will be many, many times when clean and available definitely trumps ugly."

Her heart crunching at her new friend's kindness, Deanna fingered a little pair of frilly socks patterned like ballet slippers. "I'd get up and give you a hug but you probably have some place to be before next week."

Chuckling, Val did the honors instead, bending over to wrap her arms around Deanna for a moment before settling again in her seat. Smoky ventured back into the kitchen, craning his head to listen down the hall before scooting away again. "But..." Deanna pressed one of the sleepers—a grayish pink with white polka dots—to her chest. "What if you need these again?" Val blushed, and Deanna gasped. "Oh, my God. You're pregnant."

"I'm *late*," the blonde whispered. "As in, way too early to announce. Which is why I backpedaled at the shower, because I was afraid to believe it myself. And nobody else knows except Levi."

Oh. Wow. Warmth spreading through her, Deanna reached for Val's hand. "I take it you're thrilled?"

A smile slowly crept across the blonde's mouth. "If it sticks? You have no idea."

"Then I am, too. And I won't breathe a word, I promise."

"Thanks. And don't even worry about the stuff," Val said, waving her hand over the messy stacks on the table. "You can always give it back when Katie outgrows it, if it's even still usable at that point. Besides, it might not even be a girl…" Her eyes glistened. "There is no doubt in my mind whatsoever that Levi loves Josie and Risa every bit as much as their father did. But when I told him I might be pregnant, the look on his face…"

Now Deanna's smile felt frozen in place. Not that she wasn't delighted for Josh's brother and sister-in-law, but damned if she didn't feel cheated, that the look on *Phillippe's* face had been more a cross between panicked and furious. Still, before the self-pity demons got their clutches in her, it struck Deanna she was only the second person to know about this baby. True, she'd guessed, but Val could've kept her secret if she'd wanted to. And wasn't it crazy, how good that made her feel? How…included.

Val and the girls stuck around for maybe a half hour or so, at which point Josie—and Val—insisted on taking Austin home with them. Even though the silence left in their wake was so profound Deanna could practically feel it. But the solitude, the stillness, also enveloped her every bit as cozily as her old shawl, which she wrapped up in before walking out onto the hacienda's garland-draped veranda. Not to mention the sparkling clear light, the crisp mountain air, on this icy afternoon.

The memories. Of other early winter days, when her mother was still alive and the house *reeked* of Christmas, when she and Josh would saddle up their horses and ride out probably farther than their parents ever realized, not even caring when their butts went numb from the cold. She certainly hadn't felt hamstrung then, had she? If anything, she remembered a kind of contentment she hadn't felt since.

The thought brought her up short. As did the rustle of wings from the top of a nearby piñon—a hawk, its harsh keen knifing the quiet, prompting Thor to jerk awake from his spot on the veranda's sun-drenched lip to bark at the bird.

She'd missed this. All of it. Dogs and hawks and the sky, dotted with great big fluffy clouds. The peace.

Her breath catching in her throat, Deanna shut her eyes, letting the admission wash over her. Embracing it, even if she didn't have the foggiest notion what to do with it. Much as she still had no idea why she'd as good as admitted to Josh two days ago what she'd felt when they were kids. Seriously, why even bring up something neither one of them could have done anything about then? That still had absolutely nothing to do with *now*.

Never mind that she'd barely slept the past few nights, since he and Austin moved in. Although who could sleep with an octopus inside her? So much for the baby settling down once the head was engaged. Except the thing was, Octobaby's hyperactivity also gave Deanna way too much time to think about stuff. Okay, Josh. More to the point, how manly and funny and caring and crazy he was. The same as she remembered, only the grown-up version, which was proving a whole lot harder to ignore than she'd thought. Hoped.

How her poor sleep-deprived hormones had clearly made it their mission to torment her with images of Josh sleeping right down the hall. Or, far worse, wondering what his reaction would be if she asked him to give her a back rub. Yeah, those hormones were being stinkers of the highest order. Although would somebody please explain to her why in the *hell* she'd feel this hot to trot when she couldn't even walk from her bedroom to the john without getting winded?

Jeezy Pete, her thoughts were whistling through her brain like the wind through the trees.

Thor nudged Deanna's hand, his ice-cold nose making her jump. Chuckling, she bent over to give him some loving, a move which made her back twinge. She ignored it. Tried to, anyway. Really, she should waddle back inside, put away all the clothes Val had brought. Except then she'd think about Josh putting together the crib, or horsing around with his son, or thanking her for making dinner…

Sighing at her own silliness, Deanna and the dog trudged out to the barn—well, she trudged, he did more of a fox-trot—where her old horse was stabled, thinking maybe she'd let her out to enjoy the air. Or she could at least open a stall, right?

The cold only made the barn smell sweeter—Josh was meticulous about keeping the stalls as clean as possible— of hay and horse, overlaid with the slight tang of piñon smoke that permeated the air this time of year. Starlight immediately came over when Deanna got closer to the stall, the space bigger than her bedroom in her "fun"-sized DC apartment. Her father had always taken damn good care of his horses, too, another poignant memory that only spiked her grief. For things she'd had and lost, for things that had never been hers. Not really. Not entirely.

For things she'd like to be hers, even if she had no earthly idea how to get them.

"Hey, girl," she crooned to the mare, who laid her muzzle in the crook of Deanna's shoulder, her horsey scent intensifying the yearning. All she wanted, she realized, was home. But where was that? *What* was that—

"Oh!" she breathed out on a short gasp when the twinging suddenly morphed into something…different. Releasing the horse, she stepped away to grasp the top of the stall door and bend forward, trying to ease the pressure in her back…

She felt a weird, painless prick…followed by roughly five thousand gallons of water rushing down her legs.

Well, crap.

"Stay calm," she muttered to herself, fumbling for her phone. Never mind she was shaking so much she could barely see it. "It's all good, nothing to worry about..." She took a breath. Then another. Then looked at the phone again.

Focus, focus, it's okay...

Except for one tiny problem:

There was no signal!

Josh had been back on the road maybe twenty minutes when his sister-in-law's call came through on his truck's Bluetooth device.

"Hey, Val," he said, keeping an eagle eye on the rusted-out clunker a couple hundred yards up the road. A light snow had begun to fall. No biggie, though. "What's up—"

"I've been trying to get you for the past fifteen minutes," she said, and his heart went ba-da-*boom* against his ribs.

"Sorry, signal's pretty sketchy up here—"

"So Deanna hasn't called you? Well, if she couldn't get through—"

"Val! What's going on?"

"Probably nothing, really. But when the kids and I were out at the Vista a little bit ago she was complaining about her back hurting."

Josh relaxed. Some. "Yeah, she's been doing that a lot. Since before Thanksgiving."

"That's what she said. Still. I've got a feeling."

"But you didn't think she was in labor."

"Then? No. I wouldn't've left if I thought she was. Except then I got home, and..." He heard a soft, slightly nervous laugh. "Sorry, I'm probably sounding crazy."

"Not hardly," Josh said, knowing from experience that

when a woman said she had a "feeling," a smart man paid attention. "I take it you tried calling her?"

"Of course. Only she's not answering, either."

Damn. Josh glowered at the dude ahead of him, moseying along the road like he owned it. And of course this was the stretch where it was nearly impossible to pass. Especially with a stupid horse trailer hitched to his truck. "What about my mom? EMS?"

"Billie was about an hour away from the Vista when I called, she's on her way. And we're out of luck with the ambulance, they're out on another call." Unfortunately one of the major disadvantages to living in the boonies was that small-town volunteer emergency crews weren't always readily available. "And I'd go back over, but I've got the kids. Including yours—"

"No, no—it's okay. When did you last see her?"

"Maybe forty-five minutes? Oh, and it's started to snow."

Josh sucked in a steadying breath, releasing it on a rush of gratitude when the slowpoke finally turned off the road and he could step on the gas. Only a few miles left before the highway.

"I'm about a half hour out. At the most," he said, hoping to hell no state trooper was lurking in the bushes. Because right now the speed limit was only a suggestion. Unless the snow decided not to play nice...

"Keep trying to get her, and I will, too. But I'm sure she's fine," he said, more to reassure himself than Val. But the instant he disconnected the call he started praying harder than he ever had in his life.

And God laughed and ripped open the sky, instantly coating the countryside in white.

The first contraction hit while Deanna was still staring at her phone in disbelief, the pain almost enough to distract her from the absurdity of standing in soaking-wet leggings, in a freezing barn, with no other human being for miles. One of those things she'd probably find funny, ten, twenty years down the road.

At the moment, however…

At least, she thought when the pain let up enough *to* think, she'd be able reach someone on the landline.

Back at the house.

Way, *way*, back at the house.

That is, if she didn't die of hypothermia first, she mused as she inched out of the barn and that first wave of ice-cold air smacked the bejeebers out of her. At precisely the moment another contraction viced her lower belly like a sonuvabitch, pretty much bringing anything even vaguely resembling forward motion to a dead halt. And…wait.

Snow?

Okay, not exactly a blizzard, but still. Judging from the bigger, badder clouds rapidly moving in from the north, blizzarding was definitely a possibility. Soon. As in, probably sooner than she was going to make it to the house. Honestly, she didn't know whether to laugh or cry—or maybe both, what the hell—but since one was inappropriate and the other self-defeating, she nixed emotion altogether.

And, since she couldn't move, anyway, checked her phone. One bar. She'd take it. Only now, feeling like a jailbird who only got a single call, she was momentarily stymied as to who she should call first. A quandary she pondered as she took advantage of the break between contractions to continue her agonizingly slow trek toward the house, Thor now snapping at snowflakes as though he'd never seen them before—

"Jeebus!" she yelled when the phone rang, making her jump out of her goose-bumpy skin.

"Thank God," Josh said when she answered. "You okay?"

"Not even remotely."

"Wrong answer."

"Tough." Deanna looked up at the sky, which was now spitting snow in earnest. "Where are you?"

"Close."

"Woman in labor, here. Need specifics."

"Ten minutes, maybe—"

"It's snowing," she said, inanely, holding out her hand to catch a few flakes, like she used to do as a child.

"I know. You'll probably want to crank up the heat. How far apart are the contractions?"

"You don't wanna know."

She heard him sigh. "What're we talking? Every ten minutes? Five?"

"Um…two? Ish?"

The next word out of his mouth was colorful, to say the least. "I thought it wasn't supposed to happen that fast."

"Yeah, well, this kid clearly doesn't know from 'supposed to.' But the good news is…" Finally, *finally*, she made it to the veranda, which under other circumstances she might've knelt down to kiss. Although under other circumstances, she wouldn't have wanted to. She stopped, her eyes squeezing shut as she grabbed the nearest post to hang on.

"The good news is…?"

"I'm not…in the barn…anymore…"

Silence. Then: "Hang on, honey… I'm almost there…"

But she didn't answer him, because that blowtorch thing? Yep.

Too bad the heat wouldn't dry out her pants.

Chapter Nine

Over his hammering heart, Josh desperately tried not to think about how he might have to deliver this baby. So of course that was the only thing he could think about. Sure, he knew all about foaling horses, but for the most part his participation had been limited to watching. Or arriving on the scene after the blessed event had already happened. Horses were efficient like that. And since Jordan hadn't bothered to let him know Austin was coming until he'd already arrived, he hadn't even witnessed his own son's birth.

And not seeing his mother's pickup in front of the house wasn't exactly making him calmer. Although rising to the occasion was clearly his lot in life, so...

The trailer rattled like thunder when he slammed into the dirt drive. Thor bounced up to his door, barking his head off. *Geez, human, what took you so long? Lady person foaling, here, get the lead out!* Josh tumbled out of the truck, the dog beating him to the door.

"Dee?" he bellowed, his voice echoing off the great room's rafters. "Where are you, honey?"

"Bathroom!"

Hers, he assumed, his boots skidding on the tile when

he hit her doorway. Breathing hard, he stopped at the entrance to her bath, where she stood in the tub, of all places.

"I'm here," he said…and Dee took one look at him and completely lost it.

"Hey, hey…" Climbing into the tub with her, what the hell, Josh wrapped her close and kicked his own panic to the curb. "It's okay, honey, it's okay…"

"Those are t-tears of re-relief, doofus," she said, hiccupping a little laugh as she scrubbed her face, then tried to push away. "Eww, I'm all wet—"

"So I noticed," he said, which got a shaky little smile before she grabbed his arms like she was about to fall off a cliff. The moan started low and soft, only to rapidly escalate into something like out of a horror movie.

"Look at me, honey," Josh said, ignoring his own quaking stomach when her eyes squinched shut. "Dee! Look at me!"

"Can't," she panted out. "Hurts."

"I know, baby. Okay, I can guess," he said when she shot him a death glare. "But the breathing will help. Trust me."

Somehow, she obeyed, and he hooked his gaze in hers and started breathing slowly, deeply, encouraging her to follow his example, even as it nearly killed him to see how much pain she was in. How scared she was. And not, he didn't think, only about giving birth.

And at that moment, he hated the jerkwad who'd done this to her with the heat of a thousand suns. The jerkwad who obviously didn't give a damn about her or his daughter.

Even stronger than the heat, though, feelings Josh couldn't even identify rippled through him, that the woman the jerkwad had done this *to* had chosen to have this baby, raise this baby, *love* this baby…

That Dee had more courage than the jerkwad could

even dream about, a thought that made a knot swell in Josh's throat.

After what seemed like a year, the contraction let up, and Josh figured he had a pretty narrow opportunity to get her someplace other than the damn tub to have this baby.

Which begged the question, "Why are you standing in the tub, anyway?"

"Trying to figure out how to get these wet pants off. Seemed as logical a place as any. Except now..." She shrugged. He got it.

"You okay with me doing the honors?"

"You really have to ask? And how do you know about breathing?"

"Mom has these movies, Levi and I got curious one day. Okay. I won't look, I promise."

"Believe me—right now, I do not care who sees what. I just want this kid out of me."

"We can do that," he said, proud of how confident he sounded, even as worry replaced the pain in those big brown eyes.

"I'm not gonna make it to the birthing center, am I?"

"That would be my guess," he said, crouching to help her remove the soggy pants. "Roads are already pretty slick."

"And it was such a great birth plan, too," she muttered, and he smiled.

"Although the good news is my mother's on her way."

Dee's forehead bunched as her hands tightened around his shoulders. "What? How? When—"

"Val." He tugged as gently as he could, but the only experience he'd had with getting wet bottoms off a wet bottom was with skinny little boys. Not curvy nonboys. With giant, baby-filled bellies. "She had an inkling something was going on, so she called you after she left, to check.

But—" the soaked pants landed with a plop in the bottom of the tub "—you weren't answering your phone. So she called me. And my mother. And apparently half the county. Okay, put your arms around my neck and hang on," he said, scooping her up into his arms before she had a chance to realize those arms were against her bare bottom. And for him to fully register how heavy a full-term pregnant woman was. Damn.

His phone went off again, buzzing against his chest. "Get it out of my pocket," he said, trying not to grunt as he carried Dee over to her bed.

"It's your mother."

"Who you probably need to talk to more right now than I do."

"Good point. Hey, Billie," she said as Josh lowered her to the bed as gently as his muscles would let him. "Uh-huh...yep, he made it...a little while ago...every two minutes, maybe...no, not yet." Sitting on the edge of the bed, she handed him the phone. "She wants to talk to you."

"So the roads are total crap," Mom said in his ear as Dee's face crumpled again. Josh mimed steady breathing, but she wasn't paying a whole lot of attention. "Although I'm doing my best to get there. How close do you think she is—"

"Oh! *Oh!*" Dee grabbed for his hand, nearly cutting off his circulation. "Oh, *man*, do I want to push!"

"Never mind, I heard. Okay, listen to me. It could still be a while yet. Although considering how fast things are already moving, maybe not." Yeah, not encouraging. "So put your phone on speaker," Mom said, "I'm gonna talk you through it. Josh? You hear me?"

He did as she asked. "Got it. Okay, on speaker now."

"Good. Now go get a bunch of towels to put underneath

Dee and wash your hands. Y'all got a baby to welcome into the world!"

At Dee's halfhearted giggle, something shifted inside Josh, replacing the last scraps of fear with something far more powerful. More important. He thought about all times in her life men had let her down or abandoned her or shut her out or whatever.

Damned if his name was about to get added to that list.

Sitting on the edge of the bed, he reached out to cup her jaw, earning him a very startled glance.

"Let's do this, sweetheart," he said, and her trembling smile broke his heart.

Listening to the snow softly snick against the bedroom window, Deanna shifted the solid little bundle in her arms to kiss her silky forehead for probably the hundredth time since her birth two hours before.

She couldn't stop looking at her perfect little daughter.

She couldn't stop thinking about Josh.

But most of all she couldn't unknot her thoughts long enough to figure out which of them were worth hanging on to and which needed to be ditched. Like cleaning out the closet in her head.

Especially now, when Josh sat on the edge of the bed, softly chuckling when Katie screwed up her tiny face, her mouth puckering into an itty bitty O. Billie had finally arrived an hour after Katie did, basically to "tidy up," she said, since the birth had been textbook perfect, and was now in the kitchen tending to that casserole Deanna hadn't gotten around to making. But right here, right now, it was just the three of them cocooned in her bedroom while the out-of-nowhere storm continued its assault on the landscape outside.

As her memories of this amazing experience—of Josh—assaulted her from within.

He'd been her rock through the whole thing, not even flinching when the sensation of pushing out a cannonball might've made her scream, a little. Okay, a lot. Not to mention childbirth was a messy business. Hadn't even fazed him. Then again, he was a rancher, the man knew from messy. Also, she supposed this was fitting payback for the time she'd had to mop up *his* blood after he'd whacked his head on an unseen tree branch when they'd been out riding. Gosh, she'd forgotten all about that. How old had she been? Twelve? Thirteen—

"I've seen you make faces exactly like that," he said, and she looked at him looking at the baby, her little spidery fingers curled around his index finger, and thought, *Hell*.

"Hey," Josh said gently, his gaze shifting to hers. "What's with the tears?"

"Hormones, probably," Deanna said, trying to smile, even as a whole new slew of feelings threatened to take her under. Because in that sweet, tough gaze she saw... everything. Everything she'd ever wanted, everything she didn't dare let herself want. Because what good ever came from looking to someone else to fill the blanks in your life? Your heart. Even someone who'd been there for her in a way no man, no *one*, ever had.

Even if for only this moment—

"I think I'm transfixed," he said, and Deanna smiled. "Tell me about it."

Grinning, Josh propped his fist against the mattress on the other side of Deanna's legs, cupping the baby's capped head with his free hand. A hand that gripped reins and tickled little boys and hammered fence rails into place, banged up and scarred and callused, the nails jagged. *Real*. Like the rest of him—

"I missed this with Austin," he said quietly.

Deanna swallowed, then frowned. "How old was he when you first saw him?"

"Two weeks? Something like that."

"You're kidding?"

"Nope. Apparently Jordan had been having second thoughts."

"About?"

"Including me in our child's life," he said, tenderly stroking Katie's downy cheek. "Until she realized she was in way over her head, trying to do it by herself."

Deanna felt her face warm. "Some women can, you know."

His gaze flicked to hers, then away. "Some women, yeah. Not Jordan. Of course I had no idea when she showed up with this wailing baby that 'not doing it all by herself' would eventually turn into 'not doing any of it.' Although to be truthful I wasn't surprised. Gal definitely wasn't the maternal type."

"And you are," Deanna said, and Josh chuckled.

"Apparently so. Still. For a long time it irked me, that I missed seeing my son's entrance. That Jordan stole that from me."

"You still angry with her?"

"For leaving?" His head wagged. "Not so much anymore. Although I was at first. For Austin's sake, though, not mine. Frankly it was a relief, not having to deal with all that negativity." He sat up straighter to face her, his half smile masking his pain even less than his words. "But people are who they are. No sense hanging on to bad feelings about stuff you can't change. *People* you can't change." A soft laugh puffed through his lips. "I may've been stupid as hell, but at least I learned something from the experience."

"Which was?"

"To be a lot more careful about who I get involved with. Making sure we're on the same page about stuff. Or at least compatible. Honesty, too. That's a biggie. If not *the* biggie. If Jordan and I had been up front with each other from the beginning…" He humphed. "Of course I wouldn't have Austin, so there is that."

Deanna was quiet for a long moment, watching her sleeping daughter. Thinking about what Josh had just said about compatibility. Being on the same page.

Honesty.

"I'm glad you were here," she said softly, her gaze flicking over the freshly painted wall, now devoid of Lorelai's and Rory's grinning faces. "Not just grateful, I don't mean that. Although I am. But…" Her insides melted at his slightly puzzled smile. "But that you were here to share this with me. That it *was* you."

And she meant it. Sure, it hurt that neither of her parents were still alive to meet their granddaughter. But not once, not even for a split second, had she found herself regretting Phillippe's absence. Not even right after the baby's birth and it was Josh, not the baby's father, wrapping her up and putting her on Deanna's chest. That it was Josh grinning like hot stuff at the two of them, not the man who'd gotten her pregnant. Yes, what'd happened with Phillippe was ten kinds of wrong, no getting around that. And she doubted she'd ever forgive herself for being so naive. But Josh being here couldn't have been more right.

Another second or so passed before he said, "I'm glad I was here, too. But not nearly as glad that you didn't have this kid in the barn."

Deanna laughed. "*You're* glad? Believe me, the Mary-in-the-stable scenario was definitely not on my agenda. Hey, buddy," she said when Thor cautiously clicked into the room, his tail wagging when he came over to the bed, sniffing. He'd stayed well out of the way until now, most likely because her yelling had scared the bejeebers out of the poor dog. "It's okay, puppy, come see the new person. That's right, come on…"

When the dog inched closer, Josh carefully scooped Katie out of Deanna's arms—and yes, she felt the loss immediately—to lower the baby so the dog could check her out.

"Whaddya think, guy? Cute, huh?"

The baby squeaked and the dog cocked his head…then bowed, butt in air, and barked, his tail madly wagging.

"Sorry, dude," Josh said, chuckling as he gave the baby back to Deanna, his breath soft in her hair, his scent making her heart stutter. "She's too little to play." The dog barked again. "Yes, seriously—"

"So how're we doing in here?" Billie said from the doorway.

"Good." Deanna smiled down at her daughter, her heart turning over in her chest. "Really good."

"I can see that. Josh, why don't you take little bit for a moment so I can check out mama? Dinner will be ready in a few minutes."

"Glad to," he said, gathering Katie in his arms again, and Deanna watched Josh leave the room with her daughter, her heart constricting at how carefully he held her, his gentle smile as he talked silly to her the same way he did with his son. Billie sat on the edge of the bed to take Deanna's blood pressure, nodding in apparent approval at the reading.

"See? All you needed to do was give birth."

Deanna chuckled, then sighed. "Your son was…amazing."

"No surprise there. Boy never has been shy about stepping up, doing whatever needed doing."

"Like with Austin, you mean?"

"With anything." She stuffed the blood pressure cuff back in the bag she'd left earlier on the nightstand. "He even helped with Granville's nursing care, there at the end. Before poor Gus keeled over from exhaustion. Spent every night with him, sleeping in the chair beside your daddy's bed."

"He did? I didn't know that."

"That doesn't surprise me, either. Okay, let me just check to make sure everything's as it should be, then Josh can bring your daughter back…"

A minute later—all was well—Deanna repositioned herself and said, "How is it even possible to love something—some*one*—that much?"

Billie gave her a weird look. "Funny how that happens, huh? Now let's get some food in you, mama…"

A few days later, Josh came through the back door after picking up Austin from his folks' house to find Dee standing at the stove with the baby strapped to her front, stirring something that smelled like angels had been cooking. As usual her phone was docked to the Bluetooth adapter on the counter, filling the kitchen with a huge chorus belting out some Christmas carol. As was she, pausing every so often to "conduct" with the wooden spoon. She stopped midnote, though, when Austin giggled, grinning for the boy when he ran over to her to wrap his arms around her hips.

Her expression soft as an angel's, she cupped Austin's snow-flecked hair. "You have a good day, cutie-pie?"

"Uh-huh," he said, then pulled away to stand on tiptoe, trying to see into the pot. "What's that?"

"Soup," she said, gently tugging him away from the stove. "With all kinds of yummy things in it."

"Like what?"

"Oh…chicken and corn and carrots. Among other things. Whatever I could find. There's also corn bread. And brownies for dessert."

Austin made a face. "With nuts?"

Dee laughed. "Only on top. I'll be happy to eat yours if you don't want 'em."

"'Kay—"

"But only if you try the soup," Josh said, hanging up his barn coat on the hook by the door. "And go wash your hands."

"But I washed 'em at Grandma's!"

"When?"

Screwing up his face, he scratched his head. "Before lunch?"

"Then you get to wash them again. Go on, scoot."

Sighing mightily, the kid slogged off to the half bath and Josh came nearer to get a better smell. Of dinner, Dee, whatever. Yeah, the soup wasn't the only thing getting stirred, that was for sure. And wasn't it crazy, how much he wanted to slip his arm around her waist, nestle his chin on her shoulder to see the baby. Who was sound asleep, all cuddled next to mama like that.

Instead he settled for grabbing a clean spoon out of the drawer and snitching a sample taste.

"Hey!"

"Damn, this is good."

Even though she didn't look at him, he could see the smile toying with her mouth. "Thanks. Like I said, it's just stuff I found in the pantry or whatever. You can make soup out of pretty much anything."

"*You* can make soup out of pretty much anything. But might I remind you, you just gave birth three days ago?"

The look she shot him had *Seriously?* written all over it. "It's dinner, Josh. Not plowing the back forty. I think

I'm good. Also I was bored out of my ever-loving mind. Newborn babies aren't exactly great conversationalists."

Smiling, Josh cupped Katie's little head, cocooned in a knit cap barely big enough to cover his fist, a move that brought him even closer to her mother. A move that apparently made Dee suck in a sharp little breath, like he was breaching some boundary or other. Although if you asked him any and all boundaries had already been breached three nights ago when he'd helped guide this little person into the world.

But, you know. Women.

"I have news," she said quietly, staring at the bubbling soup, and Josh removed his hand, stuffing it in his pocket. "Oh?"

"I sort of got a job offer today."

"I thought you had a job."

"Okay, a better job offer." She rattled the lid back on the soup pot. "Much better, actually."

Josh frowned. "What? Where?"

Finally her gaze met his. "From another gallery in DC. One of those crazy things, someone knew someone who'd attended one of our showings, of an artist who was apparently very appreciative of my work, and long story short... totally out of the blue, this gallery owner emailed me, asking me if I'd consider coming to work for him. As in, big-time gallery owner, someone who showcases artists who've *already* arrived."

Quashing what felt ridiculously like disappointment, Josh gripped the counter edge behind him and said evenly, "You gonna take it?"

Dee turned to reach for soup bowls in the cupboard next to the stove. "Aside from the salary, which is already twice what I'm making, the commission potential...it's really good. Theoretically I could make as much from the sale of one work as I now do from selling three or four."

"Wow."

"I know, right? I was totally up front with him, though, said I had a new baby, wouldn't even be back until probably sometime in January, and wanted to work flexible hours." She set the bowls on the table. "He seemed fine with all of it."

And she seemed…not that excited, actually. "So… what's the problem?"

The baby squirmed; Dee palmed her daughter's head, kissed it through the hat. Then she laughed. If you could call it that. "This is absolutely the perfect fit for me. And it's mine for the taking. And yet…" Her shoulders lifted, gently bumping the baby.

"You sound like you need convincing."

That got a sigh. "Which is nuts, because the last thing I want—or need—is anybody trying to talk me into anything. Or out of it, whichever."

Josh frowned: what the hell was up with the waffling routine? But you know what? After her speech the other day about needing to figure stuff out for herself, damned if he was gonna pry. Even if it nearly killed him not to.

"So it's a good thing, then," he said, "that I'm the last person who'd do that. Since I learned a long time ago that people are gonna do what they want, anyway."

Her mouth tucked up on one side. "So basically you're no help whatsoever."

Josh crossed his arms, waiting out the mule kick to his gut. "A friend's job is to listen. Be a sounding board. But anything more? That's just asking for trouble."

"Friends?" Dee's eyes narrowed. "Like we were before, you mean?"

Okay, why did he feel like somebody'd just switched the

channel on him? "And will always be," he said cautiously, desperately trying to figure out what was going on. If anything. Because God knew he was no stranger to imagining things that weren't there. "I'll always have your back, Dee. But I'll never push you into something you don't want. Or try to talk you out of something I think you really do."

Chuckling, she turned to the fridge for a jug of milk, a pitcher of tea. "I need more friends like you," she said, setting the containers on the counter, then surprising him by curving one cold hand over his where it still gripped the edge. A nontouch, really, with little to no meaning behind it. Certainly nothing that should've scorched his skin the way it did. Not to mention a few other things. "Thanks," she said, and he smiled.

"Anytime."

Although once she left his *friendship* would be moot, wouldn't it?

The first three nights Katie had only woken up once, leading Deanna to foolishly believe she'd gotten one of those dream babies who'd be sleeping through the night in no time, and she'd breeze through this new motherhood thing like a champ.

Then Night Number Four arrived, and with it her daughter's apparent newfound goal to never let her mother sleep, ever again. The problem was, Deanna had always been a Sleeper, never even being able to pull an all-nighter in college because her body had simply said, *Um…no.* So when this little critter woke up at midnight…and two… and four…screaming as though she'd never eaten in her entire short life…

Muttering things loving mothers probably weren't supposed to mutter, Deanna somehow roused herself from what felt like a drugged sleep to turn on the low-wattage lamp on the dresser, then lean over the bassinet. How on earth could something that small be so fricking *loud*? And hungry? Close to tears as she tried to shake herself awake enough to change her, Deanna fumbled for a clean diaper and the wipes, only to jump a foot when she heard her door squeak open.

"Somebody giving you trouble?" Josh whispered behind her, and she swallowed, hard. Because wussiness was not an option.

"Sorry."

"For what?"

"Waking you?"

"You didn't," Josh said, gently shoving her aside and taking over the diaper changing duty. "She did. It's what babies do."

"You don't have to—"

"Hey. You made dinner. Fair exchange."

Far too gone to argue, Deanna stood with her arms crossed under her leaking, achy breasts, watching Josh efficiently clean and rediaper Katie's bottom in the chilly room. The old heating system never had worked very well in the bedrooms, and Deanna was too paranoid to use a space heater, no matter how safe they were supposed to be. Billie had only laughed and pointed out that's what sleep sacks were for, the kid would be fine.

"You're good at this," she said, watching him snap up the baby's sleeper, then stuff assorted limbs into a little fleece sack big enough to hold three of her.

Josh hmmed. "Between Austin and my nephews, I've had a lot of practice. It doesn't really get gross until they start eating solids, though."

"Thanks for the heads-up." Deanna yawned, then raked a hand through hair that felt like a freshly scythed wheatfield. Charming. Somehow, the wailing got louder. "What if she wakes Austin—"

"She won't." Josh stuffed the dirty diaper into the lidded garbage can by the table, then hauled Katie against his chest. Even in the dim light—and through the fog of exhaustion—that soft T-shirt left little to the imagination. Hers, anyway. "Kid sleeps through anything. Where do you want to feed her? Chair or bed?"

"Bed. It's warmer."

"Then get back in, I'll bring her to you."

Yawning again, she did, stuffing two pillows behind her back and hiking the covers up to her waist before reaching for Katie. But instead of Josh handing her the kid and returning to his own bed, he set about making a fire in the fireplace. A small one that would burn out fairly quickly, but still. Deanna's eyes burned. And not from the fire.

"That's..." She swallowed. "Lovely. Thanks."

"You're welcome." Apparently satisfied with his handiwork, Josh stood, staring at the flames for a moment before facing her, his forehead crunched. "I could hang out here until you're done—"

"You don't have to do that—"

"And I'm not taking any chances on you falling asleep before putting her back to bed."

Deanna had to smile. "And you won't?"

"Nope. I'll just sit over here..." He settled into her mother's old rocking chair, crossing his arms over his chest. Tightly. "You got an extra blanket or something, though?"

Oh, for pity's sake... "Why don't you get into the bed with us?"

Brows crashed. "You sure?"

As if. Especially since the double bed wasn't exactly roomy. "Of course."

Josh still hesitated, then crossed the few feet to the bed

and climbed in beside them, his scent, his body heat immediately swamping the space, making Deanna feel small
and warm and safe and scared out of her wits. Because
she had this ambivalence thing *down*, boy. Josh crammed
the other two pillows behind his own back, then his arm
behind his head.

"We should have a movie to watch or something."

Deanna chuckled. "Aside from there being no TV in
here…what would that be?"

He shrugged. "Dunno. Anything but a chick flick. Or
one of those things where everybody's talking in a weird
accent."

"God, you are such a rube."

"Yep," he said, shifting a little in the bed, much too
close. Much too *there*. "This is kind of nice, actually."

"If weird."

"Weird is subjective. And that's as profound as I get at
four in the morning."

Then he scrunched down under the covers on his side,
his head propped in his hand, and it occurred to her that
her whole idea of having a man in bed with her had just
gotten turned on its head. That in this moment, under piles
of bedclothes and fully dressed—well, except for the half-
exposed boob so her daughter could feed—she felt closer
to this man than she ever had naked with anyone else.

Weird? Heh. Not even close.

"So you decided yet about that job?"

She managed a weary laugh. "Can I get back to you on
that after I've had some sleep?"

"I'm serious. Because it sounds perfect for you."

"And you sound pretty sure about something you basically know squat about."

"I don't need to. But I'm guessing you do." He poked
her hip. Through three layers of bedding. "Which is why

that dude is so hot to get you on board. So you need to ask yourself—is this what you really want? Would it make you happy?"

Deanna looked down into that dear, sexy, aggravating face, forgetting for a moment how wiped out she was. "And what happened to not taking a position one way or the other?"

"Doesn't mean I can't encourage you to do something I really think you want to do. Or…am I wrong about that?"

"No, but…" Focusing again on her daughter, she tucked the blankets more tightly around her, shoving aside a disappointment she didn't even fully understand. "You make it sound so simple."

A moment passed before Josh said, very quietly, "I think the problem is, most people make things too hard. Harder than they need to be, anyway. But then, that's always been the difference between us, huh? Even when we were kids, you'd think things half to death before making a decision, while I'd go with my gut." He paused again. "Mostly, anyway. Since my gut and I didn't always agree. I'd hear it, sure. But I didn't always listen."

"Sounds like there's a story there," Deanna said, trying to lighten a suddenly heavy mood.

The covers went every-which-way when he sat up again, leaning much too close. And not nearly close enough. "All I know is," he whispered, looking at the baby, who'd sacked out in Deanna's arms, "people have a right to be happy. Otherwise, what's the point of living? She done?"

"Um…yeah. It's just…" Tired as she was, she smiled at her precious little girl, then barely touched her soft, soft cheek. "She feels so good, right where she is. It's hard to give her up."

Josh's rumbled chuckle vibrated through her, gentle and warm. "I can see that. But you're not going to be much good to her if you're dead on your feet. So hand her over, cupcake. I'm the best burper in these parts."

So, reluctantly, she did, her heart doing a slow turn in her chest as she watched him snuggle her child against that broad chest, as though she were the most precious, fragile thing in the entire world. Her eyes stinging, Deanna rehooked her nursing bra, her eyes immediately going heavy as she sank back underneath the warm bedcovers, barely hearing Josh getting up to put Katie back into her bassinet. And for a moment she felt the way home was supposed to make you feel, safe and loved and peaceful.

For a moment, she thought as tears pushed at her eyelids, she could almost believe in fairy tales.

"*Now* can I put stuff on the tree?"

His hands full of silver tinsel garland, Josh grinned down at Austin, a half dozen ornaments dangling from the kid's grimy fingers. It'd nearly killed the boy to wait while Josh strung the lights on the nine-foot fir. Especially since this was the first year Austin really understood that Christmas—and cookies and Christmas trees and *presents*—was an annual event.

"Go for it," he said, figuring he'd work the garland around his son's enthusiasm. Which would probably fade after five minutes, anyway. If that. Focusing wasn't a huge part of a preschooler's skill set.

He'd managed to hold off on getting the tree until two weekends before Christmas, although Josh wasn't sure who'd bugged him more about it—Austin or Dee. But even through the holiday excitement, not to mention the preparations for the party, Josh couldn't completely shake the dread of knowing what came after, that the ranch would go on the market, and most likely sell to some random stranger who'd do God knew what with it.

That he and Austin would have to find someplace else to live.

That in all likelihood Dee would take that new job back east. And very likely never return. Because why would she?

Josh glanced over at her, sitting cross-legged in leggings and a baggy, sparkly sweater on the couch, chattering to her daughter as Thor guarded them both, his head on her knee—

"I don't know where to put this one, Daddy. There's no room!"

Hauling his head out of his butt, Josh chuckled. The kid had hung five of the six ornaments on the same branch. "Come over where I am. Yeah, like that. See? Plenty of holes to fill up."

Austin flashed him the dimpled grin that shredded his gut every time. Then Dee called Austin over to where dozens of boxes of glittery decorations lay all over the floor, the coffee table, the other sofa.

"Did you see the box of birds, sweetie?"

"Where?" he said, looking every which way. Smiling, Dee touched his shoulder, gently steering.

"Right…there, that's it. Those were my mother's favorites. Mine, too, actually. Mom told me she brought them home from a trip to Germany when she was a teenager."

Austin had already carefully pried one of the jewel-like ornaments from its tissue paper nest, cradling it in both hands like it was a real bird. "Where's Germany?"

"It's a country in Europe. Far away from here."

"Like Albuquerque?"

"Even farther. We can look it up together on the globe later, how's that?"

Meaning the giant antique globe in the study, where Josh had caught Dee and his son "exploring" more than once in the past few days, their heads touching, her arm around his waist...

"'Kay," Austin said, gingerly carrying the bird across the room, where—after several seconds' serious consideration—the child who routinely broke every toy he'd ever received reverently placed it on the perfect branch.

"Good job! Only eleven more to go!" Dee said, and Josh realized she hadn't told the child to be careful, even though the delicate ornaments had to hold a special place in her heart. What kind of woman trusted a four-year-old like that?

The same kind of woman who showed little boys where to find countries on a globe. Who calmly explained breast-feeding like it was no big deal. Who never lost her cool when Austin did spill or break or mess up something. Who understood he was a child without ever treating him like one.

In other words, he thought as his son solemnly found a "home" for the next bird, the woman was seriously mess-ing with Josh's head. And that's not even counting that night he'd spent in her bed. Okay, not a whole night, and not exactly in a way most people would define that sen-tence. Still. Who knew there could be such intimacy in innocence? That seeing how tender Dee was with her new daughter, that watching her sleep after he'd put Katie back in her little crib, had aroused him in ways he wouldn't've thought possible? Hell, all he'd wanted to do was crawl back under the covers with her and wrap himself in her warmth, wrap her in *his*, keeping her safe from whatever made her forehead crease as she slept.

Whatever had caused that single tear to trickle down her cheek.

Even though he'd meant what he'd said, his own brow creasing as he moved to the back side of the tree—that she needed to do whatever made her happy. Made *her* happy, not anybody else. Certainly not him. And for damn sure not the ghosts still lingering in the house. No, he didn't believe in all that supernatural mumbo jumbo, spirits moving stuff around, making doors slam shut and all like that. But memories, expectations—the crap inside a person's head—could haunt a person every bit as bad. If not worse.

And he could tell, Deanna was haunted. By what, he wasn't sure. Nor was he sure he was the one to shine the light on her fears, convince her they weren't real.

Never mind that's exactly what he wanted to do. As in, so badly it almost hurt. Even though he wasn't sure about why that was, either.

Releasing a breath, Josh turned back to the tree to twist the garland around the next soft, sweet-smelling branch, finally admitting to himself how much he ached to be what he knew she'd never let him be. What Jordan had never let him be, either. Oh, sure, his ex had done all but shove the baby at him—she'd had no qualms about letting him take care of their kid. Not that he'd minded. Especially since the alternative—that she might've taken him from Josh entirely—would've been far worse. Any more than that, though...

Of course, Jordan just didn't want the obligation that came with being in a real relationship, the give-and-take of it. Dee, he strongly suspected, was simply flat-out scared.

And Josh had no idea how to get past that. Or even, frankly, if he should try. Since when all was said and done, they wanted very different things from life. On the same page? Hell, they weren't even in the same *library*.

Austin's laughter blending with Dee's made Josh peek from behind the tree as he tucked the garland's end into a branch. The kid had smushed up against her, giggling when Katie screwed up her face as her mama talked to her, like she was trying so hard to figure out what Dee was saying...and it was this frickin' picture-perfect moment like he'd always dreamed of, even if he didn't know it until *this* moment. His throat got all tight, that history was repeating itself, that he was falling in love with a woman he knew was all wrong for him, even as he watched her with his son and saw how right it could be.

For all of them.

Josh shoved out a soundless laugh—clearly the fumes from this damn tree had hallucinogenic properties. But he really did have to wonder why, in the name of all that was holy, that God, or Granville, or who*ever*, would plant Deanna Blake smack in front of him, like the grapes the fox could never reach in that dumb story he read to his son the other day.

Although, unlike the stupid fox who decided he was wasting his time trying to reach a bunch of probably sour grapes, Josh knew full well these grapes were sweet as could be.

Which made not being able to reach them all the more frustrating.

Chapter Ten

Inordinately pleased with herself, Deanna leaned against the archway separating the great room from the dining room, a glass of sparkling cider nestled in her hand and a smile touching her lips. To be sure, between the band's no-holds-barred rendition of "A Holly Jolly Christmas" and the laughter, the madness of God knew how many kids running around and thousands of twinkling lights and shimmering decorations, her senses had given up trying to cope an hour ago.

In other words, it was a perfect party. For everyone else, anyway.

And that was all that mattered, wasn't it?

"Lookin' good, Mama," Val shouted over the din as she came up beside Deanna, a zonked-out baby Katie in her arms. More people had held this kid tonight than had probably held Deanna in her entire life. "That dress is the bomb. Especially with that necklace."

Black velvet. Straight, short and a little more snug than it had been prebaby. And the bib necklace had been a birthday gift from Emily, the chunky red stones appropriately festive for the occasion.

"Thanks. You, too."

"Is it okay? I'm not one for dressing up much."

"It" was a lovely lace top worn over a pair of jeans, loose enough to hide the merest suggestion of a baby bump. A pair of dangly, glittery earrings and a messy updo had the little blonde looking every bit as chic as anyone Deanna had ever seen at one of the gallery openings. Which she told her.

Val laughed. "Levi just said I looked hot."

"Then what more do you need?"

"True," Val said, gazing over the crowd. And a crowd, it definitely was, bigger than Deanna ever remembered from when she was a kid. The band leader, a Willie Nelson clone if ever there was one, asked if anyone wanted to do a sing-along, which got an instant chorus of approval. Val turned to Deanna, her eyes soft underneath newly cut bangs.

"*Now* they're saying goodbye. To your dad, I mean. In a way he would've wanted."

"I know," Deanna breathed out. "Which is why I agreed when Josh suggested it. Why…" Her gaze took in the giant, stately tree at the far end of the great room, glittering with the hundreds of glass ornaments her mother had loved so much, most of which Dad had bought for her. "Why I did all this. To soften the blow."

"Oh, honey…" Val shifted the baby to one arm to tug Deanna to her side. As much as she could, anyway, since in her heels Deanna was nearly a head taller than her new friend. "I think they all understand a lot more than you're giving them credit for. Tradition might be the thing that holds this town together, but adaptability is what keeps everyone going when tradition falls on its sorry butt. And since my husband is giving me that look, I guess I need to give you back your child…"

A moment later, gently bouncing her daughter, Deanna retreated from the raucousness to the marginally quieter dining room. The goody laden table—she sent up yet another prayer of thanks for Annie and AJ, who'd happily catered the affair—glowed not only from the candlelight of her mother's treasured wrought iron candelabras, but from the luminarias lining the edge of the veranda outside. Not to mention the driveway and roof, a labor of love from all the Talbot men.

"You want to look outside?" she whispered to her daughter, kissing her downy head as she carried the baby over to the ceiling-high paned window, the shutters open to what could only be called a magical view. Another light snow had fallen, golden in the hushed, softly flickering light from hundreds of candle-filled paper bags. Deanna blinked back tears, practically *seeing* her parents, her mother with her head on her father's shoulders as they watched the last of their guests leave after a party much like this, their entwined figures limned in the same burnished glow.

And oh, how Deanna would practically shimmer with her own expectation for the holiday to follow, infected by her mother's love for the season. More images floated past her mind's eye—the almost worshipful look in Dad's eyes when Mom would set the Christmas roast on the table, their laughter as they cleaned up afterward.

Together. Always together.

A silent, shuddering sigh left her lungs. Her parents' love for each other was never a question. But that wasn't enough, was it, to overcome her mother's crippling loneliness—?

"Hey," Josh said behind her, his voice barely audible over the singing in the other room. "You okay?"

Nodding, Deanna hastily wiped her cheek, startled to realize she'd been crying.

"Just…remembering."

"That good or bad?" Josh said, taking the baby from her, his smile gentle when Katie did her funny little frowny face before settling back to sleep.

"Not sure. Don't suppose it's surprising, though, stuff popping into my head I haven't thought about in years." She smiled at him. "I'm glad we did this. Thank you."

Tucking Katie's head under his chin, Josh gave Deanna a look she couldn't quite define. "Closure?"

"Oh. I hadn't thought of it like that, but…maybe. Speaking of which…my current boss called today, badgering me again about when I was coming back to work."

"And?"

"And I quit."

"Ballsy," Josh said, and Deanna laughed.

"You have no idea. But I realized… I deserve better than that. No matter what happens."

A long pause preceded, "Does this mean you've decided to take the other job?"

"It means I'm free to take the other job, if I want—"

From the great room, a great roar went up from the crowd. Josh turned to her, grinning.

"I'm guessing Santa's here. Come on," he said, his hand going to her waist to steer her back to the party. Never mind that she hadn't finished her sentence.

Then again, maybe it was just as well. Since she wasn't entirely sure she could.

"So did you have fun tonight?" Josh asked, finally getting his son into bed nearly two hours past his bedtime. Nodding, Austin yawned, grabbing for his ratty Kanga, a gift from Josh's parents two years ago that had inexplicably become The Toy, although Roo had gone missing ages ago.

"Uh-huh," his sleepy little boy said, yawning again. "'Cept I know that was Grampa playing Santa."

Josh chuckled. "Oh, yeah?"

"Yeah. But don't tell 'im I know, 'cause I don't wanna hurt his feelings."

"Got it. Okay, buddy, I need to get back to help Dee clean up—"

"Are Dee and the baby really gonna leave after Christmas?"

Remembering their conversation—not to mention the pain in her eyes all those memories had obviously dredged up—Josh felt his chest go tight. "As far as I know, yeah."

Austin's forehead pinched. "How come?"

"Because she doesn't live here, guy. She was only visiting."

The little boy tugged the kangaroo closer, and Josh could practically hear the wheels turning. "But she *feels* like she lives here. Like this is her house. She feels like…"

Gently, Josh brushed his son's hair away from his face. "Like what?"

"A mom."

Josh started, thinking, *And how do you know what a mom feels like?* But he'd had enough examples, hadn't he? His grandmother, for one thing. And more recently Val with her girls. Not to mention the other mothers in town who brought their kids to the church day care. The kid was four, not blind. Or immune to the concept of feeling like something was missing.

Something Josh knew all about, didn't he?

"I know, squirt—"

"You need to make her stay."

Oh, jeez… "Can't do that, buddy."

"How come?"

"Because trying to make people do something they don't want to do isn't good. Dee would have to want to stay. Otherwise she'd be unhappy." Never mind how easily she fit in tonight, crouching to talk to kids she'd never met, completely tuned in to whatever they were saying; laughing at old people's jokes; freely dispensing hugs. Giving Josh a grin and a thumbs-up at one point when it was obvious the party was a hit. "And you wouldn't want that, would you?"

"Noooo, but…" The frown got deeper. "So how do we make her want to stay?"

"We don't. Sorry. But maybe—" Because he was not above grasping at straws. "Maybe after Dee goes back to DC, we can go visit her sometime. And you can see where the president lives. And there's a great big museum there where they have all kinds of neat stuff, like a whole bunch of really old airplanes. And dinosaur skeletons. Wouldn't that be cool, to go see all that?"

That got several seconds' worth of *Not buyin' it, dude*, before the kid's eyes got wet, and Josh remembered that for a four-year-old, *today* was the only thing that mattered. The only thing you could count on. Even *tomorrow*, in most cases, was sketchy. Even so, it wrecked Josh something fierce, that some things, you couldn't promise a kid. No matter how much the kid might want them, or how much you might want to make those promises.

Or want those things yourself.

Yeah, sometimes being a parent sucked. Especially when you could see in your kid's eyes questions he didn't even know how to ask, that you couldn't answer even if he did. Questions that would probably surface one day or another, questions like *How come my mother left?*

Or *Why does loving somebody hurt so much?*

"Hey," Josh said, gently tickling Austin's tummy and getting a tiny smile for his efforts. "You got any idea how much I love you?"

The smile got a little bit bigger. "Lots?"

"Oh, way beyond *lots*. Like, so much more than *lots* it can't even be measured."

"More than God loves me?"

Josh smiled. "Maybe not more than that, He's pretty big. But as close to that as a person can get, how's that? And I'm not going anywhere. Or Grandma and Grandpa. Or a whole bunch of other people who love you like nobody's business. So. Are we good?"

A moment passed before Austin lurched onto his knees to throw his arms around Josh's neck, and Josh wasn't sure which one was holding on harder. Or whose heart was being squeezed more.

"I take it that's a yes?" he said, and his son nodded against Josh's neck, then slipped back down onto his pillow, Kanga strangled in his arm.

"How many sleeps until Christmas?" he asked.

"Let me see…six."

"That's *way* too many."

Chuckling, Josh stood, his fingers in his front pockets. "It'll be here before you know it. Now go to sleep, and when you wake up, guess what?"

"What?"

"It'll only be five."

Grinning, Austin squeezed shut his eyes and was somehow instantly asleep, and Josh sent up a short prayer of thanks: *one crisis averted, a million and three to go.*

The house, as he walked back down the hall toward the kitchen, shimmered with the calm-after-the-storm silence that had always followed these shindigs as long as Josh could remember. The elves—as in, his family—had already cleaned up and, apparently, left. But he found Dee and Katie in the kitchen, the infant asleep in a baby seat a safe distance away from the woodstove, the cat on one side, the dog—who looked up when Josh came in to thump his tail—on the other. Dee stood at the counter, wrapping up leftovers, softly singing along to the "Hallelujah Chorus." That, he knew. Not well enough to join in, no, but at least he recognized it. And even liked it. Kind of.

But instead of announcing his presence, Josh stood in the doorway, his hands slugged in his back pockets, watching. Listening.

Longing.

How do we make her want to stay?

Damned if he knew. What he did know was how effortlessly she meshed with the town, his family. His life. That the way she'd interacted with everybody tonight, her smiles and laughter, the way she'd *glowed*—that'd been the real Dee, whether she realized it or not. Sure, there was still *stuff*, if her subdued mood when he'd found her in the dining room was any indication. But everybody had *stuff*. That didn't mean—

Dee turned, her face flushed and her lips tilted in a questioning smile, and the longing turned into something more…insistent.

Foolhardy.

"Hey," she said, the smile softening. "Didn't know you were there."

"Everybody else gone?" Josh asked, his heart rate picking up speed. Like a freaking runaway train.

"Yep. It's just us," she said, forking a hand through now limp spikes, and the train ran right off the damn track. "Josh?" she asked, questions swarming in her eyes as he approached her…cupped her face in his hands…kissed her…

And damned if she didn't kiss him back.

Hallelujah, was right.

Not until that very moment, when Josh's lips touched hers and his tongue slipped into her mouth—cowboy was not shy, that was for sure—had Deanna realized she'd been wondering what it would be like to kiss Josh Talbot since she was fourteen years old.

Well, now she knew.

And all she could think was, when he claimed her mouth again with a second kiss so deep it threatened to eviscerate her soul, *And aren't we in a whole heap of trouble now, missy?*

As in, nipple-prickling, clutching-his-shirt, please-don't-stop kind of trouble.

Except—big sigh, here—*somebody* had to, and that particular ball would seem to have landed in her court. Before other balls landed in other courts and, well, yeah. But no.

Because at least this time, she *knew* she was needy.

At least this time, Deanna knew from the outset there wasn't a chance in hell this could work. The same as she always had with Josh, for pretty much the same reasons—that they were too different, wanted different things from life. And it would kill her, to break his heart. Let alone Austin's.

Not to mention she wasn't all that wild about getting hers broken again, either. Especially since she wasn't all that sure it was fully healed after the last debacle.

So, with an oh-so-mighty effort, she unclutched his shirt to press her hands to his chest, refusing to look at him as his heart hammered against her palms, and took a very...deep...breath.

"Oh, Josh," she said, in this stringy little voice that didn't even sound like her.

He let her go as though she'd just caught fire.

And laughed.

Frowning, Dee finally met his eyes, full of Joshness. And still, if she wasn't mistaken, arousal. Even though he

briefly clamped his hands around her shoulders to place
a quick, brotherly smooch on the top of her head before
releasing her again.

"You're not…mad?"

His brows dipped. "After a kiss like that? Why would
I be mad?"

"Because… I…" She blew out a short sigh. "Because
we can't. Okay, *I* can't."

"Yeah, I figured that's what you'd say," he said with a
shrug, then lifted the plastic lid off the nearest container
to snag a stuffed mushroom, which he popped into his
mouth. "But to be honest I've been wanting to do that since
I was fifteen. And I figured, since I might not get the opportunity again, to go for it while I had the chance. Can't
say as I'm sorry." He filched another mushroom. "Damn,
Dee…where'd you learn to kiss like that?"

Her face warmed. "Is that your usual modus operandi?
Kissing someone whether or not she's indicated she's good
with that?"

The mushroom hung suspended six inches from his
mouth before he lowered it again. "No, Dee," he said softly.
"It's not. And frankly I never have before this. Before *you*.
But you know what?" Tossing the mushroom in the trash,
he backed away, hands up. "I take it back, I am sorry. More
sorry than you have any idea. Because you're right, that
was a real dumb move on my part. And I promise you, it
won't happen again."

Then he left the kitchen before her tongue came un-
glued from the roof of her mouth long enough for her to
point out the obvious, which was that she had kissed him
back—with more enthusiasm than she'd ever kissed anyone back in her entire life, actually—so she was every bit
as complicit in what had just happened as he.

And he would've been totally justified in calling her on it.

That he hadn't only balled up everything in her head even more.

Even though Deanna apologized to Josh the next day for her reaction—an apology he seemed to accept graciously enough—there was no denying the tension now present in every conversation, every interaction, that hadn't been there before that kiss. Honestly, it was ridiculous, how hard they were trying not to offend each other. And this... carefulness between them hurt far more than she could have imagined. As though one little make-out session had somehow turned them into different people. Into strangers.

So she was beyond grateful when Val invited her to meet up with her and Mallory and all the kids in town to do some last-minute Christmas shopping. Despite the heaviness clogging her heart, Deanna had to smile at the same tacky decorations she remembered from when she was a kid, how several businesses still decorated the spruces in the town square with everything from miniature chile *ristras* to traditional cornhusk figures to giant, glittery globes the size of basketballs. And the air was crisp and clean and smelled of woodsmoke and evergreens, and the frosted mountains sparkled against the deep blue sky, and little kids sprinted from tree to tree, laughing, their innocent joy wrapping around Deanna's heart, soothing it. Healing it.

Confusing the hell out of it.

They'd gotten churros and hot chocolate from Annie's and were sitting on one of the battered benches in the square—well, Val and Deanna were on the bench, Mallory was in her wheelchair—bundled against the cold, although at this altitude the glaring midday sunshine kept the frostbite at bay. Mallory had commandeered Katie, practically invisible inside a snowsuit that used to belong to the toddler now shrieking back to a crow pretending to be a tree topper. They'd brought Austin, too—of course—and it almost frightened Deanna how much she'd grown to love the sweet, funny little kid in only a few weeks.

Although that wasn't nearly as frightening as how she felt about his father—

"Ohmigosh, Dee," Mallory said, sweeping her long red hair back over her shoulders as she grinned at the baby. "She is so freaking gorgeous. And don't you love how they can sleep through—" Risa shrieked at the crow again, the sound echoing around the square "—anything?"

"Except at night," Deanna said on a sigh. "Kid wakes up if I breathe too loudly."

"Because, hey," Val said beside her. "Twenty-four-hour dairy bar. Right?"

Deanna looked at the blonde, hunched into a pile-lined hoodie worn under a down vest, her cowboy-booted feet crossed at the ankles. "So you breastfed, too?"

"I did. Probably will this time, too." This said with a smug grin, bless her heart. The secret was no longer a secret, since keeping the news to himself was apparently beyond Josh's twin.

"One question." Deanna lowered her voice. "When does the dripping stop?"

Val laughed. "Yeah, the fun part. I swear I felt like an automatic sprinkler system for weeks. But it does get better. Eventually." She chomped off the end of her churro, then wiped the pastry's cinnamon sugar from her chin with a napkin. "Does make things awkward for a while, though."

"Things?"

"As in sex," Mallory said, still staring at the baby. "Bras and nursing pads—not exactly alluring."

Val snorted a laugh through her nose. "You kidding? *Willingness* is alluring. At least in my experience."

Deanna blushed so hard her cheeks actually hurt. "Not an issue for me," she muttered, biting a hunk from her own churro in the ensuing, deafening silence.

"So," Val said brightly, "you're staying through the holidays?"

"Might as well," Deanna said as nonchalantly as she could manage. Although after that kiss? She'd considered leaving as soon as she could book a flight home. But while on the surface that might've been the easiest solution, it was also the most cowardly one. And if ever a time called for big girl panties, this was it. "Since it'll be easier to get a flight after the New Year…"

God, did that sound as lame to everyone else as it did to her?

Austin ran over to throw himself across Deanna's lap, grinning, cheeks pink underneath a triple-cuffed beanie, and Deanna's heart nearly burst out of her chest.

"Jeremy an' Landon and me are playing airplanes! It's so fun! Watch!"

Then the little boy zoomed off, arms outstretched, to join Josh's oldest nephew and Mallory's son, the natural leader of the pack. Deanna had missed this as a kid, not having siblings or cousins close by, living too far outside of town to hang out with the local kids very much. Except for Josh, of course—

"He clearly adores you," Mallory said softly, making Deanna start. Val popped up off the bench to see to Risa, who'd tripped over nothing and landed hard on her tummy. "I remember those days of being worshipped."

Oh. She'd meant Austin. Of course. Except…

"Only Austin's not mine."

Instead of responding, Mallory shifted the baby in her

lap, sweeping a strand of coppery hair off her cheek. "So no nibbles yet on the Vista?"

Mallory's attempt to shift the subject to safer, more neutral territory, Deanna assumed. Oddly, it wasn't. "It's not even going on the market until after the New Year—"

"Oh, please. Realtors are masters at letting things 'slip.' And the Vista is prime property."

Her forehead bunched, Deanna turned to the woman holding her daughter. Prime property indeed. Especially for Hollywood types hankering to play rancher during their downtime. And the used-to-be film star undoubtedly still had connections.

"You have a buyer."

Amusement danced in Mallory's soft gray eyes. "I do. Me."

Deanna blinked. "What? Why? You already have a place—"

"Not to live in, for a therapy facility. I've been thinking about looking for a place for a while now, actually. Ever since Zach took me to the one that got me riding again. And Zach understood…"

The other woman cleared her throat. Deanna already knew Mallory had been a champion barrel racer as a teenager back in Texas, before Hollywood. And long before the skiing accident that had left her in a wheelchair and derailed her acting career. And that Josh's older brother had been instrumental in helping Mallory reembrace something that'd clearly meant the world to her at one time.

"He understood what you needed?" Deanna ventured.

Smiling softly, the redhead met Deanna's gaze. "Even if I didn't." She looked back over the square, her breath misting around her face. "Which is how it so often goes, isn't it? Somebody else seeing what you can't? I came here to escape. Didn't work out that way."

And clearly she was not in the least unhappy about that. Mallory's words prickling her consciousness, Deanna took a sip of her hot chocolate. Except it'd gone cold and cloying, nearly choking her. She cleared her throat. "Escape? From what?"

"Life? Myself? A pity party that'd gone on five years too long?" Mallory shrugged. "But Zach knew it wasn't escaping I needed. What I needed, what he *knew* I needed, was to reclaim my...dominion. And now...well. Wouldn't it be lovely, helping other people get past their fears like I did?"

"It would," Deanna got out. Somehow.

"Also, from what little I knew of your dad, I think he'd be pleased, don't you? Knowing his family home was being put to good use?"

Would he? Even though those weren't the plans *he'd* envisioned for it?

For Josh and her?

Deanna's eyes cut to Mallory's. "So whose idea is this, really? Yours? Or Zach's?"

Mallory laughed. "As it happens, I was about to bring it up to Zach when he beat me to the punch. I swear, sometimes it totally freaks me out, how much we think alike." Her smile softened. "Almost as much as how against all odds this incredibly good man landed in my life. And I thank God every day that he didn't give up on me—on us—when *giving up* would have seemed the most logical choice."

Deanna smiled, even though Mallory's words, not to mention her I-don't-give-a-damn-who-knows-it happiness, made her even squirmier than she already was. "I didn't know Zach all that well when I was a kid, since he's so much older. But I do remember he was a good guy, even then."

"I gather all the Talbot boys were. Are."

"Well, the jury was out on Levi for a long time," Deanna said, ignoring Mallory's subtext as she smiled at Levi's newly pregnant wife playing hide-and-seek with all the little kids behind the sparkly trees. "In fact, you'd've never known he and Josh were twins, they were so different. And who knows about Colin."

"Ah, yes. The mystery man. Zach's not even sure he'll come to the wedding." Set for some time in the spring, Josh had said. "But back to my proposal…it's a serious offer, Dee."

"Didn't think it wasn't. But Josh doesn't know about it yet?"

"I thought I'd feel you out first," Mallory said gently. "Since it's your home—"

"Only half mine, now." She faced Mallory again, her heart pounding painfully against her sternum. "But even before, the Vista was every bit as much Josh's as mine. In every way that really counts. Especially since I haven't even lived here in more than ten years."

"So what if I buy *you* out," the redhead said, excitement making her cheeks brighter than the cold already had, "and Josh could keep his half interest and keep living there with Austin, since Zach and I are perfectly happy where we are. The therapy end would be entirely separate. It could definitely be a win-win for both of you."

Deanna looked away, her stomach churning, even as she knew this could be a perfect solution. Josh could stay right where his heart had always been, and Deanna would still have plenty to invest for Katie's education. Not to mention this would be a painless way to sever her ties without hurting Josh—

Josh? Or yourself—

"This way the Talbots could still keep all the traditions alive," Mallory said, as though assuming Deanna's silence meant she needed to up her sales pitch. "Whispering Pines…"

Mallory smiled down at Katie, making cute little baby faces in her sleep. "What I loved most about this town, the whole area, when I first came here years ago, was that sense of real community I remembered from when I was a kid in Texas. And the people here…from the get-go they made Mom and me feel like one of them. We were…"

She smiled. "Embraced. Welcomed. A lot more than I would've expected, since I do know small towns aren't always like that. But this one is. After so many years of not actually feeling connected to anything real, to have finally found home again…there's no price to be put on that. So if I can in some way help keep intact whatever makes Whispering Pines so special—and I think the Vista plays a huge part in that…" Her eyes touched Deanna's again. "I'd be very honored."

Katie woke up, started to whimper. Deanna stood to take her daughter from Mallory, almost overwhelmed by the wave of protectiveness that washed over her.

"I'll have to talk it over with Josh, of course."

"No rush. Really. Only promise me you'll give me first rights of refusal?"

The baby tucked against her chest, Deanna smiled down at Zach's fiancée. "But you don't even know what we're asking for the property."

"Not an issue," Mallory said, a smile teasing the corners of her mouth. "Now—" she pivoted the wheelchair to face the square. And the small herd of children in it. "I suppose we should corral these little critters before they freeze…"

Deanna hugged her daughter more closely as it occurred to her that everything she'd worked toward the last few weeks was almost effortlessly falling into place. She'd have funds for Katie's education, Josh would get to keep the ranch...a perfect solution, really.

So why didn't she feel happier about that?

Chapter Eleven

"Hey, squirt," Josh said, grinning for his kid when he came storming into the kitchen, where Josh was fixing himself a sandwich. He grabbed the kid to swing him up on his hip, kiss his cold cheeks. "You have a good time?"

"It was *so* fun," Austin said, linking his hands around the back of Josh's neck. "An' DeeDee and me bought you a present, 'cause she said Santa only brings 'em for kids, not for grown-ups." His smooth little forehead pleated. "That true?"

"Mostly, yeah," Josh said, trying to keep a straight face. "But I don't think you're supposed to say you got something for me."

"DeeDee only said I couldn't tell you what it is. And I'm not gonna. 'Cause it's a secret."

"Good. Where is she, anyway?"

"She went to feed the baby in her room. C'n I go play with Thor out back? I already ate."

"Okay, but only as far as the Big Tree."

"I *know*," the boy said as Josh lowered him to the floor. "I'm not a baby, sheesh."

Josh sighed as kid and dog ran out the back door, then chomped off a big chunk of the sandwich before going down to Dee's room, where he stood at the door warily spying on her. Seated in her mother's old rocking chair wedged into a corner of her bedroom, she softly chattered to Katie while the baby nursed, her hand batting at Dee's chest. Chuckling, Dee caught the tiny hand and kissed it, holding it to her lips as the baby continued to suckle.

And Josh's gut knotted, that no matter what choice he made when it came to Dee, it never seemed to be the right one. Instead of maybe giving her a reason to reconsider her move, to reconsider him, all he'd given her was even more reason to leave.

More reason to remember *all* the reasons why they wouldn't work.

And yet, for all Dee's insistence on returning "home," he couldn't help wondering what, exactly, she was returning *to*. Since Emily had let it slip that Dee's social life hadn't been exactly hopping *before* the pregnancy. That for various reasons Emily had become her only real friend, and her aunt and uncle…well, who knew what was going on there. Nothing good, as far as he could tell. She had her little apartment, and what could be a good job, he supposed. But that wasn't exactly a life, was it?

Still. Although he was obviously a fool, he wasn't so much of one as to bring that subject up with her. Because God knows he'd had enough of those "talks" with Jordan that no way was he going down that particular road again. Like he'd said to Austin, Dee had to want to stay here. *Want* a life with him and his son. Clearly she didn't. And never let it be said he couldn't learn from his mistakes.

Apparently sensing his presence, Dee looked over with a slightly nervous smile curving her mouth, and Josh wanted to smack himself, for letting a single, stupid impulse ruin what had been good and right and honest between them. That he hadn't let well enough alone.

"Ah. You're here." Dee nodded toward her unmade bed. "Have a seat."

"That sounds ominous."

She sort of laughed. "Not at all. In fact, it's good news. At least I think so."

The old Navajo rug absorbed his boots' clomping as Josh crossed to the bed and lowered himself to the edge, then leaned forward to link his hands between his knees. He caught a whiff of those rumpled sheets, smelling of baby and fabric softener, faintly of her perfume, and his libido stirred, intrigued. He told it to go back to sleep.

"So Mallory and I got to talking while we were in town," Dee said, "and...she'd like to buy my half of the Vista."

It took a second for her words to register. "You serious?"

"Well, she certainly seems to be. To turn it into a therapy ranch. Partly, anyway, since she fully expects you to keep your enterprise going, too."

He couldn't tell from the tone of her voice how she really felt about this turn of events, although her refusal to look at him told him something. What, exactly, he wasn't entirely sure.

The thing was, on the surface it wasn't a bad idea. At least, a helluva lot better one than selling the ranch outright to some stranger, of Josh losing his home as well as whatever chance he'd convinced himself he might have with Dee. Even if that second thing was now obviously a nonissue. The minute he started peeking below the surface, however, things started feeling sketchy.

"I suppose," he said carefully, "we could consider it."

"That's what I told her." Dee shifted the baby up onto her shoulder to burp her, smiling when the kid released a belch loud enough to hear across the state line. "Not until after the holidays, though. If you're okay with that." When he didn't say anything—because he honestly wasn't sure what that would be—she went on. "This could be the perfect solution, don't you think? Especially since it would keep the ranch in the family."

His frown gouged his forehead. "Whose family, Dee? The ranch belonged to the Blakes. Not the Talbots."

"Technically, maybe. Although you know as well as I do your family's connection to the Vista runs every bit as deep as mine did." She fiddled with her top to put the baby to her other breast, and Josh felt another kind of pull that went way beyond sex. She paused, looking out her bedroom window, where they could see Austin romping with the dog. "Your connection, especially."

For the first time he heard something he hadn't before, although he supposed it'd always been there: sadness. Not bitterness, or boredom, but something more like grief, if he had to put a name to it.

As in, the Vista held some pretty bad memories for her. Memories he now finally, fully realized trumped whatever good ones there might've been, whatever glimmers of hope he might've thought he'd seen in her interaction with his family, the community. Hell, her mother had died here; her father had more or less ignored her before sending her away. Those two things, on top of the isolation she'd already felt...no wonder she wanted to get away. Again.

"You really were miserable here, weren't you?"

A huge sigh left her lungs before she smiled again, forced though it might've been.

"Not all the time," she said. "There were...moments. But there was a reason I glommed on to you. Because you made it bearable." The smile brightened, slightly. "Even fun, sometimes. Still. The moment I returned I remembered..." Glancing around, she sighed again. "How abandoned I'd felt here. Yes, you did your best. And Gus, God bless 'im. But none of that changed how I felt, even if those moments temporarily alleviated it. And then...*then*..." She looked down at the baby, her mouth pulled tight. "There's that whole manipulation business."

"Your father, you mean."

She grimaced. "All I wanted, when I was a kid, was for him to really pay attention to me. A real connection. Like you have with Austin. Like I pray I do with this one," she said, smiling for her daughter. "Not to be made to feel like a chess piece to be moved at will."

"The same way you felt manipulated by Katie's father."

A pause preceded, "Because what else do I know, right?"

And, oh, how Josh wanted to plead that he wasn't like that. And wouldn't be. But even he knew if you had to argue your case, you didn't really have one to begin with. If she didn't know who he was by now...well. Nothing he could do about that.

"Except if Granville sent you away because you were unhappy here—"

"He sent me away," she said flatly, "so he wouldn't have to deal with me. Because..." Josh saw her swallow. "Because I wasn't Mom and he couldn't deal with that. So *now* he wants to fix things?" She scoffed, then lifted her face to his, apology swimming along with the tears in her eyes. "And please don't take offense, because none of this has anything to do with you."

"Good to know," he said, and she pushed out a tiny laugh.

"It's only, when you think of home," she said, looking out the window again, "you should get a warm, fuzzy feeling, you know? Good memories, good associations—"

"And what's in DC for you?" Josh blurted out, earning him a justifiably startled glance. But dammit, somebody had to say it. "Seriously? Because it sure as hell doesn't sound like you've got a whole lot of good memories from there, either—"

"A *future*," she lobbed back. "Or at least a promise of one. Opportunity—"

"That job offer, you mean?"

A second, then another, preceded, "Yes."

"And there's more to life than work."

"There's nothing for me here, Josh," she said, sadly. But more than that, as though the very thought exhausted her. "Maybe if I felt more nostalgic—"

"Screw nostalgia," Josh said, angrier than he probably should be. "We're talking about now, dammit. And *now* there are people here who care about you, who could help *take* care of you—"

The words were no sooner out of his mouth than he realized how deeply he'd put his foot in it. Especially when she gave him almost a pitying look.

"People?" she said at last. "Meaning you? The person who said he refused to get involved with anyone else unless he was sure he and that hypothetical someone else were on the same page?"

Did she even realize what she was saying? Or was he sorely misinterpreting things? Which was entirely possible. See, this was what he hated about trying to talk to women, how they never came right out and said what they meant, but danced around the subject like it was up to you to figure out the coded message.

Except, even if he wasn't, no way in hell was he going to push. Because that had worked out so well before, hadn't it?

"As a friend, Dee. A *friend*. Like I said. And what's so awful about that? About letting somebody be there for you?"

Their gazes tangled for a good, long moment before she said, very gently, "That wasn't just a *friendly* kiss, Josh. And aside from all the other stuff, I can't..." Her throat worked again. "I can't be what you and Austin need. Who you need."

"And that's just crazy talk—"

"Which only proves my point, that there's way too much stuff in my head to sort out for me to be in a relationship with anybody. If nothing else..." She looked down at the baby, then released a breath. "My last experience with this one's father was a wake-up call. Just like yours was with Austin's mom. Only in my case..."

Her gaze brushed his again. "God knows I still have a lot of growing up to do, but at least my eyes are a little more open than they were before. And for Katie's sake, for yours and Austin's, I'm not about to take a risk on something where the odds aren't exactly in our favor to begin with. I can't come back, Josh. Because I can't *go* back to being who I was before."

"And who is that?" Josh said through a tight throat.

Her smile was soft. "The little girl still looking for somebody to connect with. To...complete her." He saw her eyes fill, and his own burned in response. "And it would be way too easy to let you be that person."

Holy hell. The room positively reeked of her fear, rolling off her in waves. She was right about one thing, though— whatever was going on in her head had nothing to do with him. Not deep down. So maybe he should be grateful she was giving him an out.

"Well," Josh finally said, "I expect Mallory will be pleased."

Dee shut her eyes for a moment, then nodded. "So you're good with her proposal?"

"I think that's what they call the best of a bad lot," he

said, then left the room, yanking his barn coat back on to walk outside, listening to his son's laughter, the dog's barking, as his gaze swept over the land he'd never imagined might be his one day. That now, after coming close to losing it altogether, would be his forever. Or at least half of it. Which was more than he could have ever hoped for a few months ago.

So how come he'd never felt more empty in his life?

When Josh returned, Deanna suggested she and Katie move to the foreman's cabin. Josh, however, not only pointed out that moving all of the baby's stuff would be a pain in the butt, but if Deanna needed him in the middle of the night he could hardly leave Austin alone in the Big House, could he?

"Anyway," he'd said, not looking at her as he loaded the dishwasher after a meal that redefined *awkward silence* once Austin left the table, "it's only for a few days. I think we can muddle through this like grown-ups."

In other words, this was stacking up to be one helluva crappy Christmas. Although God knew she wasn't any stranger to those.

As least Austin's infectious excitement took the edge off Deanna's increasing regret. Not that she'd made the wrong decision, but that she couldn't figure out how to make it right with Josh. Or Austin, who clearly hadn't yet reconciled himself to the inevitable.

"But I want you to stay!" he'd say, over and over, until Deanna thought her heart would crack right in two and fall out of her chest. As if the look in Josh's eyes, whenever she was foolish enough to let their gazes mingle, wasn't doing that already.

Most of which—leaving out the gaze-mingling-with-Josh-part—she shared with Val as they pushed their daughters' strollers along Main Street on Christmas Eve eve, barely glancing in windows they'd both seen a dozen times before. But then, shopping wasn't the point, as Val pointed out when she'd called that morning simply to chat, and after barely a minute declared Deanna clearly needed to get out of that house before she lost it. Of course, it was obvious she'd only called to begin with because Deanna was guessing Josh had said something to his twin, who'd then said something to his wife, because that's how small towns worked. Not to mention families, Val said with a shrug when Deanna had confronted her about her motives behind the invitation.

"Trust me," the blonde said when they stopped in front of a bookstore/gift shop to put Risa's mittens back on for the third time in five minutes, "No one is immune to that it-takes-a-village thing they've got going on here. As in, nailed." Straightening, Val got behind the stroller and resumed pushing.

"And you're not part of that?"

"Oh, hell, yeah," the blonde said, tossing Deanna a grin. "Except I'd like to think, because I've been on the receiving end of all that helpfulness, that I can be an impartial listener. Which I'm guessing is what you need most right now. And unlike a guy, I won't offer any advice."

Deanna glanced down at Katie, sacked out in her own stroller, her precious little cheeks stained pink from the cold. "They do tend to do that, don't they?"

"You kidding? Loose ends tend to make men real twitchy. Especially those men."

A frown bit into Deanna's forehead. "Loose ends?"

Her new friend chuckled. "I get that you feel leaving's the best thing for you. Not about to argue the point, because who am I to say? But I will say you don't sound all that happy about it, either. So, yeah. Loose ends. Trust me,"

Val said on a sigh. "I've been there. So I know what you're saying, that you have to figure out your own life, nobody else can do that for you. That doesn't make the limbo period before you do any easier." She paused. "Don't know if this helps or not, but with Levi and me…" Val's breath frosted in front of her face when she blew out. "Knowing what I wanted didn't make me any less afraid of it. In fact, it petrified me."

"What makes you think—?"

"Oh, honey…" Val turned to her, something close to pity shimmering in her pretty blue eyes, and Deanna sighed.

"Is it that obvious?" she said, and now Val laughed, only to sober a moment later, her forehead scrunched.

"Like I said, not gonna offer any advice. Don't know you well enough to do that, for one thing. But in my case, I finally had to ask myself whether I'd be happier with Levi or without him. If protecting whatever I thought needed protecting was worth giving up what I thought I needed protecting from."

"And is it weird, that I actually understood that?"

Val chuckled again as they approached a storefront with a For Sale sign in the grimy window. "Being happy…it's really not about where you are, is it? It's about *who* you are. Who you're with. At least, that's what I finally figured out." Tenting her mittened hand over her eyes, Val peered inside for a moment before meeting Deanna's gaze again.

"I've got everything I need," she said, "right here in this two-bit town. Although I sure didn't feel that way when I was a kid, when I couldn't imagine ever being happy here. Now I couldn't imagine being happier anywhere else." Underneath her heavy hoodie, her shoulders bumped. "Things change. *People* change. And I'm a firm believer that happiness—or misery—is more of a choice than we sometimes think. And that's all I'm gonna say about that."

Then she tilted back her head, looking up at the store's faded sign. "I remember this place from when I was a kid."

"Same here. They sold tacky tourist crap." Deanna grinned. "Coolest store, ever."

"Seriously. I heard the owners moved to Tucson, the kids aren't interested in keeping the business going." Laughter from a couple of bag-laden nonlocals emerging from a nearby gift shop briefly diverted the blonde's attention. "You ask me, though, the place won't stay vacant for long. Not the way those ski resort types spend the big bucks, according to Annie. And wouldn't it make a perfect gallery?" Her gaze slid back to Deanna's, a smile snaking across her mouth. "Snag 'em before they find their way down to Taos—"

From her pocket, Val's phone chimed. "Shoot, I didn't realize it'd gotten so late, I need to pick up Josie from school and get back to my pies for tomorrow—"

"No problem." Deanna smiled. "But it was nice to get out of my own head for a bit. So, go." She shooed Val away. "Fetch. Bake. I'm good."

"You sure?"

"Of course."

"Okay. But if you need to talk more," she said over her shoulder as she started down the street, "call me. Or text, whatever."

Then she was gone, leaving Deanna standing in front of the empty store. Following Val's lead, she peeked inside...

Her phone rang, scaring the bejeebers out of her. She smiled, though, when she saw Gus's number on the display.

"Just callin' to check up on my girl," the old housekeeper said. "Both of you, actually. So how's it going?"

The phone to her ear, Deanna squatted in front of the stroller to rearrange the baby's little cap, which had somehow fallen down over her eyes. Another clump of tourists wandered by, shopping totes in hand, smiling at Katie as they passed.

"It's going okay," Deanna said over the knot in her throat as she got to her feet again.

Gus paused, then said, "Josh tells me you're gonna sell your half of the Vista to Zach and Mallory?"

"Mallory, yes. To use as a therapy facility."

Another pause. "Win-win, huh?"

"Yep. So how's things by you?" she said, staring inside the vacant shop again.

"Good. Really good, in fact. Like I'm finally where I belong."

Deanna frowned. "You didn't feel like you belonged in Whispering Pines?"

"When your daddy was still alive, sure. And you know I always felt like an honorary Talbot," he said on another short laugh. "But it really didn't feel like home anymore. This does."

"Get out."

Another belly laugh preceded, "Crazy, huh? Especially after a million years of thinkin' I'd rather jab a stick in my eye than come back down here. But you know what? God has a way of puttin' us where we belong, not where we think we're supposed to be. So I'm glad I listened. Although if you'd asked me six months ago if I could see myself living down here again…" He laughed again. "I'd've said you were loco. So. When you going back east?"

"Um…right after the New Year."

"That soon? Okay, keep in touch, honey—"

"Mom hated the Vista, you know," Deanna blurted out, not even knowing why. "And eventually it killed her, being so unhappy. I remember, how trapped she felt. Same as I did—"

"No," Gus said, his voice surprisingly strong. "Not the

same at all. Holy hell—is that what you've thought all these years? That your mama hated the ranch?"

"Kinda hard to miss, Gus."

"Meanin' your father never told you the truth about that, either." On a huge sigh, the old man muttered something in Spanish Deanna didn't entirely get. "If that sweet lady was trapped by anything, it was her illness. Not the tumor, what she lived with for years before that. The doctors, your daddy—they tried everything, but—"

"Gus—what are you talking about?"

"Depression. You really didn't know? From the time she was a girl, they said. Although it apparently got worse after you were born. She had good days, sure, but…"

Deanna pressed her gloved hand to her chest as images, incidents, that had always felt fuzzy around the edges flooded her thoughts, suddenly in almost painfully sharp focus. Of course now, as an adult, it made sense—her mother's withdrawals and not wanting to get out of bed, her false cheer when she was awake. But then…

"I remember," she said softly. "Oh, God… I remember."

Gus pushed out another breath. "Your daddy—he wasn't thinking straight, after your mama died. And for a long time after. Never did get over feeling like he'd failed, somehow. Even though it wasn't his fault. And then your aunt came out, and she convinced him—"

Deanna's blood ran cold. "I'd be better off with her."

"Or at least better off not there," Gus said in a tone that strongly suggested there was no love lost there. "And your father was grasping at straws. The Talbots tried telling him it was only you being a teenager that made you moody, then grief after your mama died. And that even if you had been ill like Mrs. Blake, sending you away wouldn't've 'cured' it. But your daddy did what he thought was right. And nothing and nobody was gonna change his mind."

"I thought…" She cleared her throat. "So it wasn't about Josh?"

"Oh, that played a part in it, sure it did. Because your father was definitely scared you'd end up falling for each other, and then…well."

"History would repeat itself. Which is what I'd always figured, about why he'd sent me away."

"Except there was more to it than that. A lot more."

Tears blurring her vision, Deanna sagged against the grimy window. "Holy crap. Only…eventually he realized he'd made a mistake?"

Gus sighed again. "Lookin' death in the face does that to a person, I guess. But you gotta know, honey—your mama loved the Vista, she really did. Just like she loved your daddy. And she loved you like I've never seen another mother love her child."

Blinking, Deanna looked down at her own daughter, feeling her heart shatter. "I know she did."

"And your daddy loved you, too. Even if he had a weird way of showing it."

She snuffed a little laugh. "By pushing me away, you mean."

"By doin' what he could to protect you."

A sudden, sharp wind zipped down the street, making her shiver, even as she felt as though a boulder had finally rolled off her chest. "Thanks, Gus. For telling me all that. Seriously—"

"An' there's something else you need to know. When you were little, I never saw anything but a happy little girl who loved to be outdoors and ride horses and go tubing in the snow. If you were lonely…well. I sure as hell never saw it. An' I think I would've. Since you never were any good about keeping whatever you were thinking or feeling from showing in that sweet face of yours. And *Dios mio*," he said with a chuckle, "you weren't afraid of a damn thing back then. Some of the stuff you pulled scared the crap out of all of us. I remember thinkin' to myself, there's a gal who's gonna get whatever she puts her mind to."

And now she could hardly breathe. Or hear, for all those words crashing and clanging in her brain.

Words she'd clearly needed to hear, crashing and clanging aside.

Swiping a hot tear off her nearly frozen cheek, Deanna said softly, "I love you, Gus. Merry Christmas."

"Aw, I love you, too, honey. And send me lots of pictures of that baby, you hear?"

"Absolutely," Deanna said, then disconnected the call, turning away from the next round of passersby so there'd be no witnesses to her losing it right out in public.

Which meant she was facing the empty store again...

Her breath hitched. Oh, hell, no.

No.

Because Gus's words didn't change anything, really. Her life wasn't here, hadn't *been* here in years...

Because it wasn't enough, simply *wanting* something. Was it?

She leaned closer to the window, like some Dickensian orphan seeing hope and promise and dreams-come-true inside, and she sputtered a laugh.

"Get real," she mumbled to herself, steering her sleeping baby back toward where she'd parked the truck, as the strains of "O Come All Ye Faithful" spilled out over the square from the Catholic church's PA system, a block away.

Joyful and triumphant? *Not so much*, Deanna thought as she hauled little Miss Dead Weight out of the stroller and strapped her into her car seat, telling herself it was the cold making her eyes sting.

Although she couldn't blame the temperature for her heartache.

Chapter Twelve

"Looks like she's doing great," Zach said, patting the horse's rump before frowning at Josh. "Which is more than I can say for you."

"Me? I'm fine."

The stall door banging closed behind him, Zach snorted. "Please. You haven't been *fine* since Deanna returned. And the closer she gets to leaving, the less fine you are."

Josh's fists clenched. Too bad he'd dropped off Austin, aka Mr. Big Ears, at his folks earlier. Because nothing put the brakes on a dicey conversation like a four-year-old.

"Then I'll be fine once she leaves and things get back to normal."

That got a smirk. "I seem to recall telling myself something similar when I thought Mallory was going back to LA. Until I realized I was being an idiot of the first order, thinking there was nothing I could do to stop her."

Josh met his brother's gaze dead-on. "Only in my case, there isn't."

"You sure about that?"

"Her life's not here," Josh muttered as they walked out to Zach's truck, the dumb dog dancing around their legs. "I told you about that job offer, right?"

"You did." Seemingly in no hurry to catch up, Zach said behind him, "So you're good with Mallory's proposal?"

"Sure."

"Not hearing a whole lot of conviction there, buddy."

"It is what it is, okay? Although I'll tell you one thing— I'd give up the Vista like that—" he snapped his fingers "—if it meant…"

Damn. He couldn't even finish the sentence. Pathetic.

"She really hates it here that much?" Zach said. Almost kindly.

"Can you blame her?"

Under his cowboy hat's brim, Zach's face folded into a frown. "I know the place has some sketchy memories for her. But I'm guessing it's got some good ones, too. Memories she's afraid of owning. Because if she does that…" He shrugged.

For a good two, three seconds, Josh actually considered not taking the bait. However, since it wasn't like he could feel any worse… "And what memories might those be?"

"And you can't be that dense. It's not the *Vista* that scares her, numskull. It's you. The ranch is only an excuse."

Josh gawked at his brother for several seconds before pushing out a dry laugh. "And how on earth did you come to this conclusion?"

"I didn't. But Mallory did. And Val. And I'd trust those two's intuition with my life. They're also of a mind that Deanna's not all that crazy about going back east, whether she'll admit that out loud or not. Only you haven't exactly given her a reason to stay, have you?"

Ramming his hands in his pockets, Josh stared out toward the house. "It's…complicated."

"So let's break it down into small bites. Does she even know you love her?"

"Dammit, Zach—" The dog danced out of the way when Josh spun around. "Loving a woman isn't enough to make her stay if she doesn't want to! And no *way* am I going there again."

A beat or two passed before Zach said, "So much for you telling everybody it was 'just a thing' between you and Jordan."

Josh grimaced. "I was feeling stupid enough as it was. Decided I'd rather have people mad at me than pity me."

"As in, Mom and Dad?"

"As in, anybody."

"Deanna's not Jordan, buddy."

"No kidding. Which is why I'm not even remotely interested in making the same mistake with her. Because nothing shuts down a woman faster than telling her you love her when that's not what she wants to hear. And she's been through enough without me putting any more pressure on her."

His brother held Josh's gaze in his for far too long. "So you're just going to let her go."

And no jury in the land would convict him if he killed his brother right then. "Okay. Even if the whole here-or-there thing weren't an issue, even if I told her how I feel, she's made it more than clear she's got to figure stuff out on her own, that her problem is…how'd she put that? Looking for somebody to complete her."

"Because she's been hurt, idiot. By her dad, by Katie's father…" Zach shook his head. "For God's sake, Josh— the woman is probably *petrified* of being abandoned again. That whole *I gotta figure this out for myself* shtick? Oldest defense mechanism in the world."

"Oh, and like telling her that is the way to win her over? Dude. Not *that* stupid."

"And if you don't tell her *something*…" Zach squatted

to pet Thor, then looked back up at Josh. "The animals I see who've been abused, the ones who're the most skittish—they're ones who need the most love. *And* the most patience. People are no different. Yeah, it's a risk, I get that. You might fail. She might leave anyway. You might even piss her off so much she'll never want to speak to you again. And hell, maybe she really does feel she belongs in DC, what do I know? But I do know if you don't put your ass on the line, you'll definitely lose her. Also, since I'm on a roll, here," he said, standing again, "being there for a woman isn't the same as trying to complete her. Not even close."

"Except if she doesn't see it that way—"

"Then make sure she does," Zach said, clapping Josh on his shoulder before climbing back into his truck. But before he slammed shut the door, he said, "You really want to show her you're willing to let her make her own choices? Then make sure she's got all the information she needs to make 'em. Just be prepared—"

"To let her go. Got it."

Zach's eyes softened behind his glasses a moment before the old truck roared to life. "Showing a woman you love her enough to risk rejection? No better gift in the world."

Fists jammed in his coat pockets and his forehead crunched, Josh watched his brother drive away, his pickup bumping over ruts in the dirt road leading out to the main drag. Part of him—a pretty big part, actually—thought Zach was talking out of his butt, that what was all well and good in theory had nothing to do with the reality that was him and Dee. That, however, would be the part that didn't much cotton to accepting anything Zach—or anyone else, for that matter—had to say. Because Josh was pigheaded like that. As his parents regularly pointed out.

The other part, however—the part that'd reluctantly cozied up to adulthood along about the time Austin appeared—knew Zach was right, that there was no reward without risk. That nothing worthwhile came easy.

Or without being completely honest. With himself as well as with Dee.

He whistled for the dog and headed back to the house, ignoring the cold sweat trickling down his back.

After putting a sacked-out Katie in her crib, Deanna had gone out to the great room, where she plugged in the Christmas tree lights and lowered herself to the Navajo rug to sit cross-legged on the floor, stroking Smoky's silky fur as she stared up at the lit tree. Like she used to when she was little, letting herself become one with the pretty colors, the heady scent of fresh fir, the soothing, mesmerizing strains of familiar Christmas carols. There'd usually been a cat then, too, she thought, smiling at this one as he stretched a paw across her knee, his purr rumbling through her. Straw-colored, late afternoon light tumbled through the tall windows to tangle with the sparkling tree, and Deanna remembered how her mother would sit with her on the floor and look up at the lights, too…how the good days had been very good, how much Katherine Blake had loved the holidays, loved her…

How much Deanna *had* loved this house, the ranch, once upon a time. Just as Gus had said.

And the tears came. Copious and hard, the kind that made her chest hurt and her breath come in fitful, choking gasps. So hard, in fact, she didn't hear Josh come up behind her, let alone even react when he lowered himself to the floor, dislodging the cat before pulling her into his lap. Cradling her head to his smoke-scented chest, he pressed his lips to her hair, again and again, and Deanna's sobs only intensified, as she keened for everything she'd lost, everything that had been ripped from her...

Everything she'd been so afraid to grasp for fear of losing again.

And all she wanted, in that moment, was to stop pretending.

To not be afraid anymore.

And so, she thought as she clutched the front of Josh's shirt and brought their mouths together, she wouldn't be.

After his brain stopped sizzling from that *What the hell?* kiss—not to mention finding the poor woman in a pool of tears—Josh cupped Dee's face in his hands and held her back just far enough to see into her eyes. Waterlogged and slightly crossed though they may have been.

"I don't understand."

"Me, either," she said, swooping in for round two. "Just go with it—"

Josh grabbed her hands. Definitely not how he'd imagined this playing out. Nor was he about to let himself be derailed. "And what, exactly, is this *it* I'm supposed to be going with?"

One thing about fair-skinned women, when they blushed, they blushed *big*.

He almost laughed. Granted, there would've been a time, not all that long ago, when his younger self wouldn't've questioned the turn of events, but would've gone with it, as she'd suggested. Eagerly. Not to mention gratefully. However...

"Not happening, honey," he said gently.

Dee froze, then clumsily shoved off his lap and to her feet, raking a hand through her straggly hair as she walked over to the nearest window, her arms tightly crossed. Cautiously, the cat writhed around her ankles, giving Josh the stink eye—because clearly this was all his fault—before warbling a series of hugely concerned *mrreow*s.

You okay, Human? You'll still feed me, right? Another glance in Josh's direction. *What the* hell *did you do to her? Fix it!*

"Sorry. I..." Dee blew out a breath. "Sorry."

Braving the cat's glare, Josh came up behind Dee to turn her toward him, kiss her forehead. "Come here," he said, steering her toward the nearest sofa, where she collapsed beside him, still strangling her rib cage. Until the cat jumped on her lap again, clearly daring Josh to pull a fast one. Not to mention Thor, who crept into the room, took one look at the cat and tiptoed out again.

Dee scrubbed at her cheek, folded her arms again. "And now that I've made a total fool of myself—"

"That wasn't a rejection, honey."

"Really."

"Okay, I wasn't rejecting *you*. What I was rejecting was the temptation to go down a path I never want to again. Because the last time a woman said something similar to me I ended up a daddy. Not that I'm not crazy about my son, but the next time I become a parent—if there is a next time—I'd like to have an actual say in the matter. And since I don't have any protection and I'm guessing you don't, either..." She grunted. "It's called being practical, honey."

Although she didn't seem inclined to move out of his arms. So there was that. Whatever that was. "And speaking of practical..." Josh reached out to pet the cat, who shot him a *You gotta be kidding me?* look that made him think better of it. "You only gave birth a month ago—"

A pause preceded, "I figured we could be careful?"

Now he did laugh. "Trust me—after all this time of wondering what it'd be like to get naked with you, *careful* is the last thing I'd want to be. Except for the part about making more babies, I mean. So you want to tell me what this is really about? Because I'm also not partial to being used to salve whatever wounds you're looking to salve."

Dee sat up so fast the cat shot off her lap and stalked off, only to stop a few feet away to lick his mussed fur.

"I would never do that! Especially..." Blushing again, Dee looked away. "Especially not to you."

"Even though you're going back east in a few days? I presume, never to return?"

She faced him again, her mouth twitching. "Wow. You sound kind of...pissed."

And with that, he was. Monumentally pissed. Pissed like no man in love had probably even been in the history of the world.

"Damn straight, I'm pissed. And you know what?" Josh surged to his feet, sending the poor cat streaking from the room. "What I said before, about being careful? I'm done with that. Done with tiptoeing around letting you know how I feel, because I...hell, I don't even know why anymore. Because it's like Zach said, how can you make a choice if you don't have all the options—"

"You were talking about this with your brother?"

Josh smacked away the interruption. "He brought it up, it's what this family does, in case you haven't noticed. But he's right. What's the worst that can happen if I admit I want you to stay? That, hell, I want to marry you, and be Katie's daddy, and for you to be Austin's mom? You'd tell me to go screw myself, and you'd leave anyway. Which you have every right to do, don't get me wrong. But at least..."

Josh pointed at her, only to realize his hand was shaking. Right along with the rest of him. "But at least you'd *know*." He gulped down the next wave of shakes. "At least I would've been up front with you, instead of pretending...

of pretending everything's okay when it isn't. Pretending I'm okay with the idea of losing you when I'm anything but." He lowered his hand, his heart beating so hard his chest ached. "At least you'd know I loved you enough to let you go. But if...*if*..."

Swallowing again, he let his gaze melt into hers. "I don't know if what I have to offer is even remotely enough for you. I'm never gonna be anything but a country boy, never gonna like the opera or the ballet or any of that fancy stuff you do. But whatever I am..." He shoved out a breath. "At least you'd have all of me. Everything. Until my dying breath, swear to God. Because the one thing I'm good at is keeping promises. And if you truly hate the Vista, if you really can't shake yourself loose from whatever's haunting you about it, we can still sell it. Because no property, not even this one, is worth losing you over. I can promise you that, too."

From down the hall came Katie's fierce little cry. It seemed to take Dee a moment to hear her before she broke their gaze and got up to go to her child, not seeming to care that Josh followed her. He stopped at the doorway to the baby's room, listening to Dee coo to the softly babbling baby as she changed her diaper and apparently soggy sleeper. When she was done, she lifted her infant daughter to her chest and faced Josh again, a tiny crease wedged between her eyebrows, and Josh released a sorry-assed laugh.

"What am I saying? Your dream job...jeebus. I can't ask you to sacrifice that for, what? A life out here in the sticks—"

"No. You can't. And I won't let you."

By now his throat was so tight he felt like he was trying to swallow a baseball. Especially when she walked past him with the baby and back down the hall, where she curled up in the corner of the sofa to feed her kid.

Without even thinking, he went to the kitchen to get her a glass of water.

"Thanks," she said quietly when he handed it to her. She drank half of it before setting the glass on the end table, then smiled for her daughter, noisily sucking away. Josh sat on a nearby chair, tightly gripping the arms. After a moment, Dee looked up, letting her gaze sweep over the room.

"When your life is based on lies and half-truths," she said quietly, "it tends to... I don't know. Contaminate what *is* true? What..." Her gaze touched his, a small smile on her lips. "What was good and pure and lovely. But then, if you're very lucky..." She smoothed her fingers across Katie's chick-fluff hair. "Something, or someone—or several someones—opens your eyes, and you see through all the muck to what was real all along. That the sweet memories always win out over the bad ones. If you give them that chance. And sometimes, if you're very, *very* lucky..."

Watery eyes lifted to his. "A very *special* someone comes along—or back along—who helps you trust again. Who makes you believe. Not in fairy tales. But in truth." She smiled. "In yourself. Even if you're not sure you can do that. Because it's scary."

Josh did some fast blinking himself. "It is for everybody, honey."

A moment passed before she nodded, then sighed. "I don't hate the house, Josh. Or the ranch. Or Whispering Pines. I never did, really. Any more than my mother did, I realize. What I hated was being lied to in the name of 'protecting' me. Of people making decisions for me instead of asking me what I might've wanted. Needed. Because leaving me out of the loop left me vulnerable and naive." She snorted a soft laugh. "*Un*protected, actually. Which I doubt was my father's intention. Although it was probably my aunt's," she said, her mouth yanked flat.

"Your aunt—"

"Later," she said, then sighed. "But it was the lies, the *secrets*, that were so stifling, even if I didn't understand that until a little bit ago. Not the place. What I'd like to do now, though…" Another sweep of the room preceded, "is reclaim what was taken from me. Including…" She smiled at Josh. "You."

Josh hesitated, his heart thundering in his chest, before moving from the chair to squat in front of her, taking Katie's tiny hand in his. "Even if that means your father wins?"

Dee's laugh floated up to the beamed ceiling. "I suppose I'll have to cede this one to him," she said, and Josh pushed himself up to palm her cheek and kiss her, her mouth soft and yielding under his. Then he leaned back, and what he saw in her eyes made hope burn in his chest, glittering and bright.

"But that job…?"

Her mouth screwed to one side, she looked back at the baby. "It would be perfect. For someone else."

"You sure?"

"I need…" Her eyes shut for a moment as she hauled in a breath. "To push myself past what's safe. Because *playing* it safe hasn't exactly been a winning game plan."

"And why do I get the feeling there's more behind those words than you're saying?"

Laughing, she cupped the baby's head and said, very softly, "You know that old gift shop on Main Street that's for sale? It would be perfect for a gallery. Not that I have any clue how I'd go about financing it, but…simply the thought of it, that it'd be *mine*…"

By now Josh's heart was pounding so hard he could hardly hear his own thoughts. But the one he *did* hear…

Dee's brow creased when Josh pushed himself up to sit

beside her on the couch, tugging over a nearby ottoman to prop his boot on the edge.

"Okay, what's with the grin?"

"I bet between us we could swing a half-decent down payment." He smiled into her startled gaze. "Whaddya think?"

Now her eyes nearly popped out of her head. Only to immediately squint. "And that wouldn't be you trying to buy me, would it?"

He actually laughed. "Even if that were possible—since you're the last person on earth who could be bought—we're talking a piece of property, honey. Hell, you can make it a loan, if that makes you more comfortable. But when I said everything I have, or am, is yours... I meant it."

Dee turned away, staring toward the tree. "You'd really be willing to risk it? On me?"

Chuckling, Josh swung his arm around her shoulders to tug her and the still nursing baby closer. "Trust me, laying my butt on the line with you like I just did? That was far scarier than investing in your new gallery could ever be."

Her breath actually hitched before she said, "*Our* new gallery."

"Oh, no—that's all yours. I'll stick with horses and ro-deos, thank you. Since what I know about art you could write on a gum wrapper."

Several moments of silence passed before she said, real softly, "No one's ever..." Then she shook her head, and Josh kissed her hair, and she knuckled away a tear before shoving out another choked little laugh.

"I suppose this means I have to marry you now," she said, and Josh's heart banged against his ribs hard enough to hurt. "Since I doubt anyone's ever shacked up at the Vista before."

"And God forbid the ghosts talk smack about us."

Her chuckle rumbled through him. "God forbid."

"But *only* if you want to. No pressure."

"Got it." Then Dee looked up at him, her eyes all shiny. "What was always true still is, you know."

"And what's that?"

"That I love you," she said softly. "That I *trust* you. That you'll always be my best friend."

"Same goes," Josh whispered as the dog stuck his head back in the room, cautiously wagging his tail. Chuckling, Josh smacked his leg to bring the dog closer. "Merry Christmas, sweetheart," he said, more content than he'd ever been in his life. "Or should I say, *Marry* Christmas?"

Dee groaned, then laughed so hard Thor got on his hind legs to shove his face in hers, making sure she was okay.

"You ready?"

Sitting beside Josh in his SUV, both kids strapped in their car seats behind them, Deanna blew out a breath, then nodded. Next year, he thought, they'd do Christmas Eve at their house—a thought that still, less than twenty-four hours after Deanna agreed to marry him, sent a thrill racing up his spine. But tonight they were all gathering at his parents' place, and it would be crazy and loud and a trial by fire for the girl whose childhood had been so lonely and quiet most of the time. But if she was truly opting for this life, best she know what she was really getting into.

He leaned over and kissed her, her lips cold and smooth even though the truck's heat had kicked in almost as soon as they'd left the ranch. Once she'd told him about her and Gus's conversation, when she'd learned about her mother's mental health struggles, her aunt's role in her father's sending her away, a lot of things made sense that hadn't before. For both of them, but especially for Dee. And Josh was well aware that it wasn't going to be a walk in the park for either of them, watching her feel her way through to the other side after all the crap her family, in some misguided effort to shield her from her own pain, had actually dumped on her to deal with later. At the same time, that she trusted him enough to do that...

Well. You really couldn't put a price on that.

Austin naturally ran off to play with his cousins the moment they entered the cozy little house, filled with the traditional New Mexico Christmas Eve scents of roasting turkey and spicy enchiladas and posole. Val appeared out of nowhere to claim Katie, who was taking in the sights and sounds with big dark eyes and pursed lips.

"Auntie time," his twin's wife said with a wink, as if she knew. Then again, knowing Val, she probably did.

Still in their coats, Josh took Dee's hand and led her into the jam-packed kitchen, filled to bursting with Talbots. Or soon-to-be Talbots. And immediately the chattering and laughter ceased, all eyes turning to them. Expectantly, Josh thought.

Then Dee took a deep breath and said, "I'm staying," and Austin popped up again out of nowhere and said, "An' she's gonna be my mom! For real!" and all *hell* broke loose.

In the best possible way.

Several minutes later, after the poor woman had been hugged within an inch of her life and Josh's back had been slapped so hard he was sure he'd have bruises, he tugged his fiancée into a back bedroom to kiss the stuffing out of her. Then she smiled up at him and whispered, "Thank you for loving me," and he saw so much promise in her eyes he almost couldn't stand it.

But he'd manage, he thought, pulling her into his arms with a big old grin on his face.

Epilogue

Several weeks later

Dude definitely hadn't been kidding about not being *careful*, Deanna thought with a satisfied smile as she gradually came awake in the new king-size bed in the house's master bedroom.

The bedroom she now shared with the warm, naked man in whose arms she'd awakened. The man responsible for that satisfied smile. The man who'd finally banished the ghosts from this house—her thoughts—forever. Or at least, was helping *her* banish them.

Dee lay in the silence of the deep winter morning, still gray and soft and velvety, cherishing the moment. The peace. The...*knowing*. That she was safe, and loved, and right where she belonged. Where she'd always belonged, if she were being honest. And where her daughter would grow up cocooned in love, in laughter and shenanigans, surrounded by family.

Thank you, Daddy, she thought, blinking back the suggestion of tears. Whatever mistakes her father might have made—even from the best of intentions—in the end, he got it right.

So right.

From his dog bed in the corner, Thor whup-whupped in his sleep, probably disturbing the cat, who'd taken to cozying up to the mutt, much to the dog's shock. It'd be a good hour before the kids woke up—Katie had been sleeping through the night for weeks, God bless her, in Dee's old room, now girlified within an inch of its life. Although her wicked, wicked mother-in-law had said not to get used to it, the next one probably wouldn't. A thought that pushed a silent chuckle from Deanna's chest. Not that she and Josh were in any hurry to add to their brood—they'd only been married a week, for heaven's sake, a no-frills justice of the peace affair with a reception at Annie's—but maybe next year…

She snuggled closer, breathing in Josh's scent, reveling in his solidity, his *there*ness. It'd been a crazy few weeks, including her returning to DC long enough to close up her apartment, arrange for shipping stuff here she wanted to keep, sell off what she didn't. Enduring an endless evening with her aunt and uncle to show off Katie, practically choking on the rampant disapproval, that clearly her aunt's plan to *rescue* Deanna had backfired so spectacularly. Then again, once Emily's wedding was over, she doubted she'd ever see them again. No reason to, really.

And, since the sale to Mallory was no longer an option—not that her future sister-in-law seemed at all unhappy about that—Josh instead offered to rent her part of the spread for her therapy facility since so much of the ranch was underutilized, anyway. And those funds would go into the kids' college funds, as well into the gallery, which Deanna planned on opening in the spring—

Josh stirred, then yawned and stretched before pulling her closer, his early-morning beard haze tickling her neck, his fingers skimming the slim gold band on her finger before finding their way to her no-longer-leaking breast, hallelujah.

"Mornin', wife," he murmured, his voice thick with sleep as he thumbed her nipple, making her toes curl.

"Morning, husband," she whispered back, turning into a mass of tingles when Josh gave her an impish grin.

"How much time we got?"

"Enough," she said, laughing when he disappeared beneath the covers to stoke fires that, to be honest, didn't need all that much stoking. And she melted at his touch, his tenderness, the message behind them both—*I'm not goin' anywhere, darlin'*—breathing out a sigh of pure contentment when he slid inside her, filling all her empty spaces…and she saw, in his eyes, bright in the silky, filmy light, *home.*

"I love you," she whispered, and he grinned.

"Oh, just wait," he said, and she laughed, thinking, *I am a lucky, lucky girl.*

* * * * *

*Colin Talbot finally returns home in the next book in
Karen Templeton's WED IN THE WEST
series, coming in February 2017
from Mills & Boon Cherish*

MILLS & BOON®

Cherish™

EXPERIENCE THE ULTIMATE RUSH OF FALLING IN LOVE

A sneak peek at next month's titles...

In stores from 17th November 2016:

- **Winter Wedding for the Prince** – Barbara Wallace *and*
  The More Mavericks, the Merrier! – Brenda Harlen
- **Christmas in the Boss's Castle** – Scarlet Wilson *and*
  A Bravo for Christmas – Christine Rimmer

In stores from 1st December 2016:

- **Her Festive Doorstep Baby** – Kate Hardy *and*
  The Holiday Gift – RaeAnne Thayne
- **Holiday with the Mystery Italian** – Ellie Darkins *and*
  A Cowboy's Wish Upon a Star – Caro Carson

Just can't wait?
Buy our books online a month before they hit the shops!
www.millsandboon.co.uk

Also available as eBooks.

MILLS & BOON®

EXCLUSIVE EXTRACT

Crown Prince Armando enlists Rosa Lamberti to find him a suitable wife—but could a stolen kiss under the mistletoe lead to an unexpected Christmas wedding?

Read on for a sneak preview of
WINTER WEDDING FOR THE PRINCE
by Barbara Wallace

"Have you ever looked at an unfocused telescope only to turn the knob and make everything sharp and clear?" Armando asked.

Rosa nodded.

"That is what it was like for me, a few minutes ago. One moment I had all these sensations I couldn't explain swirling inside me, then the next everything made sense. They were my soul coming back to life."

"I don't know what to think," she said.

"Then don't think," he replied. "Just go with your heart."

He made it sound easy. Just go with your heart. But what if your heart was frightened and confused? For all his talk of coming to life, he was essentially in the same place as before, unable or unwilling to give her a true emotional commitment.

On the other hand, her feelings wanted to override her common sense, so maybe they were even. As she watched him close the gap between them, she felt her heartbeat quicken to match her breath.

"You do know that we're under the mistletoe yet again, don't you?"

The sprig of berries had quite a knack for timing, didn't it? Anticipation ran down her spine ceasing what little hold common sense still had. Armando was going kiss her and she was going to let him. She wanted to lose herself in his arms. Believe for a moment that his heart felt more than simple desire.

This time, when he wrapped his arm around her waist, she slid against him willingly, aligning her hips against his with a smile.

"Appears to be our fate," she whispered. "Mistletoe, that is."

"You'll get no complaints from me." She could hear her heart beating in her ears as his head dipped toward hers. "Merry Christmas, Rosa."

"Mer…" His kiss swallowed the rest of her wish. Rosa didn't care if she spoke another word again. She'd waited her whole life to be kissed like this. Fully and deeply, with a need she felt all the way down to her toes.

They were both breathless when the moment ended. With their foreheads resting against each other, she felt Armando smile against her lips. "Merry Christmas," he whispered again.

Don't miss
WINTER WEDDING FOR THE PRINCE
by Barbara Wallace

Available December 2016